Brady's writ[...] [...]cretly
[...]ng historical [...] to be
[...]ng on her [...]iction
[...]ed a cland[...] as a
[...] professor [...], she
[...]d to go public. She has since won or been a finalist
[...]ny writing competitions and now leads a double
[...]her time split between teaching music at a university
[...]reating serial killers on a laptop.

[...]e lives in Atlanta with her husband, two children,
[...]n array of furry, feathery, and scaly things.

Visit her website at www.katebrady.net

Praise for Kate Brady:

'Kate Brady's debut novel is ... scary, sexy, pulse-
[p]ounding, and page-turning. Remarkable characters,
[pit]ch-perfect pacing, and a memorable villain make *One
Scream Away* a standout book. A winner'
New York Times bestselling author, Allison Brennan

'Snappy Dialogue, good police procedural details and
[t]visty psychology create white-hot tension that thriller
fans will love'
Publishers Weekly

'Kate Brady has made her mark with a taut, masterful
debut of chilling suspense that grabs you by the throat
and heart and won't let go ... Prepare to stay up all
night, then sleep with the lights on'
N[...] [...]laire

writing career began in the closet, se...
...sagas when she was supposed...
...doctoral dissertation. Writing...
...estine hobby during her career
...and conductor, but eventually...

New York Times bestselling author, Roxanne St Clair

ONE SCREAM AWAY

KATE BRADY

piatkus

PIATKUS

First published in the USA in 2009 by Forever, an
imprint of Grand Central Publishing, a division of Hachette Book Group, Inc.
First published in Great Britain as a paperback original in 2010 by Piatkus

A CIP catalogue record for this book
is available from the British Library.

ISBN 978-0-7499-5265-5

Typeset in Palatino by Action Publishing Technology Ltd, Gloucester
Printed and bound by Clays Ltd, Bungay, Suffolk

Papers used by Piatkus are natural, renewable and recyclable
products sourced from well-managed forests and certified
in accordance with the rules of the Forest Stewardship Council.

Piatkus
An imprint of
Little, Brown Book Group
100 Victoria Embankment
London EC4Y 0DY

An Hachette UK Company
www.hachette.co.uk

www.piatkus.co.uk

Acknowledgments

Writing seems a solitary venture, yet there are many people to whom I am indebted for making this book a reality:

To my fabulous agent, Jenny Bent, for her belief in the manuscript and her unwavering support at every step along the way.

To my wonderful editor, Celia Johnson, for her unflagging patience, skill, devotion, and kindness throughout the process.

To Carol, Elaine, and Shirley, for things only you can understand; and to Emily, wherever you are.

To Tom and Carolyn and my years at Garth's Auctions, for teaching me just enough about antiques to make up the rest.

To Ken, for being there after all these years and guiding me through proper police procedures (not that my characters listened).

To Linda, for being my personal statistics and research guru, and so much more.

To Rocki, for being the greatest cheerleader in the field.

To my dear friends—Fran, in particular—for understanding that I can't talk on the phone, have dinner, or go shopping when someone is bleeding to death on my computer.

To my in-laws, for their genuine excitement and support; to my late father, for instilling a love of words; to my mother, for her love and strength of character in all matters; and to my sister, for her genuine pride in this endeavour, even though her books do a lot more good in the world.

To my children, Kaitlin and Kyle, for understanding that Mom's mind is scarier than other mom's minds.

And to my husband, Brady, for picking up the slack at home, for listening through endless possibilities, and for not being afraid to share a bed with a woman who is always plotting murders. But mostly, for loving me so well.

Chapter 1

Bighorn Butte, Washington
2,780 miles away

A chilly night with just a wedge of moon, mist brewing on the water and congealing in gullies. Six thousand feet below, Seattle glittered in a haze, but here on the butte the air was thin and clear, steeped in eerie stillness. No light but the blue-white column of a halogen flashlight. No movement but the trusty reels of an old cassette tape recorder. No sound but the strangled sobs of a woman about to die.

Chevy Bankes looked down at the woman. Lila Beckenridge, her driver's license said, the photo showing razor-sharp cheekbones and hair scraped into a bun. A dancer, he'd decided while roping her ankles—calloused feet and spaghetti-thin body, the faint odor of perspiration layered beneath her perfume.

And a screamer, a good set of lungs. Well worthy of her role in the performance that began here tonight.

Chevy stilled, the enormity of the moment weakening his knees. He'd had women before, he'd killed before, but never with such *purpose*. He'd never killed one woman to

1

give to another, or taken a life for something greater than his own immediate need. In that sense, the dancer was unique. A first.

A perverse sort of gratitude washed over him, and he bent to stroke her cheek. She spit at him.

"Bitch!" He wiped his face with the edge of his shirt, snarling, and the rage jumped in him. How dare she? That wasn't in the plan ...

Who killed Cock Robin? I, said the Sparrow, with my bow and arrow, I killed Cock Robin ...

Chevy covered his ears. "No," he said, but the song threaded in—a haunting little folk tune like a mosquito buzzing in his ear. He slapped at the air around his head, trying to shoo it away, then drew back his foot and kicked the woman on the ground. Her jaw gave with the sound of wood snapping in a fire, a moan of pain ripping from her chest.

The song slipped away.

Chevy waited, forcing himself to breathe. Control. Silence. There could be no singing tonight, not when a plan seven years in the making was finally under way.

Shaking, he uncovered his ears, eyes wide as if he might be able to see the voice and ward it off if it came again. He glanced at the cassette—ten, maybe fifteen minutes of tape left—then at his watch. It was late, and he still had a phone call to make. Besides, his little sister was waiting, and she didn't like to be alone. Poor Jenny had spent enough of her young life alone and waiting for Chevy.

"Not much longer, Jen," he whispered, as if she might hear him. He turned off the recorder and picked up the box he'd carried all the way up the butte. It was two feet

2

long and about a foot deep, not overly heavy but awkward, and he set it on the ground beside the dancer and opened the flaps. Styrofoam peanuts fluttered to his feet as he pulled out the fragile bundle and unwound the tissue paper, layer by layer, round and round until—

"Jesus." Chevy's breath caught even though he'd seen the face before: dark, soulful eyes, vacuous smile, thick ringlets of human hair. He swallowed and sifted through the stack of insurance statements in the box, making sure this was the earliest doll in the set: *1862 Benoit. Bisque head and breastplate, wood body. Rare opening/closing eyelids. Appraisal: $40,000–$50,000.*

Chevy tilted the doll upright then tipped her down again—up and down, up and down—studying her eyes. Despite what the insurance appraisal said, this doll's eyes had never closed. They remained open and watchful, taking in every little thing.

Who saw him die? I, said the Fly, with my little eye—

"Stop it," Chevy snapped, his teeth grinding together. For the space of five heartbeats he listened, then blew out a breath. Get on with it: The woman needed work. He laid the doll on the ground, several feet away in case there was splatter, then pulled an X-Acto knife from his pocket and went back to the dancer.

She squeaked and he stopped. Shit, he'd almost forgotten.

He pushed Play and Record at the same time, then crouched to one knee beside the dancer's shoulder. Whimpers reeled onto the tape, garbled now by the broken jaw but stunning all the same, her terror rising to a fevered pitch as he bent over her.

Just a few screams away, now.

Heart galloping, Chevy went to work, glancing often at the doll, fighting to keep his hand steady. When he finished, he sat back on his knees and let the cries wash over him. A few minutes, no more, then, *click*.

Out of tape.

He opened his eyes and looked down at his handiwork. A little messy, but good enough. He dug his .38 Ruger from a bag of supplies and wiped off the woman's temple. She was beyond noticing, her cries just snags in her breaths now, as if she knew it was over. Chevy measured an inch straight up, marked the spot with an eyebrow pencil, and placed the barrel of the pistol exactly on the spot. Squeezed.

A blessed silence rolled in behind the shot. Chevy held his breath, but he knew the singing wouldn't come now. It never came when the cries were good.

He untied the dancer and arranged her limbs to his liking, then spent ten minutes gathering the things a crime scene team would spend hours looking for: X-Acto knife, gun and shell casing, tape recorder, the rope and tent stakes—all of it, into his gym bag. Every last Styrofoam peanut. Once, as he shoved a peanut into his pocket and pulled his hand back out, he dragged out some snack trash. He noticed and picked it up, a pulse of relief tapping at his chest. Being smart was key; being careful was critical.

Being lucky didn't hurt.

One last look around, and Chevy hiked back down the butte, carrying his bag and the box, stopping to check the dancer's cell phone about every twenty yards. He got

4

halfway down before a cosmic little tune trickled out: service.

His pulse picked up. This was the moment he'd been waiting for, the call he'd been dreaming of for seven long years.

Let the games begin.

Arlington, Virginia

Midnight, the house tucked in, the child long asleep. A hundred-watt bulb glared down at a yellow mat in the basement, the air thick with the odors of perspiration and leather, the usual silence scuffed by illogical sounds of violence. Grunts, thumps, pants of breathlessness. The occasional screech of rubber soles.

The telephone.

Beth Denison scowled. She drew a deep breath, the air settling in her lungs like wet sand, then pulled herself back. Inhale, focus, balance. Strike. Her fist slammed into a hundred-and-fifty-pound sandbag. A hard left hook followed, a roundhouse spinning her around to land a kick that would have crushed an attacker's windpipe. She ducked from the rebound, pivoted, and jammed her heel where the average man's balls would be.

The ringing stopped.

She braced her hands on her knees, panting. No eerie message this time, no moans or heavy breathing. Maybe the caller was getting bored. She straightened and uncurled her fingers, wincing as each knuckle stretched through the pain. Tomorrow, she'd pay for not bothering to wear protective gear. Tonight, she needed sheer physical exhaustion to smother thought—about the future of

5

the antiques firm, about Evan, and about phone calls from some jerk who apparently had a phone book, a few spare minutes in his evenings, and a flair for the perver—

Ring.

She whirled and turned a dangling red speed bag into a blur, the flurry of sound beating at her ears. Not loud enough, though. The phone still sang out over it. Four rings, five. He wasn't hanging up this time.

"Damn it." She threw up her hands and took the stairs two at a time, planning to ... what? Pick up and tell the caller what she was wearing? Tell him to go to hell? She eyed the kitchen phone, frowning at the number that dribbled across the caller-ID screen. Area code 206. Seattle, again, but she didn't recognize the number.

Six rings, seven. The answering machine picked up, her own cheerful voice spinning out: *Hi. You've reached the Denisons, or rather, our machine. You know what to do. Beeep.*

"Hello, doll."

The voice was low and clear. A finger of fear pressed down.

"Beth. I know you're there. Pick up the phone."

Beth? The finger turned into a fist. She shot a worried glance toward Abby's bedroom. No sound, no stirring of the bedcovers. Thankfully, Abby had sunk into the kind of sleep nature reserves for the very young.

"Be-heth. It's been seven long years. Don't you want to talk to me?"

Her lungs seized. *No. Please, no.* It couldn't be.

"Yes, Beth." And his voice lowered. "Surprise."

The past sputtered to life, the chilling drops of memory trickling down her spine.

6

"I bet you thought I'd never find you," he said. "But I'm a resourceful man. In fact, I'm so resourceful that I've arranged some *very* special gifts for you. I can't wait until you see them." He paused, as if he knew she'd had to grab the back of the kitchen chair to stay upright, and that her world was suddenly careening into orbit.

Idiot, Beth said to herself. Of course he knew.

So don't answer. Just ignore him and don't pick up the—

"By the way, Beth, how's your daughter?"

She snatched up the phone. "*Bastard.*"

"Ah, there you are. For a moment I was beginning to worry."

Red sparks burst behind her eyes. "H-how?"

"How, what? Oh, I guess you haven't heard. Well, it's no wonder, of course. Why would anyone think to contact you with the news?"

"What are you talking about?"

"Freedom. Comeuppance. Getting what I've been denied all these years."

The room seemed to be in motion. Beth couldn't even swear her feet were still on the floor. She closed her eyes. Think, *think*. Why, no, *how* was he calling her? "I don't understand," she said.

"I'm sure you'll find the whole story on the Internet with just a few keystrokes. For now, suffice it to say that I'm free. I've been free a while now, in fact, using the time to arrange the details of our reunion."

Nausea crawled up the back of Beth's throat, lodging there like a burr. *Free?* Hold on. Stay in control. If he was out of prison, there was only one reason he would contact her. And he couldn't possibly want to dredge up the past to get it. "I'll call the police. I'll tell them every—"

He chuckled. "No, you won't. You think you have everyone fooled, living your pretty life with your pretty daughter, but you've forgotten: I know your secrets."

She gripped the receiver so tight cramps screamed up the tendons in her arm. "You don't know anything."

"Really?" he asked. Something clicked on his end, and for a second Beth thought he'd hung up. Then he was breathing in her ear again, a faint *whirrr* on the line. "Let's review: I know what happened to Anne Chaney. I know why you moved from Seattle, all the way across the country to Arlington, Virginia." He paused. "I know about your little gir—"

She gasped, then bit it back. Too late.

"Oh, that was nice, Beth. Do that again."

"Stop—" She spit the word but caught herself. Quiet, now. Don't make a sound. She remembered how much he liked sounds. *Scream, bitch. Cry for me.*

"Let me hear your voice again, Beth," he said. "It doesn't need to be much, not yet. Just a few small sounds to get the opus star—"

Beth hurled the phone across the room. Fear and fury coiled in her belly like snakes, and she forced herself to breathe, letting fury writhe to the top. Damn it, she had to keep her head. Even as a free man he wasn't half the threat to her that she was to him. He was the one who should be afraid. Besides, the call hadn't even come from this part of the country.

Area code 206 ... Seattle.

Reality sank to the pit of her stomach. This wasn't a dream. It wasn't some vile memory from the bowels of another lifetime. It wasn't a prank caller with a six-pack and a phone book, who'd latched on to a number he liked and kept hitting Redial.

It was Chevy Bankes.

The need to see Abby kicked Beth in the chest. She raced upstairs and peered into the bedroom. Abby lay sprawled in a puddle of moonlight, a toy cat clutched against her tummy, a real dog draped over her ankles. The dog swished his tail and lolled hopefully to his back, oblivious to the chill creeping through Beth's veins as she stood watching the rise and fall of Abby's stomach: one breath, two breaths, three. Three was the magic number. Beth always counted three breaths in a row before she went to bed at night.

This time she counted ten.

She slipped back into the hallway, the heels of her hands bullying back tears. Don't cry. God knows, tears had never accomplished anything. This wasn't supposed to have happened, but she'd always known it might. Bankes wasn't the only one with a plan.

Inhale, focus, balance. She called on years of Muay Thai to center herself, then went to the master bedroom. She dragged a rocking chair across the room and set it beside a huge Chippendale chest of drawers. It was an early New England piece with heavily carved aprons, the escutcheons all original, the patina rich and dark. Still, she hadn't bought this dresser for its age or beauty. She'd bought it for the cornices.

She climbed onto the tottering rocker and wrenched the finial on the top right cornice of the dresser. It creaked and gaped open.

A folded piece of paper sprang out. Beth tucked it

under a sweatband on her wrist and reached back into the secret compartment. Her fingers curled around the butt of a 9 mm Glock, cool and powerful, neglected but never forgotten. She lifted it, straightened both elbows, and sighted the little red light on the phone across the room.

She could do it. If she had to—for Abby's sake—she would.

She lowered the gun, climbed down, and unfolded the list of names from her wristband. Cheryl Stallings, her sister-in-law. Two attorneys, one who had authored Beth's will and another who had a reputation for winning at any cost. Three Early American furniture dealers, each of whom had offered cash for a few of Beth's finer pieces and would buy them, no questions asked.

Reviewing the list had a calming effect, a tangible reminder that she had a plan and the resources to achieve it. She took a deep breath. Despite the hour, she picked up the phone, then paused. The digits 9 and 1 seemed to glow brighter than the rest.

I'll call the police; I'll tell them everything. But it was a bluff and Bankes knew it. She couldn't call the police. She couldn't do that to Abby.

Steadier now, she muttered a prayer—for forgiveness, just in case there was a God after all. She cleared her throat and schooled her voice into the calm, composed tone she'd perfected years ago. Dialed the top number.

The first lie would be the hardest.

Chapter 2

New York, New York

Thunder rolled in, dragging Neil Sheridan from the depths of a stupor he'd worked on for weeks. A jackhammer pounded in his skull and he reached up, expecting to find his head split in two. His fingers closed around something warm and soft. His brain? No, a breast. He moved his hand. A second one. Oh, that's right, they usually came in pairs.

The thunder intensified. "Neil. Goddamn it, open the door."

He cracked his eyelids and sunlight bleached his eyes. He twisted from it, the breasts rolling over with a soft moan.

"Neil. I'm about to have the hotel staff unlock this door. Fair warning."

"Stop yelling," he muttered, lumbering to his feet. He found a pair of jeans at the foot of the bed and humped into them, bracing a shoulder against the wall.

"Go ahead, unlock the door," the voice in the hallway was saying. Rick? Damn it. The thunder had stopped, though pain still ricocheted around in his head like a round from an M16. Somewhere outside, a female voice took off in quick-fire Spanish and Rick cut her off: "I'm a police lieutenant, lady. Just unlock the damned door."

"Hold on," Neil said, but his voice was a croak. He fumbled with the lock and pulled the door open. A maid gawked at him.

"Whoa, you look like hell," Rick said, pressing a twenty into the maid's hand. He watched her skitter down the hall then stalked into Neil's suite. "I've been calling you. Heard you quit the Sentry. You've been back in the States over a month."

"Time flies."

Rick picked up an empty whiskey bottle, bent to the floor, and hooked a lacy camisole between two fingers. He set both on a table littered with Chinese carryout boxes, peeking into one. He sniffed. "General Ts'ao's chicken," he said. "With whiskey?"

"The beverage that goes with anything."

Rick nudged a second bottle with his toe. It rolled over a ripped-open foil packet on the floor. He glanced at the bedroom door, shaking his head so fractionally Neil thought he might have imagined it. "I want you to come to Arlington with me. You been wallowing in self-pity long enough."

"I've been wallowing in Jack and Jill. And they're still waiting for me in the bedroom."

"Jack Daniels and Jill Who? Do you even know her last name?"

"Didn't ask," Neil said, dropping into a chair and bullying his brow with his fingers. His brain ached, and that shouldn't have been possible. He shouldn't even have a brain anymore. At least that's what they taught boys in high school: too much drinking, too much screwing, and your mind goes blank, your soul goes numb, you become an empty shell of a man who can't think or feel.

Promises, promises.

"Don't you wanna know why I'm here?" Rick asked.

"I know why. You think I'm less likely to eat my gun in front of your wife and kids than I am here."

A beat passed. "Are you?"

Neil closed his eyes, but the pictures came anyway: video footage of his brother visiting a refugee camp, running, running, until the ground exploded and Mitch went flying through the air. He blinked to kill the images. "Eating my gun would be too easy."

"It wasn't your job to stop the attack, Neil. The Sentry is a security organization."

"Right. And I provided security for the bastard who blew up a refugee camp and nearly killed my brother."

Rick grimaced. "Where's Mitch now?"

"In Switzerland, healing. Getting good at phrases like *mea culpa* and *fuck off*."

"I thought you held the copyright to those," Rick muttered, thumbing three tablets from a roll of Tums. "Fly to D.C. with me. I'm looking at a murder case that's interesting."

Neil looked at him as if he were an alien. "Murder cases haven't interested me in nine years."

"A woman was killed near Seattle three nights ago."

"Not interested."

"Hikers found her body early this morning."

13

"Not interested."

"She was a dancer, twenty-six years old. Had a little girl in preschool."

Neil closed his eyes.

"The murderer could be the same—"

"I. Don't. Care." Neil ground out the words, his jaw so tight that for a second he wondered if he could break his own molars. He reached for the nearest bottle, but Rick got there first and heaved it across the room.

The last precious sips of oblivion splattered all over the wallpaper.

"Well, now look what you've done," Neil groused, coming to his feet. "And that was the last bott—"

Rick sprang. In two seconds, Neil's spine was against the wall. "It looks like Anthony Russell, you stupid, self-serving son of a bitch," Rick said, his fingers digging into Neil's arms. "This murder could've been done by *Anthony Russell*."

Neil's lungs shut down. Seconds passed before he got them working again, and when he did, he broke free of Rick with a shove. "Go to hell," he said, but two strides later he spun back around. "Anthony Russell is dead. I shot him."

"After he jumped a bailiff and took off from his own arraignment. I remember." A vein pulsed in Rick's forehead. "It was never a sure thing, though, was it? That he killed that college girl?"

"He confessed. How much more of a sure thing do you need?"

"I mean—"

"What? *What* do you mean?" Neil advanced. "Anthony

14

Russell abducted Gloria Michaels after a fraternity party. He stabbed her almost dead then shot her in the head for good measure, and when he escaped from custody, I killed the bastard. So whatever this Seattle woman looks like, there's no way she was killed by Anthony Russell."

"You didn't find Gloria's body where he said you would."

A thread of doubt began to fray. Not for the first time. "The fucker *confessed*."

"In exchange for the DA lessening three other charges."

The pounding in Neil's head picked up again. Anthony Russell's reasons for confessing weren't something anyone had bothered to examine too closely. They had a confession; that's all that had mattered. "Why are you pulling Anthony Russell up on me?"

"The report about the Seattle woman rang some bells."

"What bells?"

Rick ticked them off on his fingers. "Woman disappears with her car. Car was dumped, wiped clean. Body found days later in a wooded area, and some knife-work done on it. Thirty-eight-caliber hollowpoint to finish her. Piece of candy wrapper at the scene." He paused. "Reese's Cup."

The ancient doubt began to dig roots. That did sound like Gloria. Even down to the tiny piece of candy that had been left in the car by her killer. Neil swallowed. "Raped?"

"Can't be sure yet, but—" he paused and ran a hand over his face "—it looks that way."

Fingers of dread crawled across Neil's neck. He paced, trying to talk himself out of it, but the possibilities rose in his mind like specters: The possibility that Anthony Russell had lied about Gloria in order to strike a deal with the DA. The possibility that a jury might have sprung him, had he gone to trial. The possibility that when Neil turned his back on his family in order to catch a murderer, he'd caught the wrong man.

And the right man had murdered a woman in Seattle last night.

"Neil, you knew the Gloria Michaels case better than anyone. Come take a look at it. We can catch the next shuttle back to Virginia."

Neil narrowed his eyes. "Why is a lieutenant in Arlington, Virginia, looking at a murder three thousand miles away?"

"Seattle PD asked me to check on someone. The dead woman's cell phone was used to call a woman in my precinct the night of the murder."

"Who?"

"Her name's Elizabeth Denison."

Neil combed his memory for the people he'd once connected to Anthony Russell. He couldn't come up with anyone named Elizabeth Denison, but then that was no surprise. Because Anthony wasn't involved in this. "You talk to Denison?"

"No one home. I put a car on her street to wait. Then the Gloria Michaels bells started clanging, and I decided to come see if you wanted to look at it."

Neil blew out a curse. Hell, no, he didn't want to look at it. For nine years, he hadn't concerned himself with such futile things as right and wrong, good and evil. He was nothing but an exorbitantly paid guard dog. Jungles,

16

mountains, deserts. Places where he never bothered to ask if he was guarding the good guys or the bad guys, where all that mattered was getting off the first shot.

Fuck it. That was his motto now, and it was a far cry from the words inscribed on the federal shield he'd once carried.

He braced his arm against the wall and tipped his forehead onto it. "If you're right," he finally said, "I killed an innocent man."

"Innocent? Anthony Russell was shooting at you. He left a bailiff paralyzed for life."

"He was in custody because I collared him for Gloria."

Rick stepped closer. "He was a murderer with a rap sheet as long as your dick. The only reason it matters whether you were wrong about him doing Gloria is the chance that her real killer hit Seattle three nights ago. You get that?"

I get it, Neil thought but was somehow afraid to breathe. If he did, it might infuse new life into his veins, might make him start caring about something again. He'd sworn that off nine years ago.

But even as the warnings trolled through his mind, his hand slid into his pocket, a battered piece of ribbon and plastic squeezing into his palm. He held it tight, closing his eyes against the worst possibility of all.

If he'd been wrong about Anthony Russell, then Mackenzie had died for nothing.

That thought almost buckled his knees. That, and the thud of something landing hard on his conscience. The body of a Seattle dancer.

He pulled his hand from his pocket, leaving the barrette in its hideaway. He took a deep breath and looked

17

at Door Number One, knowing he wouldn't choose it, and that Jill Something was going to wake up there alone. A better man might have felt guilty about that, the kind of man who had room on his conscience for such things.

But Neil didn't. Too many corpses there.

Chapter 3

"Lila Beckenridge of Bellevue, Washington," Rick said in a low voice after they settled into the plane seats. He pulled out two file folders and handed them to Neil. "She was leaving a rehearsal, stopped at a convenience mart, and never made it home."

Neil opened the folder containing crime scene photos. "Whoa," he said, biting back the taste of bile. A gruesome pair of eyes stared up at him. "He carved on her?"

"Cut off her eyelids. That's them on the ground."

Neil angled the page, winced. "Jesus," he said and sifted through the pictures, trying not to be disturbed by how Lila Beckenridge seemed to watch him through the crusted blood and dirt on her face. He forced himself to note more mundane details. An inch above her temple sat the bullet hole—small and black and ironically tidy, like a period at the end of a story no one yet knew. A bruise darkened her right jaw, but aside from her face, she looked almost neat: Her arms were bowed out at her sides like a frozen ballerina, her blouse tucked in and skirt pulled neat around her knees. She was stringy thin, and the close-ups of her wrists showed what appeared to be rope burns. A couple of other shots focused on holes in the ground, as if she might have been staked down before she died.

Neil swallowed and opened a second folder labeled "E. DENISON." "Is this all you've got on the woman at your end of the phone call? Driver's license and house deed?"

"Hey, I'm not FBI. Besides, there's nothing to have. Don't know why someone's calling her."

"Someone? You mean the murderer."

"Or Beckenridge."

Neil thumbed through the report. "The call was made just after midnight. Beckenridge's time of death is estimated between six and twelve."

"*Estimated.* How many times have you seen a medical examiner's opinion changed by an autopsy, especially when the body isn't fresh?"

Occasionally, Neil thought, but not often enough to assume error. Neil might have been out of the game for a while, but he hadn't forgotten the three basic rules of criminal investigation. Rule Number Two: Everyone in the chain is as dirty as its dirtiest link.

The woman named Elizabeth Denison was in a chain that included a murderer. It didn't make her a criminal herself, but it did mean she was in the loop long enough to know something about him. Something that would lead them to him.

He shifted, uneasy with the faint throb of excitement in his chest. None of this meant anything was going to change about Gloria Michaels's murder. There were

20

similarities between her case and this Lila Beckenridge—enough to raise eyebrows—but there were differences, too. Chief among them were nine years and three thousand miles. If Gloria's killer had been on the loose all that time, where had he been?

Of course, Neil wouldn't know the answer to that. Because Neil had spent that time hiding behind M16s and a convenient motto.

The plane hopped, wheels skidding on the runway. They taxied to the gate and Rick put away the folders. "You ready?" he asked.

Neil had a sudden longing for Jack and Jill.

"Come on," Rick said. "We'll find you a razor, a coat and tie. We'll pound the pavement a little, go talk to Denison. Find out why she got a phone call from a dead woman."

The lazy feel of a Saturday evening glazed Denison's neighborhood—long shadows stretching across manicured lawns, the smell of charcoal in the air, a group of kids putting together a game of four-square in the street. The kids darted to the curb when they saw Rick's car, poured back into the street with their ball and bucket of chalk after he rolled past. Half a block up, a lady getting her mail waved at them like they must be old friends simply because they were on her street, and at a driveway on the right, a man waited for his beagle to finish peeing on someone's tulips. He nodded and returned Rick's salute from the steering wheel.

"Mayberry," Neil muttered and downed a handful of aspirin with a swig of oily coffee. "Wonder what Ms.

21

Denison's neighbors would think if they knew about her buddy out west."

"Yeah, well, keep in mind that she might not know whoever's calling her. No need to go in there all scary and mean."

"You made me shave and put on a suit," Neil said. "How can I be scary and mean with my good looks hanging out?"

Rick snorted.

"It's the scar, isn't it?" Neil ran his finger along the pale, jagged ridge that ran from his left earlobe to his chin, jogging under the crook of his jaw. Made him look like his cheek had once been torn from the bone.

It had.

"It's not the scar, asshole," Rick said. "It's the way you come off all the time. Intense, dangerous. Screwing the world."

"Women go for all that dark, leashed power."

"You're not trying to get this woman in bed; you're trying to get her to *talk*. And in case you're thinking about waving pictures of Lila Beckenridge in Denison's face, forget it. We're gonna keep the murder under wraps until we're sure she's connected."

"You're kidding."

"Hey, Lila Beckenridge's cell phone coulda been picked up and dialed by anyone."

"Pansy," Neil said, but Rick didn't bite. He parked along the curb and unwrapped a new roll of Tums, popping three or four into his mouth. For the first time Neil noticed how the years had piled up: Lines were etched into Rick's broad, Slavic brow, deep grooves

22

digging around his mouth. At forty-two, he looked fifty and downed antacids like a food group.

He also, come to think of it, hadn't mentioned Maggie on the trip back. Bragged about the three boys and waved around pictures of his new baby daughter, but he hadn't spoken of Maggie even once.

Huh.

Neil cocked his head, waiting for him to finish the Tums. "You okay, man?"

"Look," Rick said, turning to him. "The department's got some legal stuff going, on account of us jumping the gun last year, screwing up a man's life. Like that first suspect from the Olympics' bombing in Atlanta, remember? Well, this guy committed suicide after we started hounding him." He paused, frowning at something only he could see. "He was innocent."

"Ah, man."

"We're in court over it right now. So no matter how much you *want* this Denison woman to know the murderer, I can't accuse her of being involved in anything until I'm sure. Besides," he said, glancing down the street, "look around. Ten bucks says any woman living here in Beaver-Cleaverville don't know squat about a murder."

"You're on," Neil said, following Rick's gaze to Denison's house. It had a quaint feel to it, with butter-yellow siding, azaleas blooming in the yard, three ferns hanging from the porch. A good match for the petite, pretty woman in the driver's license photo.

But all that did was bring Rule Number Three to mind: Things are never as pretty as they seem.

Chapter 4

The moment Chevy saw her he knew she was the next to die. She parked a ninety-something Buick LeSabre in Lot F, Row 12, a good distance from the entrance to the Fuller Cancer Treatment Center. She wore a long peasant skirt and clogs, and her stride was slow, distracted. The fact that she talked on the phone as she walked was a point in Chevy's favor. But what really sealed her fate was the colorful turban that marked her as a chemo patient.

Yes, she was the one.

Adrenaline surged. Chevy straightened, wanting to take her now. She was only thirty yards away, coming closer. Then again, it was four-thirty and broad daylight. And every second he debated it—now or later, now or later—she stepped that much farther from him and closer to the temporary safety of the visitors' entrance.

He waited five seconds too long and smacked the steering wheel.

"What's the matter?" Jenny asked. She'd been dozing in the passenger seat.

24

"Too risky. I'll have to wait."

"Fraidycat," she teased, but Chevy wasn't in the mood and turned to snap at her. Only the look on her face stopped him. She was pale and gaunt, the hollows of her eyes more pronounced than usual. Traveling had been hard on her—the late run from Seattle, then waiting for Chevy the next day while he took care of business in Boise. They'd lost a whole day on the road while he arranged to have the dolls sent on the appropriate dates, cleaned out his bank account, and emptied his safety-deposit box.

But now they were in Denver, and things were moving. Beth Denison's second gift had just walked into the hospital.

He pulled a picture of Beth from his breast pocket. It was worn, a rip where he'd torn it from an issue of *Antiques* magazine slashing through her elbow, fold lines scoring her body like the crosshairs of a rifle. But her face was clear enough, and he smiled at the knowledge that on that pretty cheek was a remnant of their time together. During all the years in prison, he'd wondered if she remembered him. The scar told him she must—every time she looked in a mirror.

He closed his eyes, turned the ignition just enough to get power, and pressed Play on the tape player in the dash.

"You bastard ... I don't understand." Gasp. *"Stop!"* Broken breaths.

Her panic touched him like the hands of a lover. The beginning of her well-deserved suffering.

Stop. Rewind. Play.

"You bastard . . . I don't understand." Gasp. *"Stop!"* Broken breaths. *"H-how?"*

Stop. Rewind. Play.

"Chevy?"

Jenny's voice snapped him back.

"Are you going to call her again?" she asked.

"I can't," he said. He turned off the tape and took a deep breath, trying to unravel the knots of tension that balled in his groin. "Not yet. You know I had to get rid of Lila Beckenridge's phone." He looked at the doors through which the turbaned woman had gone. "It won't be long until I have a new one."

"I don't know why you like listening to that tape. She just sounds mad to me."

"Scared, Jenny, not mad." An edge of anger pressed down. Chevy loved Jenny, but she didn't understand the process. She didn't comprehend what it took to silence the singing.

And she wasn't well. She hadn't been well since the night they'd met Beth Denison.

"Whatever you say," she said. "You're 'The Hunter.'"

"Stop it," he snapped. The Hunter. That's what the press had dubbed him during his trial for the murder of Anne Chaney. The prosecutor's big sound bite all those years ago had been that women weren't in season when Chevy put a bullet in Anne Chaney's back, at the edge of a lake known for its elk and eight-point deer. They took some heat for the comment, as well as for the crass reference to a second woman, dubbed "the one that got away." But the press seized upon Chevy's nickname and it stuck: The Hunter—capital T, capital H. Jenny thought it was funny, but it had always irked Chevy. He was no hunter.

26

A hunter lies in wait, unnoticed, and strikes in the blink of an eye. Snap, you're dead, and you didn't even know I was there.

Where was the thrill in *that*?

The thrill was in the preparation, the process, the control. In capturing a woman's first tiny quavers of surprise, coaching her through a steady rise of terror, and getting her to deliver the final screams of agony and surrender when the moment was right. He shouldn't expect Jenny to understand, really. Even for him, there had been a learning curve. Three women before Anne Chaney, and the first, Gloria Michaels, hardly even counted. She'd been an impulse, a compulsion in a moment of rage when the singing was too much to endure. But he'd learned from her and done the others better, each a more fulfilling experience than the last.

Beth Denison would be the ultimate fulfillment. Her suffering would be the result of a master plan and an amusing irony: a set of antique dolls that she'd never had the privilege of seeing, but that had changed both their lives seven years earlier. The night Anne Chaney died.

He reached into the console between the two front seats and got the envelope of insurance forms. The top one, for the doll that was supposed to blink but didn't, was already x-ed out. He went to the next page: *1864 Benoit. Bisque head and breastplate, kid body. Replaced cork pate with human hair. Missing from the Larousse collection until 1995. Appraisal: $20,000–$25,000.*

He leaned over to show the picture to Jenny. "Look," he said. "You always liked this doll, didn't you?"

She didn't answer.

"I'm not going to mail this one. You and I are going to hide it. You can help me find a good place, okay? We won't want anyone to find her for a long, long time." Just like the cancer patient. No one would be finding her, either. "Do you want me to get the doll from the trunk for you?"

No response. Chevy put the insurance papers away and opened the atlas, knowing he might as well be talking to thin air. "Listen, tonight shouldn't take too long. If we get back on the road, say, by midnight, then by morning we can get to about"—he did some quick calculations, following I-80 eastward—"*here*. Omaha. I've never been to Omaha," he said, tapping the word on the map. "How does that sound?"

He held the map over in front of Jenny. Nothing.

"Jen?" He sighed and put the map away. She was gone again, to that dark, silent place where no one could touch her. Where no one could hurt her.

Chevy closed his eyes on the sadness and when he opened them again, the woman who was next to die pushed through the hospital doors. He straightened, a thrill slipping down his spine.

"Okay, okay," he said, his fingers trembling with excitement. "Here we go."

There was no answer at Denison's front door, but an impressive-sounding dog began barking the minute they rang the bell.

"Bring any of those special Milk-Bones?" Neil asked and dropped off the porch. He wandered to a gate over-looking the backyard, the air smelling of freshly turned soil and flowers. A plastic wheelbarrow and munchkinsize rake, shovel, and gloves were stacked in the corner of a brick patio, with the adult-size gardening tools lounging in a pot nearby. Petunias and some tiny creeping flower Neil couldn't name sprouted from flower beds, and two flats of red-and-white cocktail begonias—the tag was still in them—sat by the gate.

Elizabeth Denison was in the middle of planting her spring flowers, teaching her kid to garden. A daughter, Neil decided. Pink-and-purple wheelbarrow, pink flowers on the miniature gardening gloves.

His heart gave a tug.

"Think she bailed?" Rick asked, coming up behind him.

Neil flared his nostrils. "Doesn't feel like it. The gardening's not finished, but things are kinda put away, not like she dropped everything in a hurry."

"Let's go talk to the neighbors. Maybe they know her schedule. Deed says she's owned this house three years."

"No husband, right?"

"All in her name."

Single woman with at least one child. Dog. Gingerbread house, complete with flower beds and ruffled curtains in the windows. Boyfriend who cuts up women? Neil had to admit that didn't seem to fit.

"Whoa, there she is," Rick said.

He nodded to the street where a dark green Suburban slowed. The driver paused, spoke to a kid in the backseat, then swung the rear of the SUV down to the garage door. She popped the locks and got out.

Things are never as pretty as they seem.

Rick walked toward her. "Ms. Denison? I'm Lieutenant Richard Sacowicz with the Arlington Police Department, and this is Neil Sheridan. We'd like to have a word with you." He pulled out his badge, letting it suffice for both of them.

Her glance flitted to Neil and he crossed his arms, accustomed to the once-over a six-foot-three man with an ugly scar always got.

"You need to talk to me?" she asked, a little tension in her voice. "Why?"

"Mommy, who's that?"

The kid, a little girl wearing a baseball cap with a ladybug embroidered on the front, had unbuckled and climbed out of the car.

"Abby," Ms. Denison said, "why don't you go let Heinz out? It sounds like he's about to leap out a window."

"Heinz is our dog." The child glanced at Neil but spoke to Rick. *Scary and mean.*

Rick bent to his haunches. "Is he friendly?" he asked.

"If you're not a cat." Abby snickered. "Hey, why did the cat cross the road?"

Rick didn't miss a beat. "Because it was the chicken's day off."

"No," she scolded, wagging a finger at him. "To prove he wasn't chicken."

"Oh, man, you got me. Hey, how does a chicken tell time?"

The little girl's eyes danced with joy. "One o'cluck, two o'cluck, three o'cluck."

Rick chucked her under the chin, and Neil had to admire the method. Rick could schmooze with anyone. Make them tell their deepest secrets.

"Abby," Denison said, holding out a key to her daughter, "go let the dog out."

Abby took the key but stood rooted in front of Rick. "Hey, what did the three-legged dog say when he walked into the saloon?" She jammed her fists against the sides of her waist, affecting her rendition of what was apparently John Wayne. "I'm lookin' for the man who shot my paw."

Rick laughed out loud. Neil wanted to. A surprise, that.

"Hey," Ms. Denison interjected, "what happened to the girl who ignored her mother?"

"It's okay," Rick said, while Abby humphed and trotted to the side door. "I could use some new material. I have a nine-year-old who thinks he's a comic." Fellow dumb-joke-survivor, Mr. I'm-a-Parent-Too. Yeah, this was definitely what Rick was good at.

"Will this take long?" Denison asked. "I can't leave this furniture out here for long."

"It's a Queen Anne highboy," the little girl called out, heading for the side door. "Worth a *lot* if Mr. Waterford is right, but Mommy says he lies through his tee—"

"Abby."

Waterford. A mental list began forming in Neil's mind. Names to check on, clues to follow. An instinct not quite dead after all. Another surprise.

Some unlikely combination of collie, husky, and who-knows-what charged out and Abby squealed. The dog flew from person to person, gathering scents, then circled Abby until she said the magic word "cookie" and they both trotted inside.

"Great watchdog," Rick said, kissing ass a little more. And, "No, it shouldn't take long."

"Okay." Denison reached into the backseat of the SUV, and Neil took her in. She was a small woman, wearing

31

jeans, Nikes, and a white tee under one of those fuzzy sweaters that open down the front. Made you want to pet her. Her build was slender, tight like an athlete. Dark hair fell past her shoulders with a few windblown bangs herded over the top of her head as she slid her sunglasses up. She turned, T-ball paraphernalia in hand, and the sunlight struck her face.

Neil blinked. A scar—a wide, inch-and-a-half-long hyphen—marched high across her cheekbone. It didn't lessen her attractiveness, wasn't garish or twisted like his. But it gave her depth, character. A story.

She popped a button and the garage door lifted. It was an enormous, two-car affair enlarged into a spacious finished basement, and brightly lit. The whole thing was filled with ... stuff. That was the only word Neil could think of for it. Furniture, dishes, baskets, toys, quilts, boxes. Books and magazines filled a counter and an ink-jet printer sat beside a computer, filled with twenty or so pages of printouts. The top page was a picture of an old-fashioned doll, and beside it, a real version of the image in the picture lay in a partially open box, the UPS label dated yesterday. The doll itself, cushioned with tissue paper and Styrofoam peanuts, stared at the ceiling.

Neil picked it up. It was fourteen or fifteen inches tall, with silky hair and a penetrating, wide-eyed gaze. "Antiques," he said. "You're an antiques dealer?"

"I'm a researcher for Foster's Antiques. Would you like to know what my research says about the value of that doll you're holding?"

He arched a brow. "Six months of my salary?"

"I doubt you make that much."

Neil bit back a smile, setting the doll down. Denison came over and tucked it deeper into its packaging, an oddly protective gesture, and his gut lurched at the sight of her hands.

He skimmed her throat, neck, face—any bare flesh that was visible. No injuries buried under makeup, no defensive bruises or scrapes. Just fresh abrasions on her knuckles. He thought of Abby, then dismissed that possibility as quickly as it surfaced. Little girls who take beatings from their mothers don't play T-ball the next day, or roll around with big dogs and tell chicken jokes to total strangers. But something—or someone—had been at the other end of Denison's fists recently.

"I need to get upstairs with Abby," she said. "We can talk in the kitchen."

They followed her up the stairs and into her family room, where Neil braced himself for priceless figurines and ancient rugs and Louis-the-Whatever furniture he'd be afraid to touch. He wasn't even close. It was warm and homey, might have graced the cover of a home-and-garden magazine in the grocery checkout line. It was neat, but not compulsively so, with Barbie dolls and plastic horses frozen in action on the hearth, a watercolor of some four-legged creature drying on the coffee table, and the scent of chocolate chip cookies lingering in the air.

An unexpected attack of warm fuzzies dimmed Neil's hopes: Rick was right. This woman lived a Beaver-Cleaver life, though Neil couldn't recall wishing Mrs. Cleaver would take off her sweater to give him a better look. Elizabeth Denison wasn't the type to know a murderer.

33

The best he could hope for was that she actually knew Lila Beckenridge.

He nursed that hope and strode past Abby and Heinz on the sofa. Followed Rick into the eat-in area of the kitchen.

"What's this about?" Denison asked.

Rick took over. "Do you know a woman named Lila Beckenridge?" he asked, showing her Beckenridge's driver's license photo.

Her brow wrinkled as she looked. "No, I don't think so."

"You're sure?"

"I've never heard the name before," she said, looking genuinely perplexed.

"What about Gloria Michaels?" Neil asked, and again, she shook her head.

"Just after midnight on Wednesday night," Rick said, "you received a phone call from Seattle. Who was that caller?"

For a fraction of a second, she froze. Then her eyes darted down and left, and Neil ground his jaw at how classic it all was.

Damn her, anyway. Beaver's mom was about to lie.

Chapter 5

And that was Rule Number One: Everyone lies, everyone. Criminals, witnesses, victims, sexy young mothers with cute little girls.

Wives.

"The call we're wondering about came three nights ago at twelve-oh-nine," Rick said. "Was it a friend of yours?"

"No."

"Then who was it?"

"Look," she said, "I got an obscene phone call late Wednesday night. That's all."

Neil cracked a smile. "That's a good story; stick with that."

She glared at him and Rick cut in. "The call lasted eighty-two seconds, Ms. Denison. That's a long time to listen to an obscene phone caller."

Her jaw closed. Neil could almost hear the *click* of it locking. He glanced at Rick: *Ten bucks, buddy.*

"So, what did the caller say?" Rick asked.

"He said the normal things an obscene phone caller says. I didn't take notes."

He.

Rick frowned. "Are you afraid of this man?"

"Of course I'm afraid. I told you, it was an obscene phone call. It was creepy."

"Then why didn't you file a police report?" Neil asked.

She crossed her arms. "Last I heard, being creepy on the phone isn't against the law."

She was right. Reports of obscene phone calls came into police stations every day, and were generally blown off by the front line of desk cops before the complaint could consume any paper. But Denison's attitude didn't make sense. A single mother who had received frightening phone calls in the middle of the night should've been oozing cooperation. She should've been relieved to have a couple of heroes knocking at her door.

"How long have you worked for Foster's?" Rick asked. Digging mode now.

"Six years, full-time. Before that I worked part-time in their Seattle gallery."

"Seattle," Neil mused.

She crossed her arms. "I haven't been back there in years, Mr. Sheridan. I moved here right after I finished my degrees."

"Degrees in what?"

"I have a BA in American History and an MFA in Art History."

She was almost defiant when she said it, a little jut of her chin and solid eye contact, as if daring him to find something untrue. Good liars did that—told the truth wherever possible to minimize errors. She was good. And she had fascinating eyes, the kind a man could fall into if

36

he wasn't careful and not even realize he was drowning. Wide, the color of black coffee, with high, slashing brows and thick lashes. Exotic, but something else, too.

Exhausted. Neil would bet his good hand she hadn't slept much lately.

"Do you travel in your work?" Rick asked.

"I sometimes attend antiques exhibitions, usually long weekends at holidays." She paused. "Not Seattle."

Neil pointed to her face. "So it isn't jet lag that put those bags under your eyes."

She pulled back. "Abby wasn't feeling well; I was up last night with her. And I wasn't aware that answering the phone in my own home was a criminal act. Do I need a lawyer?"

Neil's patience slipped its leash. She was lying, plain and simple. He moved to the telephone on the counter. "Well, you just might. Should I call the public defender's office for you?" He purposely fumbled with the phone, pushing a button. "Oh, sorry," he said sweetly, and Rick cursed beneath his breath.

"You have ... two ... new messages," said the mechanical male voice.

Denison panicked. "You can't do—"

Neil caught her wrist when she went for the phone. A caller's voice spun out, female: *"Ms. Denison, this is Margaret Chadburne, in Boise. I was just checking again on the dolls I sent you. You should have received the first one this morning."*

Denison's pulse galloped beneath Neil's fingers. He loosened his grip fractionally.

Beeep.

37

"Hey, honey, it's me. Hannah said you picked up Waterford's highboy from the gallery this afternoon. Call me as soon as you've looked it over."

The ending beep sounded and he looked down at Denison. "Who was that?"

"Margaret Chadburne, in Boise. She was checking again on the dolls she sent—"

"The other call."

"My boss. Evan Foster."

"Honey," he said, and she gaped at him. "He called you 'honey.'"

"Evan Foster wasn't in Seattle on Wednesday and didn't call me. Leave him alone."

Neil bit back a smile. "You're very protective of your friends." He turned her hand over and eyed the abrasions on her knuckles. "Is that how you got these?"

"I'm a kickboxer," she said, yanking her hand away. It was the first thing she'd said that actually fit. Tough, controlled, combative. For a second, Neil let his mind wander, envisioning that lean body in spandex, releasing all the tension that seemed to tie her in knots …

Bad move. Neil shook it off. "Where's your husband?" he asked.

"Excuse me?"

He pointed to the foyer, where he'd seen a large photo on the wall beyond the kitchen door: Denison in a cream-colored dress, a sprig of flowers blossoming in her hair and a sandy-haired man at her side. "You're wearing a ring," Neil said, "but he doesn't own this house with you. Where is he? Seattle, maybe?"

"Dead."

38

The answer came as a jolt, but would be so easy to verify there was no reason to question it. "When?" Neil asked.

"Seven years ago, when I was pregnant with Abby."

"I'm sorry, Ms. Denison," Rick said. "How did that happen?"

Her chin lifted a notch. "Adam was flying back to Chicago with my family after graduation, to look for a house. The plane crashed. My parents, my brother, my husband, and two hundred and three other people on board died. Anything else?"

Whoa, that wasn't the type of story Neil expected. Love gone bad, an affair, a divorce. Not the tragic loss of someone—everyone—she loved, in the blink of an eye.

"Okay." Rick handed her a card. "If you hear from this caller again, let me know, okay?"

She took it—planning to throw it in the trash the minute they were gone, no doubt—and Rick went back through the family room. Neil followed, trying to let it go, then thought, *Screw that*. He veered to the couch and knelt beside Abby. "I hope you feel better soon, sweet—"

"Mr. Sheridan!"

"I feel fine," Abby said. She was confused.

Neil rose, cocking his head to Denison. "Amazing how kids bounce back like that, isn't it?"

"Hey," Abby said, "what happened to your face?"

The question came out of the blue and wasn't from her arsenal of jokes. Neil touched his scar. "I had a really big boo-boo a few years ago. Kind of scary, huh?"

"No. Mommy has one, too. It just means you hurt once."

Well, there was a perspective he'd never considered. Pretty insightful for a six-year-old, but honest, anyway, which was more than the girl's mother had managed. A pang of worry thrummed in his chest: Abby had no choice about what her mother dragged her into; a child never does.

The thought haunted him as he strode down to the curb, and he fisted his right hand on the roof of Rick's car. Spasms shot to his elbow. "She's lying," he said, forcing himself to flex his fingers.

Rick made his eyes big. "Ya think?"

"Damn it, she knows him. He murdered a woman and she's lying for him." His heart was beating double time. "Take her in, man, charge her with accessory. Work her over."

"Sleep deprivation? Waterboarding, maybe?"

"Screw you."

"Obscene phone calls, Neil. That's her story and it fits. Maybe she's really afraid."

"Then why didn't she say so? Jesus, Rick, you're a police lieutenant and I'm—" He stopped. He wasn't anything anymore. "If she was scared, she'd have said so."

"She did."

"Bullshit. The creepy phone call thing was a cover for that asshole and you know it." He slid a hand into his pocket, found the broken barrette. "I have to know, Rick. Whether it was Russell or not, that fucker cost me everything."

Rick looked at him over the roof of the car. "I loved her, too."

Neil's heart jerked. "Not the same."

"No," Rick agreed, "and God willing, I'll go my whole life and never know how it feels. But you know I can't do surveillance on a woman who's under suspicion of answering her ph—"

"Look."

Rick followed Neil's gaze toward Denison's house. Through the front picture window, she could be seen picking up her phone. She carried it to the window, saw Rick and Neil, and dropped the blinds. But her silhouette was still visible, and within seconds, she hung up.

"That was quick," Neil said.

"Come on, Neil. We can't spy on the woman like this. Watching her isn't gonna tell us anything."

"Then what is?"

"Looking at Gloria Michaels's murder again, for one, and putting it up against Beckenridge. Maybe we'll find enough to get your friends at the Bureau to reopen the case."

"Friends?" Neil said and sank into the front seat. "Oh, shit."

But it was the right thing to do. They headed back to the precinct and hashed through Lila Beckenridge's murder—as much as anyone knew yet. Finally, Rick took Neil home and dumped him in the guest room. For the first time in recent memory, Neil slept sober.

He started Sunday on the phone, tracking down Ellen Jenkins at a country club, playing golf. He called for a rental car—upgraded to a 2009 Dodge Charger with a hemi when he got there—and decided he needed some-thing more appropriate to wear to meet Ellen than desert gear or ripped jeans. He came out of a department store wearing pleated blue slacks and a cream shirt with an embroidered logo above the pocket. The country-club set liked embroidered logos, he decided, though he couldn't quite make this one out. It looked vaguely like a penguin.

He rolled through Chester County, Pennsylvania, two hours later, Ellen's neighborhood marked by turreted mansions with high stone walls, four-car garages, and gated pools and tennis courts. Her country club came into view like a landscape that might be pictured on a wine bottle, and at the front gate, Neil found his name on the magic list that granted entry. The manager of the golf course was expecting him, the logo on *his* pocket recognizable as cursive letters.

"Her party just got to hole seven," the manager said and tossed Neil the keys to a cart. "I were you, I wouldn't wanna interrupt her."

"Aw," Neil said, "Ellen's a pussycat."

The man scoffed. "And the rest of us are wounded mice."

Ellen didn't look up when he got there. "Sheridan, if you breathe one word before I sink this putt, I'll use your balls on the next hole."

Neil wasn't stupid. He watched eastern Pennsylvania's fiercest DA crouch down and line up her shot, take one practice swing, then sink the ball in the cup twelve yards away.

She took a bow, the men in her foursome applauding. A caddy took her club, and one of the men kissed her on the cheek. Neil decided it was Byron, the same husband

42

she'd had nine years ago, though the poor bastard was showing his age.

"Man, you got old," she said, coming over to Neil. "Is that a penguin on your chest?"

"You'll be buying this brand for Byron come Christmas."

"I told him I'd ride with you and meet them at the next hole. You know how to drive this thing?"

"Hang on."

He got close to the eighth tee then tucked the cart between a sand trap and a wild area. He pulled off his sunglasses. "Smacking balls around agrees with you," Neil said. "You look good."

"And you look like a terrorist trying to sneak onto a golf course."

"It's the penguin."

"It's the scar," she said, and angled his cheek toward her. "I heard about the shooting afterwards. I didn't know ... I mean, it must've been worse than I thought."

"I was out of the game a little while, but now the scar helps me pick up women."

"So, you and Heather ..."

Neil swallowed. "We only made it a couple years after that."

"Okay."

And that was just about all the emotional chitchat Ellen Jenkins was capable of, not that Neil was very adept at it, either. "I need a favor," he said.

"No shit."

"I want to reexamine the Gloria Michaels murder. Anthony Russell may not have killed her."

43

Ellen's jaw didn't drop; she was too poised for that. Still, there was a tightness in her throat Neil could see. "And you brought me boatloads of evidence, I presume?"

"A woman was killed in Seattle on Wednesday night. Too much like Gloria ..."

He laid it out, and when he was done, Ellen said, "But can they show the bullet came from the same gun that shot Gloria?"

"Not that easy," he admitted. "It's a thirty-eight, but it's a hollowpoint. Hollowpoints get pretty busted up when they hit something hard."

"Like a skull," Ellen said. She took a deep breath and got out of the golf cart, wandered a few steps toward the sand trap, and adjusted her visor. Neil followed a few steps behind, letting her think. "I always wondered if that asshole Russell was lying," she said after a moment. "Why shouldn't he? Make up a story about killing Gloria Michaels and snap, no more death penalty. Hell, his attorney was orgasmic over the deal."

Neil knew it was true but bristled nonetheless. "Russell dated Gloria, and he had the right history. It's not like he didn't look good for her murder."

"Bullshit. You Feds came in because it looked like a kidnapping, then you browbeat your way through the investigation, fingered the guy, and turned him over to us."

"Hey, I'm not here to use you as a confessor, damn it. I'm here for some help."

"So why don't you call your Fed cronies?" Then she waved a hand. "Never mind. The Feds eating crow? They don't know how."

"I just want the paper, Ellen. I'll find enough to get the FBI on board."

"It's a closed case. The paper is a matter of public record."

"I don't want just the parts that are a matter of public record. I want all of it. The narratives, the photos, the impressions. The notes to each other in the margins of the reports, the e-mails. That's what I need, Ellen."

"I'm the one who handled Russell's indictment."

"And your objections to doing it are all over the record." Not only the record, but the newspaper and political gossip columns, too. Ellen wanted the death penalty, but the DA at the time, Wallace McMahan, ordered her to drop premeditated murder and go for manslaughter. Manslaughter was an easier win. And in this case, because Russell's end of the bargain was to talk about Gloria's murder, the deal came with an added bonus for McMahan: one more X in the win column.

"Wally McMahan is running for the Senate now," she said. "This could throw egg all over his face."

"You hate Wally McMahan."

A tiny smile curled her lips. "I do, don't I?" She looked at him sideways. "So give me what you've got on the Seattle woman. I'll look at it after the ninth hole. *After.* And after a shower and a couple of stiff martinis. Come by the house at six o'clock. I'll let you know."

It was the best he could hope for. Neil spent the afternoon at a coffee shop hooked up to their WiFi and making phone calls to Seattle. Seattle wouldn't tell him jack shit about Beckenridge: He wasn't a cop, he wasn't a Fed, and he wasn't a lawyer. He wasn't even a reporter. He was nothing.

He dropped by Ellen's McMansion at ten 'til six.

"I'm not sure the unsub in Seattle is Gloria's killer," she said, handing him a cardboard box full of files. "But if there's even a chance, I want you to get him."

"Ellen, I could kiss you," Neil said.

"Yeah, yeah, that's what they all say."

He was loading the box of files into the Charger when Rick called.

"I've got Lila Beckenridge's autopsy," he said. "And something else you won't believe."

"What is it?"

"Meet me at my office."

"I'm two hours away."

"So drive fast."

Chapter 6

Neil made it back to Arlington a little before nine o'clock.

Rick leaned forward onto his desk. "Another one," he said. "Maybe."

Neil went still. "What?" Then, "What do you mean, *maybe*?"

"A car was found this afternoon outside Denver, wiped down. It belongs to a single mom named Thelma Jacobs. She's missing."

Neil's heart rate kicked up, but he was afraid to let it run away with him. "Cars are found every day with their owners missing. Why do we care about one in Denver?"

"Guess who Thelma Jacobs called at seven-thirty last night."

Neil stared. "No way."

"Yup. But the call only lasted about ten seconds."

"Son of a bitch." Neil couldn't believe it. "That's the call Denison was picking up last night as we were leaving." He stood up and started pacing. "Denver? He's moving?"

"Could be."

"But no body."

"Not yet. Jacobs attended a support group for breast cancer survivors yesterday afternoon at three. That was the last place she was seen."

"Not a dancer then," Neil said. And not a college coed. He shook his head, as if jostling all the information would somehow make it fall into place. "Let's go find out if Elizabeth Denison has Thelma Jacobs on her Christmas card list."

"I already did. She says she's never heard of her. And the call at seven-thirty last night was a wrong number."

"We're supposed to buy that?" Neil fisted and flexed his right hand through a series of spasms. His heart was thumping fast. Anger, he thought at first, then realized it was adrenaline.

He was hunting again, and Elizabeth Denison was a lead.

Rick opened a folder. "Here's the autopsy on Lila Beckenridge. She *was* raped, using a Trojan condom, and her right jaw was broken, probably from a kick. And this mark right here" —he slid a photo across his desk and pointed at Lila's temple— "it's not dirt or blood. It's eyebrow pencil."

"Eyebrow pencil?" Neil looked at the line. Straight as an arrow, and one inch long.

"Revlon, charcoal-black eye pencil, I shit you not. Looks like he drew a line to mark the placement of the bullet. There's heavy stippling around the top of the line."

"So the shot was point-blank."

"Yup. Like Gloria, right?"

"Yeah."

"And Gloria was raped?" Rick asked.

"With a Trojan. And she was carjacked, beaten, cut up, and left in a woods; her car was wiped down like Beckenridge's, and a smear of Reese's Cup chocolate was found on the front seat. But she wasn't marked with any damned eyebrow pencil."

Rick shrugged. "So it's not a hundred percent. It's still plenty to justify another look. The question is, did you convince the ADA of that?"

"She's the DA now, and yeah. I have the files on Gloria's case in my trunk."

"So let's sit down with them. Order a pizza or something."

Neil nodded and started for the door, then narrowed his eyes on Rick. Rick was pretty anxious to dive in—at nine-thirty at night—to a case that barely touched his precinct. It struck Neil that there was an awful lot on Rick's plate to be beating time with this. It also struck him that there were deep, dark gullies dragging under his eyes.

"Hey, you been home yet?" Neil asked.

Rick thumbed through the yellow pages to P. "Not tonight. Been a little busy."

"Uh-huh. And last night? Maggie said you came back here after you dropped me off."

"Had some work to finish."

Neil looked around the office and felt his chest tighten. There were little things he'd been too distracted to notice: a blanket folded across the back of the sofa, pillow underneath, dopp kit on the floor with a toothbrush sticking out. His heart dropped. "Ah, jeez, man," he said, shaking his head. "How long?"

Rick glanced up, then sank against the back of his chair. "A few weeks in the den. The last couple here in the office."

"Christ." So it wasn't just the job pulling Rick under. Neil came back to the desk and closed the phone book. "Screw a pizza. We can look at paper at your house as well as we can here."

"Maggie sorta wants some time alone, man."

"Then she shouldn't have married you and had four freakin' kids. Besides, even if you're not sleeping together, it's not like you don't have an extra bed in that house."

"Hey, I ain't sharing with a guy who has a penguin on his chest."

"Bigot. I'll drive."

The kids were in bed by the time they got to Rick's, but Maggie wasn't. Neil ordered the pizza, adding green olives for Maggie, and the three of them shared it. The tension was right there on the surface; Neil's heart ached with it. He couldn't imagine a world in which Rick and Maggie Sacowicz weren't together. They were the gold standard in marriage.

Eventually Rick dragged a pillow to the den, and Neil read for another hour, then slept, dreaming of his own mistakes. That last phone conversation: *I'm sorry, pumpkin, Daddy has to go back to work, but I'll be home as soon as I can ... Damn it, Heather, I can't deal with this right now; handle it yourself. I have to find Anthony Russell ...*

By Monday morning, the adrenaline surge from the

50

evening before had morphed to restlessness. Nothing to do. Neil thought about catching a plane to Seattle or Denver, then remembered the unaccommodating nature of police working an active investigation. He had no place in the investigations of Lila Beckenridge or Thelma Jacobs. If not for the fact that Rick had been asked to look up Elizabeth Denison, they wouldn't have even known about them.

But he did know and, further, he knew Elizabeth Denison knew something. And while Rick might be bound to playing it safe when it came to talking to her, Neil had no such restraints. He had no badge, no shield, no career to protect.

No rules.

"You look terrible," Evan Foster said, holding Beth's chair at his favorite lunch spot. It was a Caribbean grill on Barrett Road, complete with saltwater aquariums and palm fronds.

"Thanks," she groused, stuffing a loose strand of hair behind her ear. "I've been a little under the weather. Spent the weekend in bed."

Spent the weekend on the Internet and working through her list was more like it, but she couldn't tell Evan that. She still hadn't completely wrapped her mind around what was happening. For almost a year, Bankes had been out of prison. His was one of a rash of over-turned convictions that had the internal affairs department of the Seattle PD routing out dirty cops in collusion with a dirty DA.

"If you were sick," Evan said, "why didn't you bring

Abby over so Aunt Carol could watch her and you could get some rest?"

"I can take care of my own daughter, Evan. I do it all—"

"All the time. Yeah, yeah. A regular Wonder Wo—"

Beth heard no more. Ten feet away, Neil Sheridan was being seated by a hostess. He stretched his long legs out under his table, looked at Beth, and winked.

Her belly somersaulted. Damn him. What was he doing here?

"Beth." Evan's voice. "I asked how Abby's T-ball is going."

"Oh," she said, twisting her napkin into tiny cyclones on her lap. "Abby hates it."

"Then don't make her do it."

"It's good for her," Beth said. Evan. Concentrate on Evan, not Sheridan. "This is spring break week at school, and I'm going to take her to spend a few days with Cheryl and Jeff. I'm hoping Jeff can coach her a little and get her excited about it."

"Sure. Let your brother-in-law turn her into a boy for you."

"I'm not trying to turn her into a boy. I just want her exposed to things—"

"Adam would have exposed her to. So take her to a ball game."

"I'm not into ball games. That's the problem."

"Then let *me* take her to a ball game." Evan reached into his pocket and held up three tickets. "Orioles, in three weeks. Right behind home plate."

Beth went silent. "Evan, no," she finally said. "It might mislead Abby into thinking—"

"That I'm someone special? God forbid." He slid the tickets back into his breast pocket, his expression changing from charm to genuine bewilderment. "Tell me something. Don't you get tired of going to bed alone? Of not having anyone in your life who can name your favorite color or deepest fear?"

"You?" Beth asked.

He managed a smile. "Your favorite color is blue. Your deepest fear is loving again."

Wrong on both counts, Evan, she thought, but wished to God he was right.

The phone in her purse rang. Beth looked. She'd missed a call from the same number earlier when she was dropping Abby off at T-ball, but there hadn't been a message. She put the phone away. She wasn't anxious to take calls from unknown numbers these days.

"So tell me about Waterford's highboy." Evan was back to business. "Is it any good?"

"The back is made up, on both pieces. Six, maybe eight thousand dollars, tops."

"Shit."

"Kerry Waterford is a con artist. I've been telling you that."

"Then it's gotta be the dolls, Beth. That widow's dolls better be worth a fortune."

"They might be. I've only seen one so far, but it's a legitimate Benoit. And early—1862." She let a sparkle into her eyes. "It almost reminds me of the Larousse dolls."

"Larousse?" Evan leaned in. He was no doll expert, but he knew of the Larousse collection. It had been held by a wealthy collector's family for nearly a century.

53

"Don't get excited. I checked. The Larousses haven't sold anything; that collection is still intact in Vancouver. But this one's still good."

"Is it in good condition?"

"The blinking mechanism in her eyelids doesn't work, but otherwise, she's nearly perfect. Thirty or forty thousand dollars, I bet, even without repairing the eyes."

"Cha-ching," Evan said, smiling now. "How many more are there?"

"I don't know. The owner is a widow in Boise whose husband had them in an attic. I met her at the Dallas show in September after Kerry tried to con her into buying a fake Benoit. It's taken me this long to convince her to sell, but she called this morning and said she sent me two more."

Sheridan's voice rumbled from across the aisle. Beth blinked. For one shining moment, she'd forgotten about him. Now, he thanked a blushing waitress for a club sandwich and coleslaw, then picked up his glass of water and tipped it toward Beth in a toast.

Her skin shrank two sizes. She spent the rest of the meal torn between wanting to tell Sheridan to go to hell and wanting to plead with him to keep Bankes away. But there was too much at stake for the latter.

When Evan reached for the tab, Beth stopped him and picked it up. "I'll get it," she said. "I'm going to stay a few more minutes and return some phone calls, have a cup of coffee."

Time to have it out with Neil Sheridan.

Chapter 7

Evan Foster kissed Beth Denison before he left. Just on the cheek, but that was Denison's doing—that instinctively feminine maneuver of her chin in the last second. She'd talked about Abby and T-ball and antique dolls, munched salad and breadsticks, and tried not to get caught shooting nervous glances in Neil's direction. She and Foster had discussed nothing that could be construed as even remotely related to murder or kidnapping. In fact, Beth Denison made such a pretty picture of innocence that Neil began to wonder if his bullshit detector had gone on the blink.

Then his phone rang. Rick. "Denison got a call a little while ago on her cell phone."

"Yeah, I know," Neil said. "I'm with her now."

"You're what?"

"Not *with* her, exactly. But we're in the same place. She had lunch with Evan Foster."

"Did she answer her phone about forty minutes ago?"

"No. It rang and she checked the number, then let it go. Why?"

"That call came from a cell phone in Omaha, Nebraska. It's the second call from that phone today. It lasted fifty seconds."

Neil's hackles rose; he didn't like the direction Rick was going. "Omaha?"

"The owner of the phone may have gone missing there this morning. She hasn't been gone long enough to be official, but the family is worried and reported it."

"No way, man."

"I'm gonna pull Denison in for questioning, just in case. Where are you?"

Neil told him, his pulse picking up. Another one? He stared at Denison.

"Don't do anything stupid, Neil," Rick said. "There's no crime in Omaha yet. We're just talking." Beat. "Neil?"

"I heard you."

He disconnected just as Denison gathered her purse and stood. She headed past Neil, slowing at his table to slide her tab under his.

Neil might have smiled if he wasn't so pissed. And confused. He gave her a minute just in case she really was using the restroom, then left enough money for both checks and followed her to the back of the restaurant. He found her in the outer lobby of the restrooms with her back to him, her cell phone pressed against her ear. Checking the message from Omaha, no doubt.

He stepped closer, then stopped. She wasn't listening to a message.

"So, you got the jewels?" she asked in a hushed tone. "Okay. Take them to the lockbox. I'll call Vito and arrange for the drop. Be careful. They may be onto us."

"Cute," Neil said.

She turned. "Oh, my!" The fingers of one hand splayed over her breastbone. "Mr. Sheridan. I didn't know you were there."

"I suppose Vito's last name is Gambino?"

"Wouldn't you like to know?" She squared her shoulders, the cell phone dead in one hand. "You're following me."

"I stopped for lunch. Don't you ever run into friends at lunch?"

"You aren't a friend. You aren't a police officer, either."

Neil was impressed. "The lady does her homework."

"Stay away from me, or I'll file charges. Harassment, impersonating a police officer."

"I didn't impersonate anyone. I used to be FBI. Lieutenant Sacowicz invited me along to talk to you because the man calling you may be the same man I hunted in a murder case several years ago."

She went suddenly pale, her body rigid as steel. "I told you, I don't know him."

Neil took a step closer. "But you're lying."

She started past him and Neil reached for her elbow. She exploded. Air hissed between her teeth as her right elbow went for his throat and her knee jammed upward. Neil twisted, blocking the blows out of sheer instinct and no small degree of luck, and in two seconds he jostled her up against the wall, pinning her wrists over her head.

"Let go of me," she said, breathless.

"What the hell was that?" Neil's heart was thundering. He couldn't believe she'd caught him so off guard. More than that, he couldn't believe she'd reacted so strongly to

57

the mere grasp of her arm or that, even now, crowded against the wall, she seemed to be gauging the details of their positions, considering some fancy Jackie Chan move. An ex–FBI agent and Sentryman, for God's sake, nearly twice her size. "Bad idea," he warned. "You may be some sort of black belt or something, but I know every trick you do plus a dozen you never thought of."

She squirmed and he moved closer—a man holding his lover, murmuring sweet nothings against her ear, in case anyone should see them. Except that holding Beth Denison was like handling fire. "I want answers," he said.

"Let go of me."

"Why did you try to kill me just now?" Christ. That wasn't what he should have asked. He should have asked her about the phone call. But his brain had short-circuited. Sensory overload. The fragrance of berries in her hair, the throb of her pulse in her wrist, the brush of her breasts against his rib cage. "Answer me," he said. "Why did you go off like that?"

"You grabbed me," she snarled.

"I touched you. There's a difference."

"You're still touching me. Let go."

Neil held her eyes then couldn't resist letting his gaze drop to her lips. It was the tightness there that shook him free of the spell. Pinching back secrets.

He cursed and let go, but she came after him the instant she realized he'd wrenched her phone away. "Damn you," she said, stomping her foot. "What do you want?"

"I wanna know what makes a woman lie to police, then walk around ready to rip a man's throat out," he said. "But I'll settle for finding out who called you during lunch."

58

"What?"

"Your cell phone rang about forty minutes ago. Lieutenant Sacowicz thinks the call came from Omaha."

She blinked, as if genuinely surprised, and Neil arrowed down her phone screen.

"You have no right to listen to my phone messages! I'll sue the police department."

Her conviction was so righteous he almost chuckled. "I'm not a member of the police department, remember? Of course, you could file charges against me for assault or stealing your phone, but it would be one of those he-said, she-said situations." He cocked a dark brow at her. "And *I* haven't already lied to the police this week."

"Give me my phone."

He pushed her hands away and punched Okay. The screen came up with a number: area code 402. Well, shit. "You didn't answer your phone during lunch," he said, "yet this call was almost a minute long. Guess that means there'll be a message here, huh?"

Denison ground her heel into the floor. Neil punched Okay again and put the phone to his ear. *"Ah, Beth, where are you? Answer the phone, doll. I need to talk to you."*

His blood turned cold. Not a woman, not the owner of the phone. Was this the voice of Gloria Michaels's killer? He turned off the phone and looked at Denison. One more chance. "Who is this?"

"How would I know? *I* haven't heard the message."

He pushed the appropriate buttons and held the phone to her ear. She listened, and the blood drained from her cheeks.

"Ms. Denison?" he said, but she didn't seem to hear

him. He touched her shoulder and she jumped like a startled cat. Neil frowned. Thirty seconds earlier, the woman had been spitting nails. Now, she looked scared to death.

But there wasn't time to think about it. A pair of uniforms came through the restaurant, and Neil slid the phone back into her purse. He dropped back as they walked into the lobby.

"Ms. Denison," a balding officer said, "Lieutenant Sacowicz would like for you to come with us to the station."

"What?" She looked at Neil, shock and anger swimming in her eyes, then back to the officers. "What the hell for?"

"Just questioning, ma'am," said the other uniform, a striking blond who might have been of legal drinking age. He schooled his features into an expression he'd probably practiced in front of a mirror, adding, "Unless you wanna do it the hard way."

Denison looked as if she'd gone numb, but for the sheer betrayal in her eyes. She stared at Neil, the cops flanking her out the door, and a memory stabbed him in the chest. *Damn it, Heather, I can't help if you're not gonna be straight with me . . .*

He cursed.

Déjà fucking vu.

Omaha, Nebraska
1,159 miles away

Chevy shoved the woman's arms into the driver's seat of the Honda. He stepped back and peered over the edge of the

60

ravine, a hundred-and-fifty-foot bluff that sank into an abandoned quarry like the end of the earth. It made for a long hike back, but here he wouldn't have to worry about anyone finding the woman. That was critical to his plan. This woman needed to be *missing*, like the one from Denver.

He propped the doll on the dead woman's lap, smiling a little at the idea of all that money about to go over the bluff and into oblivion. *Eighteen sixty-four Benoit, original clothing. Bisque head and breastplate, kid body. One of a pair missing from the Larousse collection until 1995. Appraisal: $20,000–$25,000.* Another precious doll that Beth would never see.

Damn, he wished he hadn't thought of her again. The only flaw in his plan so far was that she hadn't answered her phone this morning, hadn't given him the chance to turn the thumbscrews a little. Leaving a message was risky, but Chevy had finally given in. He'd had to hear her voice, even if it was just in voice mail, and know that when she got his message, the fear would start thumping in her chest. He had to know she was suffering.

Not like Mother. She had never suffered; she was gone between one heartbeat and the next. Incessant, lilting little folk tunes on her lips one second, death rattling in her throat the next. A .38-caliber pistol in her hand.

Chevy shook off the memory and wrenched the gearshift into neutral. He walked to the back of the Honda, lodged his shoulder against the bumper, and gave it a shove. The wheels turned, the front end of the car dipping as the tires edged toward the ravine. Breathing hard, he pushed until the car crept another inch, then two, then picked up speed as the front wheels rotated down the slope and past the edge. A second later, momentum hurled it into the ravine.

He listened for metal crunching into the earth, the ribbon of sound swirling up from the bottom of the bluff like a scream. He pulled out the dead woman's cell phone and started to dial Beth, then stopped.

He looked at his watch. Two o'clock, and an hour later in Virginia. God, he wanted to talk to Beth, but this woman's phone wouldn't be good for much longer. It might not even be safe now. The date book in her purse showed she'd had a hair appointment at nine o'clock this morning. It could be someone had noticed her missing already, maybe even reported it. Normally, there would be no need to worry so soon. But on the heels of Lila Beckenridge and Thelma Jacobs, the authorities just might take the report of a missing woman seriously enough to look into it without waiting the usual twenty-four hours.

He studied the cell phone, the frustration of not hearing Beth's voice causing almost physical pain. But the risk of this phone being watched increased with every passing moment. No sense in taking chances.

He turned off the phone and with a pitcher's windup, hurled it into the ravine. He pulled a pen from his pocket and marked off the insurance form for the doll that had just gone over. Already thinking ahead to his next stop, he turned to the fourth page.

Ah, yes. *That* doll. A thrill shot through him. Better pick up a couple of blank tapes for that one.

"Ah, Beth, where are you? Answer the phone, doll. I need to talk to you ..."

Beth sat at a cold metal table in the interrogation room, eyes closed as the recording of a phone message from Omaha streamed from a digital recorder. It was the third time the lieutenant had played it for her, but if he expected repetition to wear her down, he'd be sadly mistaken. She simply blocked it out.

"Ms. Denison?" Lieutenant Sacowicz said, punching off the message. "Is there anything you'd like to say?"

Find him. Kill him. Take him out of my life. "No."

"Care to explain the gun in your purse?"

"I'm a single woman with a daughter to protect," Beth said, referring to the .22 derringer she'd started carrying again. "I have a permit."

"Martial arts, kickboxing, a pistol. You take protection pretty seriously."

Yes.

The lieutenant stared at her with eyes the color of pewter, then suddenly hit the recording again. Beth hadn't prepared for it this time. A tidal wave of panic washed through her at the sound of Bankes's voice. Gorge rose in her throat.

Hold it down. Don't let the fear rise up. Omaha is still a long way away.

But the trembling began anyway, deep in the center of her bones. She clutched her arms over her chest, trying to contain the shivers. It didn't help. "I need to go," she said, trying to keep her voice from shaking, too. "Abby will be finished at T-ball in half an hour."

The lieutenant rubbed a hand over his face. "The problem is, Ms. Denison, I think you need some time to think this over. See if a name comes to mind."

"What? Abby will be waiting. I have to get her." The lieutenant set his jaw. Beth couldn't believe it. "I haven't been charged with anything. You can't keep me here."

He shook his head—a slow, weary gesture that made him look older than he probably was. "Have it your way." He sighed. "You're under arrest for obstruction of justice and failure to cooperate in a police investigation. You have the right to remain silent, not that I need to tell you that," he editorialized. "If you give up that right, anything you say—"

"Wait! What about my daughter?"

"Is there someone you can call to go get her?"

Desperation clawed at Beth's heart. *I'm in jail, Evan; would you go get Abby? Hannah, would you mind keeping Abby until they release me from jail?*

"All right," Sacowicz said, taking her silence as his answer. "I'll take care of her. Shaw Park, right? Coach Mike's team, the Ladybugs."

"Wait," Beth cried, shocked at the raw terror that seized her. *Chevy Bankes! His name is Chevy Bankes. But you can't touch him. He's free and he's coming and as far as the law is concerned, he has every right* ... She was stunned by how close the words came to spilling out. "Please," she whispered.

"Please what?" he asked, bending close. "You can stop all this right now and go get your little girl and take her home. Just tell me the name of the caller and walk out of here."

So simple. As if giving the devil a name would end it.

She couldn't do it; she had to think about Abby. Keeping her mouth shut today would affect Abby for a couple of hours, maybe for the rest of the afternoon. Naming Chevy Bankes would haunt her daughter for a lifetime. About that much, anyway, Adam had been right. *Never tell, Beth. No one will understand.* And just this morning, hadn't her lawyer confirmed that? *Keep quiet, Ms. Denison. The best thing you can do for your daughter is to never tell a soul and pray we can convince Bankes to leave you alone.*

Beth grabbed the edge of the table, looking at the lieutenant through blurry eyes. "Please, Lieutenant." She hated the tears but was helpless to keep them from running down her cheeks. "You said you're a father. Please. Don't let Abby be afraid. Whatever else happens, please don't let my daughter be afraid."

Sacowicz cleared his throat. "I'll take care of her, Ms. Denison."

He started for the door and Beth said, "Wait." Her voice was barely loud enough to stop him. She cleared her throat. "I want a lawyer."

Chapter 8

The attorney blew in like a tornado, Neil thought. Her name was Adele Lochner, tall and slim, with a slick bun, sharp cheekbones, and a nose one size too big.

"Harassing good citizens again, Lieutenant?" she asked, looking at Denison through the one-way glass. She turned to Neil. "Who are you?"

"Neil Sher—"

"He's former special agent Neil Sheridan, with the FBI."

"Former," she said. "Who is he now?"

"I asked him to consult with me. He has knowledge of a related case," Rick said. "Could we talk about the case now?"

"Sure. Obstruction of justice? What kind of charge is that?"

"It's a charge to shake the woman into identifying a man calling her on the phone," Rick said. "A man we think committed a murder nine years ago and might be at it again."

She straightened. Hadn't expected that, Neil thought. "Tell me," she said.

Neil told her first about Gloria Michaels, then Rick laid out the dead Seattle woman and the missing Denver woman, and their phones being used to call Denison.

"Did my client admit to talking to anyone?" Lochner asked.

"She claims they're obscene phone calls."

She rolled her eyes. "You guys are incred—"

"Whoa, there's more," Rick said. "Denison got another call about two hours ago. From the cell phone belonging to a *third* woman whose family says she disappeared this morning in Omaha. And this time, we got the recording of the call."

"Shit," Lochner said. She drew a breath through her narrow nose. "Have you told Denison this man is a murderer?"

"Not yet," Rick said.

"And why is that? Afraid of another lawsuit, Lieutenant?" She looked back and forth between them, a smug look growing on her face. "You're not sure this caller murdered anyone at all, are you?" Rick opened his mouth, but she held up a hand. "The Seattle woman's phone has never been found, so anyone might have used it. And what about the Denver woman? You're not even sure she's the victim of foul play."

"That's bullshit," Neil said, but Rick cut in.

"Maybe not."

"What?" Neil asked, and Rick looked at the floor.

"A little while ago, Denver FBI got Thelma Jacobs's support group counselor talking," Rick said. "The day she

67

disappeared, Jacobs had learned the cancer wasn't gone. She was despondent, talking about not wanting her son to have to deal with her care and all that."

"Ah, man," Neil said.

"So," Lochner speculated, "the counselor believes she might have run off, or killed herself."

"And wiped down her own fucking car?" Neil shot. "Made a phone call to the same woman as Beckenridge?"

Lochner was undaunted. "And let me guess: The Omaha woman isn't officially *missing*. You said she disappeared just this morning."

"She skipped an appointment, that's all," Rick said. "But her family insists that's not like her." He suddenly looked beat. People thought cops got ulcers from criminals. They got them from attorneys.

Of course, if Neil was being totally honest, the information about the Denver woman threw him for a loop, too. Maybe they didn't really have two missing women. Maybe they had one woman with cancer who ran away, and another who simply forgot about a hair appointment this morning and was scaring her family to death. Maybe the Seattle woman's phone really was picked up by a random stranger, who made a random phone call to Elizabeth Denison. And maybe all those likenesses between the murders of Gloria Michaels and Lila Beckenridge were just figments of Neil's imagination.

And maybe pigs fly.

"Even if you dismiss the two missing women, what about my case?" Neil asked. "There are too many similarities between Gloria Michaels and this dancer in Seattle."

"Like what?"

He ticked them off and Lochner listened, then went silent for a long, long moment. Finally, she squared off to Neil. "And based on those similarities, has the DA reopened that case? The FBI?"

Neil glared.

"That's what I thought." She picked up her briefcase. "Excuse me, gentlemen. I'd like to go speak to my client now."

Neil watched her disappear into the interview room, frowning at her back. When the door closed, he turned to Rick. "She didn't ask the logical question."

"Huh?"

"You told her we had a recording of the last call to Denison, and Lochner didn't ask what was on it."

A crease burrowed between Rick's eyes. "You think she already knows?"

"I don't know how she could. We've been on Denison since before the call came." A thought hit. "Unless Denison had already told her about the calls."

Rick rubbed a hand over his face. "If that's the case, then she's known for a while she was in trouble. Otherwise, why bother with a lawyer?"

Neil thought about it and came up with nothing. There was a reason Denison was lying, and Lochner seemed to have had a heads-up about the calls. But there was also a reason Beth Denison went around every corner with her fists balled up, ready for a fight.

"I barely touched Denison today, and she just about gelded me," Neil said.

"What?"

"I'm beginning to think she is scared. You saw the way

she was shaking in there talking to you. It's like she was on crack or something."

"Then why doesn't she tell us?"

"Maybe she's more scared of him than us. Maybe he's got something on her."

"Or ... you think she's in love with him?"

The image of Beth Denison loving some faceless murderer drove a knife into Neil's gut. He remembered too well what a woman would do to protect a man she cared about.

Anything.

"We gotta find out how this guy's pushing Denison's buttons. Tap her phones."

Rick blinked. "I know you didn't just say that," he said, heading for his office.

"Why not?"

"Why not?" Rick moved faster. "Patriot Act aside, Neil, police departments are queasy about tapping personal phone lines."

"The Sentry's not."

Rick stuck his fingers in his ears and rounded a corner. He began to hum.

"The Sentry taps everyone it guards, secures all lines to and from."

"I can't hear you."

"I've still got some connections there."

"She's lawyered up," Rick said between hums.

"I'll keep the police department out of it."

Rick got to his office door, looked around to see who was listening, and stopped. He pulled his fingers from his ears. "Out of what? Did you say something?"

"Right." So, that was settled. Neil looked at his watch. "What are you gonna do about Abby?"

Rick already had his Rolodex out, dialing. He put the phone on speaker and a woman with a smoker's voice answered: "Shirley Barnes. Child Protection Services."

"Shirley. How's my favorite CPS caseworker?"

"Sacowicz. I paid off those parking tickets with the Ramez kids, remember? A crew of seven, and you busting my chops to keep them together. Not an easy thing to do, by the way."

"But you're our resident miracle-worker."

"And you're our resident shit-flinger. What do you want?"

"I've got a mom in custody, but not for long. I need to cover her kid for a little while."

"File the papers and we'll send someone. You know the drill."

"Man, there's no sense in that—it'll only be another few hours. Maybe not even that."

"You're suggesting . . ."

"Maggie'll watch her, no need for anything formal. You come with me to pick her up, we swing by the house, get waylaid, and before you know it, her mom shows up."

"So you don't want the daughter to get entered in the system, but you don't wanna get charged with kidnapping."

"I'm funny that way."

Silence. "Meet me downstairs. And Sacowicz, you owe me. Again."

"Next time you're in jail, I'll arrange for the *special* menu."

71

Chapter 9

Adele Lochner sat down at the table while Beth thought about burned pot roast. A strange thing to think about when you've just been arrested; nonetheless, her mind filled with the sharp aroma of gravy bubbling into pungent black blisters at the bottom of her oven, charred meat and vegetables huddled in a dry clump in the pan, the smoke alarm singing through the air. And Adam, joking about having married a woman who was hopelessly domestically challenged.

How surprised he'd be at what she'd become. The woman Adam married had two advanced degrees and an ambitious career. She'd never been touched by violence, lifted a weight, or thrown a punch. She traveled widely, dealing in outrageously expensive antiques, attended museum exhibits and law firm dinner parties, and rarely attempted a meal that wasn't microwave-ready and botch-proof.

Now, she made a kick-butt pot roast. And princess-castle birthday cakes and the neighborhood's best chocolate chip cookies. Her home wasn't the flashy urban condo she'd always imagined, but a quaint little haven where she both lived and worked, a painstakingly created bubble for her and Abby on Ashford Drive, complete with a picket fence, flower beds, and a mutt from the pound.

And a state-of-the-art gym, where she'd spent hours each week getting strong, never letting herself forget there was a time when fear and weakness had almost cost Abby her life.

"Are you listening to me, Beth?" Adele Lochner touched her arm.

"No," she admitted. "I was thinking about Adam and Abby. I'm sorry."

"Tell Abby you're sorry when you can only talk to her on the phone once a month."

Beth quailed, and Adele Lochner seized the moment. "You came to me this morning wanting to know what to do. Now I'm telling you: Keep your mouth shut."

"I did."

"So far. But the authorities haven't pressured you yet."

"They haven't?"

"They haven't even begun. I know how these guys work. If the police decide you're the link to someone they want, they'll bulldoze you under to get to him."

"Sheridan knows about Anne Chaney. He said the caller may have committed a murder several years ag—"

Adele Lochner put up a hand. "They don't know."

"You're sure?" Beth asked, wanting with all her heart to believe it. "Then why are they hunting for Bankes, without even knowing who he is?"

"It doesn't matter why they're hunting for him."

"What do you mean, it doesn't matt—"

"I mean, if you want me to be your lawyer, nothing matters but doing what I say. And I say *keep quiet*. I can tell you honestly that right now the authorities are looking for Bankes based on pure speculation; that's why they haven't thrown the book at you yet or charged you with anything real. As long as you don't give them any morsels to chew on, nothing is going to come of this. Even if Bankes does show up, you can send him away with a buttload of money and no one will ever be the wiser." She gave Beth a cutting look. "But if you break down, the whole story will come out. Then, Ms. Denison, you can't win, your daughter can't win, and I'll drop you like a hot potato."

Single-minded bitch. But then, that's why Beth had chosen her. "They've filed charges against me."

"Smoke and mirrors. I'll have them dropped within the hour. If you want, I'll bring charges of harassment against the police department, and I could manage a restraining order against Sheridan, too."

"I don't care about any of that. Just get me out of here."

"Fine. But there's one more thing to do before you go." Adele Lochner crossed to the door and summoned a uniformed officer. "My client would like to file a complaint," she said to the officer.

"What for?" he asked.

"She wants to report obscene phone calls."

Neil stayed out of sight until it looked like the paperwork was done, then strode to Denison's side.

"Need a ride?" he asked.

Her eyes flared. "I'll call a cab." She signed on one more line, and the receptionist handed over her purse, phone, and derringer. "Where do I go to get my daughter?" she asked the woman at the desk.

"Daughter? There's nothing here about a custodial child."

"What? What do you mean?" Her voice began to shake. "Oh, God. Where's my daughter? Lieutenant Sacowicz was getting her! Where's my daugh—"

"I'm checking, ma'am. Are you sure the lieutenant—"

She spun to Neil, on the sharp edge of horror. "Where is Abby? Where is Abby?"

"Abby's fine," Neil said and couldn't help but take her by the shoulders. She was trembling. "Abby is in good hands. I came to take you to her."

A sound passed her lips—relief and even gratitude, maybe. "You're sure?"

"Lieutenant Sacowicz didn't want her to be taken into protective custody for the night, that's all. He called in a favor with one of the caseworkers and made other arrangements."

"What other arrangements? Where is she?"

Neil was hard-pressed not to smile. Christ, she loved that little girl. And Christ, she seemed fragile and small just now. It touched him in a place he'd thought was long gone.

"Maybe you should talk to her," he said, pulling out his phone. He dialed and asked for Abby, then handed the phone to Denison.

"Honey? Are you all right?" she asked.

Silence.

"I'm coming to get you, sweetie, right now. I'll be there soon." Beat. "What?" Denison looked stricken. "No. I'll see you in a little while. I love you, baby."

She handed the phone back to Neil, looking perplexed.

"Something wrong?" he asked.

"She's mad I'm coming. She wants to stay longer."

Neil chuckled. "See? Nothing to worry about." She was finally calm. "So, I'll make you a deal. Forget the cab, come with me, and in thirty minutes, you'll have her back."

She gave him a skeptical look. "What's my part?"

"Excuse me?"

"You said it was a deal. What will it cost me?"

Neil looked at her. He could ask anything of her right now, and she'd do it. Anything for her daughter. "I misspoke," he said, finding his voice a little stuck. "There's no deal; some things are just wrong, that's all. A mother shouldn't be separated from her child."

She looked at him with open shock.

"Come on. I won't even grill you about the phone calls along the way." When she still hesitated, he drew an X over his chest. "Hope to die."

They rode in a rental car—a sporty Dodge about ten cuts above your standard rental car. Beth tipped her head back against the leather seat, a mixture of exhaustion and emotion making lucid thought nearly impossible. Two more days until Cheryl and Jeff got home and could take Abby, and meanwhile, Beth could almost feel Bankes getting closer. Pray God, it would take him another few days to get here; pray God that when he did, it would be as important to him to keep their secret as it was to Beth. Maybe she could get him to leave them alone. She had money to bribe him, and she had Adele Lochner to threaten him. She had a place to hide Abby. She had the financial solvency to run if necessary, and if he followed, she had her Glock ...

"Are you cold?" Sheridan's voice was oddly quiet. "I can turn on the heat."

Lord, she was shivering again. Damned chills. "I'm fine."

He turned on the heat anyway. Five minutes passed before he turned it off and spoke again. "Are you in love with him?"

He meant Bankes, of course. "What happened to 'hope to die'?"

"I said I wouldn't grill you about the calls. This is ... personal." She gawked at him and he shrugged. "So sue me for finding you attractive."

A tingle raced across Beth's skin for no good reason. She clutched her arms over her chest.

"Are you in love with him?" he repeated.

"No."

He wheeled around a corner, pulled up to a light, and stopped. "Then I have another question. Personal, that is." He looked right at her, eyes like blue crystals. "Have you got a thing going with Evan Foster?"

Beth shook her head. "No."

"And if I asked him, would he give the same answer?"

She looked at her lap.

"Uh-huh, that's what I thought," he said, going back to the road. He rolled through the intersection, his wrist dangling over the top of the steering wheel, a pose so casual he might be discussing the weather rather than something so intimate as Beth's love life. She chanced a glance at the side of his face, her emotional barriers dangerously flimsy. She had the strange feeling that if he chose to, he could simply reach inside and help himself to a slice of her soul. "So, seven years after your husband died, you're still wearing your wedding ring, you haven't given any other man the time of day, and your social life consists of T-ball games and PTA meetings."

"I don't see that it's any of your business," she said.

His big shoulders moved a little. "It just seems like a long time to be alone, that's all."

Alone. She closed her eyes on the word, her lids so heavy she wished she didn't have to open them again. Alone was the key to survival. Alone was the way to never experience such loss again. Alone was the way to protect secrets only Adam had known. *Never tell. Trust me, Beth; I'll handle everything . . .*

"Ms. Denison."

She jerked and found Neil Sheridan standing in the open passenger-side door. His fingers smoothed a strand of hair from her face. "You slept for twenty minutes," he said, answering her unvoiced question. "Abby's here."

Beth got out of the car, still muddled. They'd stopped in a nice neighborhood, in a driveway lined with red and yellow tulips. "Where are we?" she asked.

Sheridan's hand settled on the small of her back. "Sacowicz's house."

The lieutenant had taken Abby to his home? A spark of anger ignited, then she remembered the alternative:

protective custody. And Abby, on the phone, saying, *Mommy, puh-leeze ... Can't I stay and play longer?*

Before she'd decided whether she should be angry or grateful, the front door opened.

"Uncle Neil! Uncle Neil!" Three boys spilled past a woman, racing down the steps and lunging for Sheridan. He hunkered down in his coat and tie, scooped up the first boy in a bear hug, then rolled him over his back just in time to field the next attacks. They wrestled and laughed until Sheridan called a halt, then he ruffled their heads and smoothed a hand down his cockeyed tie. He came up to the porch. "Thanks for helping out today, honey," he said, kissing the woman's freckled cheek.

"No problem."

Beth's mind reeled. *Uncle Neil. Sacowicz's wife. Honey.*

"I'm Maggie Sacowicz," the woman said, holding out her hand to Beth. "Come on in. Abby's in the family room."

Abby dived into Beth's arms. "Mommy, there's a little baby girl here. I helped change her diaper. And wait'll you hear all the jokes Ritchie told me." She whirled to Sheridan, whose crisp blue eyes showed the briefest flicker of panic. "Hey, why did the butterfly get kicked out of the dance?"

"Uh ... Because he didn't know the jitterbug."

Abby thought about that for a second, then frowned. "It was a moth ball. That's why the butterfly got kicked out."

Sheridan grunted. "Mine was just as funny," he said and followed the boys outside.

Abby dragged Beth into a playroom. Tonka trucks and

bulldozers lay wrecked all over the floor, a baseball bat and Superman cape littered the sofa, and the computer idled on some sort of shoot-'em-up space invaders game. In the far corner stood a playpen, and in it an eight-or nine-month-old baby girl sat wearing a baseball hat, gnawing on a half-human, half-beast action figure. She was the pale spitting image of her mother.

"Abby's been taking care of the baby for me," Maggie said. "Playing mommy."

"That sounds like Abby. I've tried to get her interested in ball games and trucks, but she likes the girlie things."

"We need another double-X chromosome in this house. I'm way outnumbered, especially now that Neil's here."

Beth couldn't resist. "Are you his sister?"

Maggie raised her eyebrows, then shook her head. "Neil was married to my sister, Heather. A long time ago."

Beth blinked. So, Mr. Screw-the-World had loved someone once? Couldn't be.

The French doors opened and a woman with a crew cut blew a puff of smoke and came inside. A county employee tag hung around her neck, the letters CPS at the bottom.

"Mrs. Denison?" she asked, coming straight to Beth. "Aw, never mind. Abby looks just like you." She headed for the front door, waving Maggie off when she started to follow. "I can find my way out. Maggie, tell that husband of yours he owes us both."

Maggie chuckled, a dry sound. "You tell him. You'll see him before I will."

"Whoa!" An earsplitting wail came from outside. The boys had conned Sheridan into another round of wrestling.

"Go on, sweetie," Maggie said to Abby. "You can play with them, too."

Abby went to the patio, lurking on the perimeter as she watched three boys and a big man attack, retreat, roll, and attack again. Sheridan saw her, then eased the group nearer and shoved the boys off all at once. He grabbed Abby's hand and pulled her in, a *whoop* flying from her lips. Beth's breath caught.

"Don't worry," Maggie said. "He won't let Abby get hurt."

He won't let Abby get hurt. The words spiraled to Beth's chest. It was true, she realized, shaken. Sheridan had Abby right in the thick of it, gave her a fair share of pushes and flip-overs, but always had an arm loose around her like a shield, always cushioned her falls with his body. Beth found herself laughing when he tossed Abby into the air, caught her, and spun her round and round to back off the boys. She found herself cheering when the kids dropped him to his knees to tickle him, and he let them. She found herself staring when it was over and he stood, absently straightening his clothes and turning a thousand-watt smile on Beth. It shot through every nerve in her body.

"Okay, that's enough," he said, plucking the kids from his sleeves like bugs. "I'm an old man; I can't do it any longer. C'mere, Abby. I'll show you how to get away from the boys." He seized a football from a basket on the patio and pulled back his arm with the easy skill of a pro quarterback. "Whichever one of you guys catches this gets ice cream after dinner."

The ball spiraled through the air, the boys chasing it in

81

a mob. Sheridan swung Abby over his head to straddle his neck and ducked under the doorframe and into the house.

"You're terrible," Maggie said as the boys tangled over the ball.

"I think you're fun!" Abby said, wrapping her arms around his neck.

He plopped her down and touched her nose. "But I think your mom's ready to go."

"No," Abby whined.

"Sorry, honey, it's getting late. We have to let Mr. Sheridan take us home."

Her face brightened and she whirled to Sheridan. "*You're* taking us home? Yippee!"

It was almost eight when Neil pulled onto Ashford Drive. Abby hadn't lasted five minutes before falling asleep in the backseat; Neil didn't think her mother could go on much longer, either. She looked ready to drop.

He got out and bent into the back to unbuckle Abby. "Show me her room; I'll carry her up." Ms. Denison hovered so close she bumped him. "For God's sake, I'm not going to drop her."

"I can carry her. I do it all the time."

"This time you don't have to. Wanna be useful? Open the garage door and go turn down Abby's covers." Somehow he just knew Abby's bed was made.

She tucked Abby's jacket around her shoulders and inserted an electronic key card beside the garage door. It lifted with a dull grind. Inside, Heinz greeted them with impartial enthusiasm, and Denison flipped on lights here and there as she led Neil through the cozy family room, past the homey kitchen, and up the stairs.

He was doing fine until he stepped into Abby's room, then his breath caught. Lemony walls, sunflowers everywhere. Toys and books and a bed draped with white princess netting, a hammock hanging in one corner and overflowing with stuffed animals, while a half dozen more sat on the bed. Her favorites, Neil supposed, and he could see her with them: tucking them in at night, dragging them around with her in the mornings.

His throat closed up.

"Mr. Sheridan?" Neil blinked. Denison tugged Abby's shoes off, whispering, "I need to go let Heinz out. I'll be right back."

She slipped out and Neil laid Abby down. She stirred.

"Mommy'll be right back, sweet pea," he said. "She's letting Heinz out."

"Tell her it's okay to sleep in here if she gets scared again."

Neil bent over her. "What?"

"If the dreams come."

Neil frowned. "Dreams?"

"The scary ones that make her cry."

A sliver of concern slid under his skin. "Does Mommy have them very often?"

"Just lately. But she can sleep with me tonight if she wants. Heinz will make room."

Neil's chest tightened. "Okay, pumpkin, I'll tell her."

Denison reappeared, got a weary hug from Abby, then stood looking down at her for a long moment, her eyes following the rise and fall of the covers. Finally, she turned off the light and led the way downstairs.

Leave it alone, Neil said to himself as he trailed behind, past the pictures of her husband and through the foyer. *Her* secrets, *her* nightmares. *Her* daughter.

She opened the front door for him.

Walk away, Neil.

"Bad dreams?" he asked, stopping on the porch. She pulled a face. "Abby says you can sleep with her if the nightmares come back."

She stiffened. "Oh, okay. Fine."

Her eyes were downcast, the porch light gilding her features and her lashes casting long, dark shadows over the scar on her cheekbone. A cut of some sort, but not clean. A wide, messy gash that must have lain open for a time. He wondered about the internal scars that came with it and if they had healed with the same tough, nerveless finish as the wound on her skin. He wondered if they were the same wounds that kept her awake at night.

And on the heels of that thought came a pure, physical response to the image of Beth Denison in bed, *not* sleeping.

Walk away, Neil.

"What keeps you from sleeping, Ms. Denison?"

She let out a sigh. "Dolls, that's what. Just because Abby's off school this week doesn't mean I'm off work. I'm appraising a set of dolls; they're rare, and the research is end—"

"I'm not talking about working late. I'm talking about nightmares."

"That, from a six-year-old."

"But it's true, isn't it?"

"I can handle things myself. I'm stronger than I look, Mr. Sheridan."

"Handling things alone doesn't mean you're strong. It just means you're alone. Let someone help."

"Someone?" she challenged, lifting one winged brow.

"Me. Sacowicz. There's more than one person in the world willing to help you. I'd even step back and let Evan Foster take care of you if I thought you trusted him."

"I trust Evan."

"No, you don't," Neil said, with the sudden certainty that he was standing too close. He could smell the scent of berries in her shampoo, remembered the electrical charge in her body when he'd held her at the restaurant. "A man who goes to kiss you and you offer your cheek? A man you lie to about staying for a cup of coffee? No, you don't trust Evan Foster." He took a chance and tilted her chin with a finger. "Is it just him? Or do you dodge any man's kisses?"

"Don't be stupid," she said. "I don't dodge a man's kisses."

He let his gaze drop to her lips. "Prove it."

Chapter 10

It started that way—a stupid dare, proof that she wouldn't dodge him. Beth stood still as he bent his head, his hands cradling both cheeks and lips touching hers. His palms were warm and calloused, and his fingers slid into her hair as he angled her face upward and coaxed her lips apart. For a second, she tensed, sensing he could swallow her whole, but then something in her chest began to unfold and swell, something that might have been hope.

And desire. It was so unexpected her heart lost track of its beat. Reason slid from grasp, driven out by exhaustion and loneliness and fear, and some absurd craving to be coddled and safe and warm. She didn't even feel cold in Sheridan's hands. Heat surged through her body instead.

That wasn't right.

"Stop," she said, pushing away.

He pulled back, and for half a second, Beth felt as if she couldn't stand on her own. She groped for the doorframe and missed.

God, get a grip.

She got her balance back and lifted her chin. "Proof enough?"

"Proof of something," he said, his voice a little ragged. "Maybe proof that it's been a long time since you've been kissed like that."

Oh, yes.

"Beth." He hesitated, and the sound of her first name on his lips did something strange to her belly. "Evan Foster. Has he ever ... hurt you?"

"Of course not. No."

"Okay." A metallic edge slipped into his voice. "I didn't want to have to kill him."

A ludicrous comment, but it flipped Beth's heart sideways. The idea of someone looking out for her was so foreign she didn't know what to do with it. As if she'd just been gifted with a tool, but she didn't know how to use it. She only knew it felt sweet to cradle in her hand.

Until she thought of what it could do to Abby.

"You should go," she said.

"Why?"

"Because she told you to."

Both of them looked toward the voice.

"Evan," Beth said, wondering where the hell he had come from. "What are you doing here?"

His gaze locked on Sheridan. "Do I know you?"

"No," Sheridan said, and Beth noticed he made no further attempt to introduce himself. Two big dogs, sniffing each other out. The idea that she could be in the middle of some sort of romantic triangle was so ludicrous she almost laughed.

She looked at Sheridan, hoping her cheeks weren't red.

"Thank you for bringing us home."

He held her gaze long enough to set her pulse skittering, then dipped his chin. "Someone will call you in the morning about getting your car back."

He left, revving the engine of the Charger a little more than necessary, Beth thought, and Evan stepped up onto the porch. "What's going on? We had cops at Foster's this afternoon, asking a lot of questions."

"About what?"

"About Kerry Waterford. Dealers we know in Denver and Omaha. You."

Great. "Then you know as much as I do. They've been asking me questions, too. That was one of them. Well, not a cop, but he's working with them."

Evan humphed. "You gonna invite me in?"

She looked up. "No. Please, Evan, not tonight."

"Then when?"

"I told you. What happened between us is over. It never really even got started."

"In my world, going to bed with someone is getting started. Yours, too."

"But it's over now. And I have work to do. Did two more dolls come to Foster's today? Mrs. Chadburne said they should have gotten here today."

"I didn't check," he said, trying to nuzzle her. "Come on, Beth."

She pushed him away. "Evan, stop."

He straightened, at first seeming surprised but then gathering his pride. "Call me when you change your mind."

Voices. A bump. Figures creeping close, huddled low.

88

Neil's senses rocketed to red alert. He tensed, every muscle and tendon poised to strike. He could place the leader just beneath the left side of the bed. The others—two, if his radar was working accurately—were crouched near the foot.

He let the band close in, just inches away, then launched from the bed with an animal cry. He caught one in a headlock and tripped the others with his leg, toppling them. "Noooo!" squealed the leader, fighting. The smaller ones thumped to the floor, gasping for air.

"No?" Neil said, pulling Richie down onto the carpet. He threw a leg over Justin. Shawn weaseled out and climbed on his back. "What kind of a sneak attack was that? I heard you guys a mile away."

"Did not," said Justin. "You were snoring until Rich was right on top of you."

"Smart aleck," Neil said. He went for the back of Richie's pants, intending a memorable wedgie, until Shawn lost his balance and tightened his arm on Neil's throat. He flipped Shawn to the floor, and the wrestling match got going again. It drew Maggie to the guest room like a magnet.

"All right, stop it," she said. "If you're going to kill each other, do it outside."

They untangled themselves, managing a few pushes and shoves as they reclaimed their limbs from the pile.

"Are you coming, Uncle Neil?" asked Justin.

"Sure, for a few minutes," he said, rubbing a hand over his face. "Just let me get some breakfast first."

"Breakfast," Shawn said, tagging the others down the hall. "It's twelve o'clock!"

Neil's brows went up and he glanced at the window.

Sure enough. It was pretty bright outside. He lumbered to his feet.

"What time did you come back last night?" Rick came up behind Maggie, a mug of coffee in his hand. He handed it to Neil.

"I dunno," Neil lied. "Late."

"Anything happen with Denison?"

You mean, did I lose my mind and kiss her? "Not that I saw. She worked most of the night down in the basement." He sat on the edge of the bed and sipped the coffee, a little embarrassed that he'd bothered staking out Beth Denison's house. What had he expected? That Gloria's murderer would knock on her door? That Evan's BMW might stay all night? That she might put on something sexy and invite Neil to come chase away the nightmares?

Christ.

"This sounds like cop talk," Maggie said, excusing herself. She slipped through the doorway past Rick, not touching him.

Neil arched a brow. "Did you stay here last night?"

"Nah. I went back to the station." He shifted, looking down the hall after Maggie. "It's where she says I want to be, anyway."

"You two ... You gotta get it back together, man. If you two don't make it—"

"Yeah," Rick said, his eyes giving away the pain even if his words didn't. "Look, I gotta get back. I'm in court today. You got something on the agenda?"

"Gloria's parents. I need to talk to them."

"Ooooh," Rick said, shaking his head. "That's one conversation I don't envy." He contemplated his shoelaces for a minute. "Listen, Neil. There's something else you should know. Heather called."

Neil's heart might have jumped a beat.

"Not about you; I mean, she does it now and then. Calls Maggie. Not very often."

"How is she?" Neil asked, almost afraid to hear the answer.

"Married again. Third time, I think. She can't seem to get pregnant, or at least carry to term. She's had a couple of miscarriages, I guess. You can ask Maggie."

Neil walked over to the mirror. Ellen Jenkins had been right: He looked old. For a minute he wondered what the years had done to Heather, if she was still slender and creamy-skinned and freckled, with red hair like Maggie and Evie. Given what she'd been through, life had probably left her looking pretty beat-up, too, but he preferred not to think of her that way. Especially since he was responsible for a lot of it.

"Sometimes you gotta let it go, man," Rick said.

"And sometimes you don't," he said, looking Rick right in the eyes. "The job's not worth sleeping alone, Rick. I oughta know."

"Yeah."

Rick left and Neil sat down, a world of hurt seeming to lay its hands on him. Heather. Rick and Maggie. Beth Denison. The family of Gloria Michaels. The families of Lila Beckenridge and the women who were missing, even the family of Anthony Russell.

His brother, Mitch, and thirteen people who died in an explosion Neil hadn't even tried to stop.

He pulled out his cell phone, dialed a whole bunch of

numbers, and waited. The voice at the other end was that of a stranger. "Yes?"

"This is Neil Sheridan," he said. "I want to speak to my brother."

Chapter 11

Indianapolis, Indiana
593 miles away

The woman who was next to die had entered the shopping mall three hours earlier, alone, hauling a purse the size of a suitcase. Tall and lithe, she had blonde hair clipped high on the back of her head, too much makeup, and bright red Kewpie-doll lips. She'd been dressed for summer, wearing a short skirt and sandals that showed off good legs. Great legs, actually.

Legs to die for.

Chevy leaned back against the driver's seat of his car, stretching as much as he could manage. Wait, wait, wait. That was the problem with the mall: A woman could stay inside so long the waiting alone was murder.

Still, he had to be careful now, even though the clock was ticking. If he finished at a reasonable hour this evening, by tomorrow he'd be home—back to that hellhole of a little town in eastern Pennsylvania where he and Jenny had grown up. And from there, well, Arlington was only a stone's throw away. The thought sent a ripple down his spine.

So he waited, even though Jenny was antsy and Chevy was hungry. Miss Legs was worth waiting for. The right woman in the right time and the right place.

Or wrong, depending on your perspective.

A little security truck with the mall logo on the side rolled up in Chevy's driver's-side mirror. He frowned. It was the second time in the last half hour the guard had tooled this way.

"You're in trouble now," Jenny said, and Chevy pushed her back down into hiding.

"I'll handle it. Keep quiet."

He pulled a gold band from the car ashtray and slipped it on his fourth finger, wiggling it down into place. He tugged at the collar of his shirt and pulled down the visor mirror. Practiced the benign smile he'd perfected in college for the role of Jim in *The Glass Menagerie*.

Just as the oversize golf cart passed again, he got out of his car and waved a hand at the passing security guard. "Excuse me," he called out, and the little truck rolled to a stop.

"Can I help you, sir?" the guard asked, leaning across his seat toward Chevy. The guard puffed up his chest a little, suddenly important.

"Well, I hope so," Chevy said. "I've been waiting for my wife for half an hour—she just got a job this week working at the food court—but her shift's been over now for twenty minutes." He scratched his chin, using his left hand. Nothing like a wedding band to lend a man the air of respectability.

The security guard peered around Chevy into the front seat of his car, but Chevy knew all he could see was a gym bag and a dark jacket covering a lump on the floor and an empty cup from Burger King. "Did she say she'd come out the public entrance?"

"Public entrance? Is there another one?"

The security guard snapped his fingers, having solved the problem. "Most of the employees use the entrance around that corner. Your wife is probably waiting for you there."

Chevy managed to look embarrassed. "Oh, thanks. I think she did say something about—" Then, from the corner of his eye—Miss Legs. There she was, emerging from the mall with her enormous purse and three shopping bags, walking a little more slowly than before.

Adrenaline shot to his toes.

He tossed a smile at the security guard. "Oh, man, she did tell me that. Well, that would explain it, then."

"Yup. You can just pull around that way," the guard said, pointing.

Chevy was already in the car, turning over the engine.

"Hey," the guard said, and Chevy tried to look at him and at the same time keep an eye on Legs. If she got to her car before the jackass security guard got out of sight, the whole day would be lost. Chevy couldn't stay in Indianapolis. Beth was waiting.

"What?" he asked.

"I see your plates are from Washington. You a Seahawks fan?"

"No."

"You know, they were close these last couple years, and I keep thinking if the draft goes right and the Seah—"

"I said I wasn't a fan." Chevy revved the gas, rage

95

swelling in his chest. *Get the hell away from me*, he chanted inside and had to clamp his jaw together to keep from saying it aloud. The guard had already placed Chevy's tags as Washington and had a conversation that just might be memorable. "I don't follow football. But thanks for the tip. I gotta go find my wife now."

"Yeah, okay. Good luck."

The guard settled back into his cart and tooled away as Chevy pulled out to intercept Legs. Her car was fifty yards in front of him, cutting right then left around aisles of parked cars. Chevy found two empty parking spaces head-to-head and cut through, saving himself going to the end of the aisle, but she'd gotten ahead of him and was nearing the traffic light at the exit. He gunned the gas, heart thundering, and wheeled too fast around the end of the next aisle. A car backed out and Chevy slammed on his brakes.

He smashed the heel of his hand against the steering wheel. "Fuck!" he said, then hit it about five more times. "Fuck, fuck, fuck."

The singing began. Mother's voice.

"Shut up!"

"Chev?"

Jenny. She must have heard Mother, too. That incessant la-dee-da-ing, senseless lyrics floating from her lips. *Who killed Cock Robin? I, said the Sparrow, with my bow and arrow . . .*

He caught his breath, trying to block out the song and deal with Jenny, but he couldn't take the time to help her up into the passenger seat. The driver he'd almost hit was trying to maneuver out of the way; Chevy laid on the horn, backing up.

"Hold on," he said to Jenny, gunning the gas.

Legs made it through the light, out of the parking lot and into traffic. Chevy whipped his car around, hot on her trail, other drivers honking and a pair of pedestrians diving from his path as he swerved in and out to catch her. He pulled up to the same light as it turned from yellow to red and peeled through.

Just in time.

Neil drove to the little town near Harrisburg where Gloria Michaels's family still resided, about an hour and a half from West Chester University. Gloria had been a senior there. She'd lived on campus, majored in broadcast journalism, and led a typical—if not pristine—college life. Partied a little too much, failed biology the first time she took it. Liked the boys.

Anthony Russell, a thirty-year-old auto mechanic who'd once fixed her car, was one of several boyfriends Neil had found, but none of the others had been serious contenders for her murderer. With all the earmarks of a crime of passion—she'd been stabbed sixteen times—Neil had ruled out every man he could put with Gloria.

Except Russell. Who finally confessed. While his attorney had orgasms.

Neil bit back that reminder and tried to ignore the spot on his thigh where Kenzie's barrette seemed to burn through his pocket. If only Ellen Jenkins had been right about how Neil had handled the case: If only he *had* just fingered Russell then let the locals finish things up. But he hadn't. When Neil got word that Russell was on the lam, he'd made a U-turn across the median of a highway and headed back to Chester County. Called Heather and told her he needed another day or two.

A day or two became three weeks. The end of three lifetimes.

He put away the memory and pulled up to a single-story clapboard house on a two-lane road, the nearest neighbors a few acres away. Pat Michaels opened the door while Neil was still in the drive. "Agent Sheridan," she said.

Neil corrected her. "Not *Agent* anymore, Mrs. Michaels."

"I know, we heard." She stepped back and gestured for him to come in, careful not to let her eyes settle on his scar. It hadn't been there the last time he saw them. Gloria's father, Tom Michaels, stood deeper in the foyer, arms folded over a barrel chest.

"Thank you for seeing me," Neil said and held out his hand. Michaels shook it, but reluctantly. "I know I was the last person you expected to hear from."

"It's fine," said Pat Michaels, making a don't-mind-him gesture toward her husband. She took Neil by the arm and ushered him into the living room. Floral sofa, matching armchair, a rocker, and a painting of a hummingbird hovering over an old upright piano. A set of family photos hung on the opposite wall. Gloria occupied most of it.

"She was a beautiful girl," Neil said, looking at the spread of photos. He tried to focus on something more cheerful and pointed at a photo of a scrawny, eleven-year-old tomboy. She'd been precocious and sad, and she'd had a blatant case of hero worship for Neil all those years ago.

"How's Sarah doing?" he asked, the conversation

feeling forced. "I hate to think how big she's gotten by now."

"See for yourself."

Neil turned, eyes widening. "Sarah?"

"I grew up, didn't I?"

Neil chuckled. "I'll say." Blonde, curvy, legs from here to China. He glanced at her father, feeling a little like he'd been caught with his hand in the cookie jar just by looking. He covered by giving her a brotherly tweak on the nose.

Her smile faded. "Let me guess: You're not here because I'm old enough to date now."

"No," he said, and the light moment dissolved to nothing. "I'm here about Gloria."

"I can't believe it," Pat said a few minutes later. "It isn't over."

"I'm sorry, Mrs. Michaels."

"So who do you think killed this woman in Seattle?" Sarah asked.

"I don't know. But there's a good chance he's the same man who killed Gloria."

"They're alike?" Mrs. Michaels asked.

"Not entirely. There are some differences. The arrangement of the bodies, the—" He stopped. Gloria's parents had enough gory images to last them a lifetime. "But the likenesses are compelling. The murderer even ate Reese's Peanut Butter Cups."

Tom Michaels paled, running a broad hand down his face.

"I just wanted you to know that I'm going to ask the FBI to look at Gloria's case again," Neil said. "I didn't want you to hear it on the news."

Michaels stood. The years had worked on him like gravity, weighing down his shoulders, dragging the corners of his lips into a permanent frown. He looked, Neil thought, like a man who'd lost a child.

"Don't," he said. "Don't do this to us."

"Tom," his wife said, "we have to—"

"Anthony Russell killed my daughter. I don't care what happened in Seattle. Anthony Russell killed Gloria."

"Maybe not, Mr. Michaels."

The man's face began to redden, a crimson stain climbing up from the vee of his collar. "I want you to leave my little girl alone. For the love of God, let my baby rest in peace."

"Geesh, Dad," Sarah said, "it's not like it matters to Gloria anymore."

He rounded on her. "How dare you." The tendons on either side of his throat stood out, like a cobra. "How dare you say something like that about your sister."

"Dad! What if Anthony didn't kill her?"

"Anthony killed her. He killed her."

Neil stood. "Mr. Micha—"

"Get out," Tom said, his voice vibrating with tension. "Get out of my home and leave my family alone. We know who murdered our daughter, and you don't need to stir it all up again. *Just get out.*"

Neil glanced at Gloria's mother but found no help there. A second later, Sarah had his arm. "Come on, I'll walk you out."

Neil felt as if he'd just driven a knife into a man's chest.

*

He and Sarah walked to the driveway in silence, Neil on eggshells. They stopped beside his car and when she finally spoke, her words surprised him.

"You know," she said, her voice pensive, "I wanted to go to Carnegie Mellon. Or Penn State."

Neil waited. He didn't know where this was going.

"Dad couldn't stand it, the thought of me going away to college. So now I'm finishing at Bishop. It's a junior college about four miles from here. He can almost tolerate my going to classes, so long as I don't take any at night."

Neil swallowed. He didn't know what to say to that. If he could do it all over again and had the option of keeping Mackenzie under lock and key, he'd probably do it, too.

Sarah looked up, her expression filled with uncertainty. "I don't want to send him back to that place he was after Gloria died. I don't. But ..."

"What?"

She shot a glance toward the house then stepped a little closer, her voice falling to a hush. "Anthony didn't like peanut butter."

Neil frowned, a sliver of apprehension sliding in. "Sarah?"

"I know, I know," she said. Tears started. "I know Daddy told you that piece of candy had to be his. But it couldn't have been. Gloria told me. It was one of the things she said she and Anthony had in common: They both hated peanut butter."

Neil was dumbfounded. He turned, rubbing his hand over his face. "Sarah, why didn't you tell anyone back then?"

"I did. I told Dad."

"Your dad knew? Then why didn't *he* tell us?"

Sarah blinked. "You just don't get it, do you? He hated Anthony, and he does think with all his heart that Anthony killed her. He wasn't going to let an eleven-year-old's opinion about a piece of candy stand in the way of Anthony going to prison."

"Would you put that in a sworn statement?"

"That my dad believed Anthony Russell killed Gloria?"

"No, that you're certain Anthony Russell wouldn't have had a Reese's Cup."

"Are you kidding? My dad would disown me."

"Come on."

"No, really. You don't understand. Anthony's death was Dad's revenge. *You* gave him that. And if he didn't have that much, I don't think he could go on. He barely goes on as it is."

Neil closed his eyes.

"Mr. Sheridan?" Sarah touched his sleeve, looking up at him. Suddenly she sounded like a little girl again. "Should I be scared? I mean, could the guy be coming back here or something?"

Neil frowned and patted her shoulder. "Nah," he said. "There's something else going on. I don't know what, but I'm gonna find out. You're okay."

And that, Neil thought as he pulled out of the driveway, might be the biggest crock of shit he'd fed a pretty lady in a long time.

Chevy bent over Miss Legs, counting to ten. One, two, three ... He was waiting for the blood. Four, five ...

A tiny red bead squeezed out, another right behind it, and a string of liquid rubies welled up along the severed edges of flesh. At ten, he wiped away the strand, applied pressure with a cloth napkin from the motel, then sank back on his heels and started the count again.

One, two, three ...

It was taking longer than he'd thought. He should have just killed her first and saved himself all this trouble and mess. Dead women don't bleed. But they don't scream, either, and Chevy had been hurting. He needed something to carry him over until Beth.

Nine, ten. Wipe.

Done.

He looked at the photo of the fourth doll in the set, looked at Legs, and decided on one more cut. A tiny blue vein crept from the crease behind her knee, barely visible in the silvery light. He cocked his head—a surgeon, considering—decided on it, then laid the edge of his X-Acto knife flush against her skin.

Legs gasped. "Oh, God, no! Not again. I'll do anything y-you want."

Stupid bitch. She *was* doing what he wanted.

Her body tensed as he pressed down on the blade, gently, gently. The tip punched though with a tiny "pop," and her mouth opened around a glorious moan. Pleasure clutched at his vitals, the tape recorder whirring.

Easy now, not too deep. He dragged a long, darkening slit through the skin, like the line of a jagged country road on a map. A curve here, a jog there, a hundred-and-eighty-degree turn an inch below her knee. One last thin, spidery line, one last string of bloody beads to clean up. One last set of cries in his ears.

One, two, three ... Wait, wipe. Count again. Wipe. Again. Finished.

He called over his shoulder: "That's it, Jenny, I'm done."

"Wh-what?" Legs managed. " J-Jen ..."

Chevy stared at her, surprised there was any sentience left at all. "Quiet," he said. "I wasn't talking to you. I was talking to Jenny."

"J-Jenny?" She swiveled her head, as if she might actually be able to see through the blindfold. "Heelllp! Jenny, help—"

"Stop," Chevy said. "Shut up!"

She writhed against her bindings. Damn it, if she reopened those cuts, he'd be cleaning her up until dawn. Everything would be ruined.

He yanked off the blindfold and measured out the spot for the bullet, then hiked to the edge of the stream where Jenny sat alone in the darkness. Belatedly, he wondered if she might have gotten cold. Her face was stark and pale, the wide caverns of her eyes lending her a dazed, haunted look. *She doesn't feel*, Mother always said, but Chevy knew better.

"Come on, Jen," he said, gathering her in one arm. "Someone wants to see you."

Gun in hand, he carried Jenny to where Legs lay, still whimpering Jenny's name in a string of incoherent whimpers.

He knelt down close so she could see. "This is Jenny, bitch," he said through clenched teeth. "She won't help you."

Legs blinked. Her throat worked, the sight of Jenny's face stealing breath from her lungs and making the whites of her eyes glow. She gasped, a single, dumbfounded wheeze that filled her lungs with oxygen for one last time.

Chevy punched a bullet into her brain.

The crack of the shot sang through the air and he stood, cradling Jenny close, adrenaline leaking from his body like urine from the dead woman's bladder. He waited as the staid, unearthly silence that always followed a kill wrapped cold arms around him. He hated this moment; this was the danger zone—that tense, gravid interval when the singing might come.

He waited, but there was only silence. Mother wasn't here. She never came when he did it right.

He let out his breath and put Jenny down, spent another few minutes wiping off the woman's legs. Finally, she was done.

Now, for the phone.

He rooted through her purse. Cosmetics, comb, wallet. He dug some more, fingers searching for the familiar shape. Nothing. He frowned and stuck a hand in the outside pocket. It wasn't there, either.

His heartbeat stuttered. He dumped Legs's purse on the ground. Stupid—now he'd have to gather everything up or risk leaving prints at the scene. But he had to find a phone. He had to talk to Beth.

He checked her clothing then straightened, shocked. No phone. Fury caught him by the throat. A moment after that, Mother began to sing.

Chapter 12

Neil left the Michaelses' house and found a bar and a cheap motel at opposite ends of the same gravel lot. He started drinking early. He drank and tried not to think about the fact that not only had he killed the wrong man, but an eleven-year-old girl and her father had known it. He drank some more and tried not to think about the fact that he'd just ripped open the worst wound a parent can experience, and he didn't even have any authority to find the answer. He drank some more and tried not to imagine Mackenzie crying out for him in the backseat of Heather's car, of Heather hating him with every fiber of her being. Before he got around to thinking about Mitch, he was out cold.

A hangover had him in the morning, but so did a new determination. He nursed the hangover with a gallon of coffee and handful of aspirin from a gas station, then found the local sheriff and told him just enough about the present investigation to convince him to keep a deputy close to Sarah. He made a phone call to the one FBI agent who might listen to him, though he couldn't say they had parted on good terms. Then he put the Charger on the road and turned it loose, ready to go back to Arlington and do whatever was necessary to nail the bastard who wasn't Anthony Russell. For Gloria. For the Russells. For Sarah and her dad and mom.

For himself.

But he wasn't prepared for what Rick had learned.

Rick handed him two pieces of paper. The top page was an e-mail saying, "See attachment." And the bottom page—

Neil stared.

"They found her in the woods in Indiana about two hours ago."

Neil's brain simply stalled; he couldn't make sense of the photo. A woman, shot in the head, a smudge or line on her temple. She was posed, as Lila Beckenridge had been, and naked from the waist down. Her eyes appeared unharmed. But her legs ... Neil had never seen anything like it.

"It happened sometime last night," Rick said.

While you were in a bar getting wasted.

"I don't know what to say," Neil said. "This is our guy? He didn't do anything like this to the Seattle woman. Or to Gloria."

"Not to the legs, but the gunshot wound is the same caliber, same placement of the bullet, and that line is gonna turn out to be eyebrow pencil, wait and see. Same MO—being taken in her own car, killed in a woods, car found not too far away and wiped clean. En route from the West Coast to ... Jesus, maybe here. The only thing different is the legs."

"Postmortem?" Neil asked. "There's no blood."

"He cleaned her up."

Neil cringed. Then remembered: "Did Denison get a phone call?"

"No. But this vic didn't carry a cell phone. I've got the phone company on the lookout for anything coming in to Denison's number from anyplace between here and there—from pay phones, anything. Are your taps in place? Not that I know anything about that," he added.

"Yeah. It won't be in real time because a call's gotta pass through my contact guy first, but if a call comes over Denison's lines, he can route a recording here within a few minutes."

"*If* a call comes. If it doesn't, then she might be out of it: Maybe he really is some pervert who started out calling her at random."

Scary dreams that make her cry . . .

Neil drew a deep breath. He needed oxygen. "I want to talk to her."

"I've got a tail on her."

"No, I mean, I want to *talk* to her. Tell her what's going on, let her explain."

"Why? Something happen with you two that you didn't tell me? Something that made her stop hating your guts?"

"I'm done worrying about your lawsuits. We gotta put the murders in front of her."

"Fine. But here, with her lawyer."

"Damn it, just give me an hour. She's got a kid, a career, a home. She's not going anywhere."

Rick glared at him. "If she gets a phone call from

Indiana or ballistics shows this bullet is from the same gun as Beckenridge ..."

"Then pull her in. I won't stop you."

"I'll find out where she is." He picked up the phone and Neil stepped outside to check his own messages. Nothing. No voice mail from Beth Denison saying, *I'm making a terrible mistake and I need you.* Nothing from Mitch, either, damn it.

Rick stepped into the hallway, holding out the phone. "Russ Billings."

Neil took it. "Billings. This is Neil Sheridan."

"Hey, Sheridan. I told this to Sacowicz, but he wants you to hear it for yourself. She's at Chester Park right now, watching some sort of kids' T-ball practice. But you wanna know where she went first?"

Neil's hackles rose. "Where?"

With something in his voice that might have been awe, Billings said, "Keet's."

"Keet's?"

"It's a firing range," Rick said, coming in on another extension. "Anything you wanna shoot, you can shoot there. Twenty-twos to assault rifles."

Neil was speechless. Beth Denison did more than just carry a gun. She was brushing up her aim.

Samson, Pennsylvania
116 miles away

The house was nearly hidden, weeds molesting the flower beds and shrubs swallowing the porch. The steps offered up a buffet of rotted wood to termites, and the windows were clouded, as if shamed by what had happened inside.

In its day, when Mother was tending it, the house was an island of coiffed beauty. She kept it as perfect as a stage setting: calico curtains, freshly painted latticework on the front porch, trimmed bushes edging the walkways. And flowers. Mother liked flowers. Sang to them all day long.

Such a quaint, peaceful setting. The unthinkable couldn't happen here.

But it did happen. Every day.

Be careful, Mommy. You're hurting her.

I'm not hurting her; she can't feel. It's her blood. She has bad blood. La-dee-da. I, said the Fish—

"C'mon, Chev," Jenny said suddenly. "Let's get out of here. You promised you'd take me to the river, and this house gives me the creeps."

Yeah. The creeps.

He shifted his gym bag and carried Jenny past the house and into the woods. Funny, but the river hadn't seemed so far away when they were kids—probably because he always wished they could go farther. Chevy hated this property. Mother's codicil willed Chevy the only thing that mattered, so he'd sold the property, house and all, to the first person who asked. Cheap.

That was Mo Hammond, a neighbor. Mo ran a hunting ground and a gun range, and he had combined the Bankes acreage with the adjacent land he already owned. He stocked it all with deer, pheasant, even wild turkeys. Mo didn't have to worry about stocking the land with rabbits. They repopulated themselves, and he sold their feet at his store. Hard, velvety little stumps with sharp claws, dangling from metal rings.

Sick.

The shooting range was at the opposite end of the property; there was also a shop with guns for both rental and purchase, a field for target practice and skeet shooters, and the rest of the land, of course, was for hunting. It had always amazed Chevy that hunters would pay thirty-five dollars an hour to sit in a deer stand and wait for a half-tame animal to wander by, shoot it in the neck from twenty paces, and watch it convulse in a swift, silent death dance. Where was the sport in that? Chevy had seen a sign once in the hands of a protester picketing the grounds: IF HUNTING IS A SPORT, THEN WHY DON'T THE DEER KNOW THEY'RE PLAYING?

Chevy agreed. His prey always knew.

Jenny's favorite spot came into view through tiny spring buds on the trees—a shallow, dammed portion of the river, where beavers had unwittingly constructed a fine little swimming hole. Chevy had come here almost every day as a kid, watching the river from a twelve-foot-high deer stand Mo had arrogantly built years before he owned the property. Now, Chevy climbed up the rungs to the deer stand and pulled Jenny up with him, pushing away years of rotted leaves and pine straw, the pungent scent singeing his nostrils.

"Here you go," Chevy said, getting Jenny settled. "You remember how we used to come here as kids?"

"I remember. It's so peaceful. I missed it when I was gone."

Chevy's heart turned over. Gone. Jenny had been gone for so long. He remembered the day she disappeared like a movie watched in freeze-frames: Running around the

111

house, frantically looking for the baby ... His mother dabbing Clorox near her eyes, until they were red and watery and her nose was running, too ... Sheriff Goodwin taking her statement and questioning Chevy, not quite believing ... Everyone in town—from the sheriff to the minister to the school counselor—searching the house, the shed, the gardens ... Grandpap oddly silent, and Mother weeping so convincingly ...

He opened his eyes and looked at Jenny, rolling his shoulders to try to keep the tension at bay. He had her back now. That's all that mattered.

"Hey," Chevy said, "did I ever tell you that I came here after you disappeared, waiting for you? I sat in this deer stand and watched them search. They used helicopters and search teams in bright orange vests and Mo Hammond's hounds. I remember the lights and flares and sirens. Even after they all gave up and told me you were dead, I came here every day."

"I knew you wouldn't forget me. I knew you'd find me, someday."

Chevy blinked back a tear.

"Hey, c'mon, Chev. It wasn't your fault."

Yes, it was his fault. No one had believed him. Mother was too good. The tears, the singing, the flowers. She had everybody fooled.

Six months after Jenny disappeared, Chevy finally accepted that his baby sister was never coming back. Ten minutes later, he shot Mother with her own .38.

Chapter 13

Beth watched the T-ball team attack the snacks. Two of the moms handed out juice boxes and peanut-butter crackers, while the kids munched and giggled and eventually began to disperse with various parents and guardians. Beth made her way to the coach to remind him they were going to visit Abby's aunt, so Abby would miss the rest of the week of practice. He acted like it was a mortal sin.

When Beth's phone rang, her heart stopped. She forced herself to look at the number.

Boise. Margaret Chadburne.

"Hello," Beth said, sticking one finger in her ear. Abby was climbing on the monkey bars with a girl named Vanessa, their hats dropping into the dirt as they hung upside down. Beth strolled as she talked to Mrs. Chadburne. Yes, Beth had received a package this morning and the latest doll had arrived safely. No, they still hadn't seen the second two dolls, but Beth was certain they'd turn up.

Abby ran up and grabbed Beth around the waist. They nearly toppled.

"Mrs. Chadburne, I have to go," she said, laughing and putting a finger over her lips to Abby. "I'll let you know as soon as I've had a chance to look at the new doll."

She'd barely hung up when Abby grabbed her arm. "Come on, Mommy. You promised we could go feed the ducks. I saved them my crackers." She held up her package.

Beth sighed; it was their tradition at Chester Park. She trailed Abby to the pond. Abby climbed down over some rocks to the edge of the water and shook the bag of crackers. No dummies, the ducks started toward them.

"Hey," a deep voice said, "what did the first duck say to the second duck?"

Beth jumped, whirling toward the voice. Neil Sheridan strode down the bank.

"Mommy, look!" Abby cried, scrambling back up the rocks to greet him. Her face beamed. "I don't know, what?"

"You quack me up."

Abby screwed her face into thought. "You're not very good at jokes, Mr. Sheridan."

"Everyone's a critic."

"Wanna come feed the ducks with me?"

He chucked her under the chin. "Maybe in a few minutes. I need to talk to your mom first."

"Okay." She turned, watching the ducks head toward an inlet. "Mommy, can I go over there on the bench to feed them?"

Beth looked around the park. A jogger loped by and gave her a friendly wave. She recognized him, waving back and measuring his distance from the bench as she took mental inventory of the other people around: several families, a teenage couple, kids playing Frisbee.

And, of course, Sheridan. *He won't let Abby get hurt.*

"Go ahead," she said to Abby. "But don't get too close to the water."

She and Sheridan watched her go, strolling a few yards behind like lovers. Except for the fact that Beth's nerves were suddenly like live wires.

What keeps you from sleeping, Ms. Denison?

Dear God, she'd almost told him. Had Evan not appeared on her doorstep, she might have risked everything just for one more kiss, just to sink against his body and let *him* be strong.

She glanced up. Sheridan eyed the lake, a muscle twitching in his cheek.

"You had something to talk to me about?" Beth asked, the suspense killing her.

"Keet's," he said.

Beth's jaw dropped. Then she pulled herself together and lifted her chin. "There's nothing illegal about practicing marksmanship at a lawful shooting range."

"No. It's only illegal to practice marksmanship on people." He looked straight into her eyes. "Even obscene phone callers."

She blanched, and Sheridan saw it. His whole body seemed to turn to stone.

"Jesus, it's true," he said, staring at her. "My God, you're waiting for him."

"N-no."

"You want him to find you."

"I don't want him to," she snapped, "but he's going to. I have to be ready."

115

He grabbed her shoulders. "Damn it, you're in over your head. This man is a killer."

Nausea clenched her belly. *Oh, God, he knows. He knows about Anne Chaney.* But then sanity crept back in, and she remembered what Adele Lochner had said.

They didn't even know Bankes's name—they'd been trying to get it from Beth. If they didn't know who he was, they couldn't possibly know about Anne Chaney's murder, or that Beth had been there the night Chaney died. The one who got away.

Unless ... *This man is a killer.* Unless he wasn't talking about Anne Chaney.

Beth swallowed; it was like choking down sand. " Wh-when?" she whispered.

"When what?"

"When did he kill someone?"

Sheridan's gaze narrowed on her face, confused. Beth felt the shell of her armor give a little, and she knew that tiny crack was all he'd need to force his way in. But it couldn't matter anymore. "Please," she said. "I need to know. *When?*"

"Wednesday night, the night he called you from Seatt—"

"Oh, my God."

"And last night in Indianapol—"

"What?" Beth stepped away, reeling. She stumbled, looking at Abby and the ducks even as she struggled to get both her lungs and her mind to function. "Oh, no. Oh, no. Oh, God."

"Beth," he said, catching her arm. He got in her face. "The man who's calling you is dangerous. If he's got you

116

believing anything different—"

"He doesn't!"

He went still, as if that acknowledgment momentarily stunned him.

Hold on. Think. Protect Abby. *Wednesday. Last night.* Not Anne Chaney, so many years ago. Someone else. This week. Now.

She closed her eyes. Tears squeezed out. *Oh, Abby, I'm sorry. I'm so sorry.*

"For the love of God, Beth, tell me what—"

"His name is Chevy Bankes! It's me he wants." Tears spilled down her cheeks. "Why would he kill someone else? It's *me* he wants. And Abby."

"What do you mean, it's you he—"

Abby screamed.

Chapter 14

Beth ripped from Sheridan's hands. He wasn't a step behind her as she dashed down the bank to Abby, where the flock of ducks had taken to the air in a confusion of squawks and thundering wings. Sheridan actually batted birds from his face as he ran, feathers flying, and he reached Abby a heartbeat ahead of Beth.

Abby was crying. But no one was near her. She was okay.

Beth skidded to a halt as Sheridan gathered Abby up, one hand holding her ankle. Her shin was bleeding.

Beth scanned the park. The jogger who had passed earlier came down a path about twenty yards from the water, heading straight for them. *No*, Beth thought, and gave a slight shake of her head. He changed courses and veered away, cutting a wide swath around them.

"Easy, sweetie," Sheridan was saying, crooning in Abby's ear, but his eyes were on the jogger. Missing nothing. "You're okay."

"Oh, Abby." Beth was still shaking. She took Abby and

held her until the crying eased, then examined her leg more closely. "It's just a scrape, sweetie," she said, finally breathing more easily. "You'll be okay."

"I s-slipped on that rock," Abby sputtered, pointing at a boulder in the sand.

Sheridan sank into a crouch. "How 'bout a kiss for that boo-boo?"

Beth shook her head. "That's never worked with Abby. Kisses don't make—"

But he kissed Abby on the leg anyway, and her tears vanished. Wrestler, protector, kisser of boo-boos.

Emotion knotted in Beth's throat. It was crazy, childish even, to think now that she'd confided in Sheridan, he could somehow make her troubles go away. She wasn't a child. Besides, her wounds were ancient—scarred over and numb, not raw and bleeding. Her pain had healed years ago.

"Don't argue with me or ask me to explain." Sheridan spoke in her ear. "Take Abby to your car."

"What—"

He put a finger over her lips, and for some reason beyond logic, Beth didn't argue. She followed as he slanted Abby a deceptively casual smile and swallowed her hand in his.

Beth's pulse quickened as they hurried across the park, and Sheridan challenged Abby to a race through the parking lot. He buckled her into the backseat of the SUV—in short order, Beth thought distractedly. Finally, she couldn't stand it anymore.

"What happened that made you sudd—"

He shushed her with a gesture, already holding his cell

phone to his ear. "Get Billings on her again," he said into the phone. Pause. "Okay."

Beth was stunned. "Are you going to tell me what's happening?"

"Not now. I need you away from here." His eyes had gone hard. "Drive straight home and stay there until you hear from me."

"I don't take orders fr—"

"Damn it, Beth, trust me. I'll take care of everything."

I'll take care of everything. Let me handle it.

He must have seen the fear in her eyes. He took both her shoulders, his voice almost a hush. "Beth, promise me you'll go home and wait, just for a little while."

Arguments spun through her mind, but Sheridan's quiet fervor rolled the protests under. That and the surprising pressure of his lips against hers. His fingers dug into her hair, his body pressing into hers and his lips dragging an answer from Beth's throat.

"All right," she said.

Samson, Pennsylvania
114 miles away

Chevy walked into Mo Hammond's Gun Shop, an illogical little bell tinkling as he entered. Mo was helping a customer—a big, flannel-shirted redneck wearing a bandanna. Chevy wandered the store, keeping his back to Mo, browsing the handguns and pistols. Five minutes later, when Bandanna Man headed to the shooting range for an hour of free target practice, Mo locked up the ammo case and came out from behind the counter.

"Hey, there," he said. "Anything in particular I can set you up with?"

Chevy kept his face carefully downward, as if pondering the Heckler & Koch P7 in the gun case. "Could be. I heard this was the place to come." He sensed more than saw Mo's frown. "For packages, not guns."

Mo stared, then his jowls dropped to his chest. "Jesus. Chevy?"

Chevy smiled.

"Son of a bitch. Chevy." He offered a meaty hand and pumped Chevy's. "Son of a bitch."

"So have you got some packages for me, or not, you big bastard?"

"Yeah, yeah. I got 'em, Chev. They're all here, 'cept the ones you asked me to mail back to you in Seattle. I thought maybe you'd forgot about the rest of 'em. It's been a while."

"It took some time to take care of things. Hope it wasn't a problem."

"No, no, 'course not. Come on in the back. I just let 'em sit there 'til I heard from you again."

"You never opened them?"

"Now why would I go an' do that? The only time I even moved 'em was when I painted the place about two years back." He threw the dead bolt on the front door and gestured for Chevy to follow him. They went to the back; Mo unlocked a closet.

"There they are, three of 'em, right?"

Chevy glanced at the boxes, all wrapped in brown packaging and addressed to Mo by Chevy's own hand, postmarked April 10, 2002. "Right. Three of them." The first five were long gone: three mailed from Boise, and two never to be seen again. Chevy felt a rush just thinking about it.

"Damn it, Chev, you look good," Mo said, scratching his head. "Hard thing, comin' outta prison not fucked up. Never did believe you offed that woman in the woods. The Hunter, they said. Hell, the Chevy Bankes I knew never even liked to hunt. And the way you always molly-coddled that little sister of yours, why I just knew you didn't have it in you to take a woman out and shoot her in the back."

"You always did know me better than anyone else, didn't you, Mo?" Chevy asked. He was careful to say it casually, without accusation. But Mo might have caught it anyway; he shuffled his feet.

"So, you wanna take these with you now, or what?" Mo asked.

"I'll take them. I need some empty boxes, and maybe to borrow your truck for a while, okay?"

Mo frowned. "My truck, er ..." He looked at his shoes, actually dug his toe into the floor like an eight-year-old. Chevy put a hand on his shoulder. A subtle reminder of favors owed.

"Go ahead," Mo said. "I need it back by six, though."

Chevy looked at his watch: three o'clock. Arlington was less than two hours away.

Not that it mattered whether he got the truck back by six. Mo wouldn't be needing it.

The hairs on the back of Neil's neck stood on end as he watched Beth's Suburban pull away from the park.

"Rick," he said into his phone three seconds later, "the name of the man calling Denison is Chevy Bankes. See what comes up."

"Bankes." Rick was apparently writing down the name.

"And I need for you to run a plate," Neil said.

"Whatcha got?"

"I don't know, maybe nothing." But he knew better. A jogger had circled around twice after Abby's fall, rubbernecking, then gone to a Chevrolet Lumina, guzzled some water, fiddled with stuff in the trunk. Killing time, watching. Now, the man was gone, but his car wasn't.

"Shoot," Rick said, and Neil rattled off the tag numbers and letters.

Rick left the phone to call in the plates, then came back. "ID will come through in a couple minutes, and I put someone on the name Bankes. You know anything else about him?"

"No. Beth just gave me the name."

"How'd you get that out of her?"

"I told her he was a murderer. That's all it took. She almost fell apart on me."

"Ah, man. Okay. Well, I just finished reading through everything we've got on Foster's Auctions."

"And?"

"When Mike Foster died, he left the business to his wife, Carol, who hired their nephew, Evan, to run it. They never had children of their own. He's an MBA from Harvard and seems like an upstanding enough guy. I can't find any connection from the missing or dead women to any of the Fosters."

"What about a connection to Gloria? I never looked at an antiques angle with her."

"Denison was still a student in Seattle when Gloria died. What could there be connecting them?"

Neil didn't know and, for the moment, didn't want to think about. He skimmed the sea of cars, looking for the jogger. He worked his way across the parking lot, up and down the spotty aisles of cars. He came to the jogger's Lumina and peeked in. Three fast-food bags, a thermos, and several cups. Either this guy had an eating disorder, or he'd been in his car for a while.

"I also looked at Waterford, the guy whose highboy is in Denison's workshop," Rick said. "He hasn't been out of Charleston in the last two months, and his voice doesn't match the one on her phone."

"Beth's still on his shit list."

"Which does nothing for us. Look, if she's ready to talk, we're gonna need her. The thing in Indiana has turned this into interstate murder, and the FBI's putting together a task force. A guy named Armand Copeland is the Special Agent in Charge. Is he any good or just a geek with a laptop?"

"I don't know him, but don't knock it. One thing they're good at in the Bureau is geeks with laptops. I left a message for Geneviève Standlin this morning. She always liked me, didn't want me to leave the Bureau." Of course, he wasn't sure that would matter. The last time he'd seen her, he'd told her to stay the hell out of his business and leave him alone.

Neil started toward the wooded border of the parking lot, searching the trees for the jogger. Instinct made him touch his gun. The man had simply vanished.

"Okay," Rick said, "here it is—your license plate info. Chevy Lumina, two thousand one, dark blue. The owner's name is Joshua Herring. He's a—"

Neil heard a sound. He whirled and went for his gun, but too late. Everything went black.

Chapter 15

His wits surfaced when he hit the ground. He struck with enough sense to roll, the cell phone scattering shards of plastic all over the pavement, his gun dropping. He came to his knees, filaments of light spraying from his eyes like tiny, silent firecrackers, and groped for the nearest car to right himself.

The jogger rammed him back over the hood of the car. A gun arced through the air toward Neil's head. He grabbed the man's wrist and twisted, wrenching the flesh, then spun from the hood of the car. They separated long enough for Neil to scoop up his gun, but the guy hit him from behind and they both went down, rolling and snarling like two wolves.

In the distance a woman shrieked, and someone screamed to call 911. Neil dragged the brawl over the curb, into the woods and away from bystanders, but beyond that, his only salient thought was for Abby and Beth—and why this brute had been stalking them.

"Son of a bitch." He lunged and caught the guy's

forearm, slamming it up against a tree. The man's fingers sprang open, his pistol thudding to the ground. Neil drove his .45 into the bobbing Adam's apple.

"D-don't sh-shoot d-d-don't—"

"Who are you?" Neil growled. A warm river of blood trailed down the back of his neck. "And I'd better like your answer, or your brains are gonna fertilize this park for the next five years."

"ID. B-back p-p-pocket."

"Lie down."

The man dropped to his knees—Neil helping—then stretched out on his stomach, lacing his fingers obediently behind his head. Neil reached into his back pocket and dug out a wallet. He looked at the driver's license, then double-checked the next ID and sifted through a small stack of cards: VISA, American Express, Starbuck's, Block-buster, and—Jesus H. Christ—a local library card. He read the name on the license again, thought about what Rick had been saying when the world went black, and rolled the man to his back.

"You're a private investigator?" Neil asked, incredu-lous. "Watching Beth Denison?"

"Joshua Herring. Herring Investigations." He spit blood from the corner of his mouth.

"Why are you watching Beth Denison? Who hired you?"

"That's confidential infor—"

Neil grabbed Herring's shirt collar, dragged him to a stump, and spread Herring's fingers on it. He held the hand immobile and lifted his .45 in the air, as if aiming the butt of the gun at the pinky.

"No-no-no! Okay," the man sputtered, turning three shades of yellow.

"Who hired you to watch Beth Denison?" Neil repeated.

"*She* did!" he squealed. "I was keeping an eye on her daughter. Denison was afraid her ex-husband might come for the little girl."

Neil waited, needing a moment for that to sink in, while sirens wailed to a stop in the parking lot. He dropped his arm and yanked Herring to his feet, then heard the unmistakable sounds of footsteps, cocked pistols, angry voices.

"Stop! Police! Drop the weapon!"

Neil looked up, letting go of Herring and dangling his gun on the tip of his finger. "Well, shit," he said.

Silver Springs, Maryland
13 miles away

Chevy sat in Mo's truck in the far corner of the parking lot at St. Mary's Catholic Church, just outside the District. His own car was in long-term parking at the airport—safe for a while, anyway. He didn't know what was going on in the church. A rehearsal, a service, a meeting. Whatever it was seemed to have ended about thirty minutes ago. The parking lot had cleared out except for three or four vehicles parked way out here in the back forty—employees, he presumed, or die-hards who would be the last out of the building. He was counting on at least a couple of them being women. And at least one being alone.

128

He turned up the volume of the tape, sinking into the smooth, plush upholstery. Killing unsuspecting animals must be better business than he'd imagined: Mo's truck was a 2009 four-by-four, soft leather interior, double cab, a dashboard that resembled a cockpit.

State-of-the-art sound system.

"No. Please, sto-o-o-p. Please don't hurt me ..."

His latest acquisition from Indiana. Stunning.

He closed his eyes, letting the woman's cries wash over him. One of his better kills, and he was glad: He wouldn't have the luxury of taking his time with this next one. This one had to be quick and easy. No time for tapes, no time to even dump the body. Just *pop*, match the doll, and get the hell out of here.

He pulled out the next insurance form and picture: *1866 Benoit. Bisque head and breastplate, nice wood body. New blouse, but other clothing original. Superb condition. Appraisal: $30,000–$35,000.*

Yes, this one should be no trouble at all.

She came out the side door of the church—Chevy chose her the moment he saw her—and walked to the wing that was a preschool or something. She disappeared inside, then reappeared five minutes later with a large paper bag. She headed through the parking lot, coming toward him. Chevy's nerves tightened. He straightened, took stock of the cars that were left: two SUVs, a minivan, a couple of sedans. If hers was one of the bigger vehicles ...

He scanned the rest of the parking lot, his blood starting to tingle. No one else around. She passed the first sedan, the first SUV. Chevy's knee began bouncing in anticipation. Not the Honda, not the Honda. Any of the others except the little Honda—

She pushed a button in her hand, and the headlights on the Dodge Caravan flashed. A surge of excitement rushed through Chevy. The minivan: perfect.

"Jenny," he said, his voice straining, "I'll be right back."

He ran through the inventory before he got out of the truck, making sure he had everything: new pistol from Mo Hammond—a little .22; wedding ring on his finger. Oh, and don't forget the blouses. He reached under the seat where he'd stowed a J. C. Penney's bag.

The woman was thirty yards away. He started toward her, a casual walk. Chevy had sandy hair and brown doe-like eyes. He was five-foot-nine. He'd read once that five-nine was the average height for white American men, but usually he wished he was bigger. Trolling for women, though, he was glad he appeared harmless. There had been women who'd teased him during his lifetime, and some who used him. Some even felt sorry for him when they found out about his sister.

But they never feared him, not until it was too late.

This woman glanced in his direction, smiled slightly, and pressed the key fob again. The side door of her van slid open.

Chevy hastened his steps. "Whoa, you dropped something," he called out, jogging toward her. "Oh, sorry. No, I guess you didn't." A smile now. The one that never scared women. "Let me help you with that."

She stood at the side door, holding the bag, ready to thank him. He shoved as she opened her mouth. She fell across the bucket seats in the back, a shriek in her throat, and Chevy climbed in behind her—on top of her, really—struggling to get the door closed. He pressed the gun barrel about an inch above her temple—no time to measure.

Fwp. Not the echoing blast of the .38 shooting on a mountain in the Rockies or at the top of a bluff in Nebraska, just *fwp*. The woman jerked and went limp, sprawling over the console between the seats.

Chevy climbed off her and ducked down, even though the silencer had killed the sound and the windows were tinted. A few moments of caution couldn't hurt.

But no one came. Not even Mother.

He straightened as much as the van ceiling allowed, unscrewed the silencer, and pocketed the gun. He hauled the woman up and propped her in one of the backseats. Blood inched down the side of her head from the hole.

He got the bag of blouses, studied the woman. She wasn't very big. He pulled out one of the pink blouses and checked the tag. Size sixteen—way too large. Dug out another. This was an eight; that would work.

He pulled off the blazer she was wearing, then cut away the short-sleeved knit top she had on underneath. Cutting was easier than trying to get it over her head. With effort, Chevy maneuvered her arms through the sleeves of the pink blouse and buttoned it up the front. He was sweating by the time he got her blazer back over it. Dead bodies—even small ones—aren't easy to manipulate in the back of a cramped van.

But it was done. Chevy straightened the six inches he could, looked at the insurance form picture of the doll, then looked at the woman. There was a little more lace on the blouse in the photo, but the likeness was good enough.

He opened the woman's purse, looking for her cell phone. Lord, how long had it been since he'd had a safe phone to call Beth?

He couldn't wait to hear her voice when she realized where he was.

The call came three hours after Sheridan sent Beth home from the park. Abby was watching a movie. Cheryl and Jeff were due to arrive home late tonight, and Beth was planning to leave early in the morning for the four-hour drive to their house. She just had to make it through tonight.

Trust me.

She fed Abby, put in *The Aristocats*, then beat up her sandbags. Showered, stared at the phone, and wondered what Neil Sheridan was doing—now that he was the possessor of her deep, dark secret.

His name is Chevy Bankes! It's me he wants, and Abby …

Oh, dear God. I'm sorry, Abby.

Finally, Beth went to the basement and buried herself in the second of Mrs. Chadburne's dolls—the one that had arrived just this morning. She actually held her breath as she unwrapped it. These dolls were rare, and as early as European fashion dolls were known. Others—Brus and Simon-Halbigs in particular—had been made in the 1870s and later. The Benoit dolls were earlier, fewer, and their workmanship unparalleled. This one was marked 1865 and bore the standard half-crescent mark of the Benoit manufacturer on the back of her neck. Her torso was kid leather, with bisque arms and legs. Beth began peeling off the clothes to take a better look, starting with the ruffled skirt and petticoats, the bloomers—

Oh, damn. The legs were damaged. Tiny hairline fractures crawled through the bisque like a spider's web, as if something had landed on the doll once upon a time, or it had been dropped. She sighed; damage like this was difficult to repair, and even the best repairs would be visible under a black light. But as costly as the damage was, it wasn't unexpected. Some of these dolls, though originally for use as models in storefronts, had actually become playthings for children.

She sat down at her computer, wanting to lose herself and pass the time. It worked, until the phone rang.

Her heart gave a thump. *Neil?*

"Hi, baby."

Terror crashed in. Beth tempered it with fury.

"I've been missing you," Bankes said. "And I know you can't wait to see me."

"I can't wait to see you dead."

He laughed. "Such a spitfire. I would have enjoyed you about an hour ago, when the woman I was with proved to be ... boring."

A chill slipped down her spine. "What do you mean?"

"I mean there wasn't even a fight. No pain, no suffering, no pleading. She just fell into her own van and I shot her."

Oh God, oh God.

"I didn't even have the luxury of hearing her scream. But that's all right. I have others to keep me going until it's your turn."

Beth swallowed back bile, nearly choking. *Last Wednesday in Seattle, yesterday in Indiana ...* And just now, another?

"What are you doing? It's me you hate," she said. "Why would you hurt anyone else?"

"Oh, no," he whined. "You mean, I'm not hurting you? But I would swear that's *pain* I hear in your voice."

Beth sank to her knees. She might not have even realized it except that she heard the sound, *thnk*, when she landed. " S-stop. Don't hurt anyone else."

"Very nice, Beth. I love to hear you plead. It's sweet to know you're finally suffering."

Hold on, don't pass out. It's too late for deals, too late for anything Adele Lochner could help with. Too late to protect Abby. Just make him end it.

"Then come," she said low. "Come get *me*. I'm the one you want. You want me to plead? I'll plead, you bastard. I'll scream and cry all you want. I'll beg—"

His laugh cut her off, low and evil. "Be careful what you wish for, doll."

Click.

"Nooo!" The phone slid from Beth's hands. She folded down and held herself tight, then leaned back on her heels, rocking like a madwoman.

He was murdering women. Not seven years ago, now. Last week. Last night. An hour ago. All she'd ever thought about was protecting her secrets and keeping Abby safe. And all along, Bankes had been killing women on his way to her.

She went to the desk unit of the phone. Hand shaking, she punched the CID button. The number came up: area code 571.

Arlington. Oh, God.

She rooted through her purse until she found Sheridan's number, dialed. *The customer is not in the service area ... * She tried again. *The customer is not in the service area ...*

But Bankes was near. Area code 571. She had to get Abby away from here.

Stay there until you hear from me. Trust me.

Beth palmed her cheeks dry. She went upstairs, checked on Abby, who was in a movie-induced trance, and retrieved the 9 mm from its secret compartment in the cornice of her highboy. She checked the cartridge and jacked it closed, then made sure there was an extra bullet in the chamber.

Focused now, her brain guiding her rather than her emotions, Beth pulled a suitcase from the closet in the guest bedroom. It was already packed. The only things to add were Abby's toothbrush, a few toys she would have missed, and Heinz's leash and food. Beth collected the toiletries, a couple of animals and a pillow for Abby, then picked up a hedgehog that was Heinz's favorite toy. Stuffed it in the suitcase.

In three more minutes, the Suburban was loaded with Beth's purse, the dog, the toys, and the suitcase. She went upstairs.

"Hey!" Abby complained when Beth turned off the TV.

"How many times have you seen this movie?" Beth asked, forcing a smile.

Abby giggled. "About thirty-hundred-thousand."

"That's what I thought. So listen. How would you like to go see Aunt Cheryl and Uncle Jeff tonight instead of waiting 'til morning?"

"Tonight? Right now?"

"Right now. Let's hurry. Run to the bathroom first; it's a long drive."

"Okay!" Abby ran ahead, and in two more minutes, they were on the road. As soon as she got out of the city, Beth dialed Cheryl.

The first lies had been so hard. They were coming much more easily now.

Chapter 16

Neil banged through Rick's office door. Cops milled around the desk like fruit flies. They all winced when they saw Neil's battered face but were too focused on what was happening to comment.

"What happened?" he said, bulldozing his way through.

"Easy, man." Rick's brow creased. "You get sewn up?"

"I'm fine," Neil said, touching the back of his neck where ten stitches tugged at his scalp. Courtesy of Beth's private dick, Joshua Herring. "What happened?"

"A call just came in to Denison. We haven't heard it yet. Your phone is out, so the guy called me. I told him to send the dub over here." He shoved a finger at Neil's chest. "But *you* get to explain the trace to the chief."

The chief was the last thing on Neil's mind. Another call? And this time, not anonymous. Beth had identified the caller as a man named Chevy Bankes. Info had been pouring in about him while Neil was at the hospital, but so far, they hadn't made heads or tails out of Bankes's connection to Beth.

But he *was* connected; he'd just called her again. And this time, her line was tapped.

The phone on Rick's desk rang. "Sacowicz." He listened, face intent. "Stay on her. For Christ's sake, don't lose her. I'll send more cars."

He hung up and looked at Neil. "Denison's moving. She loaded up her car with a suitcase and the dog and the kid, headed north on I-95."

"What?" It took five seconds for the words to register. When they did, Neil wanted to hit something. "Goddamn it. She promised she'd stay home."

He felt the eyes of the other cops boring into him. No sooner had it dawned on him what they were thinking than someone said it aloud: "So Denison *is* in with Bankes. The bastard called her, and she's going to meet him."

"We don't know that," Rick said. "Let's wait and hear the call. Billings will stay on her."

"Just Billings?" Neil asked.

"No." Rick snapped his fingers at an officer named Fernandez. "Get her in a net. In front of her, behind her, all around. Don't take any chance of losing her or the man she meets" —he looked at Neil— "if she meets anyone at all. Remember, there's a little girl in the SUV. Don't let this turn into a clusterfuck."

"Got it," Fernandez said. He and three others were out the door in a heartbeat.

"She wouldn't do that, Rick," Neil said. "She wouldn't take off without telling me. We had a … We came to an understanding." But he wasn't sure he believed it himself. Maybe it had all been an act. The gut-wrenching emotion, the sharing of Bankes's name. Her tearful surrender to trust him. Their kisses.

"Was the call long enough to get a location?" Neil asked.

Rick went to a wall map. "Ten blocks. That's the best they could do in the amount of time he was on the line. That would mean the call came from right in here, near St. Mary's church in Silver Springs," he said, tapping an area not twenty minutes from Beth's house. "I've got uniforms around the perimeter in five-block increments, stopping anything that looks suspicious."

"Lieutenant." Another phone had rung, and a female officer held the receiver toward Rick. He took it. Silence again, and his face lost color. "Get all that to Fernandez; have them fax us everything." He hung up. "Shit."

"What is it?" Neil asked.

"We got a dead woman in a Dodge Caravan" —he paused to mark it on the map, just inside the circled area— "St. Mary's parking lot. Shot in the head."

Neil stared; Rick looked like he'd just been sucker-punched. "Get on it, Jackson," Rick said to the woman. "Take someone with you from downstairs and start canvassing the area around the church. And notify Special Agent Copeland at the FBI—don't let anybody touch anything in the van until the Feds get in there." He looked at Neil. "I'm gonna go look. Maybe something in the van will give us a lead."

"You mean another lead," Neil said, a bitter taste in his mouth. "You've already got a net around the best lead. She's driving north on I-95."

"Maybe." Rick waited, chewing his lip. Then, "You

139

wanna stay and wait for the call when the audio comes in?"

Yeah, Neil wanted to. He wanted to hear the audio of a phone call that had sent Beth running away just hours after she'd kissed Neil and allowed him to comfort Abby and agreed to trust him. He wanted to hear what it was the bastard said that made Beth jump and run when it was all Neil could do to get her to even talk to him.

More than that, though, Neil wanted to be there when they got her. See her face. Look in her beautiful, secretive eyes. Make her look into his.

Screw staying to hear the recording. Neil said, "I'll go follow Billings. Call me when you hear the audio if Bankes said anything besides, 'I'm finally here, baby. Come meet me.'"

There was something more on the audio, and Neil's heart jammed in his throat when he heard it just five minutes later.

"Listen to this," Rick said, sounding breathless on the other end of the phone. They were both in their cars, interference crackling over the line and breaking up their voices. "It's the audio of the call to Denison, ten minutes ago. Hold on to your steering wheel, man."

Neil dumped the car against the curb. The phones clicked a couple of times, then the caller's voice came through.

Threats. Intimidation. Confessions of murder. Beth, sounding shocked and frightened. Then baiting him, trying to bargain with him. Terrified.

"Jesus," Neil said. He was breathing hard, heart thun-

140

dering, though all he was doing was sitting still in his car. "Play that again."

Neil listened, then said the second prayer he could remember saying in over nine years. The first had been a little more than a month ago, for his brother. Damn if it wasn't close to becoming a habit.

Rick beeped back onto the line. "So she's not with him. That's good news, right?"

Sure. Good news. Beth was terrified and frantic, and a murderer had come all the way across the country to find her. She had Abby, was carrying at least a .22 if not the 9 mm she'd shot at Keet's, and enacting some rash plan she hadn't bothered sharing with Neil.

"Ready for some more?" Rick asked. "Denison headed west. She's not going anywhere near Bankes, and unless he tapped her phone, too, he can't have any idea where she's going."

"Do we?" Neil asked.

"Do we what?"

"Have any idea where she's going."

"Nope. That's why I called you. Want the guys to pull her over?"

"Jesus. She's got Abby with her."

"We could do it easy. One car, two officers. Try not to scare the shit out of Abby."

"You gonna let one car pull over a distraught mother who's running scared and armed with two guns?"

"So we let her go a while, let the drive cool her off."

"Yeah," Neil said. "But I wanna be there when she stops."

"Where are you? I'll come pick you up."

141

They drove for three hours, then Rick thinned the net and stayed on Beth. She wasn't a threat except to herself, and they'd crossed through five different precincts. Now they were in the mountains of southwest Virginia, and Neil wondered if she was headed to Guam.

They'd learned next to nothing about the murder of the woman in the van. The victim was a thirty-four-year-old soccer mom and Catholic preschool teacher who'd been attending a staff function. She'd been shot in the head in her own van. No ballerina-like pose, no missing eyelids, no weird carvings on her legs. Not even an eyebrow-pencil mark on her temple, and it looked like a smaller-caliber bullet than a .38. There was nothing but the phone call to Beth to connect this woman to the man who was no longer their "unidentified subject." He was identified now. His name was Chevy Bankes.

"Think she's really going?" Rick asked. "Just gonna drive until she feels far enough away to stop?"

Neil toyed with it. "No. You heard her tell him to come. I think she's gonna lure the bastard back to her house and try to kill him." He closed his eyes. "I could have helped her."

"Beth?" Rick asked, his voice low. "Or Heather?"

The old pain took a stab at Neil. "Jesus, Rick, either of them. I mean, if either one had just told me what was going on, I might've—"

"Whoa," Rick said, squinting into the darkness.

Neil skimmed the road for what Rick had seen. A pair of shiny green disks, frozen in the distance. Groundhog, maybe. Beth's car swerved around it, brake lights flashing.

"She's gonna kill herself," Rick said. "Out here on these two-lane highways, probably falling asleep at the wheel. The woman's gonna crash if she doesn't stop soon."

Neil looked at the green numbers glowing in the dashboard: 11:45. They were almost four hours outside the District, and he had no idea how far Beth was planning to go. He did know she'd been without substantial sleep for God only knows how long. She was a tragedy waiting to happen.

"Okay," he said. "Let's pull her over. Before she runs her car into a tree."

Rick nodded. He radioed Billings but stopped in the middle of the transmission. "Wait, she's getting off."

Beth took a little road whose only name was proclaimed by a tired sign reading CO. RD. 208. Neil dug out a map, using the glove-box light to see. "Covington." He thumped the map with his finger. "There's a little town six miles north on 208 called Covington, an exchange from another state highway two miles this side of it."

"What the hell's in Covington?"

"I don't know," Neil said, "but unless she's either lost or turns off at the interchange, that's where she's going. It's not an easy town to find by accident."

But she did stop at the interchange. Billings reported there were two gas stations and a mom-and-pop diner. Denison parked at the diner.

"Billings," Rick said into his handset, "stake out the intersections. We're gonna follow Denison into the restaurant." He turned to Neil with a look of resignation. "Aren't we?"

Neil nodded, but he felt a little dead inside. This wasn't the way he had imagined helping her. Damn fool that he was, he'd still believed she might come to him willingly.

It didn't matter anymore. Willing or not, she was gonna deal with Neil now.

Chapter 17

Arlington, Virginia
Ground Zero

Chevy was glad the dog was gone. He liked dogs fine, actually took in a stray once, but he didn't want Beth's sniffing around the house. He hadn't even known she had one except he'd heard it barking once in the background of a phone call. Now he saw the food and water dishes sitting in the corner of her kitchen floor. Must be a big brute, he thought, noting the size of the bowls, then saw a photo on the wall that confirmed it. Sixty-five or seventy pounds. All the better it wasn't here.

He walked through the kitchen, looking, soaking up the essence of Beth. He knew she was gone; the absence of the dog and empty spots on toy shelves indicated that she had taken her daughter and run. Alerted the police? Of course. A squad car had arrived about an hour ago and was parked down the street. A couple of cops had even walked through the house, and Chevy had barely had time to hide. He'd crouched in a basement cupboard and listened, the two cops just about pissing with excitement over the idea of a serial killer, expounding on all the ways the cops could nail him.

Chevy climbed the stairs, passing a door with the stylized letters *A-B-B-Y* hung across the top. Abby. How fortunate. He hadn't known until after he'd spoken with her former employees that Beth was pregnant when she moved from Seattle. He'd felt like the grand prize winner on one of those TV game shows. He couldn't have asked for a better tool of torture.

He ambled through the rest of the upstairs, saving the master bedroom for last. He didn't dare turn on any lights, and he'd have to wipe down everything he touched, but it would be worth it to *feel* the very things Beth had touched, to gather her scent, savor it. She was a pretty girl; he remembered that from their first encounter. But he remembered other things more. Her strength. Her silence. Her cruelty to Jenny. No woman since Mother had ever gotten away with that.

La-dee-da. Who'll dig his grave? I, said the Owl . . .

The rage was like a cancer, swelling inside, making him tremble. He gripped the four-poster footboard, closed his eyes, and battered down the fury, forcing himself to think of Jenny. In the end, Mother hadn't won. Despite all her efforts, Chevy had found Jenny, nursed her, and cared for her.

And then, beginning with Gloria Michaels, he'd learned how to silence Mother. One woman at a time, and each one better than the last.

Until Beth. She'd ruined everything.

But how sweet the taste of vengeance now. Already when he listened to tapes of their phone calls, he could hear the raw terror underlying her voice. Already her fear had grown to something that was almost tangible, that lived inside her day and night and hour after hour. And soon, when she figured out the dolls, she'd be able to look ahead to each one and know what was coming.

Then come ... I'm the one you want. I'll scream and cry all you want ...

Chevy closed his eyes. *Oh, yes, you certainly will.*

The sign for the restaurant had once read RON AND SALLY'S DINER, but Ron's name had a thin coat of paint over it, and the word *Diner* was missing the vowels. Inside, the atmosphere was homespun, smelled of simmering vegetables and overcooked beef, with a display of desserts in the lobby that could bring on diabetic shock in a perfectly healthy person. There were a fair number of customers, given the hour. Most appeared to be travelers; most of the license plates in the parking lot had been out-of-state. But a few were probably residents of Covington, giving all-alone Sally their business.

Beth Denison and Abby were already in a booth when Neil and Rick walked in. Another woman sat across from them.

"Whoa. Let's watch," Neil said, and Rick let out a weary curse.

"You think she's gonna talk to her friend, see the light, and come running to you to save her? Give it up, Neil. The lady's got a plan, and you aren't part of it."

"I'm hungry," he grumped. "Let's watch."

Thirty minutes later, Abby was fading, her head on Beth's lap. Beth appeared almost at ease, despite her stifled yawns. She and the other woman had talked, eaten bowls

147

of the house vegetable soup, played table games with Abby. They could have been two girlfriends, meeting for a late-night snack. Except for the suitcase beside the table and Heinz in the SUV.

When they paid the tab and went to the lobby, Beth bent and hugged Abby—fiercely.

"Jesus, they're saying good-bye," Rick said. "Who the hell is that woman?"

"I don't know, but call Billings."

Rick was already punching it in. "Kid and woman leaving the restaurant. Follow whatever car they take, call in the plates, and find out who she is."

"They're getting in Denison's car, Lieutenant," Billings announced. "No, wait. They're just taking the dog. Okay, the blue Camry, that's theirs. Local plate. Will call it in."

And Billings was gone. The woman was gone. Abby and Heinz were gone.

And Beth disappeared into the ladies' room.

They gave her five minutes, then Rick said, "You know, the gun is probably in her purse now. You sure it's Bankes she's planning to kill?"

Neil's eyes snapped up. Jesus, he'd never thought of that. Would Beth do something to hurt herself? He started toward the women's room.

"Wait," Rick warned. "She's exhausted, scared, and maybe holding a loaded gun." He caught the arm of a hostess wearing blue eye shadow and showed his badge. "Keep everyone out of the ladies' room, miss. And don't go telling everybody."

The girl nodded, eyes wide. With their hands hovering over their guns, Rick and Neil entered the restroom.

Crying. Wrenching, heartbreaking sobs filled the corner stall, the door shut. Rick made a quick check of the other two stalls to make sure they were empty, then perched a hip against the counter, a gesture that clearly said, *She's all yours, buddy*.

Neil squatted. He could see that Beth was sitting on the floor against the wall, her knees squeezed tight against her body. He stood back up; peeking under the stall door in a women's bathroom seemed wrong no matter what the circumstances. But her purse was sitting on the floor beside her, her gun presumably within reach. Or maybe in her hands already.

Jesus, she *sounded* like a woman who had decided to kill herself. "Beth," he said, and the sobbing choked to a halt. "It's Neil."

Silence. The air went still.

"I know Chevy Bankes called you tonight. We heard it." Steady, now. Voice low and calm. "Beth, I know you have a gun, at least the derringer. Is it in your purse?"

More silence.

"You don't have to be afraid anymore," Neil said. "Two police cars are following your friend and Abby now. Who is she, Beth?" Use her name a lot, let her know he's here for her. Even though it's the last damned thing she wants. "Sweetheart, Rick Sacowicz is here. I'm here. I think you have to talk to us now, Beth."

"I d-didn't know he was k-killing people."

Relief poured in at the sound of her voice. "I know; we should have told you." And they should have. Lawsuits and politics be damned. "Beth, honey, push the gun out to me."

149

A movement in the stall, and Neil held his breath. A small black object slid under the stall door. Neil frowned, picking it up. "Your phone, Beth?"

"I was calling you."

A tidal wave of something deep and protective surged through Neil. It startled him with its intensity. "I'm sorry, honey. My phone got broken this afternoon at the park." He paused. "Where's your gun, Beth?"

The .22 slid under the stall door, and a second later, a state-of-the-art 9 mm Glock.

"Christ," Neil said, gathering both. He emptied them and dropped the cartridge, loose bullets, and .22 into his coat pocket. The 9 mm he stuffed behind his back in his belt.

Now, for Beth.

"I'm coming in, Beth. Open the door." His hand was already on the top of the door as he said it, and it gave without effort. It wasn't locked.

She looked up at him, those beautiful, dark brown eyes glistening and swollen and red-ringed. "Her name is Cheryl Stallings," she said, and it took him a second to realize she was talking about the woman who had taken Abby. "She's Adam's sister. They live on Oakdale Lane in Covington. But I didn't tell them about Bankes. I couldn't."

Rick left, punching in numbers on his cell phone. Neil reached down and lifted Beth to her feet. Her gaze narrowed on his face.

"What happened to you?"

"Joshua Herring happened to me." He waited for that to take hold.

"Oh, God. Is he ... Did you ...?"

"Don't worry, he's all right. He gave up client confidentiality at the drop of a hat, though. Real tough guy," he said, dripping sarcasm. He gave Beth a scolding look. "Your *ex-husband*?"

"I had to tell him something. I didn't know what else to do."

Anger slid past worry. "But now you do. Now that you know what Bankes is up to, you decided to get rid of Abby and go back and blow his brains out yourself, is that it?" Neil tightened his grip on her arms. "I was right here all along, damn it. You should have told me."

"I couldn't."

"The hell you couldn't!" He gave her a shake. "Did it ever occur to you that *I* would keep Abby safe? Did you ever think, just once, that if you'd told me what was happening, maybe *I* could take care of both—"

She broke; the air just came out of her. Her body crumpled, tears coming fast. Neil cursed, dragging an armload of sobbing female against his chest. Nothing made a man feel more helpless.

When the worst had passed and her breathing came more easily, he pushed her back and tipped her chin. "Tell me the truth, Beth. Were those bullets for you or for him?"

"Abby needs me," she said simply.

Relief pounded through Neil's veins.

"Well," he said, "thank God for Abby."

It was hot in Beth's basement—that seemed odd. Or maybe Chevy was just sweaty. The cupboards had been harder work than he'd imagined, the position awkward and the little hacksaw from Beth's bachelorette tool kit inefficient. Still, when he finished, he had nearly five feet in one cupboard, and the back wall could be removed to get into the crawl space beneath her porch. His own private dwelling, right under Beth's nose. Literally. *Bedroom with access to a terrace,* he thought, making himself giggle.

He cleaned up the sawdust as best he could with just a penlight, and stowed away the boxes of dolls he'd picked up from Mo Hammond. He climbed into the cupboard and lay on his back to try it out, legs bent and shoulders a little cramped. Not great, but it would do, at least if he had something to use as a pillow.

He felt his way slowly through the house, mindful of the police cruiser sitting down the block. He thought about taking a couch cushion or a pillow from a bed, then decided it might be missed. He went to the laundry room, found a sweater of Beth's and the shirt she'd apparently worn under it.

That would do. Chevy held it to his nose and reeled with pleasure. Yes, that would do especially well, he thought, then straightened when he heard a sound.

A car. It was coming down Beth's driveway.

Chevy's heart kicked into his throat. He scrambled back down the stairs, wary of his steps in the darkness, trying not to panic. Just outside the garage, men's voices murmured.

Shit.

Chapter 18

Neil drove Beth's Suburban back to Arlington; Rick detoured to Covington to bring the locals in on the case and check in with the FBI. Beth's instincts for Abby's safety had been good. Covington was a peaceful, small community. The Stallings were well-known; Jeff was a strapping career military man just back from temporary duty. The only thing Neil could fault Beth for was sending Heinz away, too.

"You should have kept the dog with you for protection," he'd complained as they pulled away from the diner.

"Heinz is no protection. He would beg a murderer to pet him."

"He's noisy. That's something. More useful than Joshua Herring."

She frowned. "Herring watched out for Abby."

"Who was watching out for you?"

"I was. I do it all the time."

"Not anymore."

A promise or a threat, Neil wasn't sure, but it didn't matter: She was asleep before the words sank in. She slept all the way back to Arlington. Shivered and shook and made heartbreaking little sounds, but slept nonetheless. At four-thirty, Neil pulled into the driveway of her house and gestured to the police officer walking toward them from his cruiser. The officer jogged down the drive to meet him and shook hands when Neil stepped out of the vehicle.

"Sacowicz told me to expect you."

"Everything quiet?" Neil asked.

The officer nodded. "I came on about two hours ago. And Wilson, parked down the street. We did a walk-through when we got here, before we took our posts. No sign of anyone."

"Okay." Tomorrow—this morning, rather—when the task force assembled, they'd work out a more sophisti-cated surveillance plan with a team of off-site agents. Put some people in the neighborhood, maybe put someone inside the house, just in case Bankes showed.

At least, that's what Neil thought they'd do. It had been a while since he'd been in on a murder investigation. Once the FBI took over, he wasn't sure he'd still be in on this one.

"The lady's asleep," he said, nodding to the Suburban. "I need five minutes."

"I'll keep an eye on her," the officer said.

Neil raided Beth's purse for the key card to her garage and went inside. He went straight upstairs and found an empty suitcase, logically stored in the guest room closet. He went to Beth's bedroom. The top corner of a big

154

dresser was dismantled, the compartment just big enough to hide something the size of a Glock.

"Pretty slick," he muttered, then rooted through her closet and a couple of drawers, grabbing anything he thought she might need and folding clothes as neatly as a man is capable of doing. In the bathroom, a box of Tampax made him pause. He took it, just in case, then searched the drawers for birth control pills or something. There weren't any.

You've been alone a long time ...

Neil looked at a photograph of her husband on the nightstand. Some questions there, but he was honest enough to acknowledge they were mostly personal. Adam Denison didn't appear to be a big guy: five-nine or five-ten, with the build of a tennis player, light brown hair, and kind of an intellectual look about him. Abby didn't favor him; she was a carbon copy of Beth's exotic looks. But it was obvious from the array of photographs around the house that Beth worked hard to keep Adam alive, and his ring was the only jewelry Neil had seen her wear.

Was she still in love with a ghost?

At five o'clock in the morning, he pulled into the hotel parking lot.

"It's clean?" Neil asked when Rick met him.

"Yeah. My guys got security in place an hour ago."

He woke Beth gently, not knowing what to expect of her temper when she realized he'd taken her to a hotel instead of home. He didn't know if she still had any intention of taking on Bankes, but it didn't matter anymore. He was finished letting her call the shots.

155

"Where are we?" she asked, testing her legs as she got out of the car. She handed him the sport coat he'd tucked around her in the car. He draped it right back over her shoulders again.

"Hotel. Keep you out of sight for a little while."

She blinked but didn't argue. Probably just too exhausted.

"Abby?" she asked.

"Covington police and a couple of Feds are on her twenty-four, seven. Adam's sister will never know they're there. But if Bankes discovers Abby, we'll be on him before he can breathe."

"Okay."

"You're damn right, okay. Get your purse."

"I am getting my purse. You don't have to order me around."

It didn't feel that way to Neil. She needed someone to take care of her, God help him.

Beth frowned when he pulled her suitcase out of the car. "That's mine," she said.

"We went by your house and I picked up a few things. If there's something I missed, I'll get it tomorrow." She reached for the suitcase and Neil pushed her hand away. "I've got it."

"I can carry my own suitcase," she protested. "I do it all—"

"Damn it, Beth." He grabbed the suitcase with one hand and her elbow with the other. "You aren't alone anymore."

He piloted Beth to a suite of rooms on the eighth floor of the Radcliffe Hotel. It had a comfortable central sitting room, with two bedrooms jutting out like wings, each with its own bath. Another half bath squatted between the wings, and to the right a pair of double doors led to a small kitchen.

Rick, his sleeves rolled to his elbows and tie yanked loose, had files spread out on a coffee table. A larger table had been commandeered for a laptop, printer, and fax machine. Neil wasn't surprised at the man stationed there: thin, bespectacled, and slightly balding, he wore a black suit, white shirt, and navy-striped tie.

The Feds had arrived.

"Ms. Denison," Rick said, gesturing to the setup, "I'm sorry to intrude on you, but we need to talk to you before you go to bed."

"I'm not going to bed. I slept all the way here."

Neil stopped himself before he scoffed out loud. She sure as hell *was* going to bed. For about ten hours, if he had anything to say about it.

"This is Special Agent Jack Brohaugh with the FBI," Rick said, introducing the man with a laptop. "The rest of the task force will be assembled later this morning at Quantico. Brohaugh is a technology expert."

"Computer jock," Brohaugh editorialized. He smiled at Beth and shook Neil's hand.

"Do you know Special Agent Geneviève Standlin?" Neil asked.

"She's on her way," Brohaugh answered. "She said to tell you to take a pill, chill out."

Neil humphed. Witch. But, Jesus, he'd be glad to see her.

Rick started in with Beth: "We know about Anne

157

Chaney and Bankes. But we need you to help us figure out what he's doing now. Why he's after you."

Her cheeks drained of what little color they had, but she nodded. She picked her way around the room as if she didn't know where to sit, then perched on the edge of a love seat. Brohaugh started typing, though nothing had been said yet, and Rick settled into a chair.

"Ms. Denison," Rick began, "when did you receive the first phone call from Bankes?"

"About eight months ago," she said. "I thought it was just a run-of-the-mill prank call."

"How many times has he called since then?"

She pressed her fingertips against her temples. "I don't know."

"Two, ten, twenty?" Neil pushed.

"I don't know." She looked at Neil. "You were monitoring my phone calls, why don't you know?"

"Jesus, Beth, we weren't monitoring your phone calls. All we knew at first was the phone that called you on Wednesday night belonged to a woman with her eyelids cut off."

"Wh-what?"

Well, shit. Beth went ashen, looking suddenly like she might pass out. Neil glanced at Rick, whose face said, *Nice work, asshole.*

"Ms. Denison—" Rick stopped. "May I call you Beth? We only know of three phone calls. The one from Seattle you received at midnight this past Wednesday night, the one from Omaha we played for you at the station, and the one we tapped into tonight"—he looked at his watch—"I mean, last night. Do you remember the first call?"

She nodded. "It was a Monday night, Labor Day. I remember because I'd just flown back from an antiques show in Dallas."

"What did he say?"

"Nothing. I hung up. I thought it was just an obscene phone call."

"Okay," Rick said. "But there has to be a reason Bankes called you. It wasn't random. Think about people you've met through Foster's, maybe someone you dated—"

"It's not that." She looked up, and the words seemed to choke her. "I wasn't trying to be uncooperative. I thought he just wanted to get back at me. It's me he wants."

Neil's heart began to squeeze.

"But this last time—t-tonight—when he called, he said he'd—" She drew in a deep breath. Agony carved lines in her face. "He said he'd killed a woman in her van. Wh-what if it's true?"

"It is true, sweetheart," Neil said. "He shot a woman, just before he called you."

She jerked as if she'd been struck. A pallor like a death mask crept over her face.

"Beth," Neil said, "that was the third woman we think Bankes has killed—on *this* spree—and two others are miss—"

She shoved past him, swung the bathroom door closed behind her. She vanished so quickly Neil felt the air move in her wake, caught her scent in his nostrils. He frowned, then heard the unmistakable sounds of coughs and gags.

They gave her a few minutes, nobody talking, until Neil couldn't stand it any longer and started toward the bathroom. The door opened, and he stopped.

"It's not because of something at work," Beth said, her voice thready. "And it doesn't have anything to do with someone I dated."

Neil stepped closer. "Then what is it, Beth? Why does Chevy Bankes want to 'make you pay'?"

She looked up at him, forcing out the words: "Because I killed Anne Chaney."

Chapter 19

Silence. For the space of three heartbeats, the room went absolutely still, then Sheridan scraped out an order: "Don't say another word, Beth."

"I didn't me—"

"Stop." He shushed her with his hand, his voice so severe she blinked. His expression virtually dared anyone else in the room to continue the questioning.

"Uh . . . " Sacowicz rubbed his head, looking confounded. "Okay, get her lawyer," he said to Sheridan. And to Beth, "This might be a good time to take a break, maybe go lie down, whatever."

She opened her mouth, but Neil was already beside her, his hand on her elbow. "Do it."

An hour later, Beth sat on the edge of a hotel bed, water dripping from her hair and soaking the back of her hotel robe. There was a time she'd almost drowned herself in hot showers—it had been the only way to get warm when the chills came, vibrating on the heels of the memories. Memories now shared with the Arlington Police

Department, the FBI, and Neil Sheridan.

I won't tell, Adam, I promise.

"Beth." A rap at the door.

She smoothed back her hair and considered standing. She didn't have the energy. "Yes."

The door cracked open. "Hey."

Neil. Ex–Special Agent Sheridan, rather. She wasn't sure when she'd started thinking of him as Neil. For such a startlingly handsome man, he looked terrible—from his altercation with Joshua Herring, the long drive, the long hour spent reading about Anne Chaney and Chevy Bankes.

He stepped in front of her. "You should dry your hair. You're shivering."

So, what else is new? she thought.

"Adele Lochner is on her way. Don't say anything more until she gets here, do you understand?"

Don't tell, Beth. You'll go to prison.

"I didn't mean for it to happ—"

"Don't." He placed his finger over her lips. "Tell me later, with your lawyer."

The emotional dam threatened to crack. Damn it, she shouldn't need a lawyer to explain what happened. And damn it, she thought she'd gotten past the guilt.

Neil sat down so close the heat of his body penetrated her robe. "It was fifty-two degrees the night Anne Chaney died. You were cold."

Beth looked at him. No one had ever understood the physical legacy that haunted her all these years later, yet in the past few days Neil had seen it come over her time and again. Shivers and chills and bone-deep cold that wouldn't go away. "Sometimes I think I'll never get warm," she said.

"You will," he said, opening his arms, "right here."

It didn't occur to her not to accept; she simply leaned in. Strength. Heat. Safety. His protectiveness wrapped around her like a blanket, and she had the feeling all the evil in the world might simply fade from existence.

"Damn," Neil said, pulling back. There were new voices in the other room.

"What?"

"We need to get out there. I called an agent I used to know. That's her voice I hear."

"Oh." Beth noticed his shirt and rubbed her hand down it. "I got you all wet."

He jerked and caught her hand, something fierce in his eyes. His lashes dipped and he tugged the lapels of her robe together.

"I, uh, guess I should get dressed," she said, taking the lapels in hand.

His Adam's apple bobbed once.

"Neil, I—"

He stood. "Beth, for God's sake, don't say something to me now that some lawyer can dig out of me later. Just wait."

"Ironic, isn't it? You've been wanting me to talk for days, and suddenly when I can't, it feels like the most important thing in the world to tell you."

"There'll be time. Right now you need to talk to the FBI, police."

"Wait. What about you? Are you leaving?" she asked, alarmed.

"Leaving?" For a second he looked baffled, then he curled his fingers into the edges of her robe, pulled her in, and kissed her with a thoroughness that was loud and clear.

"Get it?" he asked when he was finished. "Or do you have any more stupid questions?"

Beth cleared her throat. "No. I think I got it."

She braved the audience in the common room ten minutes later. Lieutenant Sacowicz and the agent named Brohaugh bent over a laptop, while a fax machine behind them spit page after page into a tray. A newcomer pulled off the pages, reading them and handing them to Neil. Her hair was cut stylishly short and threaded with gray, and she wore a navy pantsuit set off with a yellow-and-blue scarf. His friend from the FBI, Beth supposed, and looked around the room. She thought she'd heard someone else, too.

Neil saw Beth and held up a hand to the newcomer. "Leave her alone, Standlin. She's going to eat first."

"It's okay," Beth said. "I'm not really hungry."

"The hell you're not."

The woman ignored him and stuck out her hand to Beth. "I'm Geneviève Standlin. I'm with the FBI. A psychiatrist."

Beth froze. *What?* She turned on Neil. "You called a psychiatrist? I'm not going to fall apart."

"Well, that's good," Standlin said, "because I didn't come to keep you from falling apart. I came to profile Chevy Bankes and give you something so you can sleep."

"Here's your profile: Chevy Bankes is a psycho," Beth

164

shot back. "And I don't need anything to help me sleep."

"Beth," Neil said, "Standlin's not the enemy. Come eat break—"

"And *you* can stop giving me orders." Her voice was strong, but a sudden, overwhelming wave of panic made her reel. She was finally prepared to tell them about Anne Chaney's death, and now some headshrinker was going to dig and poke and prod, searching for more.

Well, they weren't going to get it. Not all of it, anyway.

A brick-red blazer emerged from the middle bathroom. Adele Lochner.

Beth walked over to her. "You knew," she said, her voice vibrating with emotion. "You knew what he was doing and didn't tell me."

Lochner's spine grew a full two inches. "I told you they were hunting for him based on evidence that was pure speculation, and they were. It didn't seem prudent for you to go admitting to murder on the basis of that."

"It's not speculation anymore, is it, Counselor?" Neil said.

"My obligation was to protect my client, Mr. Sher—"

"Enough." Lieutenant Sacowicz stepped in. "We're all on the same side now. The rest was just everybody doing his—or her—job." He turned to Beth. "There's food in the kitchen. Better go grab some."

There must have been some sort of breakfast buffet in the hotel. A little bit of everything had been kept warm on the stove, and fresh coffee dripped into a pot. Decaf. "I need some leaded coffee," Beth complained.

"After you get caught up on your sleep," Neil said. "Not until."

Tyrant.

But, Lord, it felt nice to have someone looking out for her.

When she finished eating, Neil materialized at the table, holding out his cell phone. "Do you want to talk to Abby?"

"Oh, yes."

"I already dialed; just hit Talk."

He left the kitchenette, and on the third ring, Cheryl picked up. Abby was waiting for breakfast, playing with Jeff and the three-year-old. Beth could hear Heinz barking playfully in the background. The few minutes of conversation lifted her spirits and focused her energy, grounding her after a night that had the distant, ethereal quality of a dream. She still felt as if she were floundering at sea, but Abby's voice was like a lighthouse. Neil Sheridan, the lifeboat.

Beth pushed that maudlin sentiment away and snapped the cell phone closed, taking a deep breath. Time to face the music.

As much as she dared.

Chapter 20

"I was meeting with the curator for the Westin-Cooper Museum," Beth explained, her knees curled up in a wing-back chair, her audience rapt. "A prominent family had offered to sell a collection of antiques to the museum, and the curator, Anne Chaney, wanted to show it to me."

"So you were already employed at Foster's," Sacowicz said.

"Part-time. At the office, I got a message from Anne that she would have to reschedule our appointment for another night. I remember I was glad; it meant I could go to dinner with Adam and a DA who was visiting from Chicago. He was going to work in his grandfather's firm there, but he wanted to get into politics, so wining and dining this DA was a big deal. But then Anne called and said she could make it after all. I owed her a favor, so I told Adam to have dinner without me, and that I'd join them for dessert."

"So your associates at Foster's never knew you and Anne Chaney met that night," Neil said. "They thought your appointment had been canceled."

"Yes." She took a deep breath. "Anne had just moved into a gated community that backed up against a forest and a lake. I called her from my car and waited until I saw her come outside. She had some empty boxes from unpacking and went around back to the Dumpster. Bankes must have been there. When she didn't come back, I walked around the corner and saw them talking. Arguing."

"About what?"

"I don't know. But Anne was backing away from him, pulling her arm from his hand. Then Bankes hit her."

She paused, closing her eyes as if rewinding the footage in her mind and playing it back might change the way it had ended.

"I called out." *Stupid, stupid, thing to do.* "Bankes turned. He had his arm around Anne's throat and a gun. He said if I moved, he would kill us both. I ... I just froze. He shoved Anne up beside me and told us to walk."

"Where?"

"Out into the woods, behind the town houses. He was right behind us, with the gun." The panic leaked in, bleeding into her chest.

Ancient history. Keep talking.

"I kept thinking we should fight him, but Anne was hysterical. She wasn't going to help."

"Why did you think that?" Dr. Standlin asked.

"She recognized Bankes. He'd been, I don't know, stalking her, I guess."

"Chaney had told you that?" asked the lieutenant.

"No, but Bankes kept saying, 'I told you, you couldn't

168

hide from me,' and 'It's finally time,' things like that. He talked to Anne the whole time we walked, taunting her."

"Did Bankes talk to you during all that time you walked?" Standlin asked.

"Not really; it was all about Anne. I just happened to be there. I didn't know what to do. I wasn't a fighter then. I didn't know how to defend myself."

"So you just willingly walked into the forest with Bankes."

The censure in Standlin's voice struck like a lash. "What was I supposed to do? He had a gun. He had a bag looped over his shoulder and kept shifting it, but he always kept the gun pointed at us. Yes, I just walked willingly. I thought he'd kill us if I didn't."

"What kind of bag was he carrying?" Lieutenant Sacowicz asked.

"I don't know. Canvas, I think, or nylon. Just a bag, like for a gym or sports. It didn't look too heavy, but he kept . . . handling it all the way. Like there was something valuable inside."

"And talking to Anne," Standlin said.

"Taunting her. He liked hearing her cry."

"At the trial," Brohaugh said, "the prosecutor argued that Bankes had stalked Chaney for weeks, driven her to change her phone number, get new locks, move. But Chaney had a reputation for getting around with the men. Bankes's attorney argued that one of her ex-lovers might have been her stalker."

Neil looked at Beth. "Bankes didn't harass you?"

"I wasn't supposed to be there, I guess. He just pushed me against a tree and told me to sit down."

Don't do it. Fight. The impulse threaded back into consciousness like big, ugly stitches in time, unraveling. Helplessness, weakness.

"I didn't know what else to do," she said. "He had the gun. I just ... I just did what he said, and he teased Anne and" —she swallowed— "rubbed himself. Anne was crying."

"What were you doing during all this?" Standlin asked.

I was by the tree, doing nothing. While Anne cried and begged him not to hurt her.

"Don't just think it, Beth," Standlin ordered. "Say it out loud."

"I wasn't doing anything, damn it! If I went for the water, I'd freeze. If I ran, he'd shoot me. I thought maybe if we both ran, but Anne ... She wouldn't ..."

"She wouldn't run," Standlin finished.

Don't just stand there, Anne, damn it. Do something.

Beth shook her head. "She curled up in a ball and cried."

Anne, stop! You're making it worse.

"That must have made you angry at Anne."

Lochner stood up. "What the hell?"

"Don't be stupid," Beth said. "I wasn't angry at Anne." But even as the words came out, the first fat tear ran down her cheek. She didn't know why, and she flicked it away with the back of her hand. "It's just that she was making it worse. He wanted her to cry. He liked the sound of it. Then I saw him look around for his bag. He stepped away from Anne to drag it closer. It was just a second, but I thought maybe—" She swallowed. "I grabbed his arm."

170

Run, Anne! Go, damn it.

"And the gun."

Run!

"She ran. Finally, like I told her to, Anne started to run. And I fought with Bankes. And then the gun ..." *Pop. Pop.*

Oh no, oh no, oh no ...

Lochner cursed, and from somewhere in the room Neil said, "Ah, Jesus." Beth closed her eyes, but the memories were there, pulling at her, dragging her down.

Standlin stepped closer. "You convinced Anne to run, Beth? And attacked Bankes?"

Damn it, Beth, what were you thinking, attacking a man with a gun? Adam's voice, sharp with fury. She shook it off and looked at the room through blurry eyes. "I was just trying to get the gun."

"It's okay, Beth," the lieutenant said gently.

But it wasn't okay. Anne was dead.

Don't tell, Adam insisted, *they won't understand.* Later, he'd said if they needed her testimony, she could tell the police she was there. But the police never needed it. Bankes was arrested the next day and convicted in a short trial. They had evidence from his shoes that he'd been at Anne's townhome complex, an alibi that didn't check out, gunshot residue on his hands. Without ever hearing Beth's version of the story, he went to prison for life.

Now he was free.

Standlin held up some printouts. "There was blood at the scene that didn't belong to either Bankes or Chaney, and two shell casings from a thirty-eight semiautomatic. One bullet struck Anne Chaney in the back while you fought with Bankes. What happened to the other?"

"I don't know."

"Are you O-negative?"

Beth nodded.

"It was your blood at the scene, wasn't it?" Standlin asked.

"My client isn't going answer any more quest—"

"Were you shot, Beth?" Neil asked, sounding worried.

"No. No. I don't know what happened to the other bullet."

"Then what happened after Anne went down?" Standlin pressed.

Anne went down. Such simple words, yet so descriptive. Anne had finally been running, as Beth had told her to, and just ... went down. Dead, with one giant convulsion of her spine. The gun that killed her wrenched from Beth's hands. The gunshot stinging against her palm. Bankes dropping beside Anne's body, screaming, digging furiously into his bag.

And then Bankes, going mad.

"After?" Beth whispered. "He wanted *me* to scream then, for Anne. But I wouldn't. I was afraid it would make him ... " She touched the scar on her cheek. "He hit me with the gun."

"Christ," Neil said. He stared at her when she didn't say anything more. "That was it? You were knocked out?"

Not quite. Not enough that she couldn't feel the chill of the ground, or taste the retching combination of dirt and blood and bile that crawled down her throat. Not enough that she couldn't feel her cheek on fire, or his hands on her thighs. She wasn't out that much.

Don't tell.

"When I came to, he was gone. There was nothing there but Anne's body." She shivered. "I ran. I went back the way we'd come. I got in my car and locked the doors. I drove." Heat. All the way to high. "I went home, to our apartment. Adam was there." Angry, because she hadn't shown up at the restaurant. "I showered. I was dirty and bloody."

And cold. So, so cold.

"And you didn't tell anyone," Standlin said. A statement rather than a question.

"Of course I did. I told Adam."

"And?"

"He took care of me. He got a butterfly bandage from a first-aid kit for my cheek, and he helped me get to sleep."

"He didn't take you the hospital, call the police?" Neil said, incredulous.

"He would have the next morning, but he watched the news. Someone found Anne's body within hours. By afternoon, they had a suspect. It was on TV, and I saw they had the right man. I don't know what to tell you ... " She looked down, bracing herself for the guilt to begin gnawing again. "We'd just found out I was pregnant. Adam was worried about what a trial would do to me and the baby. And they didn't need me. Bankes was held without bail. Then he was convicted."

Standlin said, "You could have told all this to Sacowicz or Sheridan when they came looking for him a week ago."

"I could have. I wish I had. But I thought Bankes was coming for *me*, and I knew there was nothing I could do to send him back to prison. I thought maybe if I offered him enough money—"

173

"And if he didn't take it, it didn't matter," Neil said, his voice rough. "Because you could handle him now. You're strong."

"Don't respond to that, Beth," Lochner ordered. "He's try—"

"Stop." Beth felt as if a dam were crumbling. She turned to Neil. "You're right. I did think I had to handle Bankes myself—"

"Beth!" Lochner said.

"And I did want to kill him."

Adele Lochner sank into a chair.

"The system set him free, and I thought he was coming for me or my daughter. If I couldn't pay him off, I didn't think I had any choice but to kill him. But in the end, I didn't do it. In the end," she said, looking straight into Neil's eyes, "I tried to call you."

Chapter 21

In the end, I tried to call you. The weight of that dropped like a load of bricks on Neil's shoulders. Be careful what you wish for, said one part of his brain. But his conscience spoke louder: She needs you; don't fuck it up this time.

Ten more minutes spent hashing through the story yielded nothing new. And Standlin, digging deeper and harder, only seemed to push Beth further away.

"That's it," Neil said. "Beth needs to sleep."

He thought she looked grateful for that. For a minute he thought she might not even argue with him. Then she stood. "So, I'm staying here, I guess?"

"You're staying here."

"You said you could pick things up for me at the house. Would you?"

Neil nodded. "Of course. What do you want?"

"There's a widow in Boise who's sending me dolls. Two are already lost, but a new one is supposed to arrive this morning. It will need a signature." She paused. "And I'll need my black light and laptop so I can work."

"Police are watching your house, just in case Bankes shows up," Neil said. "I'll have them sign for the package and stop by and get it." It would be just as well if Beth had something to keep her occupied while she was holed up here. He sure as hell wasn't letting her out.

Standlin came over, medical bag in hand.

"What's that?" Beth asked, noticing the needles coming out of the bag.

"Two things," Standlin said. "One, we need blood to compare to the unidentified sample found at the scene of Anne Chaney's murder. And two, I'm giving you a light sedative."

Beth bristled. "You can have all the blood you want, but I don't need a sedative."

"You'll have nightmares. Sheridan says you always do."

Neil fielded a glare from Beth that might have wilted a lesser man. "Take it, Beth. You're no good to anyone running around half-comatose."

She scoffed. "You mean half-nuts. You're just afraid I'll crack up, slip away from you, and—how did you put it— go home to blow his brains out."

"I'm not afraid of that," he said, deciding to make things perfectly clear. "There's no way in hell I'll let you slip away from me."

Chevy lay on Beth's bed, feeling her, smelling her, sliding into dreams where she cried in desperation and screamed in pain, pleading with him to stop yet knowing he wouldn't, not until he'd milked every whimper and gasp and shriek from her body. He woke hard as a club and

176

tried to go back under again, but sunlight streamed through the slats in the blinds. He couldn't make it work.

Morning. And where was Beth? Gone, he thought. Probably at a friend's or at a motel. Maybe under locked guard already. It all depended on how quickly she'd decided to spill her guts to the cops, and how much of the truth she had decided to tell them. He rolled off the bed and slipped to the window, parting the blinds a mere fraction of an inch. Yup, there it was, halfway down the block. A gray sedan now: cop car.

So, they were waiting for him. He grinned a little, remembering the conversation of the two police officers he'd overheard as they walked through last night. They'd speculated about a setup, maybe a decoy to lure Bankes to Beth.

Chevy didn't know how likely that was, but Beth hadn't come back to her house. Maybe they *were* planning to set him up.

He liked the idea; it made him feel important. But he had to be ready. A little alteration in his plan.

He smoothed the bedcovers back, making sure everything looked as it had when he arrived. *Someone's been sleeping in my bed*, he thought and found himself smiling. He stayed low and went downstairs, helped himself to a bagel in the kitchen—*someone's been eating my porridge*—then began looking for Beth's paperwork. The logical drawers were filled with opened mail and bills. He dug around, came up with a phone bill: AT&T. Dug some more to see who provided her Internet service: Comcast.

Okay.

Down to the basement. Chevy had spent the night here,

just to be safe. Beth's computer was surrounded by books and magazines and Internet printouts that all appeared to be about dolls. The dolls themselves Chevy had found packed in the two boxes they'd arrived in, but Beth had tied a little tag around each one's wrist like a coroner might on a toe.

He enjoyed that bit of irony.

He settled down in front of Beth's computer and logged on. Even if the police were tapping her phone lines—and Chevy doubted they'd gotten that far yet—they wouldn't detect Internet use, not with two different carriers of service. The only thing he had to worry about was an unexpected visit from someone.

Her server came up, and he spent a few minutes reading headlines. The women out west were picking up some press, but Chevy wasn't the star yet. By noon, if Beth had talked, he'd be the headline.

He got into Beth's Web history, skimming through several of the sites she had visited. A strange sort of thrill tightened his skin at the thought of tracing her cyber-space footsteps—a new twist on Goldilocks: *Someone's been using my Internet.* Of course, he couldn't read her e-mails without a password, but then again, he didn't want to. He was just interested in what she'd learned about him.

Three-quarters of the way through her history list, a hit: *Chevy Bankes.*

A wave of pleasure washed over him. Chevy smiled as a string of sites came up, all referring to him. Seattle crim-inal cases and prison release dates. Court documents. Sheriff's office reports. Newspaper articles. Three dozen stories about the overturned court cases out of the Seattle DA's office.

He chuckled, thought about reading some of them, but forced himself to move on. If the cops *were* planning to set up some sort of sting at Beth's house, he shouldn't be found sitting at her computer. He got up, peered through a slat in the blinds. The cop car hadn't budged.

He went back to the computer, more conscious now of the time. He typed in "Kerry Waterford." The Web site came up, linking to information about his store, his private collection, and Internet sales. In the left-hand margin, Chevy clicked on Toys and Dolls, then went to pictures of dolls similar to the ones on Beth's desk. He spent fifteen minutes sifting through them, until he was certain he'd found the one he wanted: *1873 Benoit fashion doll, signed and dated*, the description said, but Chevy knew better. That doll wasn't a Benoit. It was a reproduction. Waterford had tried to sell it to Margaret Chadburne almost a year ago, but Beth stopped him.

And here it was. Fucking Kerry Waterford. Still the con artist.

Chevy checked the price: six thousand dollars. Shipping, to have it delivered on Monday afternoon, added forty-two dollars and twenty-five cents.

Chevy leaned back, thinking it through. He had plenty of money these days, but not the kind you could just send over the Internet in exchange for a doll. He'd need a credit card, ID.

He'd need Margaret Chadburne.

Chevy smiled. No problem there: He and Margaret were *tight*. Margaret would do anyth—

He stopped: a sound. He darted to the far window. The cop on duty was out of his car, walking toward the house. Chevy's heart stammered, then the cop veered over to a car that had just pulled up. A black Charger. The driver got out and closed the distance between them—a tall man in a suit, with heavy shoulders and long, purposeful strides. A string of recognition plucked in Chevy's mind, but he didn't know why and couldn't get a clear look. They spoke for two minutes then the cop went to his car and came back with a box—Chevy recognized that for sure. He held his breath as the man put it in the trunk of the Charger. But instead of driving away, they walked toward Beth's driveway, the big guy tossing a key fob in his hand.

Chevy freaked. Jesus-Jesus-Jesus. He started to hide then remembered the computer, went over and clicked on Shut Down, four, maybe five times. Stop it, he said to himself. The last thing you need is to freeze the stupid screen. Wait, wait. He sneaked a peek from the window. They were in the driveway.

Click. The screen went black.

Fight or flight: His lizard brain kicked in.

He chose flight.

Chapter 22

Neil hit the button for Beth's garage door opener.

"Whoa," said the surveillance cop. New guy. He'd come on duty an hour ago. "Whoa," he said again.

"She works for an antiques firm," Neil explained. Chadburne's third doll had already been delivered, as Beth had anticipated. Neil decided to go in and get the first two, as well. Beth would sleep most of today, Standlin had assured him, but later, she'd need something to do.

The cop was touching things, a little bit awed. "I always wondered what made people pay a fortune for stuff that's just ... old. I mean, look at this bowl. It's a *bowl*. An old, beat-up bowl. What's that about?"

"Got me," Neil admitted, looking around for the dolls. His nose wrinkled: The shop had the faint odor of sawdust.

"And this." The cop wandered to a mat where a two-piece dresser sat out. One piece was still partially covered, and Neil recognized the wrappings, the size. Waterford's highboy, the one Beth had been bringing home when they first met. The one she'd told Evan had a "made-up" back, whatever that meant.

He ran his fingers over the carvings on the highboy, bent down and sniffed. Maybe that was it. The smell of wood.

"Wonder what that thing's worth," the cop mused.

"Six, maybe eight thousand dollars, tops," Neil said. "The back is made up."

The guy gaped at him. Let him wonder.

Neil found the first two dolls near Beth's computer, lying in their boxes. "This is what I need. I'm good now; let's go. I gotta get to a task force meeting." It felt good to say it.

"Okay," the other guy said, trailing Neil out. "But I wouldn't pay six hundred for that thing, let alone six thousand."

Neil plunged into the bowels of the Behavioral Science Unit at Quantico wearing a fresh suit with a visitor's badge. The irony of being a visitor to the FBI didn't escape him. In some ways, having a formal escort through the windowless underground structure made him feel like an interloper. In others, it was like coming home.

The "command center" for the task force was a medium-size conference room with a large table, several laptops, video screens mounted on walls where windows should have been, and a half dozen FBI agents and police detectives buzzing around getting caught up on the case—which was quickly going public. The Special Agent in Charge, whom Neil knew only by reputation, was

Armand Copeland. He was a hefty black man in his fifties whose occasional appearances on the news had always left Neil thinking of James Earl Jones. He was conservative and irrefutable—a man who probably spent his free time loafing through conduct manuals.

Which made Neil wonder why Copeland had invited him: to involve him in the case or to get whatever information he had, then run his civilian ass off? Neil bit back a pang of worry. It had been easy being at the hub of the investigation when Rick was in charge; he just about had carte blanche. An FBI task force led by a man like Armand Copeland wasn't likely to be so accommodating.

Just try to keep me out of it, he thought belligerently.

In addition to Standlin and Brohaugh, two other men introduced themselves: an off-site agent named Juan Suarez, studiously unwrapping a stick of Juicy Fruit, and a six-five black man built like a refrigerator. Neil was just realizing he'd missed the big man's name, Harry or maybe Jerry, when Lexi Carter came in and waved at him. Neil had boxed with her husband a few times. She was fine-boned and dark-haired—like Beth—which, Neil decided, was probably why she was here. A sting in the works.

SAC Copeland was running down the plan: "... and Brohaugh will coordinate the field offices and resident agencies, pull it all together here in the command center."

"Is there any word on the two missing women?" Harry-Jerry asked.

"We're still waiting," Copeland answered as a bleached blonde joined the group. O'Ryan, Neil thought, recognizing her. Sidney O'Ryan. They'd flirted once in an elevator, and she'd flashed her shield when he got cocky. He'd flashed his back.

"O'Ryan is the press liaison," Copeland explained, and she grimaced.

"Why me?" she asked.

"It's the nose, *querida*," Suarez said in his slight Latino accent. "You're the only one with a nose perky enough to feed them bullshit and get away with it."

Copeland: "So what's the plan?"

O'Ryan said, "Standlin helped me craft a statement. She thinks we should stroke the bastard a little, let him know how smart he is and how many agents are working on him."

Copeland frowned. "He'll buy it?"

"I don't know," Standlin said. "I haven't figured him out yet; I can't see a pattern: Beth Denison and Anne Chaney were stalked; the others weren't. Two women were cut up, one was shot in her van, and two are missing, so we don't know what he did to them."

"Don't forget Gloria Michaels," Rick said.

"Right. She's a little different, but still looks like Bankes. And they both went to college at West Chester University. She was at a frat party the night she was killed."

Suarez turned to Neil, snapping his gum. "How come you didn't talk to him back then?"

"I talked to every fucking person who was at that party. Bankes wasn't there."

Suarez scoffed. "Good work."

"Hey, asshole—"

"All right," Copeland said, holding up a hand. "Put 'em away, boys. Suarez, back off."

184

He jerked his thumb at Neil. "The guy's not even an agent no more. He don't belong here."

Copeland's jaw went tight. "That's my decision, not yours."

Suarez stepped down with a show of poor sportsmanship, and Standlin went on. "We have to figure out his pattern. Serialists are smart, organized, with some powerful reason for every move they make. And they usually keep something from their kills, something so they can relive the excitement later."

"Trophies," Copeland said.

"Right. So, has he taken something from these women?"

"Their phones?" Rick asked. "He's using their phones."

"*Using* them. A trophy is more personal—a piece of jewelry, an article of clothing, a lock of hair, even a finger."

"Could he be leaving something with them instead of taking it?" Harry-Jerry asked.

Standlin gave him a what-are-you-talking-about look.

He slid a report across the table to Standlin. Neil squinted to catch the agent's signature at the bottom: Harrison. "The husband of the soccer mom ID'd her body but said he didn't recognize her blouse. Said she wouldn't wear pink lace. So: Could he be dressing them up?"

"Check it," Copeland said to Standlin, then pointed a finger at Brohaugh. "What was Bankes doing before he started on the road here?"

"Before prison, he worked in hotels. Started as a bus boy in college, became assistant manager of a halfway-ritzy place in Philadelphia by the time he graduated. He moved to Seattle in two thousand one and took a management position at an upscale hotel called the Orion. Fellow employees were all shocked when it came out that he'd murdered Chaney.

"Then, after he got out of prison, Bankes got an apartment and was rehired at the Orion. He worked there until a month ago, when the State awarded him six hundred thousand dollars in lost salary and damages for his prison term. Then he just quit coming to work."

"Hobbies? Activities?" Copeland asked.

"Neighbors in Seattle are being interviewed, but it sounds like he was low-key, easy enough to live with. Took in a stray dog once, gave it away to a guy at work. And traveled some—a weekend away here and there."

"Where did he go?"

Brohaugh shrugged.

"What about his apartment?" Neil asked. "Anyone been there?"

"They're in it now. Looks pretty normal. He maybe liked to play his music loud. Got himself a surround-sound stereo system and the walls are all insulated."

Copeland turned to Standlin: "What about all that childhood bull you like so much?"

She looked exasperated. "Give me a little time, for God's sake. Right now I'm still trying to figure out his thing with Anne Chaney."

"Can't Denison help you there?" Copeland asked.

"She gave us a rundown, but she's holding back. There's something she hasn't told us."

"So dig it out of her. That's what you're good at."

"I'll do my best."

And God help Beth, Neil thought. Geneviève Standlin was good at ripping open old wounds, then lancing them until they bled out.

"Okay," said Copeland, breathing it all in. "So we keep the daughter under wraps in Covington, watch Denison, and give her lots of time with Agent Standlin until we know the whole Chaney story. Meanwhile, get people scouring motels around the District, new apartment leases, homeless shelters—Hell, he has money, so check the upscale hotels, car rentals, everything. Put out an APB on his last known appearance and his vehicle. Harrison, you pull together everything on unsolved cases that could've been his, look for connections. Agent Carter, get in Denison's house, mimic her routines, et cetera." He stood; meeting over. "Everyone keep stuffing the files. Sacowicz," he said to Rick, "glad to have you in. Anything you want from the FBI in order to protect the citizens of Arlington, just ask."

"Oh, that was good," O'Ryan said. "I'll be sure it makes my sound bite."

"It better. That's the only reason I said it."

O'Ryan flashed a smile that rivaled that of anchor-women. She actually did have a perky nose.

"So go," said Copeland, but he looked at Neil with an unspoken order to stay put.

Unnecessary. Neil wasn't going anywhere.

Chapter 23

"I notice you didn't ask me where I want your ass," the SAC said after the conference room had emptied.

"I'm pretty sure I know where you want my ass, sir. There's no place for it on an active task force."

Copeland steered around the table to stand face-to-face. "I remember you, Sheridan. Twenty-nine years old when you left the Bureau, and SACs were already calling you for the tough ones."

A muscle twitched in Neil's jaw.

"You know what they called you behind your back?"

Neil swallowed. He knew. It was the reason he'd gone back to find Anthony Russell.

"Pit Bull. Once you got your teeth into something, you wouldn't let go."

Let it go, Neil. Come home. Please. I need you here. Kenzie needs you.

"Then you let a personal tragedy bowl you under and ruin your career."

"Is there something you wanted?" Neil pressed.

"This: An FBI task force is no place for civilians, with personal issues. You're a civilian, and Standlin says you're up to your eyeballs in personal on this." He waved a hand when Neil opened his mouth. "Don't deny it. She knows her stuff. She knows you, too."

Neil wanted to wring Standlin's neck. "You're talking about ancient history, sir."

"The loss of a child is never ancient history. Now, I don't like it," Copeland continued, "having someone who's not on the team playing the game with us. But you're a trained agent, and you know the Michaels case better than anyone else. Besides that, you've got something going with Denison. I'd be a fool not to use you."

"Use me?" Neil's pulse beat a little faster.

"I'm not a man who cares how many gold stars go beside my name. I want Chevy Bankes, and I don't care who catches him—my task force or the city cops." He narrowed his gaze on Neil. "Or an ex-agent who happens to be close to the woman Bankes is targeting, a man working alone and without sanction from this office."

"Sir?"

"Alone and unsanctioned, do you understand?"

Neil was beginning to. And he liked Armand Copeland more and more.

"Stay with Denison; keep her talking. Keep us up with any connections to Gloria Michaels. I'll give you whatever resources I can and let you sit in on the task force meetings. In return, anything you learn from Denison or because of your history with Bankes, you *share*."

Oh, yes. He definitely liked Armand Copeland. Neil nodded and started to leave, then turned back. "One thing no one noticed in there is Chevy Bankes's birth date," he said, and Copeland frowned. "Gloria Michaels was killed on his twenty-first birthday."

Copeland's brows went up. "What does that mean?"

Neil shrugged, opening the door. "Hell if I know."

When Neil stepped into the corridor, Standlin was waiting for the elevator. He tried to ignore her; couldn't. "Christ, Standlin, what did you tell Copeland?"

"I told him two things everyone but you already knows."

Neil crossed his arms. Goddamned shrinks.

"First, I told him that sixteen years ago, you were the best young criminal agent in the Bureau, and I was proud to have helped bring you on board."

Neil actually felt his cheeks burn.

"And second, I told him that nine years ago, you went crazy and never came back."

"Thanks a lot."

The elevator opened and she stepped inside. "Oh, and I told him one other thing."

Neil didn't wanna hear it. But his hand barred the door, anyway.

"I told him the best chance he has of finding Chevy Bankes is to let you at him, and if he does, he could have the best damned criminal agent in the Bureau again."

Something thumped in Neil's chest—pride, maybe, or even hope—something he couldn't quite identify. But on its heels came a bleaker, blacker emotion that he could. "I killed the wrong man."

She nodded. "And getting the right man now won't

bring him back. No more than cuddling up with Beth and Abby will bring your family back. But," she said, pushing the elevator button, "it just might bring you back."

The rest of the day was paper: every detail of Gloria Michaels, Lila Beckenridge, Thelma Jacobs. The women from Omaha, Indianapolis, Silver Springs. Neil couldn't remember anyone using the names of those last three; they'd become dead representatives of their cities.

By evening, he was caught up on what authorities in each city knew. Suarez, in the kind of nasty mood that comes from sitting in a hotel room all day long, met him at Beth's suite. He reported that she had slept for six hours, stirred—probably to go to the bathroom—and had been silent again for the three hours since. Neil walked through hotel surveillance, learning pass codes, covers, the faces of the agents on duty; then Suarez signed off for the night.

At seven-thirty, Beth staggered into the kitchenette. She wore a thigh-length T-shirt and looked like a zombie. A pretty zombie, if such a thing existed. Damned shapely T-shirt.

She was looking for a phone.

"I have to call Abby," she said. "She'll be going to bed soon. I have to call Abby."

Neil stuck a plate of lasagna in the microwave and punched in two minutes. Handed her his digital phone. "Her number is star-eight. She spent the morning at her aunt's house, went to McDonald's for lunch, and then to the park where she met a shih tzu and played with it for an hour. Ms. Stallings ran some errands—the grocery

191

store, dry cleaner, and a public library branch—and Abby's been at the Stallingses' house ever since." He winked. "Wanna know what she ate for supper?"

"Cocky jerk," Beth said, but she smiled.

She slipped into the sitting room and spoke with Abby for ten minutes. Neil listened to her talk about the shih tzu and Abby's little cousin and snickerdoodles that had apparently just come out of the oven. He smiled when Beth reminded Abby to brush her teeth and to make sure the back gate was always closed. It seemed Heinz had a history of trotting off to socialize with other dogs in the neighborhood whenever they visited the Stallings family.

Beth's voice cracked when she told Abby she loved her, and two or three minutes passed before she came back into the kitchen.

"Okay?" Neil asked softly.

"Abby's fine."

"But you aren't," he said and looped his arm around her neck. He pulled her in and dropped a kiss on her head. She felt brittle and small tucked against him, and after a day spent reading what Chevy Bankes had done to women, a wave of protectiveness surged through him. Keeper of her secrets and keeper of her safety—the desire to be both was so unexpected it hit him like a brick. The desire to be her lover came, too, not so unexpected.

He succumbed to the Great Comforter: "Come on," he said. "Lasagna."

Beth demolished two servings, their conversation covering everything *except* the case. More than once, she caught herself staring. Lord, the man was easy to look at.

"... physical therapy with special-needs kids," he was saying. "She dreams of doing it all on horseback—something called hippotherapy. She practically lives in a stable." This was his sister, who lived in Atlanta.

"Is it just the two of you?" Beth asked. They'd already gone through her family tree.

"I have a brother, Mitch. He's a photojournalist. J. M. Sheridan."

Her eyes bugged out.

"Ah, you've heard of him."

"Wow, you have a famous brother. I've seen his books. And I attended one of his exhibitions for an AIDS foundation once, with his photos from South Africa."

"That's him. Righteous do-gooder, champion of every underdog, and great revealer of government fuckups."

"I take it you're not close?"

"Mitch and I live by different mottos. He looks at something broken and can't leave it alone; he's gotta get in there and fix it. 'Change the world,' that's his motto."

"What's yours?"

"'Fuck the world.' Can't be fixed."

Beth looked at him. "I don't believe you."

He shoved a pile of dishes together and picked them up. "Then ask Mitch," he said, dumping the dishes into the sink. "He almost died in Iraq last month because I was working as a Doberman for two 'operatives' and never bothered to find out what they were operating. It was a bomb, by the way. They stole a Sentry helicopter, killed thirteen civilians, and messed Mitch up pretty good. But, hey. Fuck it."

"Oh, God. Neil." Beth studied the harsh lines of his

193

face. "I don't think you're doing so well sticking to your motto now."

A split second of surprise, then one dark brow rose. "Your fault."

Beth hoped so, but she shied away from saying it. She had the feeling he'd just given her something dear. But it also reminded her of all he hadn't shared. "Maggie said you were married to her sister."

"Heather," he said, and the tendons in his throat contracted. "We're divorced."

Beth waited, reminded herself she had no business asking, and asked anyway. "What happened?"

He walked over and stood one step away, his gaze boring into hers. "She kept secrets from me. Shut me out. And when I wasn't there, she decided she could handle things herself."

Beth swallowed. "Oh."

"Oh," he echoed. "That's all you have to say?"

She stepped back. "What do you want me to say? 'Gee, Neil, I'm sorry I tried to handle things by myself'? Or, 'Gee, Neil, I promise that if you're not answering your phone I'll sit quietly and wait for you'?"

"That would be a start."

She blew out a breath. "Look, I'm sorry I worried you by taking off with Abby. It's not like I was unprepared. I had the guns and I've done a helluva lot of training. I can defend mys—"

He moved like lightning, her spine suddenly slamming against his chest, her throat beneath his forearm. She started to strike, but his free hand wrenched her arm to the middle of her back. Pain lanced through her shoulder.

"You're a *kickboxer*," he said against her ear. "That's something they do in rings, for show, like the WWF. It's not real."

"Let go of me," she croaked. She could hardly breathe.

"Two minutes," he said. "Two minutes of this and you're out cold. Three, and you're tied up in the trunk of my car. Or, if I'm the expedient sort, I could just snap your neck and be done in three seconds."

Beth wheezed, her knees going soft. And just that fast, her lungs expanded again.

"You bastard," she said, heaving in oxygen. He relaxed his grip enough to allow air back into her lungs but not enough to free her. "Let go of me," she rasped.

"Get out of it," he said. "You think you're so by-God tough. Get out of it."

Chapter 24

Think, *think*. She was barefoot and he wasn't, so his instep was no good. He held her too close to kick him in the groin, and if she went for the eyeballs or ears he'd see it coming. Flipping him was out of the question; with her left arm in that position, he'd simply dislocate her shoulder.

But the kneecap—a hard heel jab, from virtually any angle—would hurt like hell. And would at least push him back far enough for a roundhouse to the throat.

She inhaled, and just as she moved her foot, his ankle popped up, tangling her legs. She flopped facedown onto the floor.

"I was careful not to break your leg just now," he said, his breath against her ear. "That's because I'm trying *not* to hurt you. Bankes wouldn't bother with that consideration."

"Bankes isn't as big as you," she muttered against the linoleum.

"He has a cruel streak and a sick need for vengeance.

His insanity will take him a lot further than karate will take you."

"Then what do you suggest?" She nearly stumbled when he jerked her vertical in no more time than it had taken for him to plow her down. He pulled her onto the carpet in the living room and moved the coffee table. Shoved back a chair.

"Forget your training," he said. "Fight dirty."

"What do you mean?"

"I mean, you've been learning how to get away from an attacker. What you need to learn is how to kill one."

"That's why I have a gun."

"And it will be in your purse when you need it."

More gently now, he turned her around into the same position he'd held her in a moment earlier—her left arm pinned behind her back and his right forearm crossing her chest and throat. "You still have a free hand right now. Forget using it to disable me. Use it to kill me."

"I don't understand."

"Hold up your hand, palm in, and flex your wrist." He shaped her hand with his. "Curl the tips of your fingers down tight so the heel of your hand is your weapon."

She did.

"Now jab the heel of your hand under my nose, and up. Do it hard enough, and the bones will splinter into my brain."

"Lovely."

"Yes. And it will save your life while he's expecting you to go for his kneecap."

Beth went through the motions, tentative at first, then with greater speed and strength and agility each time Neil made her practice it. By the fifth time, she was gasping for air. "That's enough. I've got it."

"You don't, but it's a start."

She made a move that should have taken him by surprise and wound up flat on her back. Neil straddled her hips, pinning her wrists on either side of her face.

"Damn it," she said, panting. "You're good."

"So are you. But you've been taught rules, and Bankes won't follow them." He glanced at their positions, and an expression that seemed half pain, half pleasure canted his lips. He muttered a curse and went utterly still. "From here, what would you do?" he asked. "Tell me."

His face was only inches away, his upper body brushing her breasts, his crotch grinding into her pelvis. With no small degree of astonishment, Beth realized she wasn't afraid. The strength and heat in his frame were a source of comfort and pleasure, not fear. "I let you maul me for a second, then bite off your tongue."

A flicker of amusement crossed his features. "No. That's letting him go too far."

"You have a better idea?"

"Smash your forehead into my face."

Beth blinked. "You're serious?"

"Deadly."

"I'll crack my skull."

"The only skull that will crack is the one not ready for the impact. You'll be the one ready because by the time a man gets you in this position, he's already thinking with his dick. But for God's sake don't wriggle," he said, squeezing his eyes closed for a minute. "You'll only feed the flame. Crack his nose with your head, and he'll either

198

roll off from the pain or straighten enough to free your wrists. But you have to be ready yourself. Use some of that focus and control you learned in Muay Thai."

Intrigued, feeling cosseted yet strangely powerful, Beth went through the motions. He mimicked the fallout, and when she started to scramble away he said, "No. Stay with it; never believe your last hit was the final one until you know he's really down. Otherwise, you're likely to get shot. Come after me again."

It was strangely invigorating, a workout like Beth had never experienced. Forget scream, disable, and run. Neil's philosophy was a lot simpler: kill.

Thirty minutes later, Beth lay on the floor catching her breath. Neil stretched out beside her. "Not bad," he said, dragging his finger along her arm.

"Good. Now let's talk about my gun."

A single dark brow rose. "What about it?"

"I want my Glock back."

"All right, tomorrow morning I'll take you to Keet's. You prove you can shoot it, and I'll give it back."

"Who the hell put you in charge?"

"You did. When you asked for my help."

"I never asked you to treat me like a child," she grumbled, sitting up.

She didn't get very far. Neil rolled her beneath him. It was a turbulent kiss, and very, *very* thorough. His mouth claimed every breath, his hands were everywhere, and by the time he stopped, Beth felt as if her body had dissolved into a pool of shuddering, raw sensation.

He pulled back, and Beth arched up for more. He ran a fingertip over her lips. "Is that adult enough for you?"

She threaded her fingers through the thick hair at his nape. "I don't know," she said, pulling him down. "Do it again, and this time I'll pay better attention."

They spent Friday morning tearing up targets at Keet's. Neil gave her a hard time, but inwardly, he was pleased. Apparently, marksmanship was one of Evan Foster's hobbies; the two of them had spent some time at it.

Not that *that* made Neil feel any better.

At Quantico, Copeland filled him on Bankes: "He grew up in a little town called Samson, about two hours from here. Was raised by his mother and maternal grandfather."

"No father?"

"Some boy in the next town, but the grandfather beat him up when his sixteen-year-old daughter turned up pregnant. The boy took off and Chevy never knew him. Peggy had a second child when Chevy was twelve, but there's no indication who the father was. The second baby was born with significant mental and physical disabilities. Her name was Jenny. She disappeared when she was sixteen months old."

"What?"

"Vanished." He snapped his fingers. "Thin air."

"What about the mother? Has anyone talked to her?"

"She committed suicide six months after Jenny disappeared, when Chevy was fourteen. Grandpa was dead by then, so Chevy went into foster care. He actually did okay. Got a scholarship to college and all."

"Jesus." Neil ran his fingers through his hair. "I need to go up there, talk to the people who knew him. He might've come through that way on his way here."

Copeland scowled at him. "I've got five agents doing that now. Active agents, you know, ones with shields who actually earn a paycheck. Your job is here, remember?"

"I'm not doing shit here."

"You're getting Denison's part of it."

"What part? What the hell else is she supposed to give us? She screwed up Bankes's plans for Anne Chaney. Now he wants to make her pay. That's all there is."

"Well, Sheridan," Copeland said, standing up, "you better hope you're wrong about that. Because if you're right, we won't figure him out until *he* wants us to."

But at the hotel, Neil was loath to push Beth into talking. Making her relive Chaney's death was like forcing her through a tour of hell. He didn't want to witness those chills again, or see the terror and guilt that filled her eyes.

He didn't want to think what more there might be.

Beth was holed up in the bathroom. He waited twenty minutes before he finally knocked, a little worried.

"Come in," she said, and Neil was taken aback. She sounded perfectly fine.

"Beth?" he said.

"It's okay. Come in."

He opened the door, chasing an eerie blue glow from the room. Beth sat on a small chair at the vanity. A doll lay on her lap, her notepad open, and a pencil over her ear. A black light was plugged in at the sink, cord stretched across the floor.

"Do you mind shutting the door?" she asked. "This is the only room without windows. It has to be dark enough."

Neil closed the door. The ghostly blue-black glow returned, and he felt like he was in another universe. A beautiful woman, a half-naked doll, and a black light, all in a hotel bathroom. There was a film-noir idea in there somewhere, but he wasn't sure how it would play out.

He stepped behind her. "What are you doing?"

"Looking for damage. Sometimes chips or repairs or hairline fractures aren't visible to the naked eye, but they show up in black light."

"Oh." Well, that was a brilliant response. "What if you find something?"

"That depends," Beth said. She removed the miniature vest and pink blouse the doll was wearing, adding them to a small stack of clothes. "It's weird with toys and dolls. If this were a plaything, condition wouldn't matter much. Folk toys, baby dolls, teddy bears—they can be torn all to heck and still bring big money. Fashion dolls are different. Condition is everything."

"No kidding." He didn't care, but Beth loved this stuff. He bent closer, watching her fingers glide over the bisque, smelling strawberry or raspberry or some-sort-of-berry shampoo in her hair. It wasn't pulled back, and the thick layers draped over her cheek as she looked down. Funny, the black light did the same to Beth as it did to the dolls: made her scar stand out.

"So what does that mean for Mrs. Chadburne?" Neil asked.

"Money, if these dolls check out. Lots of it." She set down the doll and, one article of clothing at a time, searched the seams and surfaces with the black light. Looking for stains, Neil decided; crime scene techies did the same thing. "The only thing I'm worried about is this blouse," she said, more to herself than to Neil.

"What do you mean?"

"I don't think it was part of the original outfit." She shook her head. "I'm gonna have to talk to someone who knows this vintage of dolls better. Maybe even Kerry. He's a jerk, but he knows dolls."

Neil eyed the miniature clothes, and his nape prickled. Probably nothing, but it was one of those thoughts like toothpaste: Once it's out, you can't squeeze it back in. *Her husband didn't recognize the blouse.*

"Honey," he asked, "where are the first two dolls, the ones you already looked at?"

"I sent them back to Foster's when I finished. Evan has them locked up there in the safe. Why?"

"Just wondering," he said but looked at his watch: four-thirty. If he hurried, he could still make it to Foster's before the office closed.

Even though it was probably nothing.

Chapter 25

Foster's Auctions was a three-million-dollar spread with a mansion tucked on a hillside and a sprawling gallery at the north end of the property. Manicured lawns stretched among all the buildings, giving way to several acres of natural woodlands farther out around the perimeter. The house itself was vintage, complete with the original barn, carriage houses, and slave quarters. The outbuildings were now used for the business—an interconnected maze that housed offices, storage space, garages, and the gallery.

Neil followed the signs to the main office, slipping in just as the receptionist appeared to be packing up for the day. He asked for Evan Foster and waited while she made some calls. Apparently Foster wasn't in his office.

"I think he's at the preview," came a disembodied voice over the intercom. "Try the main gallery."

Several cars, almost all rentals or from out of state, were parked outside the main gallery. It was unlocked, and Neil let himself in to what turned out to be the rear of the audience seating, now empty. He strode through the aisles of chairs, passed an antechamber, and stepped onto the main stage where several people were previewing the sale that would take place tomorrow and the next day. They talked, examined items, and made notes in their copies of the catalog. A catalog that was Beth's handiwork, Neil realized with a surprising tug of pride.

Evan Foster stood to one side, speaking on the phone, looking aggravated. When he saw Neil, he hung up and came across the stage, pointing at a plate in Neil's hand. A stupid-looking dog was painted in the middle of it. "That's Sheffield," he said. "An expensive thing to break."

Neil bit back the impulse to throw it against the wall and set it down. He nodded to the phone. "Customer relations problems?"

Evan shrugged. "Antiques junkies are kooks. But doll enthusiasts are the worst. They think of their dolls as children."

"That was the doll lady you were talking to? Margaret Chadburne?"

"She flew in from Boise this morning."

Neil's pulse kicked up. "Do you know where she's staying?"

Evan shook his head. "Why?"

"Oh, nothing, really. Beth wants to talk to her, that's all." Neil's brain was outracing common sense. A sure sign of desperation in an investigation. "Beth wants to see the first two dolls again. I came to get them."

Evan frowned, his demeanor going from cool to arctic. "Where are they? Beth and Abby."

"Mmm, sorry," Neil said without any chagrin at all. "Official FBI business."

"Damn it, I wanna know."

"Don't worry. She has your gun."

Evan stiffened, lifting a fist. "Listen, you son of a—"

Neil caught his lapels and spoke right in his face. "Bad idea, Foster," he growled. A couple of people straightened, watching. "Now, why don't you just make plans to cover for Beth this weekend, and go get me Mrs. Chadburne's dolls?"

"I won't have to cover for Beth. She promised she'd be here for the sale tomorrow."

"She's mistaken. She won't be here."

"What the hell have you done with her?"

"Jesus, Foster," Neil said, releasing his crumpled shirt before someone called the police. "Do you think I have her bound and gagged someplace? She's safe, that's the whole idea. She wouldn't be if she came here. Crowds, distractions, cars from all over the country. Give me a break, man. Tell her to stay home."

"She isn't *at* home."

"Tell her to stay with me, then."

Speculation swept over Foster's face. Clearly, that had been the wrong thing to say.

"You screwing her?" he asked.

Neil was amazed. "That's none of your—"

"It is." He went still. "Goddamn it. We have something going."

"That's not what she tells me," Neil said and met him glare for glare. Poor fool. There wasn't a man in history who hadn't loved the wrong woman once in his life. In another time or place—with another woman—Neil might have felt sorry for him. Might. "We don't want anything

206

at Beth's house to seem unusual," he said, keeping his voice down. "Keep things moving the way you would under normal circumstances. And get me the two dolls."

"Screw you, Sheridan. There's no way I'm letting an old lady's nest egg walk out of here with you. Beth knows how to unlock the safe. If she wants them, she can come get them."

So, nothing there, at least not until he got a look at the dolls. Neil called Copeland and talked him into a warrant, then returned to the hotel suite to find Suarez and Beth playing cards. Well, Suarez, anyway. Beth was pacing the floor, the cards in her hands apparently forgotten.

"Where the hell have you been?" she asked Neil.

A smile tugged at his lips. "Hi, honey. I'm home."

"Sheridan," Suarez said. "Maybe *you* can get her to stop wandering around. You ever tried to play poker with a woman who won't sit down?"

Beth crossed the room and slapped five playing cards onto the coffee table. "Full house," she said. "I win."

Suarez picked up his suit coat, shaking his head. "Good luck, *amigo*," he said, shutting the door behind him.

"Evan called," Beth said as soon as Suarez was gone. "He needs me at the sale this weekend."

"No."

"I'm the only one who knows this collection. It's my catalog, my client consignment."

"No."

"Damn it, you can't keep me locked up here like a child."

A memory tingled on his lips. "I thought we'd already established I wasn't treating you—"

"Stop it." She advanced on him. "You tuck me in here with a guard who keeps filling my wine glass and trying to get me to go lie down or play a card game or look at dolls, anything to keep me busy while you and the rest of the world are out there trying to catch a killer."

"You're the *target*, Beth. What am I supposed to do, hang you out there so he has a clean shot? Take you to visit the crime scenes?" He thought the tears might start and let out a curse. "Aw, jeez, don't do that."

"I won't let you shut me out," she said, her voice shaking. "Adam did that. He wanted to handle everything, and I let him and—"

"All right," Neil conceded. "I won't shut you out. But I will shut you *in*. You're staying under lock and key, like it or not."

She opened her mouth to say something, and Neil kissed her.

She wilted into it for a moment, then pushed him away to arm's length. "You can distract me all you want, but you still have to tell me what's happening."

Neil nodded. "Fair enough."

He sat down with her on the couch and filled her in on what they knew about Bankes. His family, his schooling, his employment. He hesitated when it came to Bankes's sister, Jenny, but told her anyway.

"Oh, God," she said, going pale. "Bankes killed her, didn't he?"

"No one knows that."

"But that's what they believe, isn't it?" Panic edged her voice. "He killed a helpless little gir—"

"Don't go there, Beth. Not until we know." He waited until it looked like she could hear him again, then picked up a napkin from the table and sketched out what they'd learned about his homestead: the lay of Bankes land bordering the Susquehanna River, the position of the house, the adjacent hunting range. "Chevy spent his teenage years in foster care, but he inherited his mother's land when he turned twenty-one. He sold it the same day, for a song, to the man who owns this hunting range here. Mo Hammond. Philly agents are trying to track Hammond down now to talk to him. Of all the people in that town, Hammond might've known Bankes best. His family and the Bankes family went way back." Neil gave Beth's hand a squeeze. "We'll find him, sweetheart. I promise."

She nodded, and he thought she actually believed him. But there was also an unvoiced question in her eyes: *Before he kills again, or after?*

He put down the pen and napkin. "Did you talk to Abby today?"

"Cheryl said they did a lemonade stand this morning—made six dollars and eighteen cents. Mostly donations, I think." She stopped, sucked in her lips.

"And Standlin came by?"

Beth scowled. "You know she did. Haven't you seen the latest additions to *my file*?"

"It's a file on the case, Beth, not on you. And yes, I read it. It said you chewed Standlin out, clammed up, and walked away."

"I'll do the same to you. Don't try."

He smiled at the fire in her eyes even as he worried about all that stalwart independence. Maybe he shouldn't push her or try to bully her into trusting him. Maybe he should just be patient and let her open up to him in her own time and manner. Or maybe he should just damn everything and peel off her clothes, show her how it would feel to—

"I know what you're thinking," she said smartly.

"Oh, I don't think so." He cleared his throat.

"Yes, I do. I know what you all think. You think I never dealt with what Bankes did. You think I avoided it by moving far away and having Abby and focusing on my career. Well, maybe you're right. But putting me in a room with some bulldozer shrink won't change it."

"She's just trying to profile Bankes."

"She knows all about Bankes. By now the FBI must have a file on him three inches thick. The only thing they *don't* know about him is where he currently is. It's me Standlin is analyzing. It's like she thinks I'm gonna snap, go off like a post office employee."

"You've been hoarding guns, doing a lot of training, and keeping some pretty heavy secrets, Beth." He stopped. He could have pressed the point but decided not to. He didn't want to talk about Standlin. He didn't want to talk about Bankes. He didn't really even want to talk about Abby. He looked down at his hands, thinking about the one thing he really *did* want to talk about.

"Evan Foster thinks I want to take you to bed." He paused. "I do."

Her breath stopped and she stiffened.

"Easy, honey, I didn't mean right this minute. I just thought I'd put the idea in your head, get you thinking about it."

"I have been thinking about it."

"Okay, then." He forced himself to stand up, get some distance. "So, you think about it some more, then. Let me know what you decide."

Neil swallowed. She'd spoken so quietly he wasn't sure he'd heard right, but when her cheeks burned pink, he knew he had. His body responded with a swiftness that shocked him. A woman's hand, a woman's mouth, a woman's body—they could all do that to him, had done it perhaps too many times and with too many women. But a woman's words? He hadn't known that was possible.

Chapter 26

She was dreaming again; Neil could hear it, and the sounds tightened in his chest like a fist. Whimpers, screams that didn't quite make it out of her throat.

Bankes was in there with her. Doing what? Tormenting Anne Chaney? Striking Beth with the butt of his gun? Something worse?

He groaned and laid a forearm over his eyes, sank deeper into his pillow. Leave it alone. It was part of the healing, he knew that. Hell, he'd dreamed about Mackenzie for years—still did sometimes. She'd be eleven now. Taking piano lessons, ballet. Playing soccer, maybe, starting to look at boys.

He got up, peeked in the door of Beth's room. She was asleep but sobbing softly. Hurting. He went to the bed.

When he touched her she jerked so hard he jumped back. She cowered into a fetal position, her sleep-drugged body not able to get away, the dreams not letting her out. The truth climbed on top of him, and he wanted to kill someone. The next ten someones he ran into.

Bankes.

Neil left the room and called the agent stationed outside. "Stay with her," he said. "There's something I gotta do."

"It's two o'clock in the morning."

"I'll be back by three."

On Beth's street, he called Lexi Carter and woke her up.

"Jesus, Sheridan," she said, a yawn in her voice. "Do you know what time it is? What are you doing?"

"Call off the dogs. I need to come by. I'm on Ashford Drive now."

She did, then came back on the line, still sounding groggy. "What the hell do you want?"

"Let me in. I'm coming up the front porch."

At first glance she reminded him of Beth, wearing a longish polo shirt with her dark hair disheveled. Which, of course, was the idea. "You shouldn't be here," she complained. "What if Bankes is watching?"

"Then he'll see me leave again in two minutes."

He climbed the stairs, not bothering with the lights until he got into Abby's room. He went to her dresser and found a comb, a couple of hairbrushes, a whole lot of ribbons and bows and barrettes. He pulled out an elastic doodad that had two big plastic beads on it and held it up to the light. A tiny mass of ripped-out hairs was tangled around the elastic.

"Reggie says hi, by the way," Carter said from the doorway. "He was surprised when I told him you were back at Quantico. Said he wants a rematch in the ring."

Neil forced a smile. "Sure."

213

"You okay?" she asked.

He pocketed the elastic band. "I'm fine. Sorry to wake you. This is all I needed."

Twenty minutes later, Neil waited at the entrance of an FBI lab. A short, bulky man in a cardigan walked up. "Christ, you got old," the man said, extending his hand.

"I need a favor, Max."

He laughed. "I kinda figured that, what with the sneaking around in the middle of the night and all."

Neil handed over the beaded rubber band. "DNA. And don't report the findings to anyone but me, okay? Oh, and—"

"I know, I know: Rush it, right?"

"If you can."

"Sure," Max said, slipping the band into a plastic bag. "I mean, it's only my career, ya know. Just a couple dozen years of work and my pension, my wife's future and kids' colle—"

"Max . . ."

He grinned, jowls jiggling like a bulldog's. "Love to see you big macho types squirm."

Neil was on his fifth cup of coffee the next morning when an agent called from the hallway. Neil opened the door.

"Dolls?" he asked, pointing at the boxes the agent carried.

The man handed them over. "Evan Foster wasn't very happy about having them taken from the premises. Copeland had to wake up a judge and get a warrant. He told me to tell you it better be worth his while."

"We'll find out," Neil said and closed the door just as

214

Beth walked in. She'd dabbed makeup on the dark circles under her eyes, but she still looked beat. And beautiful.

"Are those Mrs. Chadburne's dolls?" she asked, frowning. "What are you doing with them?"

Neil set both boxes on the table and opened the first. Gentle, now. All he needed was Margaret Chadburne or Evan Foster to sue him for destroying tens of thousands of dollars' worth of dolls. "Something you said about the last one got me thinking," Neil said, peeling off the packaging. He got through the bubble wrap and peanuts and found several sheets of tissue paper mummifying the doll. He let the tissue drop from his hands until the wide, dark eyes came into view. "This was the first one, right?"

"Right. You picked her up in my basement, remember?"

"You said she was worth more than six months of my salary. Why is that?"

A little crease dug into her forehead. "She's early, she's in good condition, and she blinks. Well, at least she's supposed to. The mechanism is broken, but it's rare to exist at all in such an early Benoit."

Neil's pulse began to race. Stay cool, stay cool.

He placed the doll on top of the padding inside her box and opened the second one. Blood moving fast now. "Was there anything unusual about this second one?"

"Unusual? No, not for something nearly a hundred and fifty years old. The bisque had some damage—hairline fractures on the legs."

Neil swallowed. "Show me."

Beth took the doll, her slender, practiced fingers

removing the clothes. A pair of lace-edged bloomers was the last thing to go.

"Ah, Jesus." Neil paced away from the table, rubbing the back of his neck. He could swear something had skittered across it. "Jesus," he said again.

"What?"

"And the third one had a blouse that didn't match, right?"

"Yes. Neil—"

"I need to make a phone call." He cupped both her shoulders. "Do you trust me?"

She shook her head. Not a negative, just confusion, as if the motion would jostle things into place. "Yes. But wh—"

"Do me a favor and package the dolls back up. I want to take them to the lab."

"You're scaring me, Neil."

"I know." He was scaring himself. "Where is Mrs. Chadburne staying? I need to talk to her."

"I don't know. All I have is her Boise number, but it could be a cell. I didn't know she was here until you told me. Neil, what's going on?"

"I think Chevy Bankes knows Mrs. Chadburne. He may be using her dolls to get to you."

She stared. "I don't understand."

"I don't, either, yet."

"Oh, God, Neil. If Bankes knows her—"

He put a finger over her lips. "You're doing it again, Beth, jumping to conclusions. If they do know each other, it's because Bankes needs her. He's not going to hurt her."

At least—Neil thought, but didn't say it aloud—not yet.

Chevy shifted, unable to get comfortable. Damned oak. Even with a quilted packing pad folded beneath him and Beth's sweater under his head, it might as well have been petrified redwood for as hard as it felt.

He closed his eyes, though they longed for light, and strained to listen for the impostor in Beth's house. He could hear her easily when she was in the family room or kitchen, not so much when she went up to the bedrooms. Right now, he was sure she was all the way upstairs. The water had turned on a couple of minutes ago. Taking a shower, probably.

Chevy could use one of those. Maybe he'd join her. Wouldn't that be a twist? From *someone's been sleeping in my cupboards* to standing outside the shower stall, wielding a knife while the *Psycho* music swells ... *reewk, reewk, reewk*.

He smiled at that, then drew in a long sigh. Not yet. He had to wait for Waterford's doll and then catch the impostor asleep. She was a trained FBI agent, on her guard, here for the sole purpose of luring in Chevy. Hell, she probably showered with a 10 mm.

But it would be safe to give a little taunt. Just in case they thought he'd vanished. They knew his name now, knew his identity. He didn't need to rely on strangers' phones anymore. What would it matter to use his own?

He reached to the bottom corner of the cupboard, felt the Coke bottle he kept near, and reached a little farther. Got the phone.

Not much, just a little taunt. Something to let them know he was still alive and well. And just a scream away.

Neil left the dolls with a technician in the lab, getting digital photos of each. In five minutes, he had color eight-by-ten glossies in his briefcase. He went down two more floors to the command center, where Copeland, Standlin, and Brohaugh were looking at a laptop.

"What happened?" Neil asked. Copeland looked wired.

"Another phone call just came into Denison's house."

"No," Neil said. "Christ."

"It was too short to trace."

"Let me hear it."

Brohaugh pushed some keys. Bankes's voice came through the speakers.

"Be-heth. Where are you?" Teasing, singsongy. He went right on, not waiting for her to pick up, and something prickled Neil's spine. "You think I won't get you. Don't you know the police can't protect you? Not the FBI, either. I'm too good. And I'm close. I can almost reach out and touch you anytime I want. I can *hear* your voice in my ears ..."

Dial tone. Neil's pulse was going like a racehorse.

"That call came from a cell phone purchased by Bankes in Seattle a month ago," Brohaugh said before Neil could get his thoughts together enough to ask. "It's the first call that's ever been placed from it. And," he said, glancing at Copeland first, "it bounced off the same towers that serve Denison's neighborhood."

Neil's gut knotted.

"Arlington PD is canvassing all the neighborhoods in that cell tower range now," Copeland said. "We could get lucky and find someone who saw him."

218

So Bankes was right there, within blocks of Beth's house, at least for the moment it took to place the call. He could've driven by, called, and rolled right out again.

"Sheridan," Copeland said, "the net's so tight around Denison's house, there's no way he could get in there."

Neil noticed that Copeland was looking at him hard, trying to encourage him—like he expected Neil to blow. They all did.

Cool, now; stay sane. He couldn't fly off the handle if Copeland was going to keep him in the loop. He had to stay focused: the dolls.

"I'm supposed to tell you what I learn from Beth, right?" Neil asked. He pulled three pairs of photos from his briefcase. Three pairs of eyes followed. "This is Lila Beckenridge, who was murdered in Seattle," he said, using a magnet to stick the first photo on the whiteboard. "Her eyelids were cut off." He stuck a picture of the first doll just beneath the picture of Beckenridge. "This is the first in a set of antique dolls Beth has been appraising. She received it from Boise, where the owner lives, via overnight-air last Friday. This doll was in perfect condition, except her eyes are supposed to close when she's lying down. They don't."

Copeland frowned and crossed his arms.

Neil put up the next photo. "Marsha Lane, Indianapolis." Her legs had tiny, bloodless lacerations snaking through grayish flesh, like spider's webs. Everyone on the task force had seen the photos; still, Neil could feel them wince when he put up the picture. "And this," Neil said, pulling out the photo of the doll with cracked legs, "is the second doll Beth received." He paused, letting everyone look.

"Holy Mother of God," Copeland whispered.

"Now," Neil said, producing one more pair of pictures, "our local soccer mom, murdered in her van and wearing a blouse her husband didn't recognize." He put up the picture of the third doll just beneath. "The blouse on this doll isn't part of the original clothing. Compared to the rest of the outfit, it's new."

Silence gripped the room, and finally Brohaugh said, "Shit."

"Does Beth know?" Standlin asked.

"A little, not all of it."

"What about the two missing women?" Copeland asked.

"The widow who owns the dolls, Margaret Chadburne, has been claiming all along that two of the dolls she sent have been lost in the mail. Beth's been waiting for them to arrive for the past week. And," he added, "Mrs. Chadburne is here. She flew in yesterday."

A sound whispered past Standlin's lips. "He's going to kill her," she said. "The minute he realizes we know he's using her, he's going to kill her."

"Or she's in on it with him," Brohaugh said. "Maybe he's paying her to deliver the dolls."

Copeland stared at the photos. "We're gonna find her body in a Dumpster, aren't we?"

"Is Denison expecting any more dolls?" Standlin asked.

"Yes, but she doesn't know how many."

"We need to figure out what dolls Chadburne has," Standlin said. "If we know what dolls Bankes has access to, then maybe we can predict what he plans to do next. Figure out his pattern."

"We'll have to find Chadburne first," Neil said. "We have a number, but it's a Boise-based cell. She isn't answering."

"I'll check hotels," Brohaugh said, "car rentals."

"And the post office. Find those missing packages," Copeland said. "Maybe the dolls inside will lead us to the missing women."

A phone rang. Everyone looked at their belts, and it was Copeland's.

A minute later, he hung up and rubbed a hand over his scalp. "That was the field office in Philly. A county sheriff just reported a missing gun owner in Samson, Pennsylvania. It's Amos Hammond—the man who bought Chevy Bankes's property."

Neil stared. They all did, as if their collective brain systems had crashed and needed a moment to reboot. No one was saying anything when Rick slipped in.

"What's going on?" he asked, taken aback.

Neil grabbed Rick's arm and headed for the door. "Road trip."

Chapter 27

Samson, Pennsylvania, wasn't much more than a wide spot in the road. The main drag had two traffic lights three blocks apart, a five-and-dime, a greasy spoon, and a run-down building with the word *Anti ues* painted on the roof. The only gas station in town, Grover's, had closed, but about a mile north, a second gas station—also named Grover's—sat at the intersection of two state routes. Grover had apparently moved out to where he might catch some traffic.

Mo Hammond's Shooting and Hunting Range was situated four more miles north. A sheriff's deputy was posted at the entrance when Neil rolled up, plotting how to talk his way through on Rick's badge. He was surprised when the deputy said, "Sheridan?"

"Yeah," Neil said, showing his driver's license.

"Special Agent Copeland called, said to clear you through."

Score one for Copeland.

They drove a hundred yards into the woods before

Hammond's store came into view. It was a one-story cedar building that had started as a rectangle and, due to ill-planned additions, wound up looking like something a four-year-old might construct out of blocks. A gray sedan with federal plates and two sheriff's department vehicles were parked in front, beside a rusty Honda Civic bearing a bumper sticker that read *Support the NRA: Shoot the Motherfucker.* A slimy pond sat to the west of the building, and to the east, several acres had been cleared for pistol lanes and a rifle range. A posse of buzzards soared a hundred feet above the rifle targets, as if hopeful something juicier than bull's-eyes would get hit now and then.

Neil took a deep breath, tension balling his right hand into a fist. Bankes had been here, he could feel it. No way did Mo Hammond disappear by coincidence.

He and Rick stepped into the store.

"No, no, noooo!" a woman wailed somewhere in the back. "You can't do this. Let me go!"

Neil started back, but a man said, "It's okay; the sheriff's back there." He came out from behind a gun case, a black man wearing glasses with lenses the size of gum sticks. "Christian Waite," he said, offering a hand, "from the Philly field office."

They made introductions while the yowls from the back room intensified. "What's going on?" Neil asked.

"Mo Hammond's wife. Sheriff Grimes is talking to her."

The back room smelled of body odor and gun oil, and a bulky man who must've been Grimes stood off to the side. Two deputies held a three-hundred-pound woman by the arms. She wore a sleeveless cotton dress, her armpits a couple of weeks out from their last shave, and her hair styled by about twelve hours of sleep. Her eyes homed in on Neil.

"Did you find him? Where is he? Can I see him now?" And, as an afterthought, "Who are you?"

"Mrs. Hammond," Rick began, and Neil stepped back. Let Rick handle her.

Neil introduced himself to the sheriff and whispered, "We need to get her outta here. This could be a crime scene."

"That's why the boys are holdin' on to her," Grimes said. "When she came in, she was runnin' around crazy."

"What does she think happened? Is she afraid Bankes might've got him?"

"Mo'd be lucky if that's what happened."

"What?"

"That woman came in here with a Remington thirty-aught-six, looking to blow Mo's brains out."

Chapter 28

Rick got the story from Hammond's wife: Mo was last seen the day before yesterday, wearing aftershave and a clean shirt, which, she said, only proved he was on his way to see "some bimbo whose thighs don' close." Neil listened for five minutes then sought out Sheriff Grimes.

"Some SAC from Quantico called," Grimes said, snorting. "Said don't touch anything 'cause he was sending in a team to dust the place. Like we wouldn't've known that, maybe."

Neil made an apologetic gesture; he understood the game. "Got a lot of crime scenes for this case. Some were messed up pretty good before the SAC could get anyone in. He's a little nervous."

"Yeah," Grimes said, and his gaze dropped to Neil's scar. Pondering which team Neil played on, no doubt: the bureaucrats or the real crime fighters.

"Drug dealer about nine years ago," Neil said, running a finger along the snarled flesh. "His aim was just bad enough to skim off my cheek instead of take off my head."

"Lucky," he said, and just like that, the dog sniffing ended. "Come on. I'll take you around. Out here, Mo has his regular inventory ..."

The store was well kept, the showcases all Windexed and the cabinets neat. There was a bathroom, a spartan office, and a storage room that housed extra guns and ammo, old boxes of office records, a retired Dell desktop computer, and an office chair with two broken casters. "What used to sit there?" Neil asked, noting a corner where dust marked off a rectangle of clean floor.

"Don't know. Could ask Andy, the guy who works here with Mo. I sent a deputy to bring him in; he might know which bimbo Mo was screwin'."

They went outside and walked the perimeter of the building, looking for footprints or tire tracks. "Lotta rain the last couple days," Grimes said.

"Looks like a few tracks from yesterday or today," Neil said, pointing to a muddy edge of the drive where several vehicles had overshot the gravel. "Can you get some casts made?"

Grimes's head bobbed up and down, one of the team now. "Sure thing."

"So," Neil said, his hands riding his hips as he scanned the rest of the land, "with Mo gone, no one's shot here lately?"

"Well, yeah. I think Andy had things open yesterday. He usually works Fridays."

Neil eyed the buzzards. "What happens to the prey?"

"Huh?"

"People come here to shoot animals, right? What happens to them?"

226

"Oh, Mo has a strict policy about that: You kill it, you take it. No carcasses left behind."

Neil was listening, but his mind hiked ahead. He started diagonally across the rifle-shooting lanes.

"What's up?" the sheriff asked.

"Buzzards."

"Buzzards?" Grimes looked up. "Oh, well, they're always around. There's always an asshole or two leaves a gut dump."

"By the targets?"

A little hesitation. "Well, no. I imagine Mo puts up new targets every couple weeks or so; that'd be a bad place for a gut dump."

That's what Neil was thinking.

Grimes stopped. "You don't think—" He didn't finish but picked up his pace to match Neil's.

They walked across the firing lanes toward red-and-white targets strung on the fronts of hay bales. Some were virtually untouched; others annihilated. The bales of hay themselves were pretty ragged, and thousands of small holes dotted the dirt wall that rose up behind.

Neil looked into the sky. The buzzards were right overhead, higher now, but not scattering. About ten yards closer, the stench hit him. He opened his mouth, careful not to breathe through his nose.

"Son of a bitch," Grimes said and pulled his jacket up over his nose. "Son of a bitch."

Neil came to the edge of the targets and put up a hand for Grimes to stay put; Mo was a friend of his. Neil stepped around the haystacks, cursed, and closed his eyes.

He went back to Grimes. "Found him," he said.

Forensics took over. Mo Hammond had been shot three times at close range with what looked like a .22, and numerous additional times—postmortem—by rifles. Any information beyond that would be hours coming to light as they took apart the crime scene an inch at a time. Neil hung around for the first hour, flexing his hand and bouncing on the balls of his feet, then phoned Copeland.

"Can you clear me to get into Bankes's house?"

Copeland sounded tired. "Sure, but we've already been through it. It looked like no one had been in there for years."

"Did your guys tear it apart?"

"No. We were careful to leave things alone, in case he came back. There's an on-site guy still there keeping an eye out."

"I'd like to take Rick and have a look."

"Go."

For some reason, Neil expected a dilapidated, ghost-like Victorian structure on a Hill or the equivalent of the Bates Hotel. Not at all. Bankes had grown up in a quaint, two-story home nestled in the woods, probably built just after the Depression. It had a deep front porch, gingerbreading under the eaves, and remnants of flower beds along the walkways. The property was overgrown, but in its day, Neil thought with surprise, it might have been lovely.

Inside, the same: neglected now, but once a home. Mo had sold off most furniture and any belongings that might have fetched a few dollars, but shadows of a family's life remained. There was a broken-legged metal table in the eat-in kitchen, and curtains still hung in the living room windows. Closets and drawers were empty but for one catchall kitchen drawer that contained a few remnants of life's detritus: a couple of ancient receipts, a spare button, a few pennies, three rusted paper clips. Neil unfolded the receipts. One was for gasoline at Grover's; he could barely make out the price in the faded ink—59.9 cents a gallon, in 1976. Ah, the good old days. The other was for a package of cloth diapers from the five-and-dime store.

He put the receipts back in the drawer and moved on. The only bathroom sat on the main floor, and three bedrooms—two dormers upstairs and one downstairs— were empty except for a couple of pieces of furniture that had been too dilapidated to sell. Half the basement seemed to have been finished off as another bedroom; the floor had carpet with indentations where a double bed once sat, and a broken nightstand crouched against the wall. Grandpa's room, Neil thought, but wasn't sure why.

Rick wandered in as Neil tugged open the nightstand drawer. An old Bible sat inside.

"Anything?" Rick asked.

"Not really," he said, picking up the Bible.

Rick let out a long breath. "If Bankes was gonna come here, he'd've done it already. When he killed Mo, maybe. He wouldn't come back now."

"Unless he's planning to bring Beth here."

Rick shook his head. "He's gotta know we're watching it."

Neil thumbed through the pages of the Bible. The first page was missing—torn out. He frowned, trying to think what was on the first page of a Bible ... an inscription or dedication, maybe? Owner's name?

His phone rang. "Sheridan," he said, setting down the Bible.

"Hey, this is Waite." The Philly agent with the skinny glasses. "Where are you?"

"Still in Samson, over at the house Bankes lived in. Hammond's property, I guess."

"Good. Sheriff Grimes just put me on a lead—a guy who knew Chevy way back when. Wanna come?"

"Say where."

"Where" was a nursing home ten miles from Samson, on the way south toward Arlington.

"It's Ray Goodwin, the guy who was sheriff when Bankes's little sister disappeared," Waite said, leading them down a wide, sterile hallway. In the last room on the right, Ray Goodwin sat in a wheelchair, his gnarled fingers tapping on the arms. A big man once upon a time, he'd lost his bulk to the inactivity of the chair. His jowls hung empty, his skin blue-veined.

"Don't underestimate him," whispered Waite, giving the old man a wink. "He'll chew you up and spit you out."

Neil smiled. Sure enough, the old sheriff's eyes were sharp as tacks. "Sheriff Goodwin," Neil said and shook his hand. He was surprised at the strength in it.

"You're FBI?" Goodwin asked but didn't wait for an answer. "You look like fucking FBI."

"Not anymore, sir," Neil said, "but I'm consulting with the task force. This is Lieutenant Rick Sacowicz, Arlington PD." Greetings done. "You were working when Chevy Bankes was a kid?"

"His little sister disappeared on October 14, 1991. I got the call at two-thirty. It was a Saturday. I was cleaning up my yard, getting ready for a reception next week for my daughter's wedding."

Neil glanced at Rick, then at Waite, who smiled: "Told ya."

"What can you tell us about Chevy?" Neil asked.

"I can tell you he was from a fucking freaky family."

"We just stopped by the house. Looked pretty normal to me."

"That's the point. Everything looked fine. A single mom taking care of her son and baby girl, and also her father for a while. Then the girl disappears one day while Chevy has her out in the woods. Mom whispers in my ear that she thinks Chevy hurt the baby; Chevy keeps saying his mother hated Jenny."

"They pointed the finger at each other?" Neil asked.

"Like I said, freaky."

"What about the grandfather?" Rick asked.

Goodwin shook his head. "He was a mean old bastard for as long as even I can remember. No surprise he scared Chevy's father off, and any other boy who looked at Peggy twice." He paused, his eyes searching for a memory. "You know, there was some talk Peggy had been pregnant once before, that Chevy was her second baby."

Neil frowned. That was something they hadn't heard yet.

"It was just a rumor. The Bankeses were pretty private, reclusive almost. Rumors went around."

A third Bankes child, older than Chevy. The wisp of a thought that had flown through Neil's mind while

231

looking at the family Bible floated back into range: *That's what was usually on the first page of family Bibles. Dates of births and deaths.*

Huh.

"At any rate," Goodwin continued, getting back to Rick's question, "the old man was sick a long time, cancer I guess, and died just after Jenny was born. Peggy went a little nuts after that—saying Jenny had inherited her problems from Grandpa. But she wasn't much for doctors. Truth be told, I think Chevy's the one who held things together after that, until his mom called it quits."

"Did anyone ever suspect that Peggy's death wasn't suicide?"

"You mean could a fourteen-year-old boy have gotten away with her murder? Chevy was smart enough. There was a school counselor who actually suggested it. But from the evidence" —he shook his head— "it looked like suicide."

"School counselor? Could we still talk to him, or her?" Rick asked.

"Her. Name was" —he scratched at a brow— "some flower, like Rose or Daisy. No, Iris. That's it. Iris Rhodes. But she turned missionary in the Philippines or some-where, traveled all over the place. I tried to reach her about fifteen years back when her cousin got killed in a car crash, and couldn't do it."

Dead end, Neil thought. But he'd check anyway.

"Wouldn't matter, though," Goodwin continued. "Chevy wouldn't've shared any deep confidences with her. He didn't like her."

"Why not?"

"Before Jenny disappeared, Iris called Children's Services to go check on her. She claimed the baby wasn't being cared for properly."

"Did Children's Services ever look?"

"Yup. Jenny was fine. I mean, she was born early, was a tiny little thing and maybe not coming along as fast as most babies. But there was nothing to make authorities take her away."

Neil glanced at Rick. There ought to be a record of that inquiry, anyway. "So it was a freaky family, but there was nothing that pointed to abuse or violence."

Goodwin took a deep breath, a measured one, like he was trying to do it without coughing. "Look, believe it or not, Chevy Bankes was an okay boy. Pretty good student, quiet kid. When Jenny disappeared, he was devastated."

"So what do you think happened to her?"

Goodwin sucked his teeth. "One of the thousands we'll never know about."

"Okay," Neil said, but frustration gnawed at him. "One more thing: Do you know of any reason Bankes would have it in for Mo Hammond after all these years?"

The sheriff's eyes narrowed for a split second. That was all it took. "Something happened to Mo?"

"Uh, we just found him shot to death up at his gun range."

"Oh, Lord." He rubbed his hand over his face then finally looked up. "Mo Hammond turns up dead, I think I'd look somewhere other than Chevy."

"Like where?"

"You ever met Mo's wife?"

Chapter 29

Copeland held off the task force meeting until Rick and Neil got back. When they walked in, the room smelled of stale burgers and french fries.

"It's about time you got here," Copeland said. "Did you get them?"

Neil handed over the Bankes family Bible and a receipt. After the interview with Goodwin, he'd called Copeland on a hunch and gone back for them.

Copeland opened the Bible. "Tell them," he said and nodded to the room. With the exception of Juan Suarez and Lexi Carter, everyone on the task force had assembled. But tonight, everyone was sitting. The fun had worn off.

Neil took a seat, too. "The sheriff who worked Jenny's disappearance said there was a rumor once that Chevy might have had an older sibling. The first page of the Bankeses' Bible is missing. I thought the lab should look at the next couple pages, that's all, see if there are indentations from something that might have been recorded on the missing page."

"And the receipt?" Copeland asked, studying it.

"It was in the kitchen drawer. It's for diapers. The ink's faded, so I can't read the date. But it was folded up with another receipt for gasoline from 1976. The date stuck in my mind because gas was only fifty-nine cents a gallon."

Harrison frowned. "Nineteen seventy-six is—"

"Two years before Chevy was born," Neil said. "So if the diapers receipt is from the same time . . ." He finished with a shrug.

"Any word on Chadburne?" Rick asked.

"Not yet," Copeland said. "She doesn't drive, so there's no license. We're checking Boise for a friend or family member who might have a picture of her. And I've got people trying to track down doll sales that might have been made to her husband. I don't hold out much hope on that score—the collection she's selling now could have been in his family attic for years. As for Hammond, we've cleared his wife—she was with a neighbor all day Wednesday, the day he died."

Neil nodded; no surprise there. As charming as Hammond's wife was, everyone knew Chevy had killed him. "What was missing from his store?"

"A shotgun and a twenty-two. And," Copeland added, "there was one drawer that had been broken into, the lock jimmied. We don't know what was in that."

"Silencers," Harrison speculated. "That's why no one heard a shot at the church."

Neil closed his eyes. Guns with silencers. That would change everything.

"Have a file," Copeland said, pushing a folder his direction and another toward Rick. "Harrison looked up the attorney who handled Peggy Bankes's will. It wasn't just the acreage and the house Chevy inherited. His mother added a codicil, leaving something to Chevy buried near the edge of the river. He got it on his twenty-first birthday."

"That's the day he killed Gloria," Neil said, straightening. "What was it?"

"We don't know," Copeland answered, "but a team will go look along the river in the morning. It's been a long time ..." He came forward in his chair, hands on the table. "What I wanna know is this: Why now? Bankes has been out of prison for over a year. What made him finally decide to hit Hammond? If he and Hammond had a history, say, Hammond knew something about Bankes from childhood—maybe about his sister's disappearance—then why wait all this time to knock off Hammond?"

"Because Hammond's disappearance isn't about something from Bankes's childhood," Neil said, studying the photos he'd stuck to the whiteboard hours ago. "It's now. Somehow, Hammond is the link between preparations Bankes has been making for all these months and the start of it all."

"The start of what all?" asked Brohaugh.

"The *chivy*," Standlin said, as if Neil's theory fit perfectly. Everyone looked at her. "It means chase or hunt. It's the root of his name. Reporters in Seattle used it as a hook for their stories and dubbed him 'The Hunter.' But it's the chase he likes, not the kill." She caught a nod from Copeland and stood up, sliding her own stack of papers across the table for distribution. "We've found two other unsolved cases in which women were stalked and then vanished. I spent the day talking to their families and the authorities who handled their cases."

Neil straightened. "What?"

"They happened *after* Gloria Michaels, but before Bankes moved to Seattle. You were gone, Sheridan. And Anthony Russell was dead. And the bodies were never found, so there was no reason to connect them to the Michaels murder."

"Son of a bitch."

"They actually looked at these cases during Bankes's trial in Seattle, but the gunshot to Chaney's back seemed inconsistent with the work of a serial sexual predator. The DA focused on an execution-style killing, by a man they called The Hunter."

Neil stared. Two more after Gloria Michaels? After he'd put her murder on Anthony Russell and left the country, left his family, left everything? "Who are the others?"

"Nina Ellstrom. She lived in New Jersey. Her parents say she was terrified before she disappeared, had been getting calls like Beth Denison's for weeks: 'Are you scared yet?' 'Let me hear your voice.'"

"In Jersey, though."

"She traveled twice a year to Philadelphia for a businesswomen's conference. Stayed at Bankes's hotel."

"Ah, God."

"And Paige Wheeler, a cellist. She played with a string quartet and went to West Chester to do some sort of residency for the music school."

"And stayed at the hotel Bankes worked at?" Rick asked.

Standlin nodded; Neil felt like he'd been sucker-punched.

"Ten," Brohaugh said. "If we count Mo Hammond and the two current missing women, plus these two who've been gone for years, that's ten people."

"Not including Bankes's little sister," Rick said, "and maybe his mother."

"His mother?" Copeland asked.

"The sheriff we just spoke to says it looked like suicide, but Chevy was smart enough to pull that off. The baby's gone so there's nothing to do there, but we could exhume the mother and grandfather. May be worth a look."

Copeland nodded and made himself a note as a woman with short curly hair cracked the door. She held out a piece of paper: "This just came from Agent Wright in Seattle, sir. He says an employee at the Orion Hotel remembers one of Bankes's trips was to San Francisco, July Fourth. One of the cross-checks shows an antiques exhibition in San Francisco the same weekend."

Neil's brows went up.

"We knew already he went out of town for long week-ends," Harrison said. "You think it was always San Francisco?"

Neil was startled. *I still attend certain antiques exhibitions, usually long weekends at holidays.* Beth had told him that the first time they met. "It was antiques shows."

Silence pulsed through the room for the five seconds it took for that to sink in. Then, quietly, Rick said, "Christ," and Copeland put his pencil down.

"That's where he met Chadburne," Copeland said.

Neil was aware of his heartbeat. He reached in his

pocket, dialed Beth, and tried to keep his voice calm. "Can you think back to last July, to an antiques exhibition in San Francisco?" He checked the page they just received. "It was held at the Hilton Northwest—"

"Sure," Beth said. "That show is sponsored by Randolph Earley. He always gives a bash on the Fourth of July."

"Did you go to it last summer?"

"No. I was going to, but Abby came down with strep. Hannah went instead."

Close enough. Bankes wouldn't have had any way of knowing Beth would cancel. "Are there others, big holiday sales or shows that someone would *know* you'd attend?"

"Pretty much every holiday there's something somewhere. Someone from Foster's always goes."

Neil nodded to Copeland, who shuffled to a specific page and handed it to Neil, pointing at the dates Bankes had taken days off work.

"Beth, where was the biggest collection of antiques dealers last Memorial Day?"

It took her only a second. "Chicago. Herbert Goshe does an Early American furniture sale every year at the convention center. On July Fourth there's the show in San Francisco, and at Labor Day," she continued without being asked, "there's a Victorian exhibition in Dallas."

"Did you attend those shows?"

"Yeah. With Hannah. Oh, no, not the Dallas one," she corrected herself. "That was just with Evan. Hannah didn't go."

"Was Margaret Chadburne there, too?"

"Actually," she said, her voice growing cautious, "that's where we first met. In Dallas."

And she'd gotten the first phone call from Bankes that Monday night, Labor Day. Neil tried to control the thundering in his chest. "Is there some sort of registration for those events, or are they open to the public and anyone can go?"

"They're open to the public, but there are always mailing lists, records of purchases, that sort of thing. Neil, what's going on?"

"Hang on, honey. Don't go to bed, and I'll fill you in when I get there. Everything's okay." He hung up, looked at Copeland. "She didn't go to San Francisco but was planning to until the last minute. On Memorial Day and Labor Day, when Bankes was taking long weekends, she was at sales in Chicago and Dallas."

"Okay," Copeland said, already looking at Brohaugh. "Check transportation from Seattle to those cities on those weekends. I know he didn't leave us any plane tickets, but look anyway—trains, buses, even records of carjackings or hitchhikers during those times. Get a list of everyone who attended those shows. And look for Margaret Chadburne's name."

Rick stood. "If he's been watching Beth for that long, what has he learned?"

"Everything," Standlin said. "What her interests are, who her friends are, where she's most vulnerable."

"Abby." Neil's heart formed icicles.

"No," Standlin said, "he can't know where she is. And even if he did, he wouldn't go for her yet; it would end it too soon. He'll save her daughter for last."

The ice thickened. Neil felt like a player running onto the field in the middle of a game, without knowing the game or the rules or the opponent. It was an opponent who couldn't be seen.

He had a thought. "Would Bankes want credit for what's happening?"

"A lot of serials like the idea that they're smarter than the authorities," Standlin said. "They like to watch themselves on TV."

"So what if we send O'Ryan with a press release, saying we've gotten a phone call from the stalker?"

"The Hunter," Standlin said, snapping her fingers. "Call him 'The Hunter.' It'll piss him off that we've pegged him wrong—again. He'll want us to know what he's really capable of."

"Fine," Neil said impatiently. "Let Bankes hear on the news that someone has claimed responsibility for one of the murders."

"He's too smart to fall for a newsbreak about it," Harrison said, coming to the edge of his seat. "Have to make it look like it leaked—something we never meant to let out."

"Then bypass O'Ryan," Rick suggested. "Leak it to some network reporter, and let the Bureau be seen running around trying to plug it up."

Copeland closed his eyes. Envisioning the public relations fallout, no doubt.

"I can do it," Neil said, "so it doesn't come from within the ranks."

Copeland rubbed his chin. Not happy. "Okay, you and Standlin put it together. But then get back to Denison. See if she can remember running into Bankes—or Chadburne—at any other exhibits. Can we make her home, work, and cell phones all ring to one of ours, give it to Denison so she can always answer herself?"

Brohaugh said, "Might take me an hour, depends who's at the phone company now."

"Wait," Neil protested. "I thought Agent Carter was picking up those calls. I don't want Beth having to talk to this bastard again."

Copeland gave him a look meant to dissolve grown men into their shoes. "Tough. And while you're at it, teach her how to keep him on the line long enough for a trace. Yes, Sheridan," he said, following Neil's thoughts, "it means you'll have to tell her about Agent Carter."

Neil cursed. He and Standlin had talked about it, decided it was better not to lay that on Beth, too. Standlin shrugged.

No choice, now.

Chapter 30

Chevy heard voices. Not in his mind, but from the TV. He could just barely make them out on the eleven o'clock report: *While the FBI earlier denounced reports that a man calling himself The Hunter had claimed responsibility for the murder of a woman in her van, a new report now confirms that information. Channel Three investigative reporter Carla Shorte has learned that FBI officials are now scrambling to ferret out a suspected leak ...*

What caller, what contact?

In addition, authorities are searching for a widow who may have been seen with Bankes ...

Chevy blocked that out. *A man calling himself The Hunter ...* He cursed. Someone had called the FBI and claimed to be The Hunter. The FBI was trying to cover it up, but someone else was taking credit. *Random murders.*

Panic rose up from the center of his being. "Don't listen to them, Jenny," he said. "They weren't random. And it wasn't some fucking hunter. It was your brother."

He tried to think, his leg cramping as the voice of one

243

reporter after another streamed overhead like ticker tape. *A caller claims responsibility ... Chevy Bankes, cold-blooded hunter from Seattle ... FBI is comparing the rash of recent murders to other cases going back ten years ... Random murders ...*

Mother started humming.

Shut up, bitch. You know who killed those women.

He needed his tapes. He could hardly think with Mother's voice layered among the news reporters.

Chevy closed his eyes. Remember the cries; the cries would make Mother stop. Remember their voices. Gloria Michaels, Nina Ellstrom, Paige Wheeler, even the beginning of Anne Chaney ... But try as he might, the only thing he could hear mingling with the TV anchors was Mother's singing, and the only woman he could see when he closed his eyes was Beth. Silent Beth. Cruel Beth.

A mistake to have let her survive that night, but he hadn't been thinking clearly. Chaney was gone, Jenny was hurt, and Denison—stubborn little bitch—wouldn't shut Mother up. She'd stood there in the clearing with Anne Chaney's blood steaming in the night a few yards away, and gritted her teeth, silent as a corpse. She hadn't made a sound, not when Chevy hit her, split her cheek, or spread her legs ... Not a sound.

But Jenny was there, needing his help. And Mother, getting louder. *Who'll dig his grave? I, said the Owl ...*

The TV clicked off, the reporter's drone ending. Chevy closed his eyes.

Anonymous caller taking credit for the murders ... An elderly woman ...

Well, it was time to set the record straight, that's all.

Bad news for Margaret Chadburne: She'd just outlived her usefulness.

Beth heard Neil in the hallway at eleven-thirty, just as the news ended. She skimmed her hands over the cards on the coffee table, pushing them into a pile. Solitaire is an awful game—something you play when you're lonely or worried or tired or bored. Or all of the above.

"Hey," he said, coming in. He crossed to the table and picked up her mug, sniffed. "Leaded?"

"I was just trying to stay up to hear what happened tonight at Quantico."

"No, you weren't. You were trying to make sure you won't sleep deep enough or long enough tonight to have nightmares." Her cheeks grew hot, and Neil said, "Jesus, Beth. I'm only in the next room. You don't think I hear you pacing around half the night, crying in your sleep the other half?"

He dropped his coat over a chair—finished. No coddling, no fussing about the nightmares. Just matter-of-fact acceptance that Beth had emotional baggage. It disarmed her, made her almost feel as if that baggage wouldn't matter to him.

"I saw the news," Beth said as he sat down beside her. "Is there really a caller?"

"No, we want Bankes to think there is. He called again today. From near your house."

"My God."

"Listen, Beth, there are some things you should know."

Neil was true to his word, catching her up on a litany of things the task force had been working on, each more

245

shocking than the last: Mo Hammond's murder; the discovery of two additional victims from years ago; the murdered women mimicking Chadburne's dolls. Beth's stomached soured as she remembered testing the first doll's eyelids and now thought about the poor woman in Seattle. And the idea that a woman's legs had been cut to match cracks in the second doll made her downright nauseous.

Neil had one more thing: Bankes had attended antiques shows.

"Dear God," she said.

"He started cozying up to Mrs. Chadburne months ago. And stalking you."

She hugged her arms to herself, trying to contain a shiver of revulsion.

Neil said, "Can you think of anything, *anything* Chadburne ever told you about her husband's doll collection? Something that would tell us what else Bankes might be planning to do with it?"

Beth shook her head, feeling her skin start to crawl. Margaret Chadburne had been an enigma. Always asking about Abby and Beth and interested in the antiques business, but not giving up much about herself.

"Okay," Neil said and shifted. "Listen, there's one more thing. We put an agent in your house posing as you."

Beth gasped. "You did *what*?"

"She's a pro, honey. Her name is Lexi Carter. We've got people all over your street watching out for her, watching for Bankes."

"And this Lexi Carter is supposed to just sit in my house and wait to be attacked?"

He cursed, which told Beth she'd pretty much hit the nail on the head, then handed her a phone. "All your numbers will ring to this now. Don't say anything that would lead him to believe you aren't there. And we need for you to keep him on the phone, set us up for a good trace."

"Ask him about his day, talk dirty to him?"

A nerve twitched in Neil's jaw. "Standlin says let him jerk you around. Act scared."

"Oh, I don't think that will be a problem," she said, pacing.

"Yes, it will, because you can't just get mad and hang up on him anymore. You've gotta play to him. Cry, whimper. Standlin thinks he'll stay on the phone if he hears you messed up."

"You mean don't make the same mistake I made seven years ago."

That stopped him. "Fuck," he said and closed the distance between them in two strides. He took her shoulders. "Screw Standlin, do you hear me? Don't say a word to Bankes unless it's 'Go to hell, you bastard.'"

Beth quailed at Neil's about-face: Never mind what Standlin or anyone else wanted if Beth decided she didn't want to do it. She gazed up at the tortured lines on his face and thought that, at this very moment, he might be willing to do anything to keep her from hurting. Even risk not being able to trace Bankes. "Why?" she asked quietly.

"Why what?"

"Why has it been so important for you to fight my monsters?" She paused. "Is it because of your wife?"

"Christ, Beth." He dropped his hands. "Where did that come from?"

So you think about it some more, then. Let me know what you decide. "I've been thinking, that's all. Like you told me to."

"About my wife?"

"About us. About the fact that we both have a history. You know mine—"

"All of it?"

Ouch. She lifted her chin. "A lot more than I know of yours."

Beth waited, watching him turn it all over in his mind, trying to decide how much he would say. For a second it seemed almost comical, the epitome of the male dilemma: How far to go to get a woman in bed? But when the moment dragged to an end and she realized Neil wasn't going to open up to her in spite of the honesty he'd demanded of her, she was amazed how deeply it hurt. "All right, then," she said and headed for the bedroom.

"I had a daughter," Neil said.

Beth stopped. "Oh, my God." She turned and stared, but Neil didn't seem to notice. His eyes were glued to a small piece of ribbon and plastic in his hands: a barrette with a lavender bow. It had seen better days.

"Her name was Mackenzie. She was almost three years old."

"Oh, no," she whispered. "What happened?"

He crossed to the sofa and sat down, fingering the barrette. "I was working a kidnapping case with the Bureau—a college girl named Gloria Michaels. She was Bankes's first murder."

Beth went still.

"I was gone on Gloria's case for a month. During that

time, an old boyfriend of Heather's showed up—Brad. He'd just split with his wife." He sighed. "Honest to God, there was nothing sexual going on; I know it wasn't like that. But Heather was a nurse and Brad was an addict. Crack, meth, heroine. Heather didn't tell me."

"She knew you'd worry, that's all."

"She knew I'd bust the son of a bitch." He drew a deep breath. "I nailed a man named Anthony Russell for Gloria's murder—the wrong man, but I didn't know that then. I was headed home when he escaped. Heather said she needed me but didn't tell me why. I told her to handle things herself until I finished with Russell."

"Did you find him?"

"Almost three weeks later, yeah. But by then, Brad was over the edge. DTs, blackouts, hallucinations. One night, Heather pulled some drugs from the shelves at the hospital and went to get him. She thought she could help him down. Kenzie was in her car seat, asleep." A muscle worked in his jaw. "Brad was scoring a deal when Heather drove up, and the dealer freaked. Started shooting."

Beth could barely breathe. Tears leaked from his eyes.

"Kenzie never woke up. A stray bullet went through her chest." For a long moment he said nothing more, just sat with his right hand flexing and fisting, flexing and fisting. Beth had seen him work that hand whenever something bothered him. She moved to her knees on the floor in front of him, taking the hand in hers.

Her touch seemed to pull him back. He splayed the hand. "I put it through a wall when they told me," he explained. "Got a couple of metal plates and screws holding it together now."

249

"Did you ever find him? The drug dealer?"

"Yes." The word was a chip of ice. He pointed to the scar on his face. "That's when this happened."

"Is he ... dead?"

"No. I wasn't alone. Geneviève Standlin, damn her, made sure a slew of federal agents went with me." The subtext was clear: If Neil *had* been alone, the outcome would have been different. "He has three more years on his sentence. Then he'll be out."

"Oh, Neil. What about Heather and—"

"Brad? Brad committed suicide. And Heather ... She never forgave me for not being there. A couple years later, she bailed."

"And you?"

"I bailed, too. Colombia. Bosnia. Iraq. Anywhere they needed a gun with no conscience to hinder it. Fuck the world. It worked okay until my brother almost died." He met her eyes. "And I met you."

"I didn't mean to drag you into my problems," she said honestly.

"Yeah, you were pretty clear about that. But everything about you set me off. Beautiful, secretive, independent. The mother of a little girl who might get dragged into someth—" He took a minute to regroup. "I couldn't walk away."

So that's why he wanted to slay her dragons. He was slaying his own.

Beth laid her cheek against his knee, and they sat in silence. One of his hands stroked her hair; the other idled with Mackenzie's barrette. There was nothing sexual in his touch, yet the moment was so intimate Beth could hardly remember what it was like not having him in her world. Like Abby. There wasn't a mother alive who could remember just ten minutes after giving birth what it was like to be childless. The new life came in and filled a place so huge it was impossible to imagine the world without it.

How empty the world must be when that life went away.

She climbed up onto the sofa and curled her knees beneath her, keeping her hand in his. "Tell me about Mackenzie," she said quietly.

And he did.

Chapter 31

At one-fifteen Neil heard Beth get out of bed. A light appeared under her door and then she ventured out, wearing a thigh-length T-shirt embroidered with Winnie-the-Pooh. He cursed. How the hell could a woman look sexy with a honeypot perched on her breast?

"Couldn't sleep, huh?"

She jumped when she heard his voice. He scooped up the cards from the coffee table.

"I guess not. What about you?"

He shuffled, the cards fluttering into a bridge. "Couldn't get relaxed."

"Are you still thinking about Mackenzie?"

"No," he said, amazed. "No, for the first time in nine years, Mackenzie feels like the gift she was, not a painful ghost. Thank you for that."

A smile curved her lips. "I'll want to hear more."

"You will. But not now. Now," he said, letting his gaze linger on the swell of Pooh, "I've got something else on my mind." He waited for the blush in her cheeks, then shuffled the cards and held out the deck. "Deal?"

She frowned. "You wanna play cards with me?"

"Hell, no," he said honestly, "but it's a start. Poker?"

"I don't know. I just came out to—"

"You came out because you can't sleep. Play some cards, Beth; be with me." The suggestion was so heavy with implications Neil's chest tightened. She knew what he was now: a man who'd failed his wife and daughter. If she still wanted him, there might be hope for his life after all.

And he understood her emotional baggage, too. Max had called. The results of Abby's hair-band were in: preliminary DNA.

Neil buried the white-hot rage that threatened and patted the sofa beside him. She sat while he dealt a hand.

"Stakes?" he asked.

"You have to pick a game before you name the stakes," she said.

"What did Suarez teach you?"

She was insulted. "What makes you think *he* taught *me*? I'm a crack poker player."

"Okay, Doc Holliday. You name the game; I call the stakes."

"Fine," she said. "Five-card draw."

"Fine," he said. "Kisses."

"What?"

"You know, where you pucker your lips and put them against—"

"I understand the activity. It's the betting I don't get."

Neil fanned out his cards and leaned back. "Simple. If I win the hand, I get to kiss you."

"What if I win the hand?"

"You get to kiss me."

She actually laughed. *That's right, Beth. Just kisses, nothing scary.* "How many cards do you need?"

She swallowed, the muscles convulsing in the hollow of her throat where her pulse thrummed. He'd put his first kiss there.

"Two," she said.

He slid a pair of cards to her and discarded three himself. Two eights and a king. Five-card draw was a good choice—each hand took only a minute or so. Plenty of winners and losers, plenty of kissing. "Whatcha got?" he asked.

"Not much." She spread out her cards. "A pair of fives."

He nipped back a smile. "Better than mine. You win."

She looked at him as he leaned toward her, tapping his cheek with a finger. She kissed him. He felt it like a brand.

He gave her the cards and she dealt the next hand. Silence.

"Two," he said and took the new cards.

She took only one, grinned.

"This one must be yours, too," Neil said, trying to sound frustrated. "I have a handful of crap."

She laid out three tens and looked at him, dubious. But she leaned forward and kissed his other cheek, lingering a little this time. He shifted.

He gathered the cards, dealt. Lost. If she ever asked to see what he was throwing out, he'd be sunk. This time, he'd discarded three hearts to screw up a perfectly good flush. He let her take the hand with three of a kind instead.

She gave him a suspicious look. "You're losing on purpose."

"Don't be a welcher." He touched his lips. "Here, this time."

Her eyes dropped to his lips, and she touched her mouth to his. Soft, tentative, almost experimental, and then she was shuffling cards again while his jeans shrank a size or two. Jeez, this was gonna be harder than he thought. No pun intended.

He lost two more hands, each of Beth's kisses becoming longer and more provocative than the one before, each one dragging him a little closer to insanity. He closed his eyes and wondered how much longer he could take it, and when four Jacks showed up in the next round, he was done. He fanned out the cards. "Beat this."

She hedged, frowning at her hand.

"What have you got, Ms. Card Sharp?"

Slowly, she showed her hand. Nothing but a pair of deuces.

"Huh," Neil said, smiling at her. "I win."

Chapter 32

The suite's phone rang at nine-thirty the next morning. Beth had been talking to Evan on her cell; Neil was in the second bedroom. She'd seen him come out earlier to get coffee, dressed in jeans and an AC/DC T-shirt. Apparently he was planning to stay in for the morning.

Play cards?

The thought shrank her skin into a spread of goose bumps. She could still taste his kisses, feel them, all the way to her toes. Skillful, openmouthed, with his tongue sweeping deep and his big hands cradling her face at first as if he were afraid he'd break her, then almost fiercely. She'd been shocked at the intensity of the desire that flooded her, an almost aching need to be touched and filled. It was a need she thought had vanished seven years ago.

And a need Neil stoked shamelessly. She wasn't naive enough to think he didn't know what he was doing— taking her to the edge of insanity then backing off. He wasn't going to take her to bed. He was going to make her take him.

Neil walked in from the bedroom just as the keypad on the front door beeped.

Suarez.

What was he doing here, if Neil was staying?

"The guard called and said you were on the way up," Neil said, making a beeline to the door. "What's going on?"

Suarez glanced at Neil, then Beth, then Neil again. Beth folded her arms. "I'm not leaving."

Neil gave Suarez an almost imperceptible nod. Damn him for getting to decide what she did or didn't hear.

"A car belonging to Foster's crashed this morning," Juan said. "One of the employees, Hannah Blake, was driving it. She'd just come from Beth's house."

"Oh, my God," Beth said.

"She's at St. John's. She's hanging on."

Neil was furious. "Why didn't anyone tell me?"

"I'm telling you. It only happened thirty minutes ago, man. Copeland says he'll call as soon as he knows something. Looks like tampering, though."

"No," Neil said. "How could Bankes tamper with a car at Foster's? Surveillance is *this* thick. No way he could get to a vehicle on the premises."

"Off the premises, then."

Neil's phone rang. "Sheridan," he answered.

Juan eased Beth away from Neil. "Your friend's in surgery, *querida*," he said. "Her husband is there and both sets of parents are on their way."

Beth reeled, half listening, feeling as if the floor were made of liquid. God, she thought. Not Hannah. "I'm going to the hospital," she said.

Neil hung up. "No, you're not. You stay here, with Suarez."

"Damn you, Neil—"

He took her shoulders. "Beth. We need you here. There's something you need to do."

"What?"

"You need to look at the next doll."

Beth's heart stopped. "What doll?"

"The one they just found stuffed under the hood of Hannah's car."

Neil swung by the accident site—nothing to do there—then he and Rick went to see Lexi Carter.

"Evan Foster called," she explained. "He told me Hannah was coming to pick up some pottery to show someone at the sale. She has a key card, so I stayed out of it."

"What time did she get here?"

"I heard the garage door go up at eight. She pulled her car up and left the garage door open. She was in here for about twenty minutes. They said her steering failed, but I watched her drive away from upstairs. Didn't see anything weird."

Rick said, "The ball joint was separated from the tie-rod. Easy to do: Take off the cotter pin and loosen a bolt. Do it just right and it holds a while, then starts shaking loose and one sharp turn makes it fly. It could've taken minutes, days, even weeks to come apart."

"We need to find out how much that car's been driven," Neil said, "where it's been, and check on anyone who went to Foster's and might've gotten to a car in the garages. Anyone who attended the preview or has a reason to have targeted Hannah."

"Copeland's got that going, Neil."

"Who's on surveillance at the antiques gallery?" Neil asked.

"Four of my guys and two Feds. Foster's is under guard, Abby's wrapped up tight in Covington, Beth's tucked in safe at the hotel. Not much else to do until Bankes decides it's time to act again. Call, or something."

"Something."

Neil went up the basement stairs into Beth's family room, took a deep breath. He remembered coming here the first time, when Abby was on the couch with Heinz and Beth was trying to be so strong, pretending she wasn't being terrorized by a psycho. The back of his neck prickled as Lexi Carter walked up beside him.

"Freaky, isn't it?" she asked.

"What is?"

"Knowing he's out there, planning another one, just biding his time."

She was right. Bankes was closer now, had called from nearby, and had struck someone Beth knew. Closer and closer, just like Standlin had said. Neil looked at Lexi: "You okay sitting here waiting for him?"

"Sure. Wish he'd hurry, though." Carter glanced around. "This place is a little too domestic for me. Starting to make me think about kids and dogs and white picket fences."

"Do I hear a biological clock ticking?"

"Screw you, Sheridan."

"Not me," Neil said, striding to the door. "Reggie would pound in my face."

*

Hotel, Chevy thought. Of course. That's where Beth was. They had her holed up in a hotel, probably with a dozen guard dogs surrounding her.

And one of those dogs was a lot closer than the others. Sheridan. Chevy could hardly believe it: Neil Sheridan. Chevy had seen him interviewed years ago after Gloria Michaels was found. Deep voice, heavy shoulders, long, screw-you strides. Chevy had laughed at him when Anthony Russell confessed to Gloria's murder, had laughed even harder when Russell escaped and Sheridan chased him down a second time.

He wasn't laughing now. Neil Sheridan was back and staying at a hotel with Beth. The rage was so intense he trembled with it, the thought of Beth receiving comfort nearly driving him mad. She should be suffering, not cuddling up with some cocky bastard like Sheridan.

A door opened a few feet away. Chevy listened, the air around him closing in. She was there, the impostor. He could feel her, almost see her, as she stood in the doorway looking around Beth's workshop. He held his breath, waiting, and she finally went back upstairs.

Chevy blew out a breath. He had to get out of here. Tonight, when things were quiet again, he'd have his chance. Catch the impostor sleeping, then move. Once out, he could get things going again, but he'd have to be careful. Margaret Chadburne couldn't help him anymore.

But there was someone else who could. Another old woman—a woman named Mabel Skinner who drove a Lexus and lived all alone on a quiet street called Lexington Avenue. He'd chosen her on his first night in

Arlington, before he holed up at Beth's. Mabel was just waiting to help him out.

She just didn't know it yet.

So hold on until tonight, get Lexi Carter, then get the hell out of here. Mabel would give him cover while he made his next move.

Covington ... Wonder how far that is?

Hannah Blake's "accident" was pivotal for the media: a twenty-four-hour feeding frenzy. By morning, the Bankes file had fattened by an inch. People who were unwilling to talk just days ago were suddenly coughing up every memory they had of the Bankes family, filling TV screens, clogging up the FBI tips line.

"Mom beat Chevy; Chevy beat Mom," Copeland said. "Chevy killed Jenny; Mom killed Jenny. Mom was pregnant *before* Chevy. There's even one faction out there talking about the grandfather now, that he was somehow responsible for Jenny's poor health."

Bullshit followed by bullshit followed by bullshit.

Neil had started out the door—he couldn't stand around for one more meeting—when a secretary intercepted him, pasty white. "Mr. Sheridan," she said, "there's a call for you. It's Chevy Bankes."

Silence, then everyone moved at once, whispering, gesturing, calling into headsets, manning a trace. Neil's heart kicked into high, and he lunged to the phone on the conference table. He stopped, looking at it as if it were a snake dripping poison from its fangs. "How long has he been on hold?"

"I came right in," the secretary said, breathless. "I told

261

him I wasn't sure you were here. It's been maybe twenty seconds, and it would've taken another thirty or forty getting through the phone tree up to this office."

"Don't answer yet," O'Ryan said. "String him out 'til they can get a trace."

"He's too smart for that," Harrison snapped. "Take it, man, take it. The bastard isn't gonna sit on hold."

A nerve jerked in Neil's jaw. He looked at Copeland, got a fractional nod.

He lifted the phone and pushed the Hold button. "This is Sheridan," he said.

A second of silence, then Bankes's amused, condescending voice came through: "She's a fake, you idiots. But it was fun anyway."

Chapter 33

"Sheridan?" Copeland's voice. "What did he say?"

She's a fake ... Neil's blood ran cold. "Get Carter on the phone."

"What?" asked Copeland.

"Carter!"

Copeland punched in Agent Carter's number on his digital phone. Neil waited, hardly able to breathe.

"No answer," Copeland said and tried again. "Christ."

"Carter's been hit," Neil said, heading for the door. "Go!"

Action exploded. A wild flurry of energy, chaotic yet organized. Orders spewed from Copeland, phones rang down the hall in response. Teams poured from the building, and Rick shouted into his phone as he ran through the parking lot behind Neil, ordering the nearest cops to Beth's house on Ashford Drive.

"No way he could get to Carter," Harrison called, keeping up. "Got a regular battalion on that street."

Neil stopped for half an instant, looking at all the

people trying to reach Carter: Copeland with a connection to Carter's cell phone, shaking his head as he listened to it ring and ring; Brohaugh talking into a headset to one of the surveillance units on Ashford Drive; Harrison contacting yet another unit.

Brohaugh looked at Neil. "He says nothing's happening, man." Ditto from two other street units, while O'Ryan barked into her phone about getting a tape recording of the call.

Neil hesitated, needing to think. The surveillance teams on Beth's house saw nothing. Maybe he was wrong about Carter, and Bankes was leading them into a trap. "He said she was a fake. Gotta be talking about Carter."

"Could be a setup," Copeland warned. He pressed a headset to his ear, pushing the microphone to his mouth. "Wait for the SWAT team to secure the house, then send in the entry unit." To the rest of them: "Let's go."

Copeland got in the house thirty seconds ahead of Neil. He passed Neil on his way out, his face a colorless hue that left no doubt about what he'd seen.

Neil's gut dropped. "Son of a bitch. Son of a *bitch*." He stood on the porch for a minute, then pulled himself together.

Lexi Carter was on the kitchen table.

"Holy hell," Rick said from a step behind. He rubbed his head, paced away a few steps, then came back. "Holy, holy hell."

Neil wasn't listening. The tang of blood and human waste clogged his nostrils. A stream of people moved in past the SWAT and entry teams and began their work as if in another dimension. Crime scene investigators collected like scavengers, securing the scene, flashbulbs popping in an uneven strobe. Except for the syncopated snap of cameras, Beth's house was deathly silent.

"Anyone call Carter's husband?" Neil asked, but no one answered, and he realized the words must not have cleared his throat. He tried again, louder.

"You can do it," someone answered. "Heard you know the guy, right?"

"Reggie," Neil said. "He's an English teacher. Boxes on the weekends."

Control broke. Neil let out a howl, spinning on his heel. Someone had set a black duffel on the floor in the foyer, and he kicked it out of his way, barely noticing the shocked blonde who rushed in to pick it up after it smashed into the wall. She grabbed it and carried it protectively out the door, and Neil ignored the astonished stares and barreled outside. He couldn't stand the smell of Beth's kitchen any longer, like the butcher's section of a grocery store.

He paced the yard as the task force members continued to arrive. Standlin pulled up last, just as the first county van pulled away, and Neil heard the driver of the van say, "Hope you didn't eat yet." Two minutes later, looking nauseous, Standlin joined the others.

"Forensics says Carter's been dead for several hours," Copeland said.

"So he got her in her sleep," Rick said.

"Had to," Harrison agreed. "That's the only way he could've overpowered her."

"But how'd he get in?" Rick asked. "Through all the surveillance. Disguise?"

"Surveillance units would've seen him, no matter how he was dressed," Harrison said. "There were no solicitors, no newspaper boys, no neighbors, not even a dog came near the house this morning."

"But Bankes got in anyway," Copeland said. "Somehow, the son of a bitch got—"

"He was already there," Neil said.

For a second everyone went still, then Neil's words hit home. Copeland actually trembled as he lifted his radio. "Secure the perimeter, secure the perimeter," he said in a frantic hush. "The perpetrator may still be on the premises."

"A CSI van just drove away," Neil said, feeling as if the truth had him by the throat. "Who was in it?"

Copeland lowered his transmitter and gaped at the empty spot on the driveway. "Son of a bitch."

"It hurts, it hurts …"

Jenny's voice, slicing through the white-hot rage in Chevy's chest. The pain was so intense he thought his soul was in flames. "I know," he said, clutching Jenny close with his free arm. Drive. Keep looking, keep going. Need to dump this van, need another car.

But Jenny was hurt. And Mother's voice, faint, beginning to sing in the back of his mind. The years threatened to melt away, back to that night in Seattle. Anne Chaney, dead without a scream. Beth Denison, refusing to perform her swan song. Jenny hurting, hurting …

"It hurts," she said.

"I know, doll," he answered, holding Jen. He wheeled the county van around a corner, too fast. God, don't do anything stupid. Slow now, careful. They weren't onto him yet, but he needed a new car. Then he could take care of Jenny.

He pulled through the lot of a strip mall, searching. Forced himself to breathe. The lot was almost full, all the way to the ends of the aisles.

"It hurts, it hurts."

He pulled between two SUVs, concealing the county logos on the sides of the van while he scanned the lot and murmured to Jenny. He needed to see how badly she was hurt, but there wasn't time. Seconds ticked away like hours, and finally a man—no, a teenager—came toward the end aisle, jiggling a set of keys. Chevy pulled out, tailing the guy as if hawking for a parking space, then stopped just short of the Ford Escort whose taillights chirped to life.

He turned off the ignition and jumped out, the duffel clutched in his free arm.

"Hey, buddy," he called, and the boy turned around. Surprised at what he saw, but more curious than afraid. "Could you help me, young man?"

"What—" *Umph.* Chevy poked him in the gut with his gun.

"Do what I say and you won't get hurt," Chevy said, careful to keep his gun hand low. He wrenched the keys from the boy's hand and tossed the county van keys a few feet out. "Give me your driver's license."

"My driv—"

"Do it." He gave the muzzle of the gun a punch.

The boy reached into his hip pocket and stripped his license from a wallet, his bony fingers shaking, dropping

267

a couple of membership cards on the pavement.

"We're trading cars," Chevy explained. He pointed at the keys on the ground. "Take those keys and get in that van. Turn right at the light. Drive for five minutes. If you make a phone call or slow down before then, I'll come to your house and kill your mother right in front of you." He held up the license, proof that he could find the boy later. "Do you understand?"

A convulsive little jerk sufficed as a nod.

"Right at the light. Five minutes."

The teenager bent to grab the van keys from the pavement and humped to the van. Wide-eyed, he climbed into the driver's seat while Chevy held his gun low between the cars but not wavering. When the van lurched past, Chevy folded into the Escort and pulled out in the opposite direction.

"It's okay, Jenny," he said, bracing her on the passenger seat with his right hand. In the rearview mirror he could see the boy stop at the light. A minute later, the van turned north and Chevy turned south from a different exit, moving back toward Beth's house. He went three blocks, then pulled around a corner to stop.

"Jenny," he said. "I'm here. I'll help you."

"You can't. No one will believe you. Mother has them fooled."

His eyes blurred with tears as he yanked open the duffel labeled Crime Scene Unit and took out his own gym bag from inside. Crying. Jenny was crying, and Chevy could barely get his hands to work the zipper. He had to get it open; he had to get to her. Like the day he turned twenty-one and found her again.

Go get her, Chevy ... Happy birthday.

The words of his mother's codicil rose like flames in his mind, cutting through the fog of tears and voices and memories. The land, the house, the sale to Mo Hammond. Get rid of it all; never look back. Just take care of Jenny.

He unzipped the gym bag and spread the top wide, his heart feeling like pulp. He looked inside. The sight wrenched a sob from his throat, and he sat rocking in the driver's seat as the memories jumped him. *Don't hurt the baby, Mother ... It's not her fault. It's Grandpa's. Grandpa gave her bad blood. She's crying, can't you hear? Stop singing so you can hear her ...*

Who caught his blood? I, said the Fish, with my little dish ...

Chevy shoved his fists against his ears.

"Help me, Chevy."

He uncovered his head. He glanced at the traffic, all moving normally, then looked down at Jenny. Neil Sheridan's handiwork glared back at him. She was hurt.

The rage swelled. A change of plans was necessary.

He pulled down the visor and looked in the mirror. Mascara trailed down his cheeks, the charcoal black eyeliner smudged. His wig sat askew and he tilted it, then saw a pair of women walking down the block toward the Escort. Shit, he had to move. If someone saw him like this, a mess, with Jenny ... Beth's house was only blocks away.

Keep your head; don't get careless. The FBI would be everywhere now, after the way he'd served up Agent Carter. Like a buffet, faceup on Beth's kitchen table, spread-eagled, her head dangling over the Formica edge and her own blood crusted in her hair. He hadn't been able to take his time and enjoy her screams too much—

269

didn't want to risk the surveillance team hearing her—so he'd gagged her, tied her down, and played with her a little, then measured out the line. Put a bullet in the spot using the silencer.

Then he called Sheridan and waited until the commotion broke out at Beth's house. People streamed in, credentials carefully checked on anyone who entered but not for those who exited. Within ten minutes of the phone call, a dozen people were in the house and more pulling to the curb, including the media. It was perfect until Sheridan blew in, threw a childish fit of temper, and kicked Chevy's duffel from his path. Panic had gripped Chevy. He'd lunged for the bag, but it hit the wall with a sickening *crrackk*.

Jenny began to cry. Mother sang. A single, mindless kick, and Mother had started singing again. Louder than ever.

She was still singing now, her voice building inside the Ford. Louder, higher, and closer in his head, like sirens wailing—

Chevy straightened, looking in the rearview mirror.

Sirens, not Mother. These were real, blowing through the intersection a block behind him like black-and-white bees. Gray sedans—Fed cars—came two seconds later.

They'd figured it out. Saw him leave the premises, maybe, or noted the missing van.

Chevy took a deep breath and turned the ignition. Within minutes, the teenage boy would be spouting his story, and the search for this Escort would be on. He needed to move onto his next hideout: Mabel Skinner's house.

Slow now, careful, obey the rules of traffic. Mabel didn't live too far away.

Jenny quieted. Mother went silent. The Doppler effect dragged the sirens away, northbound, where Chevy imagined the teenager peeing his pants about now, sitting in the van with a bunch of the nation's finest crouched around the vehicle pointing guns at his head, yelling through a bullhorn.

Stupid shits.

Chevy drove to Lexington Avenue, wishing he could have stayed to see the look on Sheridan's face when they searched Beth's basement. A block from Mabel's house, he stopped and fixed his makeup—didn't want to scare her—then pulled into her driveway and walked up to the front porch.

She opened the door, a diminutive woman with skeletal limbs, and he gave her his *Glass Menagerie* smile at the same instant he showed her the gun. He shoved her inside, the .22 pressing into her chest. A stairway in the front hallway led to a basement and he hustled her down—unnecessary, probably, with the silencer and all, but then again, there was no reason to take chances. Might as well keep things quiet.

So he got her to the basement, next to the freezer, and *fwp*.

Chapter 34

"Holy Christ."

Neil stepped forward. The technicians had been at work in Beth's house for four hours. Neil had known in his gut what he would see in Beth's basement, but it still hit him like a sledgehammer. He motioned to Rick and Billings, and they peered into the cabinets.

"Son of a bitch," Rick said.

"How long?" Neil asked one of the lab guys, who poked around in the cabinet. The shelves had been sawed out, the back walls cut to allow access to the crawl space beneath the house.

"I dunno," said the techie. "Three days, maybe four."

Neil's hands balled into fists. "He was here all along, the bastard. We put Carter in here three days ago, and Bankes was already here, holed up in this cabinet where no one even bothered to look."

"Hey," a cop snarled. He was the one who'd kept an eye on Beth that first night when Neil came by to pack her clothes. "We looked. Our guys swept the house before the Feds set up the watch. Someone checks the cabinet, and he's behind it in the crawl space. They check the crawl space, and he holes back up in the cabinet. No way they could've found him like that, and you fancy-ass Feds wouldn't've done any better, so get off our backs."

Neil glanced at Rick, whose face was ashen. The cop was right. No one did anything wrong. Bankes was just smart. And patient. And now he'd simply walked out the front door and driven away in a county van. He'd probably sat a block away in that Ford Escort watching the cops chase down a teenage boy.

So close.

Neil looked back at the cabinets, situated right next to the stairwell that led up to the family room. The hairs on his arms stood up. Bankes would have been here when Hannah drove up, might have walked around inside the house when Carter was sleeping. *A little freaky, isn't it?* she'd said. And even Neil had thought he felt close.

"Ick," someone muttered, pulling out a plastic two-liter bottle filled with a yellowish fluid. "Guess it had to be a man hiding in there. Never knew a woman who could piss into a Coke bottle."

"Got a piece of a candy wrapper, Reese's Cup," said a technician, holding it up with a pair of tweezers. "We'll get some prints, anyway."

Not that they needed any. They knew exactly who he was.

"Uh-oh." It was Harrison, and Neil followed the direction of his eyes. A gray Ford inched along the street, rolling through each checkpoint with the driver's hand hanging out the window showing his shield. Beth was in the passenger seat.

"What the hell—" Neil asked.

"I arranged it," Copeland said. "She was hearing things on the news, seeing pictures of her house. I thought she might be able to help."

Neil was furious. "You arranged for her to come see a woman tortured and staked out on her kitchen table?"

"I waited until Carter's body was gone, and you can keep Denison out of the kitchen. But this is her home. If Bankes left something behind, we need her to find it."

The ground actually swayed when Beth got out of the car. Neil had a grip on her elbow before it stood still again. "You okay?"

"I'm fine." It was a lie, of course, and he knew it as well as she did.

"Things are pretty well cleaned up," he told her, his voice a growl, "but stay in the workshop."

"She was killed in the kitchen?"

"Stay in the workshop, Beth. That's where Bankes was. Help us look around. Maybe you'll notice something we don't know to notice."

Beth could feel Bankes the second she walked into the garage. That was ridiculous, and she knew it, but knowing he'd been here, waiting like a cockroach in the woodwork ... She walked around, looking, studying, careful not to touch anything. A couple of crime lab technicians still went about their jobs with quiet attention to detail as Beth walked over to the cabinet where Bankes had been. Sawdust on the floor.

She peered inside the cabinet, tried to imagine an average-size man inside. Possible, if not comfortable, and the crawl space behind it acted almost like another room under the porch. In the center of the cabinet floor, something caught her eye: a little steel pin, half an inch long, the diameter of an embroidery needle. She reached for it.

"Wait," said a woman behind her. Beth looked up and saw the gloves and flashlight, the tweezers in her hands. "I'll get it."

"Sorry," Beth said, stepping back.

The woman knelt down and picked up the pin with the tweezers, dropping it into a small plastic bag that had already been labeled.

"Do you know what it is?" Neil asked.

Beth frowned, shaking her head. She couldn't seem to clear the haze. "It could have come from anything. It might've been in there for years, for all I know."

"Okay," he said, taking her arm again. "Come on. I'm getting you out of here."

"I need to go upstairs."

"No, Beth, you don't."

"She's ... I mean, Agent Carter. Her body—"

"Gone. But there's still no reason for you to go in there."

"It's my home, Neil, my world," she said, the backs of her eyes prickling. "I need to see what that bastard has done to my world."

Beth had bought this house for its kitchen. Not that she was any great cook or anything, because for a while it was all she could do to make macaroni and cheese from a box

275

or nuke a hot dog. But she'd always loved this kitchen. It was right in the middle of the house, where a family kitchen ought to be. Sunny and bright, with pale-lemon walls, hand-painted accents on the woodwork, and mosaic tile she'd designed for the backsplash. It was the place every day started and wound to a close with Abby, the site of watercoloring and homework and games of Go Fish. The place life happened.

And now death.

Her knees locked. Breathe. There was no body, no blood, no weapon. The room had been put back together with careful precision, everything in its place amid a deathly stillness and the sickening miasma of lab chemicals. All four chairs were pushed neatly under the table, even the center-piece had been replaced. As if the crime lab people had been preparing for company, she thought ridiculously.

Except that was the problem. Beth's kitchen never looked like company was coming. The centerpiece was always pushed to one end, so Abby had room to paint or mold Play-Doh. And one chair was kept in the far corner, so Abby could drag it to the counter when there was something to stir, or when she wanted to help with meas-urements. And the rugs, one of which was perennially crinkled in the corner where Heinz dug it up and napped, were missing completely, on their way, she presumed, to the FBI crime lab.

It's just a room. Just a—

"Enough." Neil pulled her out, piloting her back through the foyer and out the front door. "Are you satis-fied? Did standing there staring at it prove you're strong enough to take it?"

She looked up; there were two of him, and Standlin seemed to be hovering in multiples in the background. Beth closed her eyes, took three long breaths before she opened them again.

"Abby—"

"Is fine. I've been calling Covington every twenty minutes all day. Our people are all around her."

"Your people were all around Agent Carter, too."

Neil cursed, rubbing a hand over his face. "Bankes was in here first. He must've holed up while we were still chasing you to Covington Wednesday night, getting the story. He set himself up in your workshop and waited. The cops swept the house, but even if they checked cabinets you kept locked, he already had it so he could be out of sight."

"He thought it was me?"

"No. He knew Carter was a setup. She was part of his plan."

"Was Hannah part of the plan, too?"

"Probably, though he couldn't have known which employee would be driving when the joint gave out. He just knew it would be someone you worked with."

Beth stepped away, looking at nothing. Her skin felt as if little creatures were burrowing just beneath the surface. Bankes had penetrated her world. He'd been at antiques shows, at the gallery, and here in her home. Listening. Watching. Planning.

Killing.

A shout went up down the street. An officer in uniform ran up the hill. "Lieutenant. Lieutenant." He jogged toward Lieutenant Sacowicz.

Sacowicz started out to meet him. From another direction the FBI agent in charge—Copeland, Beth thought—also jogged over. A little bit of commotion had erupted where a UPS truck was trying to get through. The driver was shouting at a police officer.

Neil followed Sacowicz; Beth followed Neil. The uniformed cop was panting. "UPS guy down there has a package for this address. Said it needs a signature, came high-priority. Second-day air."

Everyone looked at Beth. "Were you expecting anything?"

"No. Not unless Mrs. Chadburne sent another doll. I haven't heard from her."

The officer shook his head. "It's not from Boise. It's from Charleston. The return address says *Wakeford* or *Winford* or—"

"Waterford?" Beth asked.

"That's it. Waterford."

Beth shook her head. "Kerry would've let me know if he was sending anything. I don't know what it is."

She saw Neil, Copeland, and Sacowicz all share a glance, then Agent Copeland said, "Let's find out."

They gathered on the driveway, noticed the media, and moved inside Beth's workshop. A woman wearing a County ID tag and rubber gloves set the box on one of Beth's counters. There were a few minutes of discussion and careful examination of the box itself, then, apparently satisfied that it wasn't a bomb, the woman received the go-ahead to slice through the packing tape with a knife. Bankes, Beth thought bitterly, would have approved of all the ceremony.

Everyone held their breaths as the box flaps were lifted. A folded piece of paper sat on top of packing paper, some Styrofoam peanuts falling out when the technician picked it up. She handed the paper to Agent Copeland.

"It's a sales receipt," he said, reading. "Six grand at a store called Days Gone By. For an 1873 Benoit, it says."

"That's Kerry's store," Beth said, "but I didn't order anything from there."

"No. Margaret Chadburne did. She gave this as the shipping address. It's dated two days ago, Saturday, April 18."

Beth reached for the receipt, but Copeland pulled it back, and the woman with the gloves held open a Ziploc bag. He dropped it in. Went back to the box and gently pulled out the doll.

Beth watched, her mind a jumble. Maybe Mrs. Chadburne had bought a doll from Kerry and wanted it to be included with the others. An 1873 Benoit wasn't in the same league as the ones her husband had left her, but perhaps she didn't know that. Maybe—

The woman with the gloves held up the doll. Beth stared. She couldn't believe it.

"Honey." Neil was at her side. "What's the matter?"

She swallowed, feeling as if a breeze could topple her. *Oh, Mrs. Chadburne. What have you done?* "I know that doll. It's not a Benoit. It's a fake."

Chapter 35

"Where are you taking me?" Beth asked. It was evening now, and Neil drove in the opposite direction of the hotel.

"A safe house. Someone might've seen you at your house today."

"Someone."

The nerve in his cheek jumped again. "The press, maybe."

Right.

Her phone rang, and adrenaline shot through Beth. Not fear, not terror. Fury. After the way Bankes had left Lexi Carter, after what he'd done to Hannah and what he might have done to Margaret Chadburne, Beth was looking forward to telling the bastard off. She dug her phone from her purse as Neil swerved off the road.

"Give it to me," he said. "I'll take it."

"I can do it."

"Beth—" He stopped. "Remember what I told you."

Screw Standlin ... Don't say a word to Bankes unless it's "Go to hell, you bastard." Yes, she remembered. But she would play whatever game she had to now. She'd do anything.

She looked at the caller's number and blew out a breath. Not Bankes, after all. It was Cheryl. She pressed Talk and listened.

Sorrow. Disbelief.

"What? What?" Neil was whispering, but she ignored him.

The news sank like a disease into her bones. She told Cheryl not to worry about it and disconnected.

"What is it?" Neil was in her face.

"It was nothing. It wasn't important." She closed her eyes. "Heinz disappeared."

"Oh, Christ." He rubbed a big hand over his face.

"It's not Bankes, Neil; it's happened before. Cheryl said Chase left the gate open."

"The toddler?"

She nodded. "Heinz will come back. He always does." She swallowed, ignoring the lump of tears in her throat. Stupid to cry over a lost dog when Hannah lay in the hospital and Mrs. Chadburne was missing and an agent had been shot to death on Beth's kitchen table.

"Sweetheart—"

"I said it's nothing. I mean, come on, he's just a dog."

"Yeah, right," Neil said, his voice rough. He pulled back into traffic. "Just a dog."

The safe house was in a set of condominiums, with guards who looked different from Suarez and his crew: no more blending in like bellhops or hotel maids or janitors. These guys were armed, heavily and visibly, like soldiers.

Upstairs, she took the first bedroom she saw. Neil followed, his mood dark, and slid her suitcase onto a dresser. He strode the perimeter of the rooms and emerged after a quick inspection of the bathroom. "Jacuzzi," he said, coming back out. "Ought to keep you warm, anyway."

She didn't bother telling him she wasn't cold anymore. Feeling had gone away.

"I'll put your equipment downstairs," he said. "I brought the doll from Hannah's car, and as soon as the lab finishes with the one that came today, I'll send for it."

"Thank you."

"I'm gonna go look around, show my face to the guards. You should get some sleep."

"I'm not tired."

He made a haggard sound. "Suit yourself."

"Are you ever going to tell me why you're angry at me?"

He'd been on his way out, but now he turned and dropped his hand from the doorknob. "I'm not angry at you," he said. "I'm angry at your ... independence. Your spine."

"I don't know what you mean."

"I mean you shouldn't have gone into your kitchen, Beth. I shouldn't have let you. You don't have to keep proving to everyone that you're unbreakable."

"Unbreakable," she echoed, thinking the word—applied to her—sounded ridiculous. Her whole life was defined by the fear of breaking. "You know," she said, "until Abby was three, we lived in an apartment above the carriage house at Foster's. Abby loved it. There's a maze of narrow old passageways connecting what used to be slave quarters to one another, and connecting the former stables and barn. We used to play in every nook and cranny."

Neil crossed his arms, waiting.

"It was safe there—there were always people around, people I knew. But eventually, I had to grow up."

"Beth—"

"No. I want you to understand. That house on Ashford Drive—the flower boxes and the curtains and the furniture—I sank everything into it to make it a place where I could live and play, even work. A protected little bubble where I could stay holed up and never have to remember there had once been a man named Chevy Bankes, who was still alive when Anne Chaney was dead and I was too much of a coward to tell anyone about it." She took a step toward him. "I needed to see it, Neil. My house, my world. I needed to see if the bubble I built had really popped."

"Damn it, Beth, you don't need a bubble as long as I'm here. I can take care of you."

She swallowed. That was probably true, and never, not even seven years ago, had she longed to lean on someone as much as she longed to lean on Neil now. Yet somehow, she knew leaning would never be enough for a man like him. He would want to carry her.

How tempting it was. To just let him take over and belong to him. In every way.

Her eyes dropped to his lips, and for a minute all she could think about were his kisses. He was velvet and steel, his body powerful and hard and demanding, yet his touch so tender that a single embrace from him had laid waste to seven years of brutal memories.

Making love with him would be the same, she thought. And she wanted to know for sure.

She leaned toward him, and a fraction was all it took. Neil pulled her in, and years of terror evaporated into thin air. His lips became her universe, and she kissed him with everything she had, taking and giving at the same time, knowing, at last, she was ready. With Neil, who felt so different from anything she remembered and so much better than anything she'd dared to dream, she knew she could do it.

She was ready.

Chapter 36

Neil drank her in, his hands closing around her upper arms. He strained to pull away even as he continued to kiss her, as if some invisible force were trying to pull them apart while some other force made it impossible for him to release her lips. Finally, he pushed her to arm's length. "No," he said, and Beth staggered back.

"Wh-what?" she asked. She looked flabbergasted.

He clenched both hands, the emptiness there an almost physical pain. But he couldn't do this. Not when there was still such secrecy between them.

He closed his eyes, then stepped back. "I'll see you in the morning."

"You said to let you know what I decided." Her voice quavered. "I'm ready now."

"Ready." Neil gazed at her, not knowing whether anger or pain was driving him. "Ready to see if you can stand it?"

"What? No."

"You go to your house to see if you're strong enough

to survive seeing your world destroyed. You go to bed with me to see if you can stand it after years of being alone. I don't want to be your litmus test for endurance, Beth."

"I decided, Neil."

"You decided to have sex with me." He looked her straight in the eyes. "That's not all I was asking you to think about."

His meaning took shape visibly, one small thought at a time. Her jaw unhinged. "You wanted me to decide whether I wanted to go to bed with you."

He held her eyes. "I wanted you to decide a lot more than that."

She turned, hugging her arms over her chest, then spun back to him. She was angry. "You're telling me that in all these years, you've always asked for a woman's heart before you took her to bed? Only slept with women who might be the new Mrs. Neil Sheridan or something?"

"I'm telling you that in all these years, I've only slept with women who never even made me *think* about a new Mrs. Sheridan, whose hearts I never gave a damn about." He paused. "*That's* the difference."

He turned to the door.

"Wait—"

Whatever she might have been planning to say died on her lips as Neil turned back, looking at her with such intensity he thought he might *will* the words out. Christ, he wanted this woman. He wanted to erase the horror of Chevy Bankes from her life forever and hold her so close she'd never be afraid again.

But she hadn't asked him to do that. She wasn't willing

286

yet to trust him with her wounds. She'd just barely come around to trusting him with her body.

He looked at her a moment longer, hands fisting with the hope that she wouldn't touch him again. This nobility shit was for the birds; if she offered herself again, he wasn't sure his honor would hold.

She stepped close, her voice a broken filament of sound. "I don't know what you want from me."

Neil couldn't help but stroke her jaw. "Then think about it some more. And for both our sakes, Beth, I hope you figure it out."

Chevy Bankes sat in the parking lot of a strip mall, in a new Lexus that smelled like a beehive. He'd thrown out Mabel's dashboard air freshener as soon as he got in the car, but the interior still smelled like fucking Honeycomb Harvest. He'd probably attract bears when he got out.

The morning had started with a small fire in Mabel's bathtub—he'd decided the next doll needed a little help—then he dropped by a thrift store for a few clothes. He spent the next three hours tooling the metro area to find a place that would do. Finally, he hit upon a shopping center in Alexandria that had just the right components: a Wal-Mart, a Hair Cuttery, a frame-and-photo shop, a private hardware store, a florist, and at the end, a Block-buster.

The Wal-Mart and the florist were all Chevy needed.

And, of course, the kid. A skateboarder about twelve or thirteen years old, wearing a knit hat, a double layer of shirts, and corduroy pants so tight Chevy wondered how he bent his legs. He'd converted the back of a Tex-Mex place into his own personal skate park and had been practicing a single move for twenty minutes: up the four steps to the restaurant's back door, drop the board and push off hard, then land at the bottom, still moving. Over and over again.

Chevy looked at his watch, wondering if using the kid to do his dirty work was just being paranoid. Artist renderings of his Margaret Chadburne persona were showing up everywhere, but chances were good that no one in the general public had yet seen any pictures of the woman Chevy had been at Beth's house, assuming there were any. Still, just in case, he'd retired both of them.

He rolled the Lexus up near the skate area, parked, got out. An older gentleman this time, though the air freshener that clung to his suit made it hard to stay in character. Still, he looked pretty good. Respectable clothes, respectable car, a slight hesitation to his steps—not quite a limp but a certain stiffness that spoke of bad joints. Enough that it was believable a jaunt into the Wal-Mart would be an ordeal for him.

He walked toward the skateboarder, digging in his wallet as he moved, as if he had a purpose. The kid noticed him about twenty feet out, picked up his board, and shot a furtive glance at the NO SKATEBOARDING sign in the corner of the lot. He held his board in front of him like a shield, deciding to stand his ground. This was an old dude: Fuck him.

"Excuse me," Chevy said, and in the last second, he decided on an English accent. An evening at the improv. "I'm sorry, chap."

The boy grunted.

"Say." Chevy stopped a couple of strides short of a normal conversation distance. No need to spook him. "I was wondering if you could help me out a bit."

"Huh?"

"I'll pay you for it." He pulled out some bills, seeming to have to search for the fifty he'd put on top. "I'm headed to my granddaughter's birthday party and I'm afraid I'm a bit late. I need a spry pair of legs to run into the stores for me, you know? Would you do that?"

"Huh?"

"She wants one of those Barbie dolls, but the male one, what is it, uh—"

"Ken?"

"Ah, yes, Ken, but dressed up like a soldier ..." A little perplexed. "They have those here in the States, don't they?"

"Like G.I. Joes?"

Chevy pointed a finger at him. "*That's* what her mum called it." He looked at the boy, then across the parking lot to the Wal-Mart, which, to a older man with arthritis, was an awfully long hike. "Would you get me one of those? And a box of red roses from that florist, with nice long stems. It will take you five minutes, and me with my legs, 'twould take half an hour."

"Uh ..." The *'twould* had thrown him.

"And just have them print a card for the flowers. It should say, 'See you in Covington, Love, Neil,' all right? That's N-E-I-L, not the other way, with an A."

"Uh ..."

"How's fifty dollars as your fee? Will that be enough for you, then?"

289

The kid's eyes lit up. "Uh ..."

"All right, then. Sixty it is." He put the bills in the boy's hand, then added money for the gifts. "'See you in Covington, Love, Neil.' Got that?"

Figure it out.

Beth took the Hannah doll from the guard who brought it to the door, grimacing at the idea that she called it that: *the Hannah doll*. Still, that's what it was—a representation of Hannah. The dolls were all representations of Bankes's murders. The one delivered with Lexi Carter had been easy: It was the same doll Kerry Waterford had tried to sell Mrs. Chadburne in Dallas. A reproduction rather than a real Benoit. A fake, like Carter herself.

But this one, Beth thought, unwrapping the doll, didn't make sense yet. Except for the obvious—oil stains from having been in a car engine—there seemed to be nothing unusual about it.

Figure it out. Neil's words, but not referring to the dolls. She tried to put him out of her mind and went back to all the dolls, one by one, taking them out and laying each on the table. It made a freakish kind of sense—the eyelids, the cracks on the legs, the mismatched blouse. Like an instruction manual for murder. Beth wanted to cry as she touched them now. Their beauty, rarity, and quality all tainted by what they were being used to represent. She'd never look at another fashion doll without a lurch in her belly.

Figure it out.

She picked up the latest. No hairline fractures, no chips, no obvious repairs. As far as Beth could confirm, the clothing was all original. She was perfect, in fact, even better than the first doll, because of the mechanics. Only the Benoits owned by Stefan Larousse were reputed to be both this early and in such good condition.

She sat down at her laptop and typed in "LAROUSSE." Spent a few minutes reading their history, even though she knew the Larousse dolls hadn't been out of their home during Mr. Chadburne's lifetime, and certainly not for sale. The Larousse family had held the collection privately for a hundred years, showing only select dolls at their pleasure to only a select audience. Still ...

One description matched the doll Beth was looking at. Dated 1867, with a bisque head and breastplate, real hair, and the slight, openmouthed smile doll collectors coveted. But what set it apart was the joints: The elbows and wrists were made so they actually bent to hold a pose. Beth picked up the doll again, recalling that one wrist joint was a little loose—

The thought took her by surprise. Not even fully formed, it whipped through her brain and left a knot in her throat. *Loosen the cotter, take out the pin from the ball joint ...*

She bit her lip. She stripped the doll's clothes and began dismembering the limbs, digging into each fragile joint like a surgeon whose misstep could cost a life. As a general rule, each chip or crack or mar on a doll dropped the price at auction by about a thousand dollars. Evan would be mortified by what she was doing, but—

There, in the left wrist. A ball joint, and Beth suddenly felt as if the temperature had dropped twenty degrees. The steel pin was missing. In its place, a tiny scroll of paper had been inserted.

It couldn't be. Yet she knew. She *knew*.

Heart racing, she held on to the joint and groped for a pair of tweezers, then clamped them down on the end of the scroll. She tugged, lost the end, and squeezed it again, pulling until the scroll came free and the wrist joint dissolved in her hands.

Shaking, she unrolled the shred of paper. Her eyes blurred on tiny, hand-printed letters: *Go ahead, Beth. Scream.*

Chapter 37

"That's her."

Neil narrowed his eyes on the video screen. Copeland had pressed Pause when a specific person came into view. It was television footage shot at Beth's house after Lexi Carter was found, one of dozens of tapes. This one was shot by Channel 5, from far enough away that the video-tech nerds at the Bureau had spent all morning trying to clarify the face. The footage had caught a tall woman in jeans and a sweater, with dark blonde, shoulder-length hair, wearing gloves and a mask. Like what about a dozen other crime scene specialists had worn when Carter's body was found.

But no one recognized this woman. She wore no ID badge.

"Every technician, police officer, and FBI agent caught on television tape at Denison's house has been identified," Copeland said, "except her."

"Him," corrected Harrison.

"You're sure we have all the tape that was shot?" Neil asked. The place had been swarming with cameras.

O'Ryan nodded. "We offered inside information on the case—newsbreakers—to the film crew who came up with something we could use."

"Better than a subpoena," Rick said, and everyone knew he was right. Forcing legalities on newspeople rarely influenced them. Promising them a big story was like offering pure gold.

"Run it again," Neil said and watched it two more times.

He didn't recognize her. A bigger-than-average woman, walked a little like a jock. No one in the Crime Scene Unit recognized her. No one on the police force recognized her. No one in the Bureau recognized her.

Him. Women didn't pee into Coke bottles.

Bankes?

The tape cut to another shot from a different TV crew, but this one was distant, just a survey of Beth's front yard. Copeland poked his finger at the screen to point out the person in question. "Right there," he said, "loading the duffel into the front seat of that van."

"Son of a bitch," Neil said.

"What?"

"I did see her. In the house." He closed his eyes, trying to place her in his mind's eye. "I kicked that bag out of my way, and she picked it up."

"The crime scene guys came up one bag short at Denison's house," Harrison said. "The techie who lost it said it was empty."

"It wasn't empty when I kicked it. Something hard inside. I heard it crack. No more pictures of his face?"

"That's the only footage we have that caught her. Him. Whatever."

"The photo lab came up with this." Brohaugh pushed a couple of buttons, and the picture changed. "This is what Chevy Bankes would look like in that woman's disguise. Not a very pretty broad."

Neil stared. Blonde hair, female style, on Banke's face. It wasn't much better than one of those late-night TV show gags where they merge photos for laughs. But no doubt, it was the person who'd looked at him angrily and then grabbed the bag at Beth's house. "Got this picture on the news?" he asked.

O'Ryan nodded. "And the boy driving the Escort ID'd her." She winced. "Him."

Harrison: "He can't stay underground too long. The only reason he got a few days from us is that he was hiding in locked cabinets before we even got going. Now he'll need a place to live, a car to drive, something. Someone has to see him."

"Yeah, but the guy was a theater major," Rick said. "Probably knows stage makeup. He could have ten more disguises." He shrugged. "Guess he carries his own eyebrow pencil."

Copeland turned to Neil, who'd begun pacing back and forth. "How's Beth holding up?"

Neil blinked. "Scared shitless. Too stubborn to break."

"What's with the dog?"

O'Ryan perked up, looking for the story. "Dog? What happened?"

Neil slumped, still stewing over the pictures. "Beth got a call from Cheryl Stallings last night. Her dog disappeared."

"Aw, geesh," O'Ryan said. "What else could happen to that poor woman?"

"Bankes?" Harrison asked.

Neil shook his head. "That was my first thought, too, but Mrs. Stallings thinks her three-year-old left the gate open. Apparently it's happened before, and Heinz has always come back."

"So Denison's taking it okay?"

Neil closed his eyes. Beth had blown off the news about Heinz like it was nothing. Just sucked it all up and offered to have sex with him. "Mrs. Stallings is putting up signs around the neighborhood," he said. "Beth's convinced the dog will turn up."

"One paw at a time in the mail," O'Ryan said.

"Get us a photo of the dog." Copeland sighed. "Guess we oughta know what it looks like."

"APBs on mutts," Harrison said.

"Should we call in the canine unit?" O'Ryan quipped.

"So if you were trying to get close to Beth Denison, and you had money and knew makeup, how would you go about it?" Copeland posed that question to Standlin, who had just slipped in the door.

"You'd get into her profession, become someone she talked to, but not someone so close she'd know you well," Standlin answered. "And you'd probably run into her, visit with her some, then go home and jerk off thinking about how well you're fooling everyone."

"Jesus," Neil said. Then, a half-formed idea congealing in his brain, he straightened. "Wait a minute," he said. "Go back to that close-up of the woman at Beth's house."

The head shot came onto the screen and Neil narrowed

296

his eyes. "Did we ever get a good picture of Margaret Chadburne?"

A couple of brows furrowed, then Harrison said, "Ya think?"

Brohaugh's fingers started flying. "There's no driver's license; we already know that. But I was just looking for a picture. I didn't check Social Security or birth certificates."

Neil felt as if his head was about to explode. Too many ideas, some so tangled he could hardly pull them out one at a time. But this one ... Damn it, this one made sense.

"Nothing," Brohaugh said. "I'll check plane tickets from Boise ..."

Copeland stood. He was vibrating. "God almighty, that woman doesn't even exist."

"It was Bankes all along," Neil said. He tried to unclench his fingers but couldn't. "Bankes didn't *meet* Chadburne at those exhibitions. He created her there."

"Have the photo lab do a mock-up of an old woman using Bankes's face," Copeland said to Brohaugh.

"He won't use her disguise anymore," Brohaugh said, "not if he thinks we're onto it."

"How will he know?" O'Ryan asked. "I can keep it out of the news."

"No," Neil said. "He knows, by now. Hell, he's probably been laughing at us all along, waiting for it. All we had to do was start looking for Chadburne. Sooner or later we'd realize we were looking for someone who doesn't exist."

"Take the mock-up to Foster's, anyway," Copeland said. "Maybe someone saw her—Chadburne—go into the garages there and mess with the cars, something like that." He rubbed a hand over his head. "I'm too old for this."

"If we're right," Harrison said, "it explains a few things, but it doesn't help us find Bankes now. He's out there, and we won't hear from him again until the next body shows up."

"Yes, we will," Neil said and looked at Standlin. "Because he won't be able to stay away from Beth. Am I right?"

"He'll contact her," she agreed. "I don't know how, but mark my words: He'll find a way."

Chapter 38

Go ahead, Beth. Scream.

Beth's fingers sprang open, and the tiny curl of paper dropped to the table. She clutched herself, careful to not make a sound. Odd, she *did* want to scream, but she wouldn't give him the pleasure of it, even unknowingly.

How had Bankes managed to get a note inside one of Mrs. Chadburne's dolls? And a *Larousse*? Was it possible this *was* a Larousse doll?

Chadburne ... Beth scrolled through everything she knew of the woman. She was one of Kerry's suckers who had latched on to Beth after Beth went toe-to-toe with Kerry and saved Mrs. Chadburne a small fortune on a fake Benoit—the same one that had turned up yesterday with Lexi Carter. Chadburne was widowed, lived in Idaho, had a small doll collection that looked more and more priceless, and had called Beth from time to time for advice.

"Beth."

She whirled. Suarez. "Didn't you hear the door?" he asked.

"Oh, no. Uhm, sorry."

He came in carrying a long box with embossed flowers on the lid, a red satin bow tied around it. "These just came for you. From guess who?" he asked, managing a grin. Then he looked at the dismembered doll. "Still looking, eh?"

Beth handed him the tiny scroll. He opened it, read it, and paled. "*Madre de Dios*," he said and let it drop to the table. Keeping it clear of extra fingerprints, Beth realized, and she might have laughed at the idea if it weren't so tragic. "Where did this come from?" he asked.

"In the wrist joint." She showed him, and he cursed and put his arm around her. Beth almost didn't notice. She was in a trance, the insidiousness of Bankes making her heart stand still.

"I need to call it in," he said, and Beth stepped away. Her blood pulsed in her temples, and she ran her hand over the box Neil had sent. She wanted to be touched by his thoughtfulness, but all she could think about was Bankes. He was like a cancer, deep inside the bones, buried in her life and maybe in Margaret Chadburne's. Beth had never known he was there.

Blankly, she pulled the ribbon and looked inside in the box.

Now, she screamed.

At the command center, the phone in Neil's pocket rang. It was Suarez. Neil's heart gave a thump. "What's wrong?" Neil asked.

"Man," he said, "me and Beth think maybe—"

The phone fumbled and Beth came on. "Neil. Get

300

Abby! You have to get Abby out of there, all of them—"

"Beth, calm down. Tell me what hap—"

"He's going to burn Abby. Get her out of there, Neil, please!"

"I am, Beth. I'm doing it." To Rick, he waved a hand. "Call Covington. Make sure Abby's okay."

"No, no, that's not enough!" Beth had heard him. "You have to get them out of there. She'll burn! Neil, she'll *burn*. There's going to be a fire—"

Neil didn't know what to do. He was frozen, helpless, thirty miles from the safe house and farther than that from Covington. And Beth sounded like she was cracking up.

Rick was on another phone, contacting Covington surveillance, saying something about Abby and the Stallingses, then nodding, catching Neil's eye. "They're okay," he said. "They're at the Stallings house."

There's going to be a fire ...

Maybe Beth had a nightmare about a fire. It couldn't have been Bankes—if he'd called Beth and threatened a fire, they would have had the trace by now. There couldn't really be a fire.

"Beth, honey, we called Covington. Abby's okay."

"That's not enough. Get them *out*!"

He thought about it for one more heartbeat, then turned to Rick, who still had the phone to his ear. "Tell them to clear out of the house."

"What?"

"Evacuate. Call the fire department."

Rick didn't question it again; everyone else in the room stood silent, hardly breathing.

"We're doing it, Beth." He heard a sob, felt her hysteria

reach through the phone lines and grip him by the throat. A minute passed, then another and another and another, then finally Rick was listening to something again.

"They're out," he said. "Two adults, two kids. They're in the cruisers now."

"Beth," Neil said, "Abby's in a police cruiser. The Stallingses, too. They're all okay. There's no fire."

Beth collapsed into tears. Normal tears, though, not the delirium of a lunatic. They sounded like tears of relief.

Suarez came back: "She's okay, man. Upset, but she's okay now." Neil closed his eyes. "But Sheridan?" Suarez said. "I think you better come see this."

Standlin went with him, worried about Beth's frame of mind; the rest of the task force kicked into high gear arranging for a safe house for the Stallings family, except for Rick, whose dad-gene kicked in. Neil heard him on the phone with Maggie, asking her to pull together some toys they could send to the safe house. Standlin had decided Abby should join Beth there. The condominiums where Beth was now being housed were as safe as anything, and just in case Covington's net had been contaminated, they all agreed it would be good for Beth to have Abby back. God willing, the dog would wander back soon, too.

When they got to the condo, Beth was pacing, her arms crossed. Suarez intercepted them.

"She's not nuts, Agent Standlin," he said shortly.

Standlin was insulted. "I never suggested she was—"

"No, I mean, there's a reason she wigged out. Wait'll you see."

Neil strode across the living room to Beth. She looked

302

fragile and small to him again, yet when he touched her that steely round of strength pulsed through.

"Abby?" she asked on a thread that barely sufficed as a voice.

"I just got off the phone with the Covington team. They're all in cars. It's taking a while, 'cause they sent decoys, will make some switches. But Abby's on her way here, and the Stallingses are being taken to another safe house. Your sister-in-law called her neighbor and asked her to put food out for Heinz, watch for him."

Beth actually smiled; it made Neil's heart melt a little more. "So, what's going on?"

She reached into a flower box Neil hadn't even noticed. She pulled out a doll. A child doll, an antique.

Scorched.

"Ah, jeez ..."

"A kid came by," said Suarez. "Some English dude paid him to deliver it. Your name was on the order."

Neil pulled Beth into his arms. Christ, she'd thought Abby was going to burn. "She's okay, Beth. There's no fire."

Beth returned his embrace then pulled back. "There's something else," she said. She showed him the dismembered Hannah doll and the scroll. Neil's gut clenched. *He'll contact her*, Standlin had said. *I don't know how, but mark my words ...*

"Listen, Neil," Beth was saying. "You know how I said these dolls reminded me of a set known as the Larousse dolls?"

He didn't, but he shrugged.

"I think this doll *is* one of the Larousses. I don't know

how Margaret Chadburne could have gotten her hands on it, but we need to check with someone in the Larousse family or their insurance records. I would swear this doll came from their collection. And maybe some of the others."

"Okay, honey, okay. That's good. We'll find out." At this moment, Neil didn't care. He was looking at the two new dolls, wondering about Bankes's pattern.

He tugged his digital phone from his pocket, still holding Beth in one arm. He fumbled with the numbers, calling Copeland.

"Hey, Sheridan, I was just calling you," Copeland said. "I—"

"Hold it. Beth got another doll. I'm sending it in with Suarez—"

"Fine," Copeland interrupted. "But you need to come back, too."

"Why?"

"Nine-one-one call just came in. Rick Sacowicz's house is in flames."

Chapter 39

Maggie and the kids weren't home—Neil received that blessed news as he sped back to Arlington. Maggie had done exactly what Rick asked and gathered up some toys for Abby, then piled all four kids in the car to deliver the toys to Quantico so they could be taken to the safe house. By the time Neil arrived on the scene, the Sacowicz home was a hollowed-out shell of charred wood and bricks, firefighters poking at pockets of still-smoldering ash, an arson investigator searching out the source of the flames. Gasoline trail, it looked like, all around the porches, front and back. Simple, effective. Any teenager could do it, and as a police lieutenant, Rick had enough enemies that it wouldn't be hard to cough up a list of suspects.

But they didn't need a list of suspects.

Neil got out of the car. The kids had been taken inside a neighbor's house, and Maggie stood in the street clutching her midriff, staring at what remained of her home. Neil opened his arms to her, then stopped cold at the sheer horror that wrenched her features.

"He's not with you, is he?" she whispered.

Neil froze. He glanced at the house, back to Maggie, then at the driveway. Through the barricade of emergency vehicles, Rick's car was partially visible. Neil's throat closed. The sedan was dumped over the curb at a careless angle, trunk lagging into the street. The driver's-side door stood open.

"Oh, God, no ..."

"We weren't here," Maggie whispered through trembling lips. "We were out delivering the toys, but he must have thought—"

"No, man ..."

A shout went up from inside the rubble. Neil stared as three firefighters jogged inside to answer the call. Two of them came back a minute later. They fetched a stretcher—and a body bag.

Maggie sank to her knees.

Neil dropped down beside her, and she grabbed his lapels as if she were drowning. Her sobs were like a meat hook in Neil's chest, but that was nothing compared to the sight of Richie and Justin and Shawn filing off the neighbor's front porch, a woman behind them bobbing up and down with the baby. The boys inched up behind their mom, a gurney wheeling past, and Maggie let go of Neil and opened her arms to them.

He backed away, and a cop in uniform drifted up beside him. "Gotta kill the motherfucker, now," he said beneath his breath. "Gotta kill him."

Neil did what he could—which was fucking nothing—for Maggie and the kids, staying on the phone with Quantico. Confirmation of the day's breakthrough wasn't long in coming: Margaret Chadburne didn't exist.

It hadn't taken long to figure out once Chadburne's identity had been cracked. She was registered in attendance at all the exhibitions on those same weekends Bankes took days off from work. At the Dallas show, Chadburne had maligned Kerry Waterford and cultivated a budding relationship with Beth, who was only too willing to save a novice buyer like the poor widow from a shark like Waterford. On and off for the past year, Beth had spoken to Chadburne in person and on the phone, never knowing she was talking to Chevy Bankes. Even Neil had crossed paths with him, twice, in Beth's house.

With Rick.

Grief welled up in a tidal wave, and Neil almost went under. He held it back with rage so sharp he could taste it, hot and sour on the back of his tongue. *Gonna get you now, you bastard.*

At midnight, when Rick's kids were finally asleep and neighbors nursing Maggie, Neil drove back to the safe house. He dismissed the interior guard and went upstairs, not hesitating to push Beth's bedroom door open and look inside. Abby and Beth were there, curled together spoon-fashion. Neil's eyes blurred as he bent to kiss first Beth's temple, then Abby's.

Beth stirred.

"It's me, honey. I'm back." He'd tell her in the morning about the fire. He didn't think he could go through it right now.

"I'm glad you're here," she whispered. She pressed Abby a little closer. "Abby was dying to see you."

307

"Soon." He paused, then shook loose the words that were lodged in his throat. "I'm not leaving again. I'm staying with you now."

The realization made him sway on his feet. To hell with Beth's secrets. To hell with his ego. None of that mattered. Maggie had convinced him of that tonight, without speaking a word, just by clinging to his lapels and weeping for her loss. A person had to have something worth weeping over when lost.

Neil tucked the covers over both pairs of shoulders and forced himself back downstairs. He stood in the shower for fifteen minutes, the hot water mixing with tears, then emptied his briefcase onto the coffee table. Through the paper. Again. And again. The key to catching Rick's killer was in here, somewhere.

He looked up. Not because of a sound or even a movement. It was just ... a presence.

"Hey." He stood, looking at Beth. "You okay? Did you have a nightmare?"

"No, no. I just ... Well, I wanted to talk to you. I hope it isn't too late."

She wasn't talking about the clock, he realized, and ten kinds of tenderness flooded him. "It isn't too late," he said, his throat tight. "I'm still right here."

"Uhm ... I've been thinking, and I think I figured it out. I know what you want from me now."

Neil was almost afraid to move. "It doesn't matt—"

"You want the rest. You want it all."

Her voice had cracked, as if the words themselves were cutting her in two. Guilt clawed at Neil's chest. Jesus, he didn't need for her to do this now; he was sorry he'd ever demanded it. He didn't need for her to rip out her heart and expose every last shred to him. He'd take her heart just the way it was, all wrapped up in pride and independence. Even secrets.

"You don't have to tell me anything more."

"I do. It might help you understand what's driving Bankes. And ... it might help you decide how you feel about me."

"I already know how I feel about you," he said, but when he glanced at her hands, they were wringing the flesh from the bone. His heart crumbled. "Okay, sweetheart. Tell me what's tearing you up inside."

"I ... I promised Adam I would never tell. I swore to myself I would never tell—"

"That Abby is Bankes's biological daughter?"

She froze, dumbfounded. "Y-you knew?"

"I had the lab check hair from one of Abby's hair bands." Neil was careful to keep his voice low and calm, but the rage climbed on top of him. "Bankes raped you the night he killed Chaney. He got angry after Anne died, hit you with his gun, and he raped you."

There was no color in her face. It took a full minute for her to say anything at all. "How?"

He stepped closer. "Things didn't add up. The way you wouldn't talk about the moment *after* Bankes hit you with his gun. The way Adam convinced you not to go to the police, like there was something more to hide than an accidental shooting." He looked at her cheek, at the pale white scar that had needed stitches and instead had been treated with a Band-Aid and lies. "The way you flinched when ..."

"When what?"

"I came in your room when I heard you having a nightmare. I touched you and you just about came out of your skin." He could still feel the white-hot fury that had gripped him when he realized what Bankes had likely done to her, when he realized she was still afraid. Not just of Bankes, but of *him*. "And I knew you had to have a reason for not giving us Bankes's name the first time we talked. There was only one thing I could imagine so important that you would risk handling Bankes yourself rather than let it out: keeping Abby from ever knowing who her father is. Keeping Adam's family from ever knowing."

"They still can't know," she whispered. "If his parents knew Abby was ..."

"Was what?"

She shook her head as if trying to understand it herself. "Look, in the Denison world, it's about bloodlines, reputations. Unimpeachable character ... Those are the things that matter."

"Unimpeachable character?" Neil had to repeat her words to believe she'd really said them. "It's a flaw in Abby's character that she carries Bankes's blood? It was a flaw in *your* character that you were raped by a lunatic?"

Her puzzlement hit Neil like a two-ton wrecking ball. In one brutal second, he understood. He'd heard of it before: abused women taking the blame for their husbands' tempers, people stricken with serious illnesses feeling guilty about being sick, rape victims thinking the attack was their fault.

Jesus, he'd been one blind, stupid son of a bitch. "All

these years, that's what you've believed, isn't it?"

Tears collected along the line of her lashes, glowing like quicksilver. "Adam always said—I mean, I know it was an accident, but I did everything wrong."

"What did you do wrong?"

"If I hadn't called out when I first saw Bankes. If I hadn't just walked into the woods when he told me to. If I hadn't attacked Bankes, or if I'd done it sooner ..."

Neil stared, astounded that she could spin hindsight so casually. Everything she did was wrong; everything she didn't do was wrong. "Is that what Adam told you?"

"He was a lawyer; he knew how it would look."

"You didn't do anything wrong, Beth. Adam should have helped you deal with it, not make you bury it. Jesus, you should never have had to carry this around for seven years." He had the strange desire to pummel a man who was already dead. "The rape isn't something you caused, Beth; it doesn't define you. It doesn't define Abby, either."

The quicksilver ran down her cheeks. "Chevy Bankes is her father."

"He's her sperm donor. Abby doesn't have a father." He paused. "But she could."

Neil met the surprise in her eyes with a gaze steadier than even he expected. The image of Maggie's upended world wrenched through him, the almost desperate, clawing need to love and care for Beth and Abby rubbing raw against his grief. "I've told you before, there's more than one person in the world willing to help you. There's also more than one man in the world willing to love you and father Abby."

Her voice was a whisper. "I wasn't sure you'd still

want me. Adam never t-touched me again. And when I turned up pregnant ..."

She paused, but Neil was speechless.

"He wanted me to have an abortion. Oh, God, Neil," she said, nearly choking, "I almost did it. I went to the appointment and everything. But I couldn't go through with it. Then Adam filed for divorce."

That stupid, unfeeling son of a bitch. Neil tamped back the rage and closed the distance between them. "I'm not Adam," he said, as certain of his next words as he'd ever been of anything in his life. "And I want you. I want you in my bed and in my brain and in my blood, and I want to go to sleep every night holding you and wake up every morning making love to you."

A smile quivered on her lips. "It's been so long ... I'm not sure I know how to be with a man anymore. I don't think it's like riding a bike."

He cupped her cheeks with his hands, his muscles straining with the need to show her how he felt. "I won't let you fall, Beth. Trust me."

"I do. It's just that ... sometimes the memories come when I don't expect them, and I know there are men who don't want to stop after a certain point—"

"I'll stop at any point if you ask me to." He said it with such conviction he almost believed it himself. "I'll probably have to put a bullet in my head to relieve the pressure, but I'll stop if you want me to."

She freed a tiny smile and rose up on tiptoe, her lips brushing his. "I don't think I'll want you to," she said.

Chapter 40

She didn't. Neil scooped her up and carried her into the spare bedroom, kissing her firmly enough to make her stop trembling, gently enough that she knew he would honor her body with tenderness. He took his time with her body, bringing every nerve to life, and Beth returned each stroke and kiss and caress with rising passion. When the moment came that he nudged between her thighs, he kissed her, murmuring, "It's me, Beth. Only me."

Not Bankes. Not Adam or Evan. Only Neil.

The sense of freedom was astounding, the response of her body a source of continuous, intoxicating amazement. The legacy that had stripped her of her sexuality and her womanhood dissipated, slowly and steadily. In its place a new legacy exploded, spiraling through every nerve and chasing tendrils of raw sensation through her limbs as Neil laid claim to her, inside and out, body and soul.

Only Neil.

Afterward, she lay in a daze, sated, her breast glowing as his tongue curled lazy circles around her nipple. "I should get upstairs," she whispered, touching his hair.

"Mmm." He released her nipple and dragged his lips lower, scorching a path down her ribs, her belly.

"I don't want Abby to find us together," she croaked.

"Then you'd better keep your voice down."

His hands slid beneath her hips, and his mouth made that first shocking contact. She made a sound in her throat, and he lifted his head. "Is this when you tell me to stop?"

"God, no," Beth muttered.

She woke in the wee hours of the morning, her body oddly boneless. Beside her, the bed was empty.

She sat up, blinking. Neil stood at the window, staring out into the darkness. She padded over to him. "Neil?" she whispered, and he turned to her. The look on his face backed her up a step. "Oh, God, what is it?"

He told her about the fire, and Beth's heart seized with pain. She hurt for the lieutenant who had taken care of Abby. She hurt for the four children who had lost their father, and the warmhearted redhead who had loved him.

And her heart nearly broke for the man who had been Rick's friend and colleague and brother-in-law. A man who followed Beth back to the bed and wept silent tears onto her lap as the rain began to fall, the world weeping with them.

Wednesday dawned wet, spitting a miserable mist that reminded Chevy of Seattle. He left Mabel's house early, wearing his Englishman's jacket and driving Mabel's car. He swung through a McDonald's for breakfast and headed out to work on the next step of his plan: the dog.

He felt sorry for the mutt, actually. Heinz. The letters were etched into a bone-shaped tag on his collar that Chevy had removed as soon as he took him. He was one of the friendliest dogs he'd ever met, big and fuzzy and just plain lovable. Chevy hated leaving him tied up so much, but he couldn't risk having someone else discover him. Not when he was this close.

Things were moving now—so said the television. The faces of Margaret Chadburne and the crime lab technician, along with every other disguise the FBI could come up with, had popped up in the news overnight. Except for the old English gentleman, Chevy thought with a sly smile. He still had a few tricks up his sleeve.

He worked his way through the pasture and up to the dilapidated shed, carrying a bottle of Aquafina water and a couple of Egg McMuffins in a bag. He could tell the moment Heinz heard him approach, the dog whining in excitement.

"Hey, boy," Chevy said, ducking into the shed. Heinz wagged the entire back end of his body. Chevy rubbed his fur, the dog sniffing the McDonald's bag enthusiastically. "Hungry, are you?" A little dog chow was left in one bowl, and about a half-inch of water in the other. "Not too much, I see. But I bet you'll like this."

He poured the water into the dish and broke out a sandwich. He took the leash off and made Heinz do the normal doggie-things for a few bites of meat: sit, shake, roll over. Beth had taught him well. Then he worked on a whistle for "Come."

It was the only thing the dog really had to know.

*

The sky was still spitting in the morning. Abby woke Beth early, worrying about Heinz, oblivious to the fact that the previous night had held a cruel combination of bliss and despair.

How many more people would die before Chevy Bankes was satisfied?

"Mommy," Abby whined, "you aren't even trying."

Beth glanced up. She looked around at the toys Maggie had delivered to Quantico for Abby, and her vision misted. Maggie's kindness had saved her own life, and the lives of her children. Apparently Lieutenant Sacowicz hadn't known that.

Abby gave a dramatic huff, and Beth forced herself back to the racetrack in her hands. A degree in engineering was needed to put the thing together, a second degree in electronics to make it work. Abby had given up about fifteen minutes earlier and was now coloring with scented magic markers, while Beth sat on the floor trying to figure out where the tab should be inserted so wire B-14 made contact with steel rod C-8.

"There he is!" Abby cried, charging across the room. Neil appeared, unshaven, with a grimness on his face that hadn't been there the day before. A sad smile for Beth.

"How're you doing, sweet pea?" he asked Abby, catching her in a bear hug so fierce Beth could almost feel it herself.

"I'm great," Abby replied. "But Mommy's having a bad day."

Neil caught Beth's eyes.

"It's just like Christmas when Santa brings toys that still have to be put together. Mommy hates that. She says

316

the elves are lazy. Right now she can't get the track together or make the cars work."

"I can, too," Beth said. Smother the pain. "I just haven't finished yet."

Neil sat on the arm of the sofa with Abby on his thigh. "Think I should help her?"

Abby lit up. "Do you know how?"

"Sure. Planes, trains, and automobiles. They're guy things."

Beth would have argued but for a startling truth: She'd be overjoyed to have Neil around to assemble the toys for Abby. And practice T-ball with her, and mow the lawn, and handle dozens of other things Beth had handled alone for seven years.

She left the racetrack in Neil's hands, astounded by the direction of her thoughts, and went to pour some coffee. She'd worked so hard to not need anyone, to not *want* anyone, and she had prided herself on her ability to carry her own burdens. But suddenly, after the sharing of both love and grief they'd experienced last night, self-reliance seemed highly overrated.

Neil strode into the kitchen and slid his arms around her. "Abby went into the den to play a computer game," he said, nuzzling her jaw.

Beth turned and laid a hand on his rugged cheek. "Rick—"

"Don't," he said, squeezing her hand. "Not now. He'd just want me to stay focused and catch the bastard."

Beth nodded, knowing what she had to do. "You want to hear about the rape now, don't you?"

He tipped his forehead against hers. "No," he said

317

tiredly, "it's the last thing I want to hear. But it might help, if you think you can do it."

The story leaked out. She told Neil everything she could remember, at first with detachment, then with tears as the details siphoned in. Neil gripped her hand as if he could keep her in the present, and Beth told him everything she had refused to let herself remember for seven years.

Anne dropped, and Chevy fell to his knees beside her. He looked inside the gym bag on the ground, and in that moment, sheer madness took over. No more taunting and teasing, as he had done with Anne. No more control. Just insane, unbridled rage.

"Nooo! Bitch!" He stumbled to Beth. "Look what you've done."

Grit your teeth. Don't make a sound. That's what he wants.

Smack. Beth stumbled to the ground, choking on the urge to cry out. The bag hung over his shoulder, and he pulled it up higher, cradling it with one hand. Then he flinched, as if he heard something.

"Noo!" He covered his ear, trying to block something out, the other hand wielding the gun toward Beth. "Stop it, bitch," he snarled, but he wasn't talking to Beth. He looked like an animal with nowhere to go. "Who killed Cock?" he sang into the air, then growled from his throat. "You did, bitch!"

He shook his head like a dog spraying water, then snatched Beth's arm and pulled her to her feet. He shoved the gun into her chest. "Don't you hear that? Mother's singing. She does that so she can't hear Jenny cry. But she'll stop if you scream." He glanced wildly around. "This is just like home. Mother can hear you here. Scream so she'll stop singing."

Beth twisted from his grasp. She went two strides, but she was wearing heels and stumbled. He grabbed her, baring his teeth, and the gun wheeled into her cheek.

She sprawled to the ground. Pain flared, tiny chunks of dirt and stone grinding into the open wound. Darkness swirled around her, and everything faded but the white-hot shards of pain in her face.

Good. She needed her cheek to hurt. Then maybe she wouldn't feel the ripping between her thighs. Quiet, now. Don't make a sound. It's what he wants.

And then, finally, he was gone.

Beth blinked. Neil's face was only inches away, his frown etched in stone. "He just left," she said, puzzled. "He finished and climbed off. He picked up the bag and" —she squinted in confusion— "he was crying, I think. And just left me there."

Neil brushed her bangs from her forehead. "You weren't doing what he needed you to do. You weren't screaming."

Beth blinked, feeling oddly calm. "That's all I can remember. Do we know anything more than we did before?"

"Just that it sounds like Bankes heard voices—his mother singing. He wanted your screams to stop her."

"You know, whatever was in that bag was precious to him," Beth said, sifting through the memories. "No matter what else was happening, he always kept it close."

"He took something from your house in a duffel. I wonder if it's the same thing." Neil stood, pacing. "'Who killed Cock?' What was that about?"

"It's what he heard in his mind, I think," Beth said.

319

"There's a nursery rhyme that starts like that. 'Who Killed Cock Robin?' It's in one of Abby's books. I remember reading it and thinking it was sort of sick." She pointed at Neil's laptop, and he nodded and brought it to her. She typed in the title. At home, she knew just where the book was, but certainly she could find the rhyme on the Internet. "I think it was a folk song about the death of Robin Hood or some other famous English figure. Abby's book gives annotations about the songs and rhymes."

Neil bent over her shoulder when the site came up.

"I'll be damned, there it is," he said. "'Who killed Cock Robin? I, said the Sparrow, with my bow and arrow, I killed Cock Robin. Who saw him die? I, said the Fly, with my little eye, I saw him die.' Jesus. Nice little rhyme for a kid. And it goes on and on. Looks like there's about a hundred verses."

Beth rubbed at her forehead. "What did Bankes say when he sang this? He said, 'Who killed Cock? You did, bitch.'" She shook her head. "I don't understand."

But Neil had picked up a thick three-ring binder and was thumbing through the pages.

"What is it?" Beth asked.

He stopped on a page, looked at it, and tapped it with his index finger. "Guess what Chevy's grandfather's name was: Robin Bankes."

Chapter 41

Chevy looked at the G.I. Joe doll, half listening to the news. Mabel's television was tuned to CNN Headlines, so the top stories got repeated every few minutes. He never had to wait long before they started talking about him again. Psychopath. Serial killer. Sexual deviant. The Hunter. No, that last one was losing favor. The Stalker, now, and even The Tormentor.

Finally, they were starting to get it.

And the talking heads were wild with speculation. People Chevy hadn't thought of since he was a teenager were being interviewed, telling one story after another. He glanced in the direction of the dining room, hoping Jenny wasn't listening. Most of the stories didn't hold a grain of truth. He wouldn't be surprised to hear someone suggest he'd killed his little sister, saved her in a freezer and eaten her, like that maniac Jeffrey Dahmer. Strange how being connected to a murderer suddenly made a person clamor to be in the spotlight, to say something no one else knew, to be the one who appeared on the morning news shows saying, "I knew him when ..."

They didn't know him when, Chevy thought. No one had ever known them. Mother made sure of it. No one could see past the flowers and songs.

Suddenly, the drone of the headlines changed. Chevy looked up to see the word *LIVE* pop up on the upper left corner of the screen. The cameras panned over a grave-yard, then closed in on a bunch of people standing in the drizzle in dark jackets, the yellow letters FBI across their backs. A backhoe sat in the picture, a few people holding shovels. The camera homed in on an empty grave, then tightened further on a small white brick marker: BANKES, 1990.

Grandpa? They were digging up Grandpa?

Another grave came into view, another white brick: BANKES, 1992. Then the camera followed the officials loading two coffins into a hearse. Grandpa and Mother.

Chevy's lungs froze for a moment. He couldn't believe it.

There was only one thing they could want with his mother's corpse: to review her cause of death. It wouldn't be the first time they'd wondered about that, and Chevy didn't care. But Grandpa, why Grandpa?

It hit him, and his chest tightened. *She can't feel. She has bad blood.*

"It's okay, Jenny," he said aloud. "I'll take care of you." But inside, he was nauseous.

Damn them, damn them all. Damn Neil Sheridan.

Yes, *especially* Sheridan. Chevy punched off the televi-sion and looked at the G.I. Joe in his hands. Sheridan had haunted him—hunted him—from the very beginning, after Gloria Michaels, and if that weren't enough, his careless actions with the duffel in Beth's house had sealed his fate. If Chevy was a different type of person, like the simpleminded killers he'd known in prison, he'd just catch the asshole late one night and pop him with one of Mo's pistols, be done with it. But Chevy was better than that. Beth cared about Sheridan—that was obvious from the rare glimpses a camera caught of the two of them together. A relationship had even been speculated upon by one reporter on Channel 42, trying to rake in the Jerry Springer audience. So Bankes was going to do more than just *kill* Neil Sheridan. He would use Sheridan's demise to up the ante for Beth.

He sat back down on the couch, pushing the news about the graveyard out of his mind. He picked up the .22 he'd used on the woman at the church and screwed on the silencer. Two of Mabel's thick phone books made the perfect bed. He laid the G.I. Joe on top, faceup, pressed the muzzle of the .22 against the doll's left pectoral muscle, and squeezed.

A thrill ran through his limbs. He couldn't wait to deliver *that* message.

The knowledge that Neil had done precisely what Copeland wanted him to—get the whole truth from Beth—sat on his shoulders like an anvil. He was now privy to new pieces of Chevy Bankes's madness: Chevy's mother sang so she wouldn't hear Jenny's crying. When Chevy got women to scream, his mother stopped singing. And at least as far as Chevy knew, his mother had killed her father, Robin.

Neil was privy to the information, but he couldn't do anything with it. Feeding Beth's rape to the task force—even to Standlin—wasn't an option. And it wasn't the only piece of new information weighing heavily on Neil's conscience.

Beth sat down across the table. A collection of doll photos was spread out around Neil's laptop. "What are these?"

"Your hunch was right." Neil tapped the insurance photos. "The dolls you're getting are part of the Larousse collection."

Beth's jaw unhinged. "You're sure?" She frowned. "But how did Bankes get them, even posing as Margaret Chadburne?"

He handed a page to her. One of the Larousse heirs had finally come clean with an agent in Seattle. "Turns out the Larousses were the family who wanted to sell pieces to Chaney's museum. The night you met Anne Chaney, some of the Larousse dolls were in the trunk of her car. She was planning to show them to you."

"I can't believe it."

"Anne Chaney's car was found two days after she died," Neil said. "It was empty, and no one except Stefan Larousse and Anne Chaney knew the deal with the museum was under consideration. Larousse, believe it or not, was in financial trouble. The doll collection was a big part of his collateral for a major loan, and being the financial mogul that he was, he opted not to report the dolls missing. Apparently, with nine missing, the rest of the collection is devalued."

"Nine? We've seen six," Beth said, and Neil wished she weren't so quick.

"We've seen six, but he's probably done eight. There were two dolls that didn't make it out of France during WWII. They were recovered in 1995."

"I remember reading about that. But I never thought … Oh, God. The two missing women?"

Neil nodded. "Despite what Chadburne claimed, those dolls were never mailed to you." He pulled out two of the insurance reports. "Bankes seems to be sending them in order from oldest to newest, so we think it's these two. This doll has a replaced pate. That's a wig, right?"

She nodded.

"The Denver woman we never found—the second woman—is a cancer patient. No hair."

Beth looked as if she would retch. Quickly, he added, "The third one, for the Omaha woman, was a perfect doll. Valued at over fifty thousand dollars. Maybe he didn't … hurt her."

Neil watched as she did the math and thumbed through the pictures. He could do nothing as the worst of it hit her. "Then there's still one more doll to go," she whispered. "One more murder."

"Two," he said carefully. "Because the doll that represented Lexi Carter wasn't a Larousse. It was a fake Bankes bought from Kerry. That leaves two Larousses that were in Chaney's car that night."

"And you know what they are? You've got the insurance reports?"

He waited. He could hardly bring himself to tell her.

"Well?" she demanded.

He handed her the pictures. "The last two dolls are a pair: a mother pushing a carriage, a baby doll inside."

325

She went still.

"I won't let him near you or Abby, Beth."

"I know," she said and cleared her throat. "I'm okay. I mean, it's not like we didn't know I was his ultimate target." She paced, seeming to talk herself into it, then turned. "But it means it's almost over. He'll finish soon."

"He won't get to finish. I promise."

She drew in a deep breath and let it out, and Neil saw her spine straighten with determination. She took the pictures of the last two dolls and went to her own laptop. "Well, I might as well study these dolls. Find out what he's planning to do to us."

The sadness took Chevy by surprise; he hadn't expected that. In his dreams, the later stages of Beth's torture filled him with anticipation and fulfillment and triumph. In reality, he didn't want the end to come.

But he could feel things pushing him to move. Jenny, so fragile and hurt. The dog, still tied out there in a shed. Neil Sheridan sticking to Beth like glue, maybe even screwing her. And the icing on the cake now: The phone had just rung.

"Mabel, I just wanted to tell you we'll be meeting at Neo's for brunch tomorrow, so bring the books. I'll see you then," the elderly voice had said on the answering machine.

Which meant Mabel Skinner would be missed by lunchtime tomorrow. Damn. She hadn't looked like the book club type.

Too bad. He liked Mabel's house, except for the ugly upholstery. Liked her car, too, the luxury Lexus. He'd wondered what an old lady needed with a Lexus.

She didn't need it anymore, not stuffed in the big chest freezer in the basement with Tater Tots and ground turkey. He hadn't enjoyed the killing of Mabel Skinner, hadn't thought of Jenny or Beth or even his mother. Her death was just a necessity, like Mo Hammond's. Chevy hadn't particularly enjoyed killing him, either.

He sighed, thinking how close he was now. Two dolls left.

He went to Mabel's dining room and got the last box— it held both of the last two dolls together, along with a spindle-wheeled carriage. Jenny watched, his dark mood rubbing off on her, and he pulled the baby doll out of the carriage and took it over to her. "Here you go," he said. "You can play with her until I need her."

She said nothing—she hadn't for a couple of days.

Damn Neil Sheridan for what he had done. No one hurt Jenny.

Resolve sank into Chevy's soul, and he went back to the table to finish with the mother doll. Sheridan's demise was all planned: Just as soon as Chevy was ready to leave Mabel's house, Sheridan's number would come up.

And after that, Beth. Mother doll Beth.

Chapter 42

Neil stayed with Beth and Abby, but he buried himself in paper and phone calls. The first call was from Copeland: "The child doll that was burned up was in good condition when Stefan Larousse gave her to Anne Chaney," he said. "So Bankes burned her."

"Which means he's past the point of matching the women to dolls. He's manipulating them himself now." So much for Beth using the dolls to try to figure out what he was planning for her and Abby.

"Even so, research is going over all the rest of the dolls now."

"Research," Neil said. "Not Beth."

"Standlin's worried about your girl. She suggested we get our own doll expert."

"Beth knows what she's looking at," Neil said. "She wants to help."

"Sure. But if that last pair shows up with a cord around the baby's neck and the nipples carved off the mother, how's she gonna handle that?"

Neil's gut lurched. Score one for Standlin. "Okay. You got everyone's butt covered who's working the case?"

"We went through the videos. Any agent or cop whose face showed up on the news now has a family tucked away in hiding. Sacowicz's wife took their kids up to Long Island."

"Yeah, I talked to her this morning. Rick's brother is there, another cop." Looked just like Rick, with the same Slavic brow and coppery eyebrows. *God. Rick.*

"We put the information about the dolls on TV," Copeland said, "and put every version of Bankes's face out there we can think of. Looks like he knows how to use padding in his cheeks and latex for wrinkles to pull off Chadburne, and heaven knows what other tricks he learned as a theater major. But we're checking fifty tips an hour now. The bastard won't be able to move. Won't have anyplace to go."

"He has the firepower and silencers he picked up from Mo Hammond. He probably popped an old woman, and he's been sitting in her living room watching the news and eating her TV dinners. Driving her car around."

Copeland let out a curse. "If that's what he's doing, we'll never find him."

But that's what he was doing; Neil knew it. He sat at his laptop for ten more minutes thinking it through, then dialed Copeland again. A secretary put him on hold, said Copeland was talking to a field agent. Neil paced while he waited.

"You got anyone checking packages at the post office and UPS?" he asked when Copeland came back on the line.

"They're using X-ray machines at the post office that serves Foster's; UPS and FedEx already scan packages to the D.C. area."

"Okay. Bankes couldn't mail a package that large from an unmanned mailbox, but what about private parcels like UPS?"

"We put drivers on the lookout for anything the appropriate size and weight. They've got pictures of him—male and female—taped to their dashboards. But if he wants to send something at this point, he'll just pay someone like he did with the flower box. Two weeks ago at a UPS store in Boise, Mrs. Chadburne paid a guy to send boxes to Beth on certain dates. Chadburne told him she was going to be out of town on the days the boxes needed to go."

Neil blew out a breath. It was a long shot.

"But listen," Copeland said, "things are moving, anyway. That call I took just now was from the lab in Philadelphia that's doing the mom's body and her father's. Hold on to your hat."

Neil straightened.

"Jenny—Chevy's little sister—still had blood work on file at the hospital where they worked on her. Tests on her grandfather's corpse show too many similarities. Looks like with Grandpa living in the house, the Bankeses were more than one big happy family."

"What?" It was taking a minute to sink in. "Incest?"

"There's no way Jenny's genes could have come from some other tree. Peggy Bankes was being nailed by her dad. That explains a few things, doesn't it?"

Neil's mind was racing—to Abby. "What about Chevy?"

"No, his father was some schoolboy named David Moore in the next town. We talked to his parents, and they said he never had anything to do with Peggy after Robin Bankes found out she was pregnant. He beat the hell out of the boy and locked Peggy up."

A mixture of nausea and relief surged through Neil. Bad enough knowing Bankes's blood ran in Abby's veins. To think that blood might have been spawned of incest ... "So Peggy Bankes was molested by her father. Robin Bankes was Jenny's father."

"And grandfather, both. Standlin's having a ball with this one," Copeland said.

"So there *could* have been a child before Chevy. Everyone says Peggy didn't have any boyfriends until Chevy's dad, but" —he stopped, wincing at the thought— "maybe she didn't need one."

"Man." Neil could picture Copeland running a hand over his head. "I'll push the lab on the Bible and the receipt you found. But either way, it looks like textbook, long-term sexual abuse. Peggy Bankes spent her life making everything look nice from the outside. Psychiatrist's playground, that family."

"Anything about Robin Bankes's death raising eyebrows?"

"Grandpa was sick in his last years; everyone says stomach cancer."

"I know what 'everyone' says. What do the doctors say?"

"We haven't found a doctor who treated him yet."

"How 'bout that?" Neil said.

"Don't get too excited until toxicology comes back. It

could've been stomach cancer just like everyone thought."

Or it could've been murder. By a woman whose dad chased away her boyfriend and forced her into his own bed. *Who killed Cock Robin?*

Neil took a deep breath, pacing like a caged panther. As much as he wanted to be close to Beth and Abby, staying cooped up was killing him.

"As for the mother's suicide," Copeland said, "the physical evidence on the body isn't pointing to murder, but Bankes still could have done it."

"But why? Even if Grandpa was fucked up, we haven't found anyone who said Peggy Bankes mistreated Chevy." But even as he said it, he remembered what Beth had divulged. *Mother is singing. She does that so she can't hear Jenny cry.*

Maybe it was Jenny she mistreated.

"Well, damn it, Sheridan, it's something. We're on a roll."

Maybe. But Bankes was on a faster roll, an inch ahead of them. Neil fingered the photos of the dolls from Chaney's car. "The first dolls were sent from Boise by the guy Chadburne paid, right?"

"Right."

"So how'd he get the others here?"

"Could've driven them," Copeland said. "We think he just drove here in his car then dumped it someplace and started using other people's cars."

"Maybe. Or the dolls were waiting for him when he got here."

"I'll tell the lab to check any dirt or cobwebs on the boxes the dolls came in. Maybe he sent them to his mother's house to be stored."

332

"If so, who signed for the deliveries there?"

They both said it at the same time: "Mo Hammond."

Confirmation came later that evening. Beth had just tucked Abby into bed; Neil was looking forward to tucking in with Beth when his phone rang. Copeland had called the resident agent for Samson, Pennsylvania, and sent him to search Hammond's gun store again, while the lab dug back into the boxes that had contained the first three dolls.

"The dolls weren't stashed at Bankes's house," Copeland reported, a weary note to his voice. "Hammond stored them."

"How do we know?"

"They matched speckles on one of the boxes to paint used at Hammond's shop two years ago. It's like you said: Hammond was the connection between Bankes's plans and his run on Beth. He must've stored those dolls for all the years Bankes was in prison."

"And what does that do for us?"

"Not a damned thing." He sighed. "I'll tell you what, Sheridan, we know so many facts about Bankes my head is spinning. But not one of them is any help in finding him."

"So pull him out. Make something happen."

"That's what I've been thinking—it's the reason I called. I wanted you to make sure Beth knew that Hannah Blake has turned the corner. She's gonna be okay."

Neil closed his eyes. For once, some news he'd enjoy giving to Beth. "Great. So what are you thinking?"

"That we're gonna have a funeral for her, anyway. See if Bankes shows up."

Chapter 43

Chevy waited near the Dumpsters. They were tucked into an alcove, as they usually were, and the mall would be opening in five minutes, at ten o'clock. Talk radio was lamenting the death of Hannah Blake—apparently she had passed away early in the morning as a result of complications from the surgery after her accident. The host was blaming the Democrats for creating the type of society in which this sort of thing could happen. Chevy thought about calling in. Wouldn't *that* be a hoot?

He adjusted his wedding ring and looked at his watch, imagining all those FBI agents gathered around a conference table, circling round and round Hannah Blake's death. Probably planning a setup to catch him at her funeral or something. A profiler on Channel 5 had been interviewed and said a murderer like Bankes would normally keep trophies of his kills, and since Bankes didn't seem to be doing that, they expected he would attend his victims' funerals to get a thrill from seeing what he had done. Hell, Chevy wouldn't put it past the Feds to fake the whole thing and try to lure him in.

Idiots. He didn't need to go to the funerals for a thrill, and he *did* keep trophies from the women he killed. He kept their voices.

Chevy shifted, growing hard with the thought. He flipped down the mirrored visor on Mabel's Lexus. The beard was a nuisance, the temporary black hair dye made his scalp itch, and the padding that fattened his cheeks and gave his face a totally new shape made him feel as if he'd just been to the dentist. The disguise probably wasn't necessary just driving around in a car that wouldn't be suspicious until Mabel was discovered missing, but he didn't want to take any chances. Even through tinted windows, some asshole might look at him sideways and try to be a hero or something. Better safe than sorry.

So wait, watch. The parking lot was beginning to fill, shoppers streaming like ants toward the mall entrance. Women mostly, alone, in pairs, often with children. The occasional man or family. Sooner or later, the right combination would appear, and the end would sneak that much closer. A quick abduction, a quick phone call to Sheridan, then, *snap*. One proverbially tall, dark, and handsome FBI agent—dead.

And Beth Denison on a ride straight to hell.

"Sheridan."

Neil answered his phone without taking his eyes off Beth. A small group of friends and family members of Hannah Blake had gathered at the Foster home—keeping up the appearance that she had died—while a funeral home was being staffed with FBI agents and undercover police officers for the next day's mock service. It was the opinion of the shrinks that Bankes might amuse himself by showing up at the funeral or at least lurking in the background.

Neil didn't think he would.

"Sheridan," the dispatcher said into his ear, "it's Chevy Bankes. He wants to talk to you."

Neil's heart stopped. The dispatcher's voice had trembled, as if she knew the significance of the call. Not a prank, then.

"Put him through," he said tightly.

Seconds passed while Neil's heart refused to beat and he stepped from Carol Foster's living room into a foyer. Finally the lines clicked and Bankes's voice came through: "Tell them to put me through faster, you asshole, or you'll never hear from me again."

Click. Dead air.

Shit. Neil glanced up; Harrison saw something in Neil's expression and started for him. By the time he joined Neil, Neil had the FBI dispatcher back on the phone.

"But I was told we needed time to activate a successful trace, Mr. Sher—"

"I don't care what you were told," Neil snarled under his breath. "Don't waste time trying to stall him on hold, or we won't get him at all. He's not fool enough to stay on the line, and even if we trace him, we'll find the call comes from a goddamned phone booth in Timbuktu. Put him through *fast* the next time."

"I take my orders from Agent Copeland."

"Damn it. Connect me to Copeland."

Copeland was on a couple of seconds later.

"Bankes is calling me," Neil said into his phone. "Tell your phone people not to dick around with him anymore."

"When?"

"Now. I gotta get off; he'll probably call back."

"Okay. I'll change the phone orders on my end, but you gotta keep him on the line, Sheridan. Even if he's using a prepaid cell, we can nail him. I have two choppers outfitted; they can be in the air in two minutes."

Neil punched End on his phone, kept it in his hand. "It was Bankes," he explained to Harrison. "He's gonna call back. Dispatch kept him waiting too long."

"Hell."

Neil caught Suarez's eyes; Suarez nodded a silent promise to cover Beth. Neil stepped out to a patio.

His phone rang three minutes later. "Talk," he said. "And then I'll give you my direct phone number."

"Give it to me now," Bankes ordered.

Neil did.

"That's very generous of you, Sheridan. Now we can talk a little. But it won't help you home in on this pedantic little gas station too far out of the way to get to in time anyway."

"For a smart man, you're taking some big chances." Play to the gamer in him. He'll like that, maybe keep talking.

"I'm sorry about Hannah Blake."

"Yeah, I'm sure you're all broken up."

"I am. I didn't even get to enjoy her death. Never got to hear her make a sound. And she was kind of a pretty thing, as I recall."

"When did you ever see Hannah Blake?"

"I had lunch with her at a show in San Francisco. She was there instead of Beth. But you already knew that, didn't you? I imagine you know just about everything now." He chuckled. "Except where I am and who I'll kill next."

"I know you're screwed, that's what I know." He looked at his watch. A tiny green light throbbed with the passage of seconds—slow as cold honey, it seemed. "You think it's so slick to use dolls to try to freak Beth out. Pretty cliché, if you ask me."

Neil heard a chuckle at the other end of the line, also the sound of a truck driving past. Damn it, he *was* at a gas station. On a pay phone or his cell, it didn't matter. He'd be long gone with no one ever noticing him, even if Neil did get sixty-two more seconds out of him. Sixty-one ... sixty ... fifty-nine ...

"So what's next, Bankes?" Neil wanted to confront him with what he'd done to Beth, but the call was being traced. He didn't dare say anything about her rape. "Tell me why a *man* has to threaten six-year-olds and women. Didn't you get your fill of hurting weaker things when you killed your baby sister?"

The air seemed to crackle as Neil waited for a response. So, he'd hit a nerve. Go ahead, fucker, he thought, get mad. Take *me* on.

"You don't know anything about my sister," Bankes ground out.

"I know it must not have taken much to kill her. An infant who was genetically fucked—"

"There was nothing wrong with Jenny! Her blood

338

didn't matter. Bad blood doesn't matter."

"Jenny was a preemie, didn't weigh twenty pounds by the time she disapp—"

"Shut the hell up!"

Neil did, afraid he'd hang up.

"I left you a gift," Bankes said. Hurried now, aware of the time. "You can find it at the home of Mabel Skinner, on Lexington Avenue."

Neil opened his mouth to speak, but would have been talking to thin air. Bankes was gone. One minute, forty-two seconds after the phone had rung.

He punched in Copeland's private number.

"We're on it," Copeland said. "The southeast chopper is narrowing in now on an area out in Southton."

Neil cursed. "He's already gone, driving on the highway right under the chopper."

"We'll set up roadblocks just in case, maybe catch him trying to get out."

And Bankes would beat them to it. Everyone knew exactly where he'd been sixty seconds earlier, but sixty seconds was all he needed to get out. "Look for a car belonging to a woman named Mabel Skinner, on Lexington Avenue. He said he left a gift for me at her house."

"I heard," said Copeland. "I'm calling in the forces. I'll call you with the exact address. If you get there first, stay the hell back."

"Why? You think the gift Bankes left me will blow?"

"It's a possibility," Copeland said. "Meet you there."

Neil hung up and looked at Harrison, who had gotten enough from Neil's gestures and one end of the conversation to have already relayed it to the agents on-site at the

Fosters'. Harrison punched off his phone.

"The TAC unit's on its way to that neighborhood," Neil told him. "Copeland will call with the exact address as soon as they get it."

"Let's move."

"Wait. Beth."

Harrison stopped. "Look, Sheridan, I'm no buddy like Sacowicz was, and it's none of my business how you handle the lady. But I don't think you should scare her, man. She's with her friends now, with her daughter. She looks cool. And she's safer here than anywhere else."

Grief hit Neil between the eyes. It shouldn't be Harrison giving him calm, sane advice. It should be Rick.

But Harrison was right. Neil and Beth had shared a night of sheer ecstasy, with Beth basking in the news that Hannah would survive and Neil taking shameless advantage of her good spirits. There was no need to put a damper on that now.

"Okay. Let's go."

Mabel Skinner lived at 1322 Lexington Avenue. The scene looked alarmingly like the one that had unfolded at Beth's house when Carter died: yellow ribbon, strobes of blue and red so dense they could be seen even in the afternoon light, swarms of uniforms fighting back cameras and shouting down reporters.

Neil pushed through the melee with Harrison and ratcheted the car into park. They jogged to the sidewalk, meeting up with Copeland and three other men and a woman, all wearing FBI jackets.

"Everybody evacuated?" Neil asked, looking at the

houses on either side of Skinner's and across the street.

"Yeah," Copeland said. "One block in every direction's been emptied out. No one around."

Except the ever-increasing crush of people gathering around the yellow ribbon, hoping for a freak show. "You gotta move everyone off the street," Neil said.

"We're doing it, we're doing it," someone answered.

"Infrareds didn't pick up anyone inside," Copeland said, his hands riding low on his hips. "They're setting up the mikes and amplifiers now."

"Okay," Neil said. It would take a few minutes, while they all stood around with their fingers up their noses and nothing to do but wait. The TAC unit had secured the exterior of the house to let the FBI's entry team work. The entry team used thermal-imaging cameras to sense collections of heat that indicated a live being, then placed sound equipment on the outside walls. The microphones could detect any sound in rooms with exterior walls. Beyond that . . .

Neil shook his head. "It doesn't feel like a trap. I don't think he's in there waiting to spring something."

"He still has those guns he picked up from Hammond's," Harrison said. "Coulda decided to bring you over here looking for his gift, then pop you from the front window."

"Excuse me," said a woman in uniform. She was a local cop. "My partner and I were in the area when you rolled in, Agent," she said to Copeland. "We'd like to help—on behalf of Lieutenant Sacowicz."

Copeland put his hand on her shoulder. "Thank you. Hold tight; there'll be something to do soon."

"I found a neighbor who knows the house."

Copeland looked at her, cracked a smile. Rick's team was good. "And?"

"She says there hasn't been anything going on the past few days. Except she saw the owner's Lexus in the driveway yesterday, and wondered about it because Skinner always puts it inside."

"Floor plan?"

The officer pulled out a rough sketch. "Front door opens into a small living room, then straight back to the dining room and opens to the kitchen on the right. Two bedrooms; both have outside walls. This bathroom doesn't, though, and there's a basement."

So if someone was in either the inner bathroom or the basement, the FBI's equipment wouldn't pick it up.

Neil inhaled, nostrils flaring. No one was in there. Not alive, anyway.

But they listened for another ten minutes before Copeland decided it was time to go in.

"So how's it going down?" the female officer asked Neil. "Stealth or force? Sacowicz always said the FBI likes stealth."

Neil laughed. Stealth, with forty agents and officers on the scene in broad daylight and TV cameras from here to the moon. *Screw you, Rick.*

And so they took a minute to organize, with Copeland calling the shots into a handset, and then the entry team took down the door. Every door, in fact, and every window, all at the same time. In less than five seconds, twelve people were in Mabel Skinner's house, and in another sixty, the all clear was given.

Now, to find out what Bankes had left.

Chapter 44

Something was happening. Something that had taken Neil away without a word except a cryptic message to Suarez: "I'll call her." Something no one was telling Beth and that left her feeling helpless and guilty and worried.

And exhausted. She'd been up much of the night. Not that she would trade those blissful hours with Neil, but a little sleep would go a long way just now.

Instead, she sat on a stool, icing cookies with Carol Foster and Abby.

"Mommy, what's wrong with you?" Abby asked. "Want a cookie?"

"What she wants is some rest," Carol said, wiping icing on her apron. "For heaven's sake, Beth, why don't you go on up to the apartment? No one's used it lately, and Abby and I are fine. Your guard dog here can wake you if Sheridan calls."

Juan looked at Beth. "Woof."

She smiled a little. "I guess. I just wish I knew what was going on."

"I'm sure the FBI will tell you when you need to know," Carol said.

"Right," she said, sending Juan a look of sheer skepticism. She went to Abby. "You stay with Carol, all right, honey?"

"Okay. But Uncle Evan bought me a kite for spring break, and we never got to fly it. He said it was windy enough today. Can we, please?"

Beth deferred to Juan, who chucked Abby under the chin. "Is there a place to fly it here at Foster's?"

"In that field behind the gallery. We tried there once before, but I let the kite get too close to the trees. It ripped up."

"Bummer," Juan replied. "A couple of my friends will go with you, okay? And stay close to your uncle Evan."

Abby screwed her face into a frown. "He's not really my uncle, you know."

"You don't say," Juan said.

Beth showed Juan the way to the apartment in the carriage house and flicked off her shoes in the living room. His phone rang a minute after they entered, and instead of going into the bedroom, she eavesdropped without any shame at all.

Juan looked at her as he talked. "Yeah, Carol Foster just bullied her into taking a nap. We're in the carriage house." Beat. "No, man, she's still awake. Hold on." He handed the phone to Beth.

"Neil? Where are you?"

"I'm sorry I ran out on you, honey. I got a call."

"What kind of call?"

"Never mind. I just wan—"

"Damn it, Neil, you promised not to shut me out."

Silence pulsed for three seconds. "Bankes called me. He killed another woman."

No. Oh, God. "The woman ... was she—"

"She was just a place for Bankes to stay and a car to drive. We found the teenager's Ford Escort in her garage."

"Then he didn't leave a doll?"

"He did, but—"

"I'll come look at it."

"You don't need to see this one." He went silent for a few seconds, and she could almost feel the weariness in his bones. "It's not an antique. Sweetheart, we're working on the house, waiting for results from the crime lab. You're doing the best thing you can do right now— gathering with Hannah's friends, getting some rest, keeping Abby happy. I'll call you again later, and I'll stay in touch with Suarez."

Damn it, there were tears rolling down her cheeks.

"Beth?"

She pulled herself together. "Yes?"

"I love you."

Neil punched off the phone. Copeland came over.

"She okay?"

"Sure. She's great," Neil said.

"You?"

"I'm fine."

"Hmm. I don't know why I asked. Bankes leaves us a G.I. Joe this time—dark hair, blue eyes, big muscles. A bullet hole in his chest."

Neil glared at him. "Don't even think about it," he warned.

"Son," Copeland said, and the address took Neil by surprise as much as the hand Copeland laid on his shoulder, "the game has changed. Bankes is targeting you now, and you're walking around bent on a massacre with your heart all tied in knots. I don't have any choice but to pull you out—"

Neil's phone rang. He looked at it and knew. Copeland knew, too, and cursed.

"Did you find the gift I left you?" Bankes asked.

Neil ground his teeth. "We found her. And the doll. I see you've decided to take on a man for a change."

"Just a little detour. And how fortunate that killing you will only heighten Beth's suffering, too. I get the impression she's grown rather fond of you. Tell me, Sheridan. When you're driving inside her, does she make that wonderful little sound, from down in her gut, every time you strike her womb—"

"Shut the fuck up."

Copeland cursed beneath his breath, and Bankes scolded: "Now, now. Insulting me is no way to keep me on the line long enough for a trace. Didn't they teach you that at Quantico?"

"Say what you wanna say."

"I went to the mall to get you another gift since you liked the first one so much."

Son of a bitch.

"Did you know what easy targets women are when they're shopping? Especially when their kids are with them. They get distracted. It's like taking candy from a baby ..."

"You're lying." Neil's gut clenched.

"So I have a woman and her daughter. They'll be at the park, waiting for you."

346

Jesus. Maybe he wasn't lying. "What park?"

"Ellis Park. Look in a culvert on the south end. Six-thirty."

"That's two and a half hours from now. If you really have someone, I want them now."

Bankes chuckled. "You know, my grandfather always said, 'Want in one hand and spit in the other. See which one gets full first.'"

"Are they alive?"

"For now."

"What are their names? Let me talk to the mother."

"No. You'll just have to take me at my word."

Copeland waved his hand, pointing at his watch, reminding Neil—unnecessarily—to keep talking. Another few seconds and they might be able to pinpoint his location.

"Oh, Sheridan?" Bankes said. "Let me save you the trouble of a trace. I'm at the Oak Wood Mall, in Clayton. I'll be leaving through the northeast exit, nearest to the food court Dumpster. Shall I tell you what kind of car I'm driving now that I've dumped Mabel's Lexus? Nah. That would take the sport out of it."

He was gone.

Copeland fired orders into his phone, sending a team to Clayton to stake out the mall exits, but everyone knew Bankes would be out of there in thirty seconds. Driving some new woman's car, with her and her daughter tied up in the backseat as hostages.

Or maybe the woman and daughter were already at the park.

Or maybe they were dead.

347

Chapter 45

"Here come the newest shots from Parks and Recreation," Brohaugh said, his fingers slapping at the computer keys like frog tongues snapping up bugs. As soon as the crime scene team had swept Mabel Skinner's kitchen, they'd set up an impromptu command center around her kitchen table. Everyone gathered around the monitor, searching the photos that came up.

Copeland shook his head in slow motion. "Bankes chose well. I've lived here half my life and never knew there was a park with so few trees and so much open space."

It's what everyone was thinking. Bankes had called back twice, short calls from pay phones, telling Neil exactly where to go. He'd described the sloping valley at the park where he would trade Neil for an unknown woman and child he claimed to currently hold. He'd described the wide-open field where kite-flying and jogging and Frisbee were popular, and a stone culvert that dipped low in the middle of one field.

The culvert was a dead end. Just drainage for the park; it didn't actually lead anywhere. Just a little stone well where supposedly Neil would find the woman and her little girl.

"That must be it," Harrison said, pointing at the screen. "Any other shots of that?"

Brohaugh searched, tapped, and fed more pictures onto the screen, each taken from a different angle—surveyors' photographs—of the culvert.

"Christ," Copeland muttered. "He can see us coming from three hundred yards."

"How good's your best sniper with a long gun?" Neil asked.

"Four hundred yards if you just want him hit. Can hit any button you specify at three hundred."

"Okay." A button at three hundred yards was pretty good.

Copeland: "Doesn't matter anyway. Bankes knew what he was doing. Look at that. Where the hell am I gonna put a sniper who can't be seen?"

"What about Bankes?" Harrison asked. "A shotgun was missing from Hammond's, along with three pistols. Bankes coulda nabbed a long-range rifle, too, for all we know. Something that didn't show up on the inventory."

"Unless he spent part of the last year belonging to some militia," Standlin said, "he doesn't know how to handle rifles. He's a torture man. Rifles are quick and clean, impersonal."

"No fun at all," said Copeland.

"You're saying he's only carrying a nice dull knife?" Harrison again.

349

"The good news is—" Standlin began.

"There's good news?" Brohaugh asked.

"Bankes is improvising. This thing with Sheridan isn't part of what he planned and prepared for. He came to town with antiques, not a G.I. Joe. So either he's desperate, and we've blocked him from doing anything else, or he's found a reason for a vendetta against Sheridan. Because he's with Denison, probably."

Neil thought about that. Bankes hadn't seemed angry when he spoke about Neil having sex with Beth; he'd sounded almost humored. He was more out of control when Neil accused him of killing his sister.

"Enough. Let's get going," Copeland said. "It's almost five. We have a plan—as foolish as that plan is," he said, looking at Neil, "but we still have to catch him."

"You mean kill him," Neil corrected, and Copeland said, "Sure."

They were set up less than an hour later on a concrete slab in Ellis Park. They used picnic tables, under a roof that probably leaked when it rained, with two vans filled with electronics and surveillance equipment. Brohaugh's cords were strung to a generator in the nearest van, in case he ran out of juice somewhere in the course of the standoff. Neil cringed at the idea it might take that long.

Five agents were in on it: Copeland, Brohaugh, Standlin, Harrison, and O'Ryan. And, of course, Neil. Copeland may have wanted Neil out, but *Bankes* wanted him in.

Neil unfastened his holster. A breeze blew his loose shirttail around.

"You okay?" Harrison asked.

"Get away from me," Neil growled. "You act like I've never gone into a hostage situation before."

"I'm guessing you've never gone up against a psycho who's hurt someone you love."

Neil gave him a hard look. "Then you don't know me very well, do you?"

Harrison's face lost a shade. Neil took pity on him. "I'm okay."

And he was. At least now he was finally *doing* something. Neil was happy to replace Beth as a target. *Come ahead, you son of a bitch*, he'd thought. *Come after me.*

And Bankes had. Unfortunately, a mother and daughter had been his tools. Neil hadn't been sure whether or not to believe him after the first call, which had indeed been traced to the Oak Wood Mall. But when Bankes called a second time, Neil heard the woman's horrified sobs in the background.

"I wanna talk to her," Neil had said. "And she better be able to talk."

"Talk, bitch. Tell the man what's happening."

A voice, shaking and terrified: "He h-has my daughter and m-me." Horror drenched her words. "He's going to k-kill us."

And then Bankes was back. "So you come, bastard. Come get the woman and kid."

He'd hung up. Been on the phone too long and knew all about tracing calls.

Neil looked at his watch—almost six-thirty. The woman and her child had likely been taken around two, as best they could figure. They still didn't know their identities; no one had reported a woman or child missing. Someone still thought they were spending the day at the mall.

Neil punched in Suarez's number, needing the touchstone of knowing Beth was safe.

Suarez answered in a quiet tone. "I just checked on her, man; she's out. Fell asleep about an hour ago. Do what you gotta do."

Copeland and Neil walked to the back of the second van where O'Ryan handled the magic of television newscasting on her headset. "You got the cameras under control?" Copeland asked.

"Yeah," she answered. "We moved them all out about twenty minutes ago. Except for that smart-ass who was fired from Channel Two last year, Corey Dunwoody. He freelances now and gave me a hard time. I threatened to arrest him for obstruction."

Copeland rubbed his chin. "I remember him from the assassination attempt on the governor last year. No scruples, no morals, and would sell his mother's tits to the devil to get something big on film."

"Yeah," said O'Ryan. "Your standard reporter."

Bankes walked a few yards behind Heinz and the dark-haired girl named Samantha. They circled through a sprawling neighborhood that backed up to Foster's land: a dad and his kid, out walking a dog. Samantha and Heinz made his best disguise yet. They cut through the backyard of a house that appeared empty.

The Fosters had maybe forty acres. None of it was fenced, and the landscape surrounding their property was

352

lightly wooded and sloped, open for a few scenic acres around the house and gallery, and bordered on the sides by a neighborhood, a highway, and suburban-type woods. The perimeter had been heavily guarded for the past few days; today Chevy thought it would be lighter. The FBI was at Ellis Park and setting up for Hannah Blake's funeral.

He smiled at the way it was working out, and how Neil Sheridan's death would play right into his plans for Beth. No matter how well Chevy had planned for these events, he couldn't have predicted that a man would hurt Jenny and be the very same man who was screwing Beth. Double duty for this murder, he thought.

Heinz pulled eagerly at his leash, and Samantha almost went down.

"Hold on to him," Chevy said. "Don't let him go until I tell you to."

"I'm trying," she said, almost whimpering. She was a simpering little thing. He'd be glad to be rid of her.

"Try harder." He nudged the .22 in his pocket, making sure she saw its shape. "Turn left, through those trees. We gotta move faster now."

Chapter 46

"Gotta move," Neil said. An early evening chill nipped the air, and the sun sank lower in the sky. "It's six-thirty."

"City cops are still getting the last of the people out of the park," Copeland said. "Giving a story about a poison gas leak through a viaduct."

"That oughta do it," Harrison muttered. He was bouncing on the balls of his feet. Everyone was. It had been five hours since Bankes had called about Mabel Skinner's house. Since then, they'd found her body, found the G.I. Joe, and set up at the park. Moving fast now, no stopping 'til it was over.

As per Bankes's instructions, Neil had removed his tie, gun, and holster, and unbuttoned his shirt so it was obvious he wore no bulletproof vest. Like hanging raw meat around his neck then walking into a lion's den.

"Here," Copeland said. "You can't go in wearing that big forty-five, but no way he'll notice this in your pocket with your shirttail hanging out. Take it. Anything suspicious moves in the culvert, shoot it."

Neil thought about it, recalled Bankes's warnings to walk to the culvert unarmed and alone. He slipped the .22 into his pocket anyway.

"Listen, son," Copeland said, "you walk in slow, straight down that path. There's a sniper just over that rise and another in that big-ass oak tree."

Neil bit back a grim smile. "Gonna shoot me? I'm the only thing he'll be able to see."

Copeland cursed. "Goddamn it, Sheridan."

Neil slapped him on the shoulder. Copeland was a thousand percent against this idea, and they'd traded a number of savage words over it. "I don't belong to you," Neil had said. "If I go out there and get my ass shot, you tell everyone what a fool I was, and that I broke ten direct orders doing it. If it works, I'll make sure you get the credit for setting it up." Suddenly Copeland had looked a hundred years old, and it took Neil a second to realize why. It wasn't the FBI's reputation or getting credit he was worried about. It was Neil.

He couldn't think about that now. "So I walk down that path with the Bureau's best sniper ready to shoot whatever peeks out of a culvert," Neil said. "Does he know it might be a woman or a child?"

"He knows. And Sheridan, if Bankes actually does give you the woman and kid, don't be a hero and sit down in their place. Get the hell out of there with them. We'll move in and cover you as soon as the hostages are out."

Neil was silent. Harrison, Standlin, and Brohaugh were silent, too. Everyone knew that wasn't going to happen. Bankes *had* chosen this location carefully. There was no way for him to escape from the park, and there hadn't been since ten minutes after Bankes had named it.

That's why they knew Bankes wasn't here.

"We could be wrong, Sheridan," said Copeland. "Bankes may have decided to call it quits. He might be sitting in that culvert waiting to take you with him when he goes."

"We aren't wrong," Neil said. "Bankes isn't there. The best we can hope for is that he actually did leave the woman and her kid there. Alive."

But no one really expected it. They expected bodies. Dolls.

Copeland's handset burped and he answered, then buzzed the snipers. "Time to go."

Neil walked toward the culvert as casually as a man could with his heart drumming like a fist. Nothing moved around him. There wasn't anything to move. ChemLawn grass, a sky going slowly from blue to pink, the soft chatter of birds. A pretty evening if you weren't walking into a grave site. Or a trap.

Fifty yards from the FBI's picnic tables, sixty. Still within range of the sniper, not yet in the range of the pistols Bankes had stolen from Hammond. A hundred yards out, Neil slowed his steps. He could see the entrance to the culvert now—a stone arch about three feet high, not quite that wide. When it rained, it emptied into a little pool around the arc, draining the park's playgrounds and kite-flying slopes. It had rained yesterday, not enough for any pools to gather, but enough that there'd be mud or spongy swamp. Enough that if a woman and her child were in there, they'd be wet, cold.

Neil took slow, deep breaths. *You could be wrong. Bankes might be sitting in that culvert waiting to take you with him when he goes.*

Neil knew he wasn't.

But someone was. Shit, something moved. He was closer now, thirty yards from the culvert. If Bankes was going to shoot him, he'd do it soon. If Bankes had left the woman and the child dead, there would be no noises creeping up from the culvert. If only a doll lay in the mud, there'd be no movement at the entrance.

"Sheridan." The voice of the sniper whispered in Neil's earpiece. The sniper had a scope that could make a beetle the size of a monster. "Step to the right. Something's moving in there."

Neil saw it, heard it, too. The sounds—sobs or whimpers, like a wounded animal. The movements—tremors, like fear rattling bones.

He shortened his steps, inched from the center of the path to the right to give the sniper clearance—God, don't let him be quick on the trigger if a hostage is alive—walking more slowly now. The new angle made the sun a gold disk in Neil's eyes, glowing behind the culvert and darkening his view to silhouettes.

Neil slid a hand into his pocket, handling the .22. It felt like a toy compared to the 10 mm he'd used with the FBI, or the .45 he carried these days. With hands the size of bear paws, Neil had always liked the bigger guns. Then again, in a bind, a .22 could make a hole, too.

He considered this a bind.

The sniper was in his ear: "A little more, Sheridan; move right." The sun flared behind the culvert as Neil moved closer, closer, and he thought about the sniper watching through a scope that didn't matter, and the photojournalists straining to get a shot they could put on the news, and the possibility that the sounds he was hearing were the sniffles of a little girl who might be hurting. And he thought of Beth and Abby needing him, and Bankes maybe surprising him, sitting in there with a gun at someone's temple, and he remembered the G.I. Joe and wondered why, if Bankes *was* there, he hadn't shot Neil yet. And then Neil came closer to the edge of the culvert, the whimpers still coming, and he palmed the .22 and took a deep breath, stepped out fast and aimed directly into the culvert, and in the last second he saw the other gun and thought, *Oh, Jesus, no.*

Chapter 47

Time to go. Chevy didn't know precisely how long the attention span of a six-year-old was, but Abby had been outside with Evan Foster when Chevy drove by in Samantha's mom's Monte Carlo. That was about a half hour ago now, and he didn't want to take the chance that Abby would go back inside while he was getting in place. As long as she was out beyond the gallery, he wouldn't have to go as close to the house as he'd been prepared to.

Besides, the excitement at Ellis Park ought to be ending soon. He hadn't heard anything on the news yet, but wanted to be well on his way out of town before Neil Sheridan got his just reward.

"Stop there," he told Samantha, and she did. Her cheeks were chafed with tears, her wrist rubbed red where Heinz had pulled at his leash as he scented familiar territory. Chevy smiled, remembering a show he'd once done that had a dog in the cast. "Dogs and kids," the director had said. "They're a lot more trustworthy than adult actors. They never miss a cue."

He walked through the trees to where he could just see Abby peering into the sky, then scouted the area until he saw two men with yellow block letters across the backs of their jackets: FBI. Fine. There might be a few more surrounding the rest of the property, but these two were patrolling exactly the part of Foster's perimeter Chevy needed them to patrol, about fifty yards apart. They were both looking into the sky just now, watching Abby's kite.

Chevy motioned for Samantha to come in front of him. Behind her, he withdrew the gun, the silencer snagging on his pocket lining for a second.

"That's it! You got it!" Abby's tiny voice sailed across the hill, and Heinz whimpered. Chevy heard the distant sound of Evan Foster laughing, watched him struggle with the string to the kite. A minute later it took a nose-dive straight to the ground. Abby moaned and ran to help pick it up.

Chevy found the perfect position, pushing Samantha along silently in front of him. When he had the right view, he stopped and shoved her to her knees. Terror stiffened her spine, but too late. He pressed his hand over her mouth, held her rigid, and put the gun to her temple.

The nearest FBI agent was busy chuckling at the kite fiasco. The other one called to him from across the field.

"You think you could do any better, asshole?"

"I could keep it up better than Foster just did," he called back, then muttered a bunch of stupid he-man insults under his breath. "Rich, spoiled jerk. Betcha he can't keep up much of anything ..."

He ground a cigarette beneath his heel and strolled a little closer to Chevy.

Move away, bastard; move away. Chevy held his breath.

His arm tightened on Samantha and he whispered in her ear: "Make a sound and I'll shoot you."

She believed him. The guard meandered away, Heinz getting antsy now, and Chevy tossed down a wiener to shut him up. He waited for the agent to move farther out and worked his way to the edge of the trees, keeping the gun against Samantha's head, the leash in hand.

No more time. It had to be now.

"Freeze!" Neil said.

He straight-armed the .22. A Glock 380 pointed back at him, a fractured, feminine voice just behind it.

"Stay b-back."

Neil blinked. It was a woman, for Christ's sake, sounding weak and terrified, the gun trembling in her hands. Neil's .22 stared back at her, both guns ready to fire from only twenty feet apart. "I'm not going to hurt you, honey. Put the gun down."

"Stay back," she said again. She was young, mid-twenties; her left cheek was gashed, an ugly mound of purple flesh and crusted blood swelling up around it. A doll sat on her lap. "I'll sh-shoot you," she stammered. "Stay back."

"Listen to me," Neil said. Get her to trust him, keep her calm. Stupid thought, given that she and her daughter had been the hostages of a madman all afternoon and Neil had a pistol—even a small one—aimed between her eyes. "I'm here to help you. I talked to you earlier on the phone."

The woman shook her head. Convulsive little

movements that told Neil she was on the narrow edge of hysteria.

"Lower the gun and I'll take you home."

"H-he has my d-d-daughter. He has Samantha." Tears poured over her cheeks. "I h-have to kill you."

What? "Listen to m—"

"I-I have to kill you, and then he'll let her go. He said that. I'm s-s-sorry—"

"Stop. Listen to me." Calm was almost impossible. Bankes had set the woman up as Neil's assassin. The *bastard*. "You don't have to kill me. Bankes won't know, and I'll help you get your daughter back, I promi—"

"H-he'll know. He said he'd kill her." She was crying but kept the gun pointed at Neil. "I have to kill you. He needs to see it on TV, and then he'll let Samantha go."

"He's lying; he's just using you. I can get your little girl back." His mind raced, a speed-of-light assessment: thirty law enforcement officers with high-powered artillery, a wide-open field, asshole photographers all waiting for a story. An idea wiggled into his brain and he lowered his gun, spreading his hands in surrender. "Listen to me," he said to the woman, hoping she was sane enough to hear him. "Don't shoot me, but listen ..."

Beth kicked the covers off the bed. She couldn't sleep, though she knew Juan thought she'd conked out. She couldn't even doze successfully. She couldn't do anything but lie there and wonder where Neil was, what he was doing. Where Bankes was.

She got up, padded barefoot to the window and looked outside. To her left, she had a view of Abby and Evan, a couple of FBI agents standing like sentries in the field. A dragon-shaped kite tumbled through the air, out of control. Beth smiled. They weren't having much luck with the kite, but Abby was having fun. That seemed more important than anything right now.

She started toward the door but stopped as she laid her hand on the knob. The television was going on the other side. Juan must have turned it on. The voice of the broadcaster was urgent, relaying some sort of breaking news. *"FBI ... Ellis Park ... the Chevy Bankes hunt ..."* Beth craned her ears. *"A G.I. Joe, reportedly damaged by a bullet to the chest ..."*

She stepped back, stricken. G.I. Joe? Damn Neil for not telling her. For telling her to go and take a nap, play with Abby, and just leave everything to him.

She tiptoed back to the bed, switched on the six-inch black-and-white television that sat on the nightstand. She turned the sound all the way off so Juan wouldn't hear, then fiddled with the channels until she saw something that looked like news. She only had to pass one station— everyone was starting to report on it. She stopped at Channel 2 and turned up the sound just enough to hear.

"... at Ellis Park where suspected serial killer Chevy Bankes is allegedly holding a mother and her daughter host—What's that?" The anchorwoman paused, listening to something in her earpiece, then continued her report. *"We're now learning that someone is going to meet with Chevy Bankes ..."*

Beth nudged the volume up a notch.

"We have Chuck Strommen at Ellis Park. Chuck, can you tell us what's going on?"

A male voice came on, the owner of the voice relegated

to a tiny square in the upper right corner of the screen. *"Well, Melissa, all we know now is that Corey Dunwoody, a freelance photographer, earlier scuffled with the FBI about shooting footage here at the park, but somehow he has now managed to get in position to film. I remind viewers that we are showing this footage live ..."*

Beth held her breath. Neil, his shirt hanging open, walked across the grass. What the *hell* was he doing?

"Channel Two News has learned that the man allegedly going to confront Bankes is thirty-eight-year-old Neil Sheridan, and is apparently operating without the consent of the FBI. Viewers may recall that Sheridan is the former FBI agent who has been on the periphery of this case from the beginning. A few days ago, he emerged as a quote, unquote 'consultant,' and was cited by some as the leak of critical information ..."

Beth watched in horror. Confronting Bankes? Without the FBI behind him? Damn him, damn him, damn him.

"... and we wouldn't be seeing any of this if the FBI had its way. As you can see from tape shot earlier ..."

The little square in the corner of the screen showed video of a reporter being pushed back from the scene, FBI agents confiscating his cameras amid shouting and shoving. The words *Taped Earlier* appeared inside the square, while on the larger portion of the screen the word *Live* flashed on as Neil continued to walk slowly down a path.

Beth rubbed her palms over her eyes and watched, trying to focus, trying to tune out the commentary, but at the same time afraid she would miss something if she did. Neil was walking into a shallow valley, hands empty, shirt open, walking without the casual grace his stride usually sported. Steady but tense, stiff.

Until something made him slow his steps. He hesitated, moved to the right, then pulled a gun from his pocket and aimed it into the culvert.

The camera zoomed in, and Beth's heart stopped. Another gun pointed back at him.

Beth couldn't breathe. Neil stood poised to shoot or be shot, the announcer's voice-over like a little boy recounting an exciting movie. Neil seemed to say something to the person holding the gun—it was a woman—then his body went tight and Beth wanted to scream, *Get away, get away!* Yet even as she thought it, he lowered his gun and spread out his hands. Beth watched in horror, praying for the other gun to come down as well, but it didn't. It flashed, and Neil dropped to the ground.

Now.

Heinz barked right on command. Chevy turned him loose.

Abby saw him, squealed with glee, and ran toward Heinz. Gape-mouthed, Evan jogged after her, the kite darting wildly in the air like a balloon with a hole in it, the string pulling at his hands. The guards flinched with their weapons, then watched as Heinz and Abby met in a joyful reunion.

Chevy whistled.

Twice. He had to whistle twice, but then Heinz ran back to him in the trees. Abby followed.

Good dog ...

Chapter 48

Shock.

Anguish.

Beth sat on the edge of the bed, frozen.

"*Melissa*," said the reporter on the scene, and his voice was higher now, his words coming fast. "*Sheridan is down, Sheridan is down! Emergency personnel are now flooding the scene . . .*"

Oh, God. Neil.

It was like a movie-of-the-week. The images were choppy and fast, zooming in and out, trying to get close enough to provide details but also trying to catch the dramatic influx of people from all areas of the park. In one of the tighter shots, Beth caught a glimpse of Neil on the ground—blood on his chest, then the camera panned out to show running rivers of emergency personnel flowing down the slopes to the culvert. They closed in around him until she couldn't see anymore—had he been breathing?—then a wall of people knelt around him, frantic, shouting at one another, but all the viewers could hear was the continuous, staccato descant of the reporter. The camera swept out to show agents with rifles, ambulances, a chopper settling lightly on a nearby rise, and everyone seemed to be running, running ... Then the shot swept to the culvert, where something was happening, someone coming out, wrapped in so many FBI agents it was hard to see.

"It looks like a woman, Melissa," said Chuck's voice. "Perhaps this is the woman who was held by Chevy Bankes. We can't really be sure of anything at this point, but there doesn't appear to be a child. Melissa, it doesn't look as if Chevy Bankes is anywhere near, and just as soon as we can figure out what is happening, we'll get it to you."

Beth sat horrified, numb. Neil. God, don't let him die.

Anger flooded in. At Neil, for shutting her out; at this woman, this stranger who had tried to take his life. At Bankes, who was sitting somewhere watching, maybe holding this woman's child, laughing at what he had wrought.

She thought he had caused her pain seven years ago. It was nothing compared to this.

Beth didn't know how much time passed as she watched the television reporters try to sort it out. She could hear the living room television, too, and someone else coming in to talk to Juan, speaking in hushed tones. The anchors started repeating themselves, showing the same loops over and over again, searching for things to report, until the chopper had flown away and the anchorwoman at the studio, rehashing things for the hundredth time, stopped, looked at a little piece of paper in her hand, and spoke to the camera.

"We have just received word that former federal agent Neil Sheridan, who went down into the culvert apparently to negotiate with suspected serial killer Chevy Bankes, has died. A spokesman for Georgetown University Medical Center reports that he was dead on arrival, from a bullet wound to the chest."

Chapter 49

Chevy listened as Beth's cell phone rang. Three times. Damn her, the waiting pissed him off. She should have picked up on the first ring, should have known he'd be calling. When the ringing finally did stop, there was no voice, only silence.

"Come with me, Beth," Chevy said into the phone. He felt like howling to the moon. Everything had played out so perfectly. *Not much longer, now, Jenny.* "Come with me and get your daughter."

"Beth isn't here. Talk to me instead."

Chevy froze. It was a man's voice, Latino accent. Bodyguard, no doubt. A fucking bodyguard was answering her phone. Rage shook him to the bone. "I want to talk to Beth."

"Talk to me, *amigo.*"

Chevy waited, gaining control. "Fine. You give her the message then."

"What message?"

"She should come to me if she wants her daughter alive."

"Where? Where are you? What did you do with Beth's little girl?"

Federal agents. No finesse, no subtlety. This one sounded strained. Obviously, someone had already reported to him that Abby was gone, from right under their noses. Evan Foster and the remaining two guards had all started running as Abby followed Heinz back into the woods when Chevy whistled, then they had all backed off when they saw Samantha run out wearing Abby's sweater and holding Heinz on a leash. The switch had distracted them for only a moment before they realized she wasn't Abby Denison, but it was long enough for Chevy to haul Abby back through the trees to the neighborhood where he'd parked the Monte Carlo.

"Why would I tell you where I am?" Chevy asked, then he couldn't help but gloat: "Did you like the way I handled your buddy Sheridan? I only got to hear about his demise on the radio, but I'm sure I'll catch it on *Nightline* later."

"How will Beth know where to meet you?"

Chevy sighed, setting the Monte Carlo's cruise control at an innocent sixty-one miles per hour. "Show her the doll. She'll figure it out."

"Wait. What if ... what if she can't? She's not acting right. She's messed up, you know?"

Again, Chevy laughed. "The doll will snap her back."

"She can't look at any more dolls. She's finally cracked up. *Loco.* Shrinks and everything. Tell *me*."

"Show her the doll. Tell her to remember our time together."

The doll in the culvert was a Benoit that Anne Chaney

370

had once had: dark hair, dark eyes, and ... mutilated. She was supposed to be part of a mother–daughter pair, but in her hands she clutched the bar of a baby carriage— empty.

"Sheridan, take this," Copeland said, handing him a fresh shirt. Neil's had red dye all over it. "You've gotta pull yourself together, son. Stop looking at that damned doll and carriage."

Neil forced himself to look up. They'd commandeered a waiting room at the hospital where he'd been taken by chopper. The woman from the culvert, Rebecca Alexander, was down the hall, getting her cheek stitched up. She'd been a trouper. As soon as Neil convinced her to put the gun down, they'd come up with a plan to reenact the whole thing, exactly the way Bankes wanted it to happen. This time, they did it on camera. Corey Dunwoody, the photographer who had scuffled with O'Ryan, was called back in. He videotaped the whole thing over the loud and bogus objections of the FBI. He'd relished the idea of shooting something ostensibly forbidden, and when it was over, dangled the tape like a solid-gold carrot to the TV station that had fired him.

Neil was stripping off the ruined shirt when his phone rang. Suarez.

"It's Abby. *Dios.* He got Abby!"

"What? No." The world crumbled. "Ah, God ..."

"What is it?" Copeland asked. "Is that Bankes?"

Neil tried to control the frantic drumming in his chest, ignoring Copeland as he listened to Suarez. By the time Suarez finished talking, Neil was in shock. The same cold, physical shock he'd experienced when they'd told him Mackenzie was dead.

"Sheridan, damn it, talk to me." Copeland yanked the phone from his hand. "Who was that?"

"Suarez," Neil answered in a fog. He wasn't sure his voice could even be heard over his heartbeat. "Bankes got Abby."

The room went still. Copeland sank to a chair. "Oh, Christ."

Neil turned to Brohaugh. "Bankes just called Beth's cell and Suarez answered—"

"Okay, I'm on it," Brohaugh said, punching keys in a rush. The rest of the room held its breath. "Trace is coming. Hold on, I'll get the sound."

"Jesus," Harrison said. "What did Bankes say?"

Neil cleared his throat. Stay sane. Stay in control. Copeland could still throw him off the case. "Bankes has Abby. He took her from the yard at Foster's and wants Beth to come meet him."

Copeland ran a hand over his head. "Get it in the APB that when they find that car, there's a little girl in it."

"At least we know what car he's driving now," Harrison said. "Rebecca Alexander's burgundy Monte Carlo. Got a chance this time."

A chance, but not a big one. It was getting dark. And they'd be two minutes behind Bankes.

And Abby. Bankes had Abby.

Neil grabbed fistfuls of his own hair, then pounded both hands on the wall. "Fuck!"

No one else said a word; that one seemed to sum it up. When he finally caught his breath again, he said, "I have

372

to go to Beth. She's asleep. Suarez hasn't told her yet about Abby." He peeled away the broken blood capsule taped to his chest. His fingers were still stained red where he'd clutched it when Rebecca Alexander fired blanks at him.

Standlin walked in while he slid into the fresh shirt. She'd been talking to the Alexanders.

"Is she telling the truth?" Copeland asked her.

"Absolutely," Standlin said. "Rebecca Alexander is cool as a cucumber. Her husband's the one falling apart now." She stopped and looked around the room, frowning. "What the hell is going on here?"

Copeland spoke softly—words he didn't want to say. "Bankes just picked up Denison's little girl."

Standlin gaped at Neil. "Oh, no. Oh, God, Sheridan. I'm sorry."

Brohaugh said, "Here's the audio of the call."

They all closed in, listening to the call that had changed everything. Bankes giving Suarez a message, Suarez sounding stricken—he'd only heard about Abby's abduction a moment earlier—but doing his best to stretch it out, get something. Bankes too smart for that.

It was the doll, Bankes said. *Show her the doll. Tell her to remember our time together.*

Neil let out a stream of hot curses. He felt the eyes of every task force member drilling into him. "No," he said. "I can't show this doll to Beth. Once she finds out Abby is gone ... Seeing this doll will kill her."

"Sheridan," Copeland said, using his James Earl Jones voice, "this doll is a personal message to Denison. By the time the research unit considers all the angles, Denison

373

could have it all figured out. He's making it sound like it's something only she can know—"

"Research has had the thing for over an hour now!" Neil interrupted. "Let *them* figure it out."

Copeland blew out a sigh, consulted notes he'd taken when he talked to the lab. "A Benoit, a woman pushing a baby doll in a carriage, 1868. Except for the missing baby, it's the last of the dolls Larousse gave to Anne Chaney. They were in perfect condition at the time Anne Chaney was called in to appraise them. Now, this adult doll is ... damaged."

Neil scoffed. *Damaged.* "There's got to be something else."

Standlin was still catching up. "So Bankes has *two* little girls now? That doesn't make sense."

"No, no." Neil shook his head. God, Suarez had told him Abby was gone, and Neil had forgotten everything else. "Suarez said the first girl, Samantha Alexander, is okay. She turned up at Foster's when Abby disappeared. Bankes managed to pull a switch using the two girls and Beth's dog."

"Dog? The dog's back, too?"

"Bankes sent the Alexander girl running out with the dog. The guards fell for it, thinking it was Abby just long enough that Bankes got her outta there."

Standlin started for the door. "I have to go tell the Alexanders their daughter was found. She's safe? She's okay?"

Neil nodded. "Suarez has her at Foster's. He said she's shaken, but she's not hurt. Carol Foster has her decorating cookies."

"Oh, boy," Standlin said. "So we got one mother and one daughter back. That's some good news, anyway."

But it didn't feel that way to Neil.

"She hasn't budged, man," Suarez said when Neil arrived at the apartment with the doll. "I checked on her the first hour or so, then she burrowed down in the covers like she was cold, and told me to leave her alone. She was out, last I looked in." He paused. "Any word on Abby?"

Neil shook his head. "No."

"Hey, for what it's worth, man, you looked good on TV. I'd've believed it myself if I hadn't known it was a hoax. Bankes took it hook, line, and sinker. He talked to me about it on the phone. Gloating."

"Yeah, I heard."

"Okay. So you think Beth can figure out where he's taken Abby?"

"We're about to find out."

He set down the box in which he carried the *damaged* doll and pushed open Beth's bedroom door. The room was dark, silent. Too silent. The hairs on his arms stood up.

He went to the bed and sat down beside the mound of covers. Beth didn't move. He laid his hand gently on top of the quilt, on what should have been the curve of her hip.

And then he knew.

She was gone.

Chapter 50

Beth stood at a pay phone, shivering. Hurry, hurry. She fished coins from her purse. Thank God she'd had her purse in the bedroom, even if Suarez had her gun and her phone.

Suarez had answered her phone, and in an instant, Beth knew it was Bankes. A minute after the call, Suarez called Quantico and relayed what Bankes had told him: He had Abby.

It had taken every ounce of her strength not to sink to the floor and scream in hysteria when she heard it. Abby had run after Heinz, but the other little girl, Samantha, had come back.

Abby was gone. Dear God.

Neil. Her first impulse was to talk to him. But she couldn't. Neil was dead. Abby was gone.

Beth had forced herself to keep listening. The doll was the key, Bankes had said. Something about the doll would tell her where Bankes had taken Abby.

Nothing else mattered anymore. Neil was dead. Abby was with Bankes.

Do something.

Evan.

She didn't have enough change for long-distance calls, so she punched in her calling-card number, wondering how long until the FBI would discover it had been used. It didn't matter. They probably didn't know she was gone yet; Suarez thought she was sleeping. She had to figure out where Abby was, and the FBI obviously didn't plan to let her see the doll.

Damn them, Neil promised.

Neil is dead.

Don't think about it. Dial.

Waterford answered on the third ring, and Beth nearly sobbed with relief. "Kerry, it's Beth Denison. Please, I need your help."

Silence. She could feel his confusion.

"Please, Kerry. This isn't about your collection; it's not business. Please talk to me."

There was another instant of silence; Beth could picture Waterford frowning. His voice came over the line sounding hesitant. "The news is reporting that no one knows where you are right now, Beth."

Oh, no. They'd already found her missing. *Think.* "That's because the FBI took me in. I'm in protective custody."

"Protective custody?"

"Please, Kerry, I need to know about a pair of dolls." She racked her brain for what the insurance report had said. "An 1868 Benoit baby doll and mother doll. It was a pair owned by Stefan Larousse."

"Larousse?"

"I don't have time to explain now, but it's important. I'm not the expert you are, and there's something about those dolls Chevy Bankes wants me to figure out."

Pounding sounded in the background at Kerry's end of the line, two or three little dogs suddenly yapping.

"Hold on, Beth," Kerry said. "Someone's knocking at my door."

"Wait. Kerry!" Beth glanced at her watch. Charleston was in the same time zone. It was late for visitors. She tried to hear what was going on through the phone lines, hindered by the sounds of traffic and the night surrounding her.

"Beth." Kerry was back. He sounded nervous. "The FBI is here. Two agents. They want to talk to me."

Oh, God. "Did you tell them we were talking?"

"No, I just said I had to finish a phone call and came in the kitchen. God almighty, Beth. What's going on?"

"They're going to ask you the same things I'm asking, Kerry. Tell me first. There's something about these dolls I need to know, or about Margaret Chadburne. Kerry, we both met Chadburne at about the same time, in Dallas. Do you remember? Bankes has been stalking me as Margaret Chadburne since then."

"I know, I've been following the news." Kerry's voice dropped. "For God's sake, Beth. I don't know what to tell you. I talked to that fruitcake in Dallas, just like you did, but I've never seen her dolls. I've never seen the Larousse dolls. Chadburne came to my booth after you told her not to buy the repro. She actually threatened me, saying I'd been cheating people. Muttered that her mother got away with fooling everyone for years, and she didn't appreciate it. I told her to go screw herself. Then she ordered that same doll from me last week."

Beth tried to make sense of it. Bankes's mother got away with fooling everyone.

Don't you hear it? Mother's singing. She does that so she can't hear Jenny cry. Scream, bitch. Make Mother stop.

They talked around it for another minute, Kerry narrating what he recalled about Margaret Chadburne, and Beth trying to put it all together with Bankes's hatred for his mother, for what Beth was supposed to recognize in dolls she'd never seen. All the while, she scanned the street for police cars or gray sedans with government plates. *The news is reporting that no one knows where you are right now.* It sure hadn't taken them long to discover her missing.

"Beth?" Kerry's voice. "That's the only time I ever met the woman. Er, man, I guess. And I don't know anything about those particular dolls. No one's seen the Larousse dolls, except in photographs, for decades."

Beth's mind was spinning. Nothing. She had nothing to go on.

Kerry had gone silent, then his voice squeezed back within hearing. "Hey, Beth?"

"Yes?"

"Is it true what the news said about the condition of the mother doll they found?"

"I . . . uh . . . well, I'm not sure how much they're reporting."

"They said she was mutilated terribly, a hole drilled between her legs, and the baby doll was missing."

379

A wave of nausea almost buckled her knees. "Oh. Well, I guess that's true."

"God almighty. That's one sick bastard."

She hung up. Think. No, don't think about what Bankes did to the doll or what he might do to Abby. Just think about Bankes. And how she was supposed to find him.

She slipped back into the car, driving with caution. She took corners slowly, making sure her stops were complete enough that the car she'd taken from Foster's lurched gently backward before she accelerated again. She didn't know how long she could drive this car without being stopped. The old pillows-under-the-covers trick hadn't bought her much time, and soon they would figure out what car she was driving. But at least she was out. It had been easy once Juan left her alone: through the apartment's back door into an upstairs passageway she and Abby used to play in, down the far cargo elevator, and into the carriage house. She never had to set foot outside, and she knew where to find the keys for any car. Like most of Foster's employees, she had driven them lots of times.

Like Hannah.

She'd chosen a dark green Taurus—Evan's suggestion. Evan, whom she hadn't wanted to involve, but whose voice was choked with fear and regret after losing Abby, and who would do anything for Beth. For Abby.

She pulled up to a traffic light, and a city police cruiser eased beside her. She looked straight ahead, pretended to fiddle with the radio, and thought she could feel the officer's eyes drilling into her temple.

Relax. They probably don't know what car to look for yet. The only thing making her feel conspicuous was the fact that it was a cool night and she was driving in a sleeveless dress with no jacket and wearing panty hose with no shoes—her pumps and blazer had been in the living room of the apartment, where Suarez waited.

And, of course, there was the fact that she was about to drive directly into the hands of a wanted criminal. If she was right about where he was.

She *was* right. She knew it. *"This is just like home. It's Mother's land. Scream so Mother can hear you."*

She had to be right. He'd gone home, to Samson, to where Beth could make his mother stop singing.

Please, God, just let him leave Abby behind.

Alive.

Neil banged through the front door of the Fosters' house, prompting a cop on the porch and one just inside to go for their guns. When recognition dawned, they both looked as if they had seen a ghost.

"You're dead," said one of them under his breath.

"Not yet," Neil answered, "but you will be if you blow the story. Where's Evan Foster?"

The second guard frowned. "He and his aunt went upstairs an hour ago. Been watching the news."

Neil started toward the stairs. "Which way?"

"Up and right. There's a big sitting room up—"

Neil took the stairs two at a time, paused outside a wide set of double doors, and heard the television reporter expound on the details of Neil's death. Christ, it was probably national news by now. He'd better make sure someone called his mother, his sister. Even Mitch.

He took a deep breath, then burst through the doors to the sitting room. Evan Foster stood behind Carol's chair. In two seconds, Neil had his shoulders shoved hard up against the wall. "Where is she, you bastard?"

Evan stammered, "You're d-dead. They said y-you died."

Neil tightened his grip, the fingers of his right hand crumpling something that felt like cardboard in Evan's breast pocket. "Where is she?"

"I don't know what you're talking abo—"

Neil slammed him against the wall. "Tell me, you son of a bitch!"

Carol Foster grabbed his arm. "Mr. Sheridan, you have no right coming in here and—"

Neil shoved Evan into the wall again, saw his eyes roll back with pain. "Beth's missing, and you know where she is."

"N-no, no, I don't know where she went."

"Beth's missing?" Carol said at the same time. She had Heinz by the collar. The stupid mutt was wagging his tail. "What's going on?"

"Beth pretended to be sleeping, then left through the passageways from the carriage house," Neil explained, growling over his shoulder. "Your nephew here called the guards a half hour ago, to say he'd be going out. Said he'd take the green Taurus and didn't wanna be followed— wanted some private time with a lady friend after such a harrowing day, right? Five minutes later the green Taurus pulls out and no one follows it because they know it's Evan, but look at this, Evan's right here and Beth is gone. You wanna explain that?"

The question was punctuated by another small smash against the wall, something falling from Evan's pocket. Carol's pleas of don't-hurt-him fell on deaf ears. Evan's face scrunched with pain.

"I don't know where she went," he said weakly.

"You gotta do better than—"

"I swear, I don't know!" He was screaming now, and Neil snarled at the tears that squeezed from the corners of Evan's eyes. "She just said she had to go. She begged me to trust her and said she could find Abby. She said you were dead and the Feds weren't letting her help, that there was another doll and she could figure it out. She begged me, said she had to save Abby ..."

"So you let her go after a madman by herself?"

Evan pinned Neil with a feral glare. "She can't live like this, you stupid asshole! Just what do you think Beth's life will be worth if Abby dies and she could have stopped it—"

"She can't stop it!"

"She *thinks* she can!" Evan shot back. His voice dropped three notches, emotion filtering through. "She just wanted me to give her a little time to figure out where Bankes had taken Abby. You guys wouldn't even let her try. You wouldn't let her *try*. I gave her a gun. She said if I loved her at all—"

And that was all there was before Evan Foster broke down, crying like the lovesick bastard that he was, weeping for the wrong choice, the wrong emotions, the wrong woman.

"What kind of gun did you give her?"

"A Ruger 9 mm."

Neil breathed again—Beth would know how to use that one, at least. He let Evan's shirt spring free of his fists and rolled his shoulders. Glared at both of them. "Keep your mouths shut."

"Sheridan." Evan bent to pick up the card from the floor, and pulled two more from his pocket. He held them out to Neil. Orioles tickets. "When you find Beth and Abby ..."

Neil gave Foster a long look, then pocketed the tickets. He started for the door but turned back to Evan. "Beth's favorite color is yellow, by the way," Neil said. "And her biggest fear? It's what she's out there doing right now."

Chapter 51

Beth drove like a zombie, her cruise control set, the voice on the radio washing over her like an arctic, numbing breeze. *Former FBI agent Neil Sheridan, dead ... A six-year-old-girl now believed to be held ... The FBI scrambling ... Distraught mother charged with the murder of Sheridan ... Neil Sheridan, dead ... Six-year-old missing ...*

A nightmare. A dream. Perhaps she'd awaken later to the sounds of Abby giggling with Heinz, to the sensation of Neil holding her, moving deep inside her, and discover this was all an ugly fantasy. Perhaps it wasn't happening.

But it was. That woman had killed Neil. Chevy Bankes had Abby. Beth's imagination took a wild ride for a moment, to all the things Bankes might do to a child, to what he had possibly done to his little sister, then she reined it all in and focused on the running white dashes on the highway.

Keep driving. Don't think.

She looked at the dashboard clock: 10:08 p.m. Another hour, about, to Samson, Pennsylvania. Then she'd find

Bankes's house. Neil had drawn it all out for her once. It was adjacent to Mo Hammond's shooting range, couldn't be hard to locate in such a small town. Neil had explained it to her.

Thank God. Thank God he'd come into her life, for just a little while.

She blinked to clear the tears from her eyes. She didn't dare think about Neil right now, not when Abby was alive somewhere, needing her. She had to find her.

You're in over your head with this.

Neil's words floated through the haze. She smothered them. Bankes wanted *her*. Certainly he'd kill Abby if a string of FBI agents showed up at his mother's home instead of her.

Doing everything alone doesn't mean you're strong. It just means you're alone.

She wished Neil would shut up and half laughed at that. She hadn't listened to him when he was alive, yet now, his words drummed through her body with every beat of her heart.

You aren't alone anymore.

She'd believed him, finally, and cursed herself for it. It hadn't been so painful being alone when it was the only thing she knew. But now, having lived outside her bubble with Neil for only a few short days—and nights—she was floundering. Alone again, driving toward a destiny she couldn't bear to think about, without the man who had been her anchor.

There's more than one person in the world willing to help you, Beth.

Oh, God.

386

Beth swerved and stopped on the shoulder of the highway. She closed her eyes. Made a decision.

Oh, Abby, please. Don't let this be a mistake.

The tears were gone when Beth finally found a gas station. Grover's. It was a podunk little place in Pennsylvania's wooded hills just outside the town of Samson, at the corner of two country roads. She needed a phone.

To call Special Agent Copeland.

A single car was parked on the gravel drive, a dented old Ford LTD jammed onto the sidewalk at the side of the building. One employee, one car. She looked around. There were bathrooms on the outside, an ice machine, and a newspaper stand. But no phone.

She got out of the car, shivering. The temperature had fallen to fifty-eight degrees, said the radio, and it hit her like a north wind. She walked over the pebbles on the parking lot. Glass punched through the sole of her left foot, and she stepped to the right, trying to avoid any more of what must have been a shattered bottle. No luck; her right foot found more. Not so bad, though. She'd gone more lightly there.

She stepped onto the sidewalk, now in better light, one hand curling around the door handle to the store. The other rested lightly on her purse, which was strapped over her shoulder. Evan's gun was inside. She prayed she wouldn't need it now. She'd find a phone, tell Special Agent Copeland everything, and let the FBI handle it.

You're not alone anymore.

She opened the door and peered inside. The cashier's counter was just ten feet away, lit up, with an open bottle of Aquafina on the counter and a candy wrapper lying beside it. The cashier wasn't in sight.

Then Beth noticed two things at once. One, a dark red stain was splattered behind the counter, trailing down the wall in a gruesome smudge. And two, the candy wrapper was from a Reese's Cup.

Chapter 52

Run.

She did, but her body snapped backward. A scream tore from her chest even as she groped at the arm trying to close around her throat.

No, no. Don't grab my arm; use the heel of your hand.

But reason came too slowly. He grunted and stumbled back, yanking her with him. She lost her balance, taking them both down, her purse strap falling from her shoulder. She grabbed it. The gun, the gun . . .

It will be in your purse when you need it.

Bankes was on top of her, sneering. His weight felt like stone, her hip screaming with pain from when they'd fallen. She couldn't catch her breath. *Think.*

"Ah, Beth," he said, straddling her. "Just like old times."

No. Things were different now. She was strong. She was trained. She'd practiced for years. She knew all the techniques for self-defense.

She rammed her forehead into his nose.

"Ahhggh!" he groaned, rolling to the side. She shoved him off, clambering to her feet to get away. Run.

Stay with it; never believe your last hit was the final one. Otherwise, you're likely to get—

Fwp.

She felt the impact before the pain. Like someone had shoved her hard from behind. She struck the ground, gravel scraping at her arms and legs, and the pain seeped into her shoulder blade. Her right arm went limp.

First she heard a chuckle, then felt herself being hauled upright. His gun, smelling freshly fired, pushed into her throat.

"Hi, doll," he breathed, and Beth felt the blood leaking from her back. Warm and sticky, it soaked the back of her dress. She looked down. A dark spot formed over her right breast, too.

"I've been waiting for you, Beth, watching for you to drive by. In fact, I've been waiting seven years." He looked at the blood on her shoulder and grimaced. "You shouldn't have made me shoot you, Beth. I don't want you to die yet."

Beth blinked, trying to pull the world into focus. Think. You can't beat him physically right now, so *think*. Standlin's instructions came back in a flood. *Act scared, cry, gasp. Let him see you as weak.*

"Go to hell," she spat.

Bankes cursed, shoving her against the door of the gas station. Her cheek smashed into the glass. Pain exploded behind her eyes, blackness seeping in. She grasped for consciousness, but it was like a banner whipping in the wind just out of reach, and she couldn't quite get hold of it. For a second, she wanted to stop fighting and just sink beneath the pain, then she remembered why she couldn't.

"Abby," she mumbled against the glass.

Bankes's lips settled at her temple, her face pressed hard against the door, and Beth had to concentrate on not throwing up. "What did you say?"

"My daughter. Wh-what did you do with her?"

He laughed, that same self-satisfied ripple she'd heard on the phone and in her nightmares. "You mean *our* daughter?"

"No," Beth cried before she could think not to, and Bankes chuckled.

"I thought so. Don't worry. I don't want any claim to her. Just because we share the same blood doesn't mean anything. Blood is nothing. Blood is nothing."

He'd repeated himself, or was she just hearing double? She tried to make sense of it. *Blood is nothing.* Could he really mean that? And if so, then what was this all about?

Sccrrattch. The sound cleaved her senses, the unmistakable screech of duct tape ripping from a roll. She tried to move but couldn't. He yanked her arms behind her and pain shattered her shoulder, his knee drilling into the small of her back to hold her against the door. A sticky length of the tape grabbed her wrists. He bent, to bite the end of the tape, she thought, and she jerked back and kicked, screaming, but he was ready for it and yanked her head back. Tape seized her lips, plastering her hair over one cheek. For the space of two breaths, she couldn't breathe, the panic causing her to stupidly try to open her mouth and gasp for air.

She grabbed a deep breath through her nose, and he

shoved her into the store, dragging her through the aisles to a back room. Beth felt his hand against her hip as he dug into his pocket. He produced a key and slid it into a tiny slot on the wall. He gave it a crank.

The lights went out.

He pushed her through the store again, out the door. Dark. He'd killed the store's street sign with the key, killed all but a single work-light inside. It would be a long time before anyone found the dead clerk in a store that appeared to be closed. She almost admired his thoroughness.

But all thought vanished when he opened the trunk of the old LTD. She kicked and fought, with a surreal sort of awareness of the fact that it wasn't doing any good, that despite all the years of training, he was in control and she was losing blood, the ability to fight leaking out of her in slow motion. The earth fell from beneath her feet, her head hitting the inside of the trunk and legs tumbling in after. He slammed her into darkness. She kicked, the scents of mold and mildew clogging the back of her nose, and as the car's tires ground over broken glass and stones, she sank into darkness, thinking all over again, *You did everything wrong.*

Chapter 53

They found the site Peggy Bankes might have been referring to in her codicil, a place along the river," Copeland
announced. Ten-thirty at night. Neil looked at his watch
again. Beth had taken the Taurus more than two hours
ago. "They're finding bodies there—bones, rather. It looks
like two women and a baby. Coroner says they've been
there eight or ten years."

"Dear God," Standlin breathed. "Paige Wheeler and
Nina Ellstrom."

"Probably. Except the baby. It's been there for more like
eighteen or twenty years."

"Jenny," Neil said.

"His mother's codicil willed him *Jenny*?" Brohaugh
asked, flabbergasted. "He dug up *Jenny*?"

"Could be," Standlin said. "We know he got *something*
from that location the night he received the codicil."

The same night he killed Gloria Michaels. Neil couldn't
believe it.

"Maybe," Copeland acknowledged and didn't seem to

want to say the rest. He swallowed. "The baby's skull is missing."

Silence. No one knew what to say to that.

Neil shook his head. At this moment, he couldn't care about Peggy Bankes's codicil or victims who had been dead for years or even baby bones. All he could think about was finding Bankes. Finding Beth and Abby.

He closed his eyes, thoughts wriggling in his mind like maggots. Chevy had loved Jenny, so said Sheriff Goodwin. Mother sang so she couldn't hear Jenny cry, so said Chevy, when attacking Beth. And more ... *This is just like home ... Mother's land ... Scream so Mother will stop.*

Jesus. That school counselor, Iris Rhodes, had been right to try to get Jenny away from that crazy place. If only someone had listened to her, maybe they wouldn't be digging up baby bones in the backyard now—

Neil froze. "He's going home," he said, more to himself than to the room.

Copeland looked at him. "What?"

"His mother's land. He wants to kill Beth there."

"How the hell do you know that, Sheridan? You got something the rest of us don't know?"

Yes. His hand fisted, the urge to tell all nearly over-whelming. "Think about it," he said, noticing Standlin's eyes on him. "Every woman, even Gloria Michaels, was killed or left in a forest, near a body of water. The place he found Jenny became his burial ground, maybe even his killing ground for the next two after Gloria. He's recreated that setting with almost every woman."

"But even if you're right," Copeland said, "there's no way he could be at that site now. It's swarming with cops and Feds. They put up floodlights, have orders to dig until it's clean."

"So he'll have to find another place to do Denison, or a place just like it," Brohaugh said.

"Find another wooded place along the Susquehanna River, remote enough to get away with killing someone in the middle of the night ...?" Harrison's big shoulders slumped. "There must be hundreds of miles like that."

"But he won't go far. He wants his mother to hear," Neil said.

Copeland was angry. "Sheridan, if you know something we don't know, spit it out."

Neil swallowed, shooting a silent plea to Standlin. *Trust me.*

"I think he's right," she said after a minute. "That might be where he is."

"But would Denison know that? She's at large, too," Brohaugh said logically, "presumably trying to meet him."

Neil frowned, trying to think. He recalled drawing out a map on a napkin for Beth: Bankes's land, Hammond's hunting grounds, the gun store ... "She might go to Samson. If she thinks that's where Bankes took Abby." An idea popped to the surface. "Could we still have a scent of Bankes from when he camped out in Beth's garage?"

"For dogs?" Copeland asked. "I don't know. But even if they can't track Bankes, they could track Denison or the little girl."

"How long to get there by chopper?" Neil asked.

"You could be there in forty minutes," Brohaugh answered. "But what if that's not where they are? We've got nothing but your hunch, Sheridan, and we're putting all our eggs in that one basket—"

"Agent Copeland." A secretary popped her head in the door. "The RA in Samson just called. They just found the car Denison was driving." Neil heart stopped. "It's at a little gas-station store four miles from Bankes's home."

"Grover's," Neil said.

"Right. One of the local cops checked the store because its lights were all out, and usually it's open all night. Clerk is shot dead, clerk's '85 Ford LTD is gone, Denison's—or rather, Foster's—Taurus is parked there."

"Jesus," Neil said, reeling.

Brohaugh slumped. "All right. So it's the right basket for our eggs."

"Jesus, Jesus, Jesus."

"Shut up," Copeland barked. "Is there surveillance tape from the store?"

"They're feeding it through right now. You should be able to access it in a minute," the woman said to Brohaugh. "But there's one more thing. Rebecca Alexander's Monte Carlo was there, too, parked inside the car wash where no one could see it."

"Mother of God," whispered Harrison. "He *is* going home."

Copeland snapped his fingers. "All right. Get those dogs; get the chopper." To the secretary: "Call the Samson RA and give him my private line. Tell him to call me directly from now on."

"Denison left Foster's two and a half hours ago," Standlin said.

"We'll see the time on the video," Brohaugh said. "Here it comes."

They all gathered behind Brohaugh, watching the gas station's security tape. Nothing happened on it at first and Brohaugh fast-forwarded the images, then Bankes entered the store and Brohaugh slowed the speed to normal. Everything happened in choppy black-and-white silence. The clerk went down—a single bullet from a handgun a foot away, right through the young man's nose, splat, and into the wall behind him. Bankes watched him slide to the floor, grabbed a Reese's Cup and ripped it open, then went around the counter and bent over the body for a second. He rose and went to the back of the store, tossing something small in his hand. The lights in the store flicked off and on once, then he left through the front door and there was nothing else for—Neil watched the numbers go by as Brohaugh fast-forwarded—five minutes, ten, twenty, thirty-five. Then the front door opened, and a woman's head poked in.

Beth.

And she must have seen something because suddenly she was gone again, and there was a flurry of activity outside the door. A minute later the camera caught the smudge of her face pressed into the glass and Bankes, a few inches taller, manhandling her from behind. Terror clawed at Neil. It wasn't happening in real time, he reminded himself; it had already occurred. He couldn't stop it; it was over. Just watch, and *think*. Panic coursed through his veins; he was unable to tell what Bankes was doing to her. The details were obscured by stickers on the glass door and the glare from outside lights through the

397

camera lens, until Bankes walked Beth back through the store and into the back. Dragging her, like she was hurt. Her mouth was swathed in duct tape, a dark stain above one breast, her hands behind her back.

And then the picture went dark. The camera kept running, but there were only shadows moving through the store. The door opened and closed. The shadows vanished.

A living, breathing documentary of something that had happened an hour ago, a hundred and ten miles away. Neil wasn't sure his heart was still beating.

The secretary returned when the recording ended, saying fresh blood had been found on shards of glass in the parking lot. "And," she added, careful not to look at Neil, "Denison's purse was found at the gas station. Evan Foster's Ruger is inside."

Chapter 54

It was chilly even to Chevy, and he was wearing a suede jacket. Beth shivered violently. Her shoulders hunched against the air, her dress torn and crusted with blood. Her wrists were bound at her back, her panty hose running in shreds up her legs, and her bare feet leaving dark smudges of blood on the ground. She looked alarmingly fragile. For a minute he worried she wouldn't last too long. He didn't dare push her too far, too fast. He needed her alert and aware. *Feeling*.

They were almost there now. The narrow column of light from his flashlight seemed to dissolve within ten feet in the damp underbrush, the inky night closing in around them. A little after one in the morning now and he wished they could have started sooner, but he'd had no choice but to take the time to deal with Abby, then hide the LTD he'd stolen from the gas station attendant.

Beth dragged silently through the forest. He'd stripped the tape from her mouth after they got far enough she couldn't be heard no matter how loudly she screamed.

Still, she hadn't given him a single sound, even though there was a hole in her shoulder, her feet were cut, and he thought he'd cracked at least one of her ribs in their scuffle at the gas station. Beth just gritted her teeth and kept silent, no matter what.

Go ahead, he thought wryly, tough it out a little while longer. Then the fun would begin. And he had a bag full of blank tapes.

Beth stumbled and he grabbed her arm. She grunted between her teeth. The sound surprised him, resonating in his crotch.

"Not as strong as you used to be, are you?" he said, chuckling. "As I recall, a little blood and a steady pounding between your legs didn't give me much to listen to the first time around. It wasn't a fair encounter, though. I hadn't had a chance to wear you down first. This time I know you're ready."

"Where's Abby?"

"You're a broken record."

She stopped and spoke through chattering teeth. "Let her go, and I swear I'll do anything you want. Please. Just don't hurt my daughter."

Tears gathered in her eyes, and they looked legitimate, not put on because she thought that's what he wanted her to do. He hadn't thought Beth Denison capable of genuine emotion.

But it wasn't genuine. He'd almost forgotten: She was as good as Mother.

He sneered at her. "You think you have everyone fooled, but not me. How does it feel to know that when you spoke to Margaret Chadburne on the phone it was really me? To know I had lunch with Hannah Blake and that I spoke to your daughter on the phone? How did you like it when you finally figured out the dolls?" He leaned closer. "*You're* the real fake. You hurt Jenny, you lie about Abby's father, then you plant a bunch of flowers and smile. You're just like Mother."

"I n-never hurt Jenny. I never even saw her. You're the one who hurt your baby sister. You killed her."

"*I didn't do anything to Jenny! Mother hated the baby, Sheriff ...*"

"*Now, son, why would you say that?*"

"*Because Grandpa gave her bad blood. He's the reason Jenny's so weak. She has bad blood.*"

Rage seized him by the throat and he whirled, kicking Beth in the belly. She hit the ground like a sack of flour. "You claim you never hurt Jenny," he seethed. "You're a lying cunt, just like Mother. For years she played in Grandpa's bed, pretending she hated it. But did she ever do anything to stop it?"

Beth still lay perfectly still and, for a moment, Chevy panicked. She'd lost a lot of blood, and here he was, almost losing control. If he wasn't careful, he'd lose her before he even got her going.

Mother started humming.

Shut the fuck up.

He grabbed Beth by an arm and yanked her up. "Keep walking."

One twenty-five in the morning. Neil stalked the gas station's parking lot, his gut lurching at the sight of bloody glass. Harrison punched off his cell phone and stepped over to him.

"That was the lab," he said quietly. "Blood here is O-negative. Matches Denison's."

Neil wondered why that news hit so hard. He'd expected the blood to be Beth's. She'd taken off her shoes in the living room of the apartment, she couldn't get them with Suarez right there. She didn't have a coat, either, and the overnight temperature had dipped into the fifties. Illogically, the idea of Beth being cold was as cruel as the dozens of other horrific images Neil had conjured up on the way here. The images preyed on his brain, stalking him like a predator he couldn't see or touch or get his hands on.

He walked toward Harrison, who was watching the crime scene unit take apart Alexander's car. *Keep moving, work. Don't feel.* God knows, he'd done that for nine years. Why couldn't he manage it now?

Harrison met him halfway across the parking lot. "They dusted the Monte Carlo, and they're about to open the trunk, see if any trace evidence can be collected."

"I can't believe he drove Alexander's car all the way up here without being noticed. There's been an APB out on that Monte Carlo since we got Rebecca Alexander out of that park."

"But he was already on his way by then. Driving in the dark, on back roads . . ."

A chopper sliced through the air overhead, and they waited until the noise had faded before going on. If Bankes *was* deep in the woods, a chopper would have a hard time spotting him. Even though the forest wasn't in full foliage yet, the trees were dense and it was dark. The better bet was the canine team. Neil had given them

Abby's T-ball hat with the embroidered ladybug, and Beth's T-shirt with Pooh and the honeypot. Dog handlers hadn't thought there was any hope of getting a scent of Bankes from the cabinet in Beth's garage, particularly after the crime scene unit had gone over it with chemicals and cleansers. But if Bankes was actually *with* Abby or Beth ...

A local deputy with a jack worked at the Monte Carlo's trunk, freeing it suddenly with a crunching sound. He wrenched his fingers under the edge and pried it open.

"Holy God!" he said, leaping back.

Neil rushed forward. The deputy was still catching his breath, and two others had stepped close to see. Neil barged through, shoved aside a uniform, and peered down into the cavern of the car's trunk.

They'd found Abby.

Chapter 55

Bankes circled like a shark. Beth stood slightly bent, dizzy and half-numb, her sleeveless dress little more protection from the elements than a slip. Every breath was a knife in her ribs. The hole in her right shoulder had soaked the back of her clothes, and her wrists were still bound together. Beth wiggled her fingers against her hips and thought maybe they'd moved slightly, but she wasn't sure. The blood on her hands felt like gelatin.

Bankes smiled, his gym bag hanging over his shoulder and the gun pointing in her direction as he walked around her. A lantern sat on the ground about five feet away; another one shed sickly light from somewhere behind her.

"Do you like it?" he asked, indicating a small clearing in the woods. "I chose this spot just for you."

"Where's Abby?"

"Who? Oh, yes. Abby. Why, telling you that would be rather like sharing the end of a story ahead of time, wouldn't it?"

Beth closed her eyes on a prayer: *God, please don't let me have walked all this way into the woods only to find Abby isn't here.*

"You didn't answer my question. How do you like my

stage? I wish you could have seen it in the daylight. The lanterns hardly do it justice."

Beth forced her eyes open, cataloging the details of the setting Bankes had chosen, even as she tried to focus on breathing. She could hear the Susquehanna lolling not too far away, and smelled fresh foliage and pine straw. Otherwise, there seemed nothing unique about this particular spot in the forest, save for a wooden platform some distance behind Bankes. It was built between two trees, ten or twelve feet up. Steep stairs climbed up one side, like a ship's ladder, and benches had been built three-quarters of the way around it. A deer stand, Beth thought. She'd heard of them before but never seen one.

The Hunter. Apparently, women *were* in season when Chevy Bankes went hunting.

And children?

"Where's Abby?" Beth asked. "Did you kill her the way you killed Jenny?"

"I told you. I didn't hurt Jenny."

"And I told you, I don't believe you."

Smack.

Beth's head snapped to the side; she gritted her teeth. *Cry, be weak. Let him jerk you around*, said Standlin. *Don't make a sound unless it's to say, "Go to hell, you bastard,"* said Neil. She closed her eyes, perversely wanting to serve Neil's memory by doing things right this time.

"Go," Bankes said, jerking his chin toward the deer stand. "I want you up there."

Beth spit at him.

The gun in his hand sailed toward her cheek. She ducked, but her reflexes were dull and it caught the side

405

of her head. She reeled with the impact, and a second later, Bankes was beside her on the ground, his voice and pistol both digging into the gash it had just made on her temple. "You want to hear from your daughter again, don't you?" Beth closed her eyes but didn't make a sound. "Then get in the deer stand."

He pushed her up the rungs, his body at her back and the gun barely lifting from her as they moved. Beth slumped into a corner on the floor. Even in the dim light, she could see that the platform seemed to have been prepared for her arrival. Leaves and other debris had been brushed off, revealing patches of moist, darkened wood that had been eaten away by insects for years, holding imprints of pinecones like ancient fossils.

Bankes opened his gym bag and pulled out an old cassette tape player. One by one, he set tapes out in a row. Beth could make out the labels on some of them: *Paige 3, Paige 4, Paige 5, Nina 1, Nina 2, Anne 1, Lila 1, 2 ...*

Abby's head lolled to the side as Neil cradled her in his arms. His heart was an aching stone. A flock of agents surrounded him, all looking as if they'd seen a ghost.

"Ambulance is coming," Harrison said. "ETA three minutes."

Neil sat down on the curb of the parking lot and jostled Abby on his lap. A moan escaped her lips. "Sweetheart," he said, shaking her gently. His voice broke. "Abby, honey, come on. It's Neil. Talk to me, please. Heinz is back; he missed you." He cupped her little face with his palm and tried to get her to face him. "Come on, baby, come on."

Her pulse was steady, respiration normal. There had

been no sign of broken bones or injuries with the exception of a few bruises on her arms—roughly the size of a man's hand. They'd examined her for head wounds or broken bones before they pulled her out of the trunk, and she didn't seem to have any.

But she wasn't waking up, either.

"Abby." Neil raised his voice. "Jesus, Abby, talk to me—"

"Hey, look here." A deputy holding a plastic bag pushed into the circle of onlookers. Inside was a medicine bottle. Neil couldn't see the name on the label, but it looked like a dark red liquid.

"Nighttime Benadryl," the deputy said. "Looks like about two capfuls are missing, and here's the cap."

Neil looked around in a panic. "He gave her drugs?"

Harrison laughed. "Man, my wife's threatened to do that to the kids a hundred times. Benadryl." He sounded downright joyful. "Knocks 'em out cold if it doesn't wire 'em like acid."

The knot in Neil's chest loosened fractionally. Harrison was still smiling. Neil hadn't even known he was married, let alone that he was a father, but he seemed to know what he was talking about. "You sure, man?"

Harrison brushed a knuckle across Abby's cheek. "If this is what he gave her, she'll sleep it off and be good as new in four to six hours. We'll tell the EMTs, but think about it, man. Chevy hated his mother because she hurt the baby sister. It's looking more and more like he had one helluva soft spot for Jenny. Hurting kids isn't his thing. His party is with grown women."

His party was with Beth.

407

Chapter 56

Beth tried to block out the sounds. Cries, screams, shrieks of total agony. The early morning birds and midges of the woods had all gone silent at the first shrill cry; the forest now, appropriately, was deathly quiet.

A leggy black spider inched across the bench. Beth had watched its erratic journey for what she presumed was the better part of a half hour now, and stupidly she wondered if spiders had ears. It was one of those things she had probably learned in fifth grade, like the names of every state capital, but she didn't remember those, either. Her heart went out to the poor, lost thing, even if it couldn't hear the agony going on around it. It was no doubt searching for the web that had been there before Bankes prepared his stage.

He took away my world, too, she thought as someone named Nina squalled. Beth closed her eyes.

Her stomach had already given up what little was in it, her heart seeming to rip from her chest with every guttural cry that came from the tiny speakers. She tried to think of something that could force the screams into the background, but every thought in her head revolved around Abby.

Nina shrieked in pain. Bankes sat quietly on the bench as if attending a symphony. The tape came to an unexpected end, and he popped it out and shoved another into the machine. His pistol lay next to his thigh. On first glance, he seemed careless with it, but Beth knew better. She was out of reach, weak and dazed, her ribs and shoulder aching with every breath, and her feet crusted with dirt-filled, bloody gashes. She slumped against the bench, telling herself it could only help her for him to think she was beyond the ability to hold herself upright, but wondering if she really was. If the moment came, would she be strong enough, physically, to take advantage of it?

The railing and bench on the deer stand lined three and a half sides. If he stepped close enough to that fourth side, where the ladder descended, and if she could just get her legs tangled in his ...

Then, what? A quick scissors cut? A kick? She couldn't think. Someone named Nina was dying in her ears. *Nina 2.* Still two agonizing hours from death.

Suddenly Bankes pushed Stop. "You're not enjoying my collection, Beth. That's one of my favorites, and here you are more interested in that asinine little spider than in what I'm trying to show you." He picked up the pistol and leaned over, squashing the spider with the butt of the gun. But not entirely. Half its little body smeared into the wood, the other half flailed, anchored to the spot by its own gore. Bankes sat back down. "I guess it's time to let you hear my most recent acquisition. Someone a little closer to home might stir you."

Oh, no. Not Lexi Carter. Beth wasn't sure she could handle listening to a woman who had been murdered in her own home.

Beth turned and stared into the forest. *Click.* The Play button caught.

Silence. More silence. Then, a tiny, tiny voice. *"Mommy?"*

Beth's eyes flew open. Chevy Bankes grinned at her.

"Mommy, where are you?" Abby was sniffling, trying to sound brave. *"I want to go home. Mommy, please. This tape is for you. Please, Mommy, come back."*

Terror transformed to red waves of rage. Blinded by it, she lunged.

Bankes shoved, and Beth smashed back against the railing. Warm liquid oozed from her shoulder again, and she vaguely realized he was working the cassette player, pushing Play and Record simultaneously.

Fear grabbed her by the throat. It was time. He would make tapes of her murder now. And it wasn't the idea of dying that clenched at her vitals and twisted everything inside. It wasn't even the idea of the pain he would force her to endure. It was the notion that Abby *might* still be alive, somewhere, calling for her mommy.

"What did you *do* to her?" Beth whispered.

Bankes breathed close over her face as he whispered, "I killed her. Or maybe I didn't. Maybe I left her alive and bleeding and crying. Maybe I have more tapes of her for you to hear."

"She's just a little girl! Why would you *do* this?"

"Why?" He straightened, his mouth curled into a sneer. "You know why."

"I know I ruined things with Anne Chaney. I know I let you go to jail. But you deserved it. Even if you didn't kill Anne single-handedly, you deserved every moment you spent in prison, and more." She glanced at the tape player. It was running, recording her stormy swan song. But maybe she could make sure something else got on the tape, too. Explanations. For the families of Anne Chaney and the other women Bankes had killed before he encountered Beth, for the families of Hannah Blake and Lexi Carter and the women whose deaths had been mimicked with fashion dolls. For Neil's grieving family—one estranged brother in Switzerland, one little sister in Atlanta, a mother in Florida.

Beth lifted her chin, speaking more clearly for the recording. "You hate me because I ended your killing spree." She glanced at the machine, oddly invigorated by the possibility of leaving explanations. Explanations she had once vowed to never reveal. "You hate me because after *you raped me,* I raised your daughter while you languished in prison. And how many other women were there before Anne Chaney? How many voices have you collected?"

Bankes's lips twitched at the corners, as if it amused him that Beth knew plenty of others had walked in her shoes. "Before Anne Chaney? Hmmm. There were three, not counting Mother." He bent down, the pistol brushing Beth's cheek. "Would you like to hear them?"

"I'd like to know what a man gets from listening to women scream in pain and beg for their lives."

"Pleasure," he said simply. "Orgasms so intense sometimes I think I'm dying. But mostly . . . silence."

Silence? He said it with such reverence Beth shivered. She wished she could take back her questions. She didn't want to know any of it. She didn't want to listen as this evil man took pleasure in reliving a string of atrocities Beth could hardly imagine.

Oh, Abby. Where are you?

Grief smothered every other emotion, and Beth had to grit her teeth to keep it from pouring out in great, gut-wrenching sobs. She forced herself to concentrate on the tape, on getting something out there in the world that would someday make sense of this man's madness. "Why did you want to kill Anne Chaney?"

He'd been pacing the long side of the deer stand but stopped. "She was a fraud. All of them, frauds." He looked at her, hard. "Anne Chaney was a lying, deceiving slut. She had lunch with her best friend at my hotel every day during a conference. They'd been friends since college; they kissed each other on the cheek and laughed and gossiped and talked about old times. And for dinner, they'd all go out—Anne, her best friend from college, and her best friend's husband. Now, Beth, do you want to know what happened after the cocktails were finished and everyone turned in for the night?"

No, I don't.

"Her friend's husband came back to the hotel. Anne fucked her best friend's husband all night."

Beth was shocked. "So you've taken it upon yourself to rid the world of adulterers? I'm not an adulterer."

His eyes glazed over, two hard copper orbs in his face. "No," he said quietly, "you're not. You're worse. You're the worst kind of fraud there is."

A chill slithered down her spine, taking a measure of Beth's resolve with it. "Is it because of Abby?"

"I told you, I don't want Abby. Blood is nothing."

"Then what?"

The gun pressed under her chin. "You hurt Jenny."

"You keep saying that. I never even met Jenny! Jenny disappeared eighteen years ago. She's dead."

He seemed to not be listening. He'd gone to his gym bag, pushed the pistol into his waistband. Gently, almost reverently, he used both hands to withdraw something from the bag, something small and round and white, something smooth and ...

Oh, God.

Beth faltered at the sight of the small skull gleaming like a silvery moon in his hands. He handled it gingerly, as if it were a quail's egg, and a tear ran down his cheek.

"Jenny, meet Beth. She's finally going to pay."

Chapter 57

Neil barged through the underbrush to where four agents were wired up. Harrison was hot on his heels. They'd gotten a call from Copeland as the ambulance drove away with Abby: The dogs had found something. Neil's heart hadn't beat a normal rhythm since.

Copeland put up a hand to stop him. "Hold on. We can't go in any farther yet."

"They got the cone?" Neil asked.

Copeland had a finger on the receiver in his ear, listening. He nodded. "The dogs picked up Denison's scent. When they narrow the cone enough, we'll pull them back." He looked away, concentrating on whatever the voice was saying in his ear. "No kidding. Really?" He looked at Neil. "Okay."

"What?"

"The lab's been looking at the baby bones we found at the river. Says the infant found there was a male."

Neil frowned. "Not Jenny?"

"Apparently not. They haven't been able to date the

diapers receipt yet, or find birth records from the Bible. But maybe there really was another baby before Chevy. A boy."

"Maybe." Neil thought about it for a minute, but he couldn't really care anymore. He had Abby back, and the dogs had picked up Beth's scent. That's all that mattered. "Fuck it," he said. "Let's go with the dogs."

"I've got twenty agents ready to go in." Copeland gave Neil a long look. "You aren't one of them."

Neil cursed and ran a hand through his hair. A second later he felt Harrison's hand on his shoulder.

"We'll take care of her, man," Harrison said, almost like a friend. Rick would have approved, Neil thought. "We're close now."

"That's J-Jenny?" Beth could hardly force out the words.

Bankes caressed the small skull like a lover. "My mother spent years in her own father's bed, and this is what came of it. A baby with bad blood. Mother wouldn't take care of her. That whole fucking town believed she took care of her; they never believed me. *I* took care of Jenny. Mother left her in her own shit and sang fucking little songs and pruned her flowers while Jenny cried. She said Jenny couldn't feel, but she could, I know it. She *can*. You know how I know that, Beth? Because I can hear when she cries. All her life, all the years she was missing. She cried until I finally found her again."

Oh, God. Beth blinked and tried to follow what he was saying, tried to fit it into what he was doing to her, what he had done to all those other women over the years. What he had done to Abby. "You found her again?"

"When I was twenty-one. Mother told me where to find her. But it was too late, then. She'd already fooled everyone."

Follow the story, try to keep up. "I d-don't know why you're angry with me." But then she thought she did. "Because I made everyone believe my husband was Abby's father? You said blood didn't matter. You said you didn't care about—"

"I don't care about Abby, I care about Jenny!" he roared, and Beth shrank back from his intensity, even as she marveled at the tenderness with which he held his sister's skull. "You hurt her, you fucking, deceiving little cunt. *You hurt her!"*

Beth blinked. Something moved in the forest behind him. Her heart did a somersault.

Pay attention, don't look. Follow his twisted mind. Think. *I hurt her. I hurt Jenny.*

"I d-don't know how I hurt Jenny."

He squatted down, still just out of reach of her legs, and everything behind him went still again. It might have just been an animal—a deer or something. It was still too dark to tell. But even as she warned herself to caution, her heart began to thump. She tested the bindings of her hands. Damn it, they were tight, if her fingers were wiggling at all. She couldn't be sure anymore.

"Look," he said.

She looked at Bankes, looked at the skull. His trembling finger circled a tiny black hole. An inch above the temple. Just where all the women in his killing spree had been shot.

"You did this, bitch."

She gaped at him.

"The night you killed Anne Chaney. After I'd found Jenny again and cared for her and together we were making Mother stop all that singing. You hurt Jenny all over again."

There were two shell casings from a thirty-eight pistol, Beth. One bullet struck Anne Chaney in the back. What about the other?

Memories flew through her mind. A shot into Anne Chaney's spine, and another shot ... wild.

"I n-never meant to, Ch-Chevy," she said, almost choking on his first name. "I never meant to hurt Jenny. It was an accident, I didn't mean to hit your bag."

"Mother sang so loud that night. She sang for the next six years while I was behind bars. I had no tapes there. I had to send them to Mo Hammond to keep for me with Jenny and the dolls. So I had nothing to make Mother stop."

Beth sat stunned. He rotated the skull slightly in his hands. "And this." He ran a finger along a jagged crack in the head. "Sheridan did this. At your house. He kicked Jenny. He deserved to die."

Bankes was so intent on Jenny's skull he wasn't looking around. Movements. More than one now. She could feel them. Oh, God, someone *was* out there.

Bankes's gaze lifted to Beth. It was black with rage. "You hurt Jenny, then pretended to be innocent and sweet. You planted fucking flowers. An Oscar-worthy perform-ance, Beth, as good as Mother's. Can't you hear her singing now?"

He leaned closer to her and she flinched.

417

"When I pound a cunt, Mother hates that the most. It reminds her of Grandpa, and she stops singing." He stared at Beth, the whites of his eyes showing. "And now," he said, digging into his bag, "it's your turn."

He came up with five new tapes. They were all labeled *Beth*.

"They're in," Copeland said and waved Neil over. "You can listen, but I'm in charge, you understand?" Neil nodded. Right now, he'd agree to anything. "Reconnaissance has them. They've got a view."

Neil got wired up and listened, barely breathing.

"They're in a tree house," came a hushed voice that belonged to a man Neil had never met named Wexler. "A hunter's stand, I guess. Suspect has a thirty-eight. The woman's on the floor."

"The floor?" Neil asked. They weren't close enough to see. Only a handful of recon agents had gone in past the dogs. The rest of them stayed in an outer perimeter, awaiting Copeland's orders. When they descended, they'd do it all at once, a shock-and-awe strike.

"She's bloody, clothes ripped," Wexler reported. "I can't tell how bad she's hurt. Doesn't look good."

Neil closed his eyes, adrenaline surging. Focus. He touched his .45 out of habit, longing for the assault rifle he'd cradled against his chest for the past nine years.

"Aw, shit," Wexler said. "He's on her."

"What?"

"He's running the pistol down her throat, over her breasts. Man, I think he's about to do her."

"Can you get a shot?" Copeland asked.

418

"Not from this angle, too many trees. Christ. He's touching her. She's trying to weasel away—she's tied up ..."

Neil ripped out the earpiece and lunged. Copeland and Harrison both grabbed him. Together, they rammed him up against a tree.

"Sheridan!" Copeland whispered, gripping him hard.

"I'm going in," Neil said. "It'll freak him out to see me alive. Throw him off."

"It'll *piss* him off, that's what it'll do," Harrison shot back right in Neil's face. "Are you listening to Wexler, man? There's a gun on your woman, for God's sake."

"I'm *dead*. I can go in there and fuck with his mind. I can push him over the edge."

"What edge?" Copeland growled, holding Neil's shirt in his fists. "The one that makes him screw whatever he'd planned for Denison and just put a bullet in her head? For God's sake, let me get the team in there." Copeland stared at him until Neil nodded, then stepped back. He touched his earpiece.

"Wexler," he said, "we're coming in." He clicked to another frequency to address the full team. "This is Copeland. Suspect is holding the woman in a deer stand and has a gun to her throat. Sexual assault in progress. On three, we go in. No one shoot; I repeat, *Hold your fire!*" He looked at Neil, took a deep breath. "One ... two ..."

The gun slid cold and hard down her throat. Beth cringed and was sorry a second later. Even that small reaction made Bankes smile. Don't react. Don't cry. Just *think*.

She would swear there was someone out there, but

what if she was wrong? She couldn't sit here and let Bankes make a tape recording of her torture while she awaited a cavalry she wasn't certain of. Still, she knew they were out there. Police? The FBI? Neil?

No, she'd almost forgotten. Not Neil.

The gun dragged farther down her body. Her spine went rigid, the pain a fire that had dulled to a constant, red-embered throb, now withering beneath pain of another nature. The barrel of the gun found her crotch. It rubbed, taunted through what was left of her dress. The duct tape held. Bankes slipped a finger through one of the gaping runs in her panty hose and yanked. The nylons shredded to nothing.

Be weak, act scared, feed his obsession. Cry, whimper.

He looked up as if a sound had caught his attention, then dismissed it, the gun still teasing the cleft between Beth's legs. He glanced at the tape player. The Play and Record buttons were both depressed, the faint hum of reels *whrring* in her ears. He smiled.

"It's time, Beth. Cry for me. I've waited so long to add you to my collection."

Beth looked at the tape, then stared him in the eyes and spoke loud and clear for the recording: "Go to hell, you bastard."

"Three!"

The shout seemed far away to Beth, yet suddenly the forest moved. Everywhere, and all at once. Figures wearing goggles and armor skittered through the woods like black mercury, then stopped so sharply the night seemed to die.

Bankes yanked Beth up against him. His gun gouged into her throat, pushing her view to the sky. She buckled her knees. If he was going to hold her hostage, she could damn well make it hard for him. Somehow the pain didn't matter anymore.

He tightened his grip, staggering around the deer stand in the weak light of the lantern, swaying, turning three-sixties. He kept moving, keeping Beth's body close against him. He wasn't going to give anyone a clean shot.

"She's mine!" Bankes's voice sounded panicked. "Stay back. I haven't finished with her. *She's fucking mine!*"

Beth gasped for air past the barrel of the gun, nearly choking. Everything that had moved two seconds before had suddenly gone still again. Silent. Deathly.

Then a deep voice rumbled, "Wrong," and Beth's heart stopped. It wasn't possible. But the voice came again, nearer this time, rolling through the silence like thunder. "Wrong, Bankes. *She's mine.*"

Chapter 58

A chorus of assault rifles flinched in unison, but Neil stepped past them. To a man he could feel the tension, the tightening of every finger on every trigger, the narrowing of each eye through the sights, and the furious voice of Armand Copeland sounding in their earpieces. Neil, already unarmed, yanked the stupid thing from his ear, dropping it with the night-vision goggles as he strode to the center of the dimly lit woodland stage. Copeland was likely to kill him, but that didn't matter now. He stopped thirty feet from the deer stand.

"Let's clear that up once and for all, Bankes," Neil said sharply. "Beth is mine, not yours."

The look on Bankes's face was priceless. The look on Beth's made his heart stand perfectly still. She couldn't see him down in the trees because her face was angled up by the gun. But he could see her. Blood streamed down the right side of her face and caked her dress. Her legs dangled as if she couldn't hold herself upright, and her feet looked as if they'd been through a blender. Her chest rose and fell in great, heaving breaths, and her clothes were bloodstained and shredded, especially at one shoulder. It was fucking fifty-six degrees.

Neil wanted to tear Bankes's dick off. Instead, he balled his right hand and tried to sound casual. "Didn't expect to see me, did you, Bankes?"

"You're d-dead," Bankes whispered.

Neil smiled. "Suck-er." He said it in a juvenile, singsongy taunt, and a surge of perverse pleasure washed through him. "We put on a little show for you at the park. Did you see it on TV? The season's biggest hit."

"Rebecca Alexander killed you!"

"Rebecca Alexander shot me with blanks. She fooled you, Chevy; we all did. How 'bout that? There doesn't seem to be a woman in the world who hasn't fucked you over."

"Shut up!"

"Neil." The word croaked from Beth's lips.

"I'm here, honey; I'm fine. We did it. Everything's going to be okay now."

"Abby—"

"Is alive. She's not hurt, sweetheart. Abby is *fine.*"

Beth closed her eyes, her face still pushed skyward by Bankes's pistol. The barrel pressed so deeply into her flesh Neil thought it might rip through her skin.

He stepped forward. Bankes had stopped swaying and doing three-sixties, probably realizing that the part of the deer stand at his back didn't make for a good sniper shot. He was right; no one would shoot him in the back, anyway. This team wasn't armed with .22s. Any bullet fired into Bankes's back from this team risked ripping through him and hitting Beth. He was safe as long as he kept Beth glued against him.

How long would he last? How long would Beth last?

Neil saw the pale sphere on the bench. The missing skull, the gift in the codicil from his mother. Jenny.

No, not Jenny. A boy.

The thought plucked at Neil's brain and he toyed with it. With the lab reports unfinished, he couldn't know for sure yet. But maybe he knew enough to mess with Chevy's mind.

"So, I see you brought your big brother to watch you in action," Neil said carefully.

Bankes's eyes slid to the skull, then skidded back to Neil. "That's my little sister, Jenny. You kicked her and hurt her. You have to pay."

Bankes jerked Beth higher against him and Neil winced. Beth didn't make a sound and Neil's heart took a wild turn in his chest, thinking she couldn't hold on. Then he realized that her silence indicated something else entirely. Strength, composure. That kind of control took focus and effort.

So she was still with him, and she was making things as difficult as possible for Bankes.

Good girl. Hang on.

One second. All they needed was for Beth to peel away from Bankes for *one second*, and he'd be riddled with holes. Six assault rifles were trained on him from positions on the ground. Two snipers sat in trees. A battalion of armed agents circled the area. Just one second.

"Jenny?" Neil asked, feigning confusion. "That's Jenny?" Then he laughed. "Jesus. Is that what your mother told you in her will?"

Bankes frowned. "What are you talking about?"

Neil pretended to enjoy himself thoroughly. "Christ, you said your mother fooled everyone. I guess she really did."

"Shut u—"

"That's not Jenny, you stupid idiot."

Bankes froze. "You're lying."

"I'm not," Neil said, shrugging, "but go ahead and believe it if you want. Jeez, you've spent your whole adult life carrying around a skull you thought was Jenny's? You poor stupid bastard. I almost feel sorry for you. Your mother really *was* good."

"You're full of shi—"

"Did Peggy never tell you about your older brother, Chevy? The one who died at birth? It took us a while to find someone who knew the story, and at first even we didn't believe it. But now we know it's true. Remember Ray Goodwin? He was sheriff when you were a kid."

Bankes frowned. Yes, he remembered. Neil could see it in his eyes.

"He remembered that your mother got pregnant before you came along," Neil continued, "and that baby didn't make it. Most people never even knew she was pregnant; apparently your grandfather wasn't too happy about it, kept her at home. His daughter, the one *he* liked to fuck, you know. The baby's body was buried by the river."

Neil stopped to let it all sink in. He could see the doubt in Bankes's eyes.

Bankes sneered. "You're lying. Mother said Jenny was buried there."

"You poor shit," Neil said. "Jenny disappeared. That wasn't her body you dug up."

425

"You didn't even find that place until yesterday. DNA testing isn't that fast. You couldn't know who it was."

"Well, forensic science is a beautiful thing, Chev. They don't need DNA to check parentage, only blood work. And bones hold the best information on blood a coroner can get. Our guys only needed the records on file for Jenny at the hospital and a quick look-see at your grandfather's corpse. Easy enough to tell how far from the tree the baby fell." He paused long enough to let that sink in. "As for it being Jenny, well, you can't tell gender from the skull, but you can from the hips."

Doubt had taken hold. Neil pushed harder.

"For God's sake, Chevy, if you don't believe me, just look at the skull. Jenny was sixteen months old when she disappeared. That one you've been carrying around is just an infant. Can't you tell the difference?"

"Jenny was small ..."

But even as he denied it, his eyes sought out the skull lying sideways by the tape recorder. Bankes inched closer to it, shaking his head, his gun hand trembling in the hollow of Beth's bruised throat. The tension in her body changed, and fear stabbed Neil in the chest.

Jesus, Beth, I'm getting to him. Don't do anything stupi—

She started humming.

Bankes's eyes widened. "Shut up!" he growled at her. Neil saw his grip tighten.

Beth sang. "Who killed Cock Robin? I, said the Sparrow, with my bow and arrow ... I k-killed Cock Robin."

It sounded thready and weak to Neil's ears, but it was

a tune nonetheless. Bankes began trembling, then covered his ear with one hand, and Beth straightened her legs and shoved. She launched the pair of them backward, wheeling past the ladder, but Bankes held on. Beth grabbed a breath and kept going, the broken, haunted tune growing louder. "Who saw him die? I, said the Fly, with my little eye ..."

Bankes wagged his head, frantic, trying to shake the voice. Beth seized the chance. She went for his kneecap. He grunted, flinching, and she dropped. For one bright second, they were separated, and in the next, even brighter fraction of time, the forest exploded with gunfire and Bankes's head splintered apart.

Chapter 59

Beth sat on a blanket, wrapped in another with her right shoulder bandaged. Her clothes, ripped and spattered with blood and dirt and Chevy Bankes's brain matter, had been taken away, and a paramedic now squatted at her feet. "You couldn't have worn shoes for this little outing, miss?" he asked, shooting her a concerned smile.

"The FBI had custody of my shoes," she answered, looking at Neil.

He cursed. "Stubborn damned woman. You might have called me."

"You were dead."

Neil flushed. He felt so helpless, he couldn't sit down, couldn't stand still, couldn't stop staring at her or touching her or even scolding her.

Beside the deer stand, two deputies hefted a body bag at each end. Neil watched Beth as she squinted into the morning sun, her gaze following Bankes's body to a stretcher. She touched the fresh bandage on her temple. The cut would be tended properly this time and would heal with hardly any scarring. Neil would see to that.

He'd see to a whole lot of things. Orioles games and Hotwheels tracks for Abby, Christmases with plenty of assembly-required toys. Peaceful, slumber-filled nights. Unrestrained sex.

Lots of that. And a ring that wasn't part of an act, one she didn't don as part of a costume to present to the world. A ring his sister Aubrey would call a BAD ring— *big-ass diamond.*

Neil turned when he heard a motor—a white scooter with a sheriff's logo threading between the trees. He glanced at Beth, making sure she was patched up enough not to look scary, then waved the scooter over. Behind the driver, Abby pulled off her helmet.

She ran to Beth, and twenty-five FBI agents, SWAT team snipers, and sheriff's deputies all stood still to watch. When Abby finally pulled back, Neil joined them.

"Mommy's crying," Abby said, and Neil smiled.

"Look around," he said, pointing to the collection of bold champions surrounding them. "So is everybody else." He squatted. "You think I could get in on this?" he asked and made it a three-way hug.

A family.

"Hey, Sheridan." It was a crime scene techie, holding up a plastic bag. "You wanted to see this?"

Neil got up, leaving Abby to examine Beth's bandages. He took the bag containing the tiny battered skull and turned it this way and that, studying it.

That skull you've been carrying around for all these years is just an infant. Can't you tell the difference?

Copeland came over. "Something wrong?" he asked.

Neil handed off the skull. "I can't help wondering," he said, "if this *isn't* Jenny—"

"Then what happened to her?" Copeland finished. "We'll find her. She's probably buried out there not too far from this one."

"Yeah," Neil said, looking across the copse at Abby. Having her missing for the brief hours she was gone had just about ripped a hole in his chest.

Copeland followed the direction of his gaze. "Looks to me like there may be some changes in your life, Sheridan," he said.

"Absolutely, sir."

"Are you up for one more?" Neil's brows went up, and a strange surge of excitement pulsed through his veins. "I'd like to have you on board—legitimately. That is, if you think you can learn to follow orders now and then."

Neil smiled. "Now and then, maybe."

"Good," Copeland said, shaking Neil's hand. "Now maybe Standlin will get off my back."

"Don't count on it." Neil paused. "Look, I need a little time first. I'd like to go see my brother in Europe. And then I think I'll take a nice long honeymoon."

Copeland clapped him on the shoulder. "Another one bites the dust."

Neil went over to Beth and Abby and crouched beside them.

"What was that about?" Beth asked. "It looked serious."

"Copeland invited me to come back into the Bureau."

"Oh, Neil. That's wonderful."

"But I told him I needed a few weeks first, that I have something to do."

"What's that?" Beth asked, holding Abby's hand.

Neil reached to Abby's hair, where a barrette had come loose. He moved it up and fastened it, then stroked Beth's cheek. "Figure it out."

Epilogue

"A bit lower," Jennifer Rhodes said, her head cocked to the side.

The maid tucked the center rose down a little lower into the vase. Two dozen red blossoms dappled a white cloud of baby's breath. One more day, and they'd be at their peak. That's when Jennifer loved them most. A love she'd apparently inherited from her mother.

"*Senorita?*" Maria spun the arrangement around for approval.

"That's fine," Jennifer said, straining for some memory of that mother. There wasn't one. Just the vague image of a sweet female voice, singing. Always singing.

Maria set the vase on a mahogany-based stand. "There," she said. "You like me to turn off the radio when I go?"

"No, I think I'll listen a little longer. I'll see you in the morning."

Maria shut the door behind her. Jennifer picked up the remote and spun her wheelchair toward the radio, punching up the volume. An American newscaster rolled through yet another agitated, long-winded narrative about the end of the manhunt for serial sexual predator Chevy Bankes and the little sister whose bones had yet to be found. A few moments later, the host opened the phone lines to take listeners' calls.

Jennifer muted the voices and closed her eyes. Chevy was dead. She didn't know whether to feel relief or sadness. Relief, because a dangerous man was no longer striking terror across a nation. Sadness, because everything he'd done—said the special agents and psychiatrists and old neighbors—he'd done for his little sister.

She slipped her hand into the pocket of her skirt, pulling out a folded piece of paper. It was splotchy and thin, like rice paper, with gold leaf on three sides and a torn, yellowed edge where it had been ripped from its binding. Years and years ago, she'd found it in a stack of discards when she and Iris were going through old photographs. Iris waved it off like it was nothing and told her to get rid of it, but something made Jennifer secret it away. Somehow, she'd always known it was important. Just as she'd always known there was more to her adoption than the story Iris told: *You were so sick, and your mother didn't know how to take care of you, and there was no one else ...*

No one else. Yet, all Jennifer's life, surrounded by Iris and the other foster kids, Jennifer had never quite believed it.

Now, she unfolded the fragile page and ran her finger down the names, touching the last three:

James Robin Bankes: b. March 14, 1976–d. March 28, 1976
Chevy David Bankes: b. Feb. 5, 1978–

Jennifer Robin Bankes: b. June 19, 1990–disap. Oct. 14, 1991

She wheeled to the end table and pulled out a pen, testing the ink on the corner of a magazine. The backs of her eyes prickling, she filled in the missing information for her brother.

Chevy David Bankes: ... *d. April 25, 2009.*

Don't miss
KATE BRADY'S
next spine-tingling
novel.

Please turn this page
for a preview
of
LAST TO DIE

Coming soon from Piatkus ...

Chapter 1

Whoops and giggles, canned music piped through speakers, the screech of balloons being bullied into bubble-necked poodles. The air smelled of soft pretzels and Belgian waffles, the sidewalks crowded with vendors and entertainers, teeming with families. Fathers walked along, poking keys on BlackBerry devices or talking into Bluetooth earpieces; mothers juggled sippy-cups and pacifiers as they steered overpacked strollers and chatted with friends. Slightly older siblings orbited their parents like forgotten moons—lagging behind, straying too far, easily diverted by the remnants of popped poodles on the ground or the call of a snow-cone vendor.

Bait, if you were a child molester or a kidnapper. Easy pickings.

The Broker was neither. No need to grab a child from a weekend carnival, as simple as that would be. Not when there were pregnant women willing to sell newborns. *Twenty thousand dollars, cash. Prenatal visits covered, certified midwife for the birth.* And the final straw, necessary for some women but oddly, the Broker thought, not for many: *Your baby will go to a rich couple who have prayed for a child for years, will have a better life than you could ever provide* ...

One such woman, one of those rare ones who had required the extra dose of persuasion, stood behind a magician's kiosk, secretly watching the Kinney family. She'd followed the Kinneys—Roger, Alana, and their four-year-old son, Austin—for more than an hour, not knowing that the Broker followed, too. At first the woman's motives weren't suspicious: She made no effort to speak with the Kinneys, simply followed a similar path. For a while, the Broker had even considered the possibility that she wouldn't have to die.

But then the camera came out. The woman was taking pictures of Austin Kinney.

Stupid bitch. She'd issued her own death warrant.

The Broker kept well behind, though there was little chance of being recognized: baseball cap, sunglasses, loose nylon jacket and boots. The Kinneys moved toward the park exit, oblivious to their shadows, Austin's face stuck in a blue cloud of cotton candy. A silver Jaguar gave a toot as the family neared, and the camera came out again.

She was getting the license plate, the Broker realized, and pulled on a pair of gloves. Stubborn, double-crossing bitch.

The Broker slipped the gun from the deep pocket of the jacket, gave the silencer a final twist, and closed in. By her own design, the woman with the camera was making things easy—she crouched behind huge bushes that separated the parking lot from the woods around the park, staying out of sight, her attention focused solely on the camera and the little boy. By her own design: easy pickings.

The Broker came in fast from behind, the gun barrel finding the woman's throat like a missile. She must have heard it coming: She whirled and opened her mouth to scream, but the bullet caught her in the larynx and the would-be scream came out *Unkh*. She dropped and the Broker was right there, on one knee, firing two more bullets into her throat for good measure then pulling back and hitting her with the gun, over and over again on the face and head, adrenaline surging. *Bitch. Stupid bitch.* Smack, smack. *No one bucks me! Take back Austin?* Smack. *I don't think so* ...

It was over in seconds. The Broker pulled away, fighting for breath, for *control*, and glanced around. No one, not back here in the woods. The woman lay on the ground, her face shredded by the gun, her legs bent at the knees and her body looking strangely like the letter Z. Geysers of blood from her throat fizzled to tiny gurgles.

That's it. Settle down, keep your head. The Broker stepped back, waiting as the high of the kill drained away, and summoned a mental list: Boots, hair, shell casings. Phone call. And the camera. Above all, get rid of the pictures.

The camera was first. The Broker slipped it into a pocket with the gun, purposely stepped in some of the blood, then used a pencil to punch a number into the dead woman's cell phone. *You've reached the office of Russell Sanders* ... An answering service: fine. The Broker disconnected. The phone went back in the woman's hand, pencil

439

and gloves into the wad of jacket. Folded all together, the jacket made a carryall to simply walk away with the evidence.

Finished. The Broker looked around—no one.

Easy pickings.

Twelve miles from Ar Rutbah, Iraq
Sunday, September 23

K-chhr, k-chhr, k-chhr.

The camera's shutter whirred. Mitch Sheridan squinted through the lens and adjusted the frame around the image: an old man crouched on his haunches, robes gathered around his ankles, rocket-propelled grenade on one shoulder. The sky made a blue-white backdrop behind him so bright it crinkled the eyes, the sun pulling ripples of heat from the sand. Row upon row of tents sagged in the distance, like soldiers too weary to stand.

K-chhr, k-chrr. Mitch let the sky and the tents go fuzzy in the background and zoomed in on the man's face. Not too small; keep the stump of his elbow in the frame—the bandage around it oozing and yellowed. Don't ask this old man's name or think about his pain or notice the rancid tang of infection that wafted from his wound. Don't remember that just three months ago, before the chopper came, this man was whole. Just shoot. Get the damned pictures, tell the story.

Pretend it'll help.

K-chhr. K-chhr. Focus. Shoot Move on.

Mitch pressed a hand against his ribs, over still-fresh scars. After the chopper, he'd spent a month barely conscious, another healing, and a third working hours a day with weights and machines. Too soon, he knew, but he couldn't stay holed up in Switzerland any longer. He needed the photos. The Ar Rutbah exhibition was scheduled to open in three weeks—in Mitch's hometown in the US, where people didn't live like this. Where people didn't live in tents and scrounge for food and worry that choppers might come dropping insurgents with bombs. Thirteen refugees had been killed in the attack, dozens more wounded. Men, women.

Children.

The memory caught Mitch by the throat: "Mister! Mister, here!" a voice cried. "Help!" Mitch looked up, a helicopter swooping low over the camp and whipping sand into windstorms. *Thwp-thwp-thwp* ... Its doors gaped open and terror poured out. Explosions, flames, death.

"Mister!"

He'd shielded his camera from whirlwinds of sand and searched for the voice. A little boy. Mitch recognized him. Nine or ten years old, Mitch had shot a series of him and a dog both rooting through trash for food. The boy had become fascinated by the Leica, followed Mitch all over camp to watch him work with it.

"Get down!" Mitch called, though the pandemonium was deafening. Mortars exploded and people screamed, while the chopper churned the sky into a raging black cloud. "Get down! Stop!"

But the boy kept coming. Mitch humped toward the child, dodging geysers of sand. His legs went out from under him and he clambered to his feet, something hot and sticky running down his thigh. Get to the boy. Get there, damn it. But the leg wasn't working. He dragged it. Thirty yards, twenty, ten—

The ground exploded. For an instant the world flashed white, then it went black for a long, long time, and Mitch was in Switzerland, safe, in the hands of doctors ...

Trembling, sweat streaming down his back, Mitch forced himself to open his eyes. He looked up at the sky. Nothing. Today, the sky was an empty, cloudless infinity, and by small degrees, the memory of the attack loosened its grip. The old man came back into focus, the rocket-propelled grenade on his shoulder, the tents in the background.

He was here to finish the pictures. Get them, damn it *K-chhr. K-chhr.*

A woman's wail pierced the air. Mitch frowned and followed the sounds. Something going on—in the third tent of the second row. He paused, watching as another woman hurried into the tent. Out of habit, he lifted the camera and focused on the tent flaps, ready to shoot whoever came through. Focus, get the story.

A hand slipped between the flaps of the tent—slender, brown, belonging to a woman. Then another hand pulled aside the other flap and a man came out carrying a bundle. A woman behind him hunched over, wailing, two friends hugging her in consolation. Mitch began snapping. *K-chrr, k-chrr.*

He followed the woman with his Leica, zooming in close on her face, catching eyes that overflowed with tears. He pulled off three more shots then moved his camera back to the old man and the bundle. The bundle—what was it?—something draped in cloths, weighing the man down only slightly yet carried with both hands, gingerly, and about the size of a—

"Jesus Christ." Mitch dropped the camera around his neck. His heart snagged in his throat, lungs refusing to fill. "No," he said, but knew it was true. Another one.

He spun on his heel, yanked the camera from his neck, and hurled it into the sand. It didn't shatter, damn the thing, and he wanted to stomp on it until it did. Instead, he stared at it: a container filled with toxic images: images of pain and suffering Mitch had spent a career seeking out and documenting, letting Russ Sanders spin them into gold, all the while pretending it helped.

It didn't. After all these years, mothers still buried their children, fathers still lost limbs, children still rooted through trash. The JMS Foundation hadn't changed anything.

A beep sounded and Mitch jumped. He looked back to the tents, where a small crowd now followed the bereaved parents toward the outer reaches of the camp to the grave-yard. The cosmic little beep came again—from the bag around Mitch's hips. The satellite phone.

Mitch dug it from its case. "This is Mitch Sheridan," he said, turning his back to the camp.

"Mitch, it's Russ. Can you hear me?"

Mitch swallowed and held the phone to his mouth. It was the size of a brick, like the walkie-talkies he and his brother, Neil, used to play with, except that what used to be static halfway down the block now allowed conversation halfway around the world. Russ was in Maryland. "I can hear you."

"Okay, good," Russ said. "I was afraid I wouldn't reach you. Where are you?"

"In the camp at Ar Rutbah, getting your fucking pictures."

"My what? Mitch, are you all right?"

The dam broke. "You wanted me to finish the Ar Rutbah shots, right? Well, I did it. So you can mount the damned exhibit and it'll be big, Russ, just like you wanted. Because it'll be my final show. I'm done watching kids die."

"Christ, Mitch. Listen."

"I'm serious, Russ. I'm retiring. You can have the foundation, for all the good it does."

"Mitch, listen. The photos aren't the reason I called. I called because—" He paused, more than just the lag in sound transmission. The space made the hairs on the back of Mitch's neck stand up. "I'm in trouble, Mitch. I need you."

Mitch frowned. "What do you mean?"

"I can't talk about it like this. You have to come home. It's about the foundation. I'm in trouble." A pause, then, "No."

"Russ?" Mitch asked.

"Mitch ... No!"

There was a grunt and shuffling, sounds Mitch couldn't make out. "Russ, what's going on?" He heard Russ's voice, distant and muffled now, and Mitch's grip on the phone tightened. "Russ!" He went rigid, straining to interpret sounds from the other damn side of the planet. A scrape. Something dragging. Dread congealed in his throat, then, as suddenly as it started, there was silence. No more voice, no more scuffle.

"Russ!" But all he could hear was the thundering in his chest. The connection was dead. Mitch stood in the desert

with his heart beating triple time. Jesus, what was going on?

I'm in trouble, Mitch. I need you.

He swallowed, then shoved his camera into its case and gathered up the sat-phone and bag. He raced back to the tent where he'd stayed, threw what few things he'd brought into a duffel, then tossed everything into the Jeep. Trying the sat-phone all the way.

I'm in trouble, Mitch. I need you.

Chapter 2

Monday, September 24
Lancaster, Maryland

Danielle Cole honked her way through traffic to a murder scene in Camden Park. *Murder* scene. It pissed her off just thinking about it. She wasn't a homicide detective; she'd told Tifton a dozen times she wasn't cut out for that kind of work. Homicide detectives spent their days behind desks or in courtrooms or morgues, on the phone and in cramped interview rooms, and had to be reminded to pull their guns from their desks before leaving the building. As an investigator in theft, Dani may not have been making her dad proud by going for forty years as a street-tough patrol officer, but she hadn't degenerated to a pussyfoot homicide dick, either.

The squad sergeant didn't give a damn about Dani's career goals. "Tifton caught a murder this morning at Camden Park," he'd said on the phone, dragging her from a restless night of dreams. "He wants you on it."

"Tell Tifton to call Scarpio," she said, still scrubbing the sleep from her eyes. "I've gotta go jack up a tenth-grade business teacher in a little while. The boys who lifted those computers didn't mastermind that scam by them-selves."

"I'll send Forsythe to the high school. You go meet Tifton. You're his until further notice."

"Aw, jeez ..."

"Nails," he'd said, using her departmental nickname, "is that a whine in your voice?"

Her jaw snapped shut. Dani Cole didn't whine.

Which is why, thirty minutes later, she knocked back her last swig of coffee and rolled onto a murder scene at Camden Park.

A uniform waved her through the park gate and into a television-perfect crime scene: yellow ribbon strung around the perimeter of a parking lot and disappearing into the woods, a half dozen black-and-whites parked at various angles, a couple more gray Chevrolets belonging to investigators. An ambulance sat square to the curb, the back open and two EMTs sitting on the bumper twiddling their thumbs—no one to save. The media were roped off at a respectable distance, as if distance mattered with the kinds of magnifying lenses they used these days, and a handful of detectives in coats and ties stood in the parking lot.

Reginald Tifton was one. He spoke with two of the uniforms, pointing in an arc behind them. Dani walked up as the officers turned and jogged off in the direction Tifton had pointed.

"About time, Nails," he said dropping from the curb and meeting her in an empty parking slot. "Your beauty routine hold you up this morning?"

Dani scowled. There wasn't an Avon lady in the world

who would call her efforts a beauty routine: three swipes of mascara per eye and a smear of lipstick. Her hair had major control issues, so she kept it two or three inches in length, tossed it with a daub of gel, and let it do its thing. In her confident moments, she thought she looked like Lisa Rinna or a dark Cameron Diaz. In her realistic moments, she knew she looked like Peter Pan with his finger in a light socket.

"You oughta try it sometime," she shot, pointing at his clean-shaven head. "Learn the wonders of hair products."

Tifton tried for a smile but didn't quite get there. He was a big man pushing forty, black, going for Wife Number Three, and had a bowling-ball head perched on a neck like a tree trunk. He spoke like a Yale graduate except when it behooved him to turn on the street charm and make a suspect believe he was from the hood. He was actually from the old-money area of Cheshire Lake, and secretly, Dani suspected he *had* gone to Yale.

"I'll borrow your hair products since they never see any action," he said, then his eyes homed in on hers. "I haven't seen you since your dad's funeral. You holding up?"

Dani shot him a glare.

"Okay," he said, showing his palms. Tifton knew when to back off. He jerked his chin toward the bushes. "Cleanup crew found a dead woman in her twenties. Shot sometime during the clown-fest this weekend."

Dani started toward the site. "And where's your partner? You drive him to early retirement already?"

"Thought you might know something on this one the rest of us don't."

She frowned. "Why?"

448

"The vic is one of your snitches."

Dani stopped, a chill creeping in. Her collection of snitches was comprised of a few low-level drug dealers, a bookie, a couple of hookers, a guy who sold tickets at the dollar theater on Barker Street. And Jed, a bum who'd lived under a bridge. That was the extent of the list, and she couldn't make any of them work at a Camden Park carnival.

She beat a path toward the bushes, Tifton following. "Hey, Dani, hold on. It's ugly back there. It's—"

The smell hit her and Dani hesitated, reminded herself to breathe through her mouth. She moved toward the body. She couldn't see the face, but the legs looked as if the woman had simply crumpled, like an accordion that suddenly lost air. She stepped around to look at the face, and her heart stopped.

"Oh, Jesus," she said, emotion clogging her throat. She turned her back. "Jesus, Jesus, Jesus."

Tifton had a hand on her shoulder. "It's her, right? Rosie?"

Dani couldn't breathe. She braced her hands on her knees and tried to get her lungs to function, the sight stirring up her stomach. "Rose McNamara."

"Okay," Tifton said, then called to another investigator over Dani's back: "I was right, Wilson, it's Rose McNamara. A hooker down in Deer Park."

"No," Dani said, and Tifton raised his eyebrows. Dani got control of her breathing, then forced her gaze back to the body. "She wasn't hooking anymore. She got off the streets over a year ago. Was working at the Big Lots on South Grimby Street, a cashier." Going to counseling, paying rent on her own apartment, getting her life together. *God. Rosie, Rosie.* She was just starting to get somewhere with her life.

The grief came in a flood. *Tough it out. Don't be a baby.* She swallowed back the lump in her throat and walked back to the body, summoning the cool detachment the job required. The victim's eyes were frozen in a moment of shock and pain, her throat sporting what may have been as many as three bullet holes, her face a mishmash of blood and torn tissue. The bugs had gotten to her: Maggots speckled her wounds like wiggling grains of rice, flies battling the medical examiner for access. She was fully clothed. A cell phone sat in her right hand, fingers lax. Rigor mortis had come and gone.

"Thirty-eight?" Dani asked the ME, who was writing in a small notebook.

"Probably," he said. "But they haven't found any shells, so we can't be sure yet."

Dani moved slowly around the body. "Are any of these facial wounds postmortem?"

"Won't know until she's cleaned up," the ME answered. "Too messy to see what's what."

Tifton bent down beside her. "So, what's the theory? You're the shrink."

"I'm not a shrink."

"You've got a degree in psychology. That makes you more of a shrink than the rest of us. Why did you ask about postmortem wounds?"

"It's not anonymous, that's all," she said. "There's a lot of anger there. It's personal. Or sexual. You don't get this kind of overkill for nothing."

Tifton cocked his head. "You're saying she knew him, or at least he knew her. That might explain why she came back here in the woods, anyway."

"Got some hairs here," the ME said.

Tifton walked over and looked. "Boo-yah," he said. Hair was good.

The dance got under way, the steps rehearsed a couple of dozen times a year in peaceful bedroom communities like Lancaster, two or three hundred times a year in bigger cities like Baltimore or D.C. or Philadelphia. Techies, uniforms, and detectives all went quietly about their jobs: studying the body, canvassing for onlookers, searching the woods and parking lot with rubber gloves and plastic bags, collecting items that would ultimately prove there had been a carnival. Dani hung with Tifton until those all-important words finally came from the ME: "We're ready to flip her," he called out.

Dani worked her way over and stood next to Tifton. The ME and one of his assistants flanked the body.

"Let me have the phone," Dani said.

The ME slid it from Rosie's fingers. Wearing fresh rubber gloves, Dani took it, then watched while Rosie's body was ceremoniously flipped. Nothing. No new wounds on her backside. No murder weapon or Dear John letter conveniently left beneath her body, no signed note saying, "I did it."

Dani walked to the parking lot with the phone, where she could breathe more freely. She pressed Power, bent over the hood of Tifton's car like a desk, and copied down numbers from recent calls, incoming calls, missed calls. When she finished, she took out her own phone and climbed onto Tifton's hood, propping her feet on the bumper. She dialed, then spelled each name and number to Dispatch.

Thirty minutes later, the dispatcher recited back the names and addresses of people who matched the phone numbers. Dani recognized several of them—friends, coworkers, a hairdresser, the landlord of Rosie's apartment complex, her mom. No one identifiable as a boyfriend or lover. No one unusual at all, at least not that Dani could tell, until the last name on the list: *JMS Foundation for Photography Art.*

She frowned and checked the time of the call. Sunday, 8:07 p.m. It had lasted just eighteen seconds.

"Careful, your brow is gonna stay that way." Tifton had stepped over to her, pressing his thumb to the frown line above her nose.

She brushed his hand away, already dialing. Voice mail picked up. *"You've reached the office of Russell Sanders at the JMS Foundation for Photography Art. Please leave a message ..."* She disconnected and looked up at Tifton. "What would a hooker-turned-cashier have to do with an upscale art guild like the Sheridan Foundation?"

"Developing an interest in photography, maybe?"

She ignored the pun. "This is Russ Sanders's direct line. And it's the last call Rosie made."

"Who's Russ Sanders?"

"The director of the J. M. Sheridan Foundation."

"Open eyes, open hearts. *That* Sheridan?"

Like there was another. "Russ Sanders was Sheridan's mentor," she explained. "He runs Sheridan's Foundation."

"Pretty posh circle of friends for an ex-hooker," Tifton

speculated. He arched one black brow. "Which begs the question, how do you know about him? You got a love for photography or philanthropy you've kept hidden all these years?"

She fished her keys from her pocket and started toward her car. "I met him once—Sheridan. Back when he was just getting started."

"Oh, yeah? What was the occasion?"

Getting disowned by my family, Dani thought before she could halt the memory. She bullied it down. "It was no big deal," she lied. "Are we almost done here?"

"Yeah," Tifton answered, watching the coroner's wagon pull away with Rosie's body. The crime scene unit was packing it in. "What's on your mind?"

"I wanna go talk to Sanders." She continued walking, then turned back to Tifton. "You coming, Ace, or are you gonna go sit behind your desk and wait for forensics to figure out who dunnit?"

Tifton scoffed, patting the last of the CSI guys on the shoulder as he passed. "When did forensics ever solve a case?"

"Last night," the guy answered. "On CBS."

Dani gunned into traffic, with Tifton following in his own car. In keeping with Murphy's Law, she made a wrong turn and did a U-turn across a bed of flowers in a median. Tifton laid on his horn behind her—Tifton liked flowers—and her phone rang thirty seconds later.

"Aw, shut up," she said before Tifton could speak. "They'll grow back."

"They won't, but that's not why I'm calling. The squad sergeant just called. Russell Sanders's son is at the precinct, hysterical."

"Why?"

"He's filing a missing persons report. Russell Sanders disappeared."